Spirit Winds

Spirit Winds

P.M. Grates

Accordion Creations
Glendale, Arizona

Spirit Winds

ISBN 978-0-9642693-5-4

P.M. Grates
Accordion Creations Publishing
P.O. Box 11977
Glendale, AZ 85318

Information: http://www.pmgrates.com
grates@pmgrates.com

To purchase this book please visit:
http://www.pmgrates.com

Part I Runaway
Chapter 1

"**O**h, Mel's," said the cab driver. "That's where all the girls meet their boyfriends."

The statement implied that Alyssa was one of the bad girls engaged in something disapproved of. She ignored it at first, but it grated on her. She started to speak but stopped short.

"I don't need to explain to anyone," she thought.

She handed the cabbie $23 of the original $60 that she had taken out of her backpack. Making eye contact, he smiled ever so slightly.

"I must appear desperate."

Her eyes were expressionless.

"Have a nice night," he said breaking into a broader smile.

"Focused and centered," she thought looking away.

The cab fare alone had consumed a chunk of cash, and she worried how long $150 would last. She had just started out.

Upon phoning again, she connected to the same machine, didn't leave a message, and managed her anxiety so that she wouldn't panic.

She tried coffee for the first time while waiting at Mel's because she knew that refills were free. She didn't like the flavor, but it was warm, and she was cold.

After an hour, she phoned Finhead John again with the same result.

When she returned to her seat, her coffee cup had been cleared away, so she decided to walk. She walked a few blocks down Sunset Strip, turned, walked back, and called Finhead again. No result.

She began to despair, and walked several blocks. She phoned again but got the machine. This time she left another message.

"Finn," she started quietly, "I'm stuck out here on Sunset Strip. It's getting late. It's cold, the tourists are leaving and all the weird-Os are coming out. I have nowhere to go. I'm scared. I'll be at Mel's or on the Strip!"

Her anxiety grew, but her situation wasn't dire. Dread of failure pushed her on, and she resisted phoning home.

She saw a man playing guitar on the sidewalk. His guitar case contained a few crumpled bills and some change. She added a dollar to the case, sat, and quietly listened to him play. The music helped her remain calm.

The guitar player had a scraggly beard and matted dark brown hair. His playing was superb. Occasionally he glanced her way and smiled. He stopped a few times to smoke. His hands shook when he lit his cigarette, and he shook worse when he took a puff. Alyssa found it odd that he could play so well despite his shaking. He had a persistent cough that was labored and deep. He moved slowly like an old man, but his skin and hair suggested youth. After about an hour he finally spoke.

"Do you have anywhere to go?" he asked in a gravelly voice. "A youngster like you shouldn't be out on Sunset at night. Every freak in the country is attracted to this place."

"I can't get a hold of my friend John," Alyssa said avoiding the details.

"I'm staying at the Good Shepherd Homeless Shelter on North Belmont tonight. They won't take minors, but I can vouch for you, and claim you're my daughter."

Tears welled up in Alyssa's eyes. The night wasn't going well, and she didn't know what to do, but she felt she could trust the homeless man.

"What's your name?" Alyssa asked.

"John Birch and no wise cracks."

"Why would I make a wise crack?"

"There was another John Birch that started a very conservative organization. I get teased a lot for having the same name, but it was before my time, and long before yours."

"My name is Alyssa Daingerfield. Yes, please take me with you."

Alyssa was surprised that John Birch had a decent car. It was a sky blue Toyota Corolla in good shape with almost a full tank of gas. When they checked in, the woman looked Alyssa up and down. She didn't look the least bit homeless.

"We either sleep here or on the street!" John Birch said to the woman.

The lady waved them through, and they got cots next to each other. They checked out a blanket and a mini pillow. The pillow seemed dirty, but Alyssa put her extra shirt over it, and immediately climbed in.

"Good night Alyssa. Pleasant dreams," said John.

"Pleasant dreams to you too John, and thank you!"

"It was nothing."

Alyssa stayed awake thinking about her predicament for a long time, and contemplated what she should do. She already sensed that she had made a mistake, but wondered how she could get out of it and save face at the same time. She felt that she was blowing all the respect and independence that she had earned over the summer. Her mind raced, but after 30 minutes of being warm, she calmed, and could organize her thoughts.

"Why do I always end up among the homeless?" she asked herself. "I'm actually sleeping with them now! Am I headed downhill? Or is this an experience I must have? It's so strange! It's as if I belong here in a Hollywood homeless shelter where every drifter in the nation ends up. The only things missing are my strange dreams, but I'm not asleep yet! I'll dream of changing bed linens!"

The thought of changing bed linens made her laugh, laughing calmed her, and she fell asleep. She was too exhausted to dream.

The next morning John was already up and staring at her when she opened her eyes.

"I've gotta go," he said quickly, "but we're supposed to be here together. For my sake, we better walk out together. I may need to stay here again in the future."

Alyssa gathered her things, and walked out proudly with John carrying his guitar case and a small duffle bag. She had survived the night again on her own in a homeless shelter.

They went to a pay phone, and this time Finhead John answered.

"I've been waiting all morning for your call! I wasn't home last night, and didn't get in until early this morning. I'll pick you up at Mel's!"

John Birch was going back to the Sunset Strip, so he gave Alyssa a ride to Mel's. When it was time to say goodbye, he handed her a guitar pick that said "Pat Travers" on it.

"Here's something to remember me by," he said. "I got this pick when I met Pat Travers at Trancas near Malibu."

Alyssa looked at him wide-eyed, "Thank you for all you've done, and good luck to you."

"Same to you," John replied, "because we both know there's no such thing as luck."

He smiled as he drove slowly away, and Alyssa wondered about his statement and the previous night. It seemed so unreal to her as if it had never happened. She wondered if somehow she had already known John Birch.

Finhead John showed up at Mel's about 20 minutes later, and they drove down to Santa Monica Beach together. They walked out on the pier, but the mood was different. It was mid-October now, and none of Alyssa's friends were to be found. They walked up to Denny's to drink coffee, and ended up having lunch. They drove over to UCLA where they first met, and spent the afternoon in the library. They tired of reading, headed back to Santa Monica, and walked out on the pier again. It was cloudy and cold. Most

4

people were working or in school. Alyssa looked intently at Finhead while he was staring out to sea. She realized his Dad was right. It was time for him to get to work.

"Did you ever find a job?" Alyssa asked.

"Yes, I'm working in Venice at that restaurant where you saw the help wanted sign in the window. I make deliveries. I like it because I'm on my own most of the time, and I get to meet people. So I'm not a bum anymore, but my Dad wants me to look for something better. I may do that. I'm starting to find out that he's usually right, and that a lot of my whimsical ideas just set me back."

"I'm starting to see what you mean," Alyssa said. "I'm glad you found something you like."

"What are you going to do?" Finhead asked turning to face her.

"I don't know. Today is a weekday. It's Monday, so I'm actually truant, but I'm not ready to go home."

"Why did you leave this time?"

"My Mom brought me over to her house. I could tell that she and her fiancé were hung over. Then they started drinking, and I felt awkward being there. So I left."

"People are going to drink Alyssa. That doesn't sound so bad to me. You have a decent place to live, and people actually want you. You're loved. There are always going to be drinkers in the world. I suggest you suck it up and go on home."

"I'm not ready to go home yet. I'm embarrassed and confused."

"Excuse me for advising a master, but it sounds to me like your ego is all wrapped up in this one. Shed the ego, and your situation will become clear. You're the one who taught me that."

"I'm not ready yet!"

"Okay, well you can't stay at my house. Do you want to go to Momma Leoni's?"

"No."

"I know of a place off the Sunset Strip where you can stay, but it's not the happiest place on earth. There are a lot of drug users that hang out there, and I think some are smoking heroin. The guy that pays the rent is bi-sexual, and I think he's a trust fund baby because he never seems to work. He always has money to hang out on the Strip. He brings home all kinds of strays."

"Did he bring you home?" asked Alyssa.

"Yes."

"Did you have sex with him?"

"No. He could tell I didn't want to. He's actually a nice guy, and he's very open about himself and his sexuality. He's male, but he's different. I think he felt sorry for me. Just for the record I'm a virgin. I've never been with anyone, but I could have been with a lot of guys. I'm fortunate, I guess, that I still have some innocence left."

"Are you interested in me?"

"Yes, very much so, but maybe not the way you think. I detect something in you that's a lot bigger than me. It's very attractive. If we end up together, then that's good, but I'm happy in what we already have. I hope it grows."

"What's your bisexual friend's name?"

"Corey."

"Corey what?"

"Corey I don't know!"

"Okay, let's go over to Corey I don't know's place," said Alyssa.

Corey wasn't home, but Robert answered the door, and invited them in. Robert was a friend of Corey's, and was waiting for Corey too. He didn't know Finhead, but invited them both in anyway. He suggested they stay until Corey arrived home.

"I've seen you around before," said Robert. "Make yourself at home until Corey gets here. Help yourself to whatever's in the fridge, and let yourselves out if it gets too late."

6

Alyssa fell asleep leaned up against Finhead's shoulder, and it wasn't long before they both were sleeping. The night passed with Finhead moving to the floor and Alyssa taking over the sofa. It was quiet, and they slept okay until 4:30 in the morning when Corey and his friends came in loud, tweeked, and still drinking from a night on Sunset Strip.

"It's the famous Finhead John!" said Corey. "One of the homeless by choice! Wealthy and homeless by choice I might add! A true rebel! Who's the girl?"

"This is Alyssa Daingerfield. She's with me. We're friends."

"You better be just friends," said Corey, "you can get time for that!"

"Like I said we're just friends!"

"Glad to meet you Alyssa!" said Corey. "There's something goin' on with you right? Why would Finn be messin' around with a kid? Are you dealin'? Is that it? You're sellin' for him!"

"Nope, I'm a runaway," Alyssa said point blank. "I need a place to crash for a few days."

"Damn! A hot little number like you!" Corey replied looking Alyssa over. "All clean and shit. You better watch yourself. You won't last long lookin' like that on these streets! How old are you?"

"I'm 13."

"Sheet Finhead!" Corey said. "What you doin bringin' a child over here? You tryin' to get me arrested?"

"It's either here or on the street," Finhead replied. "Neither of us will last long out there. We have no place to go Core! We just need a few days!"

"What you doin' with her? You could get in big trouble! You could get me in trouble!"

"She's a friend. I met her last summer in Santa Monica. She's cool. She's smart. She's all crazy and shit. It's hard to describe – kind of a voodoo way about her. Like a witch doctor. Yeah! Like a

7

witch doctor. She's got some sort of hex on me. I just do what she says."

"I'm not a witch!" said Alyssa. "I'm the same as everyone else! People say that! I hate it! I'm a normal girl. A little troubled, but normal, I assure you."

"No, he's right," said Corey. "There's somethin' deep and dangerous in your eyes. You look like you've been around. Normal 13 year olds don't look like you! You look like fire and ice all wrapped up in one. The famous Finn is right. You're dangerous."

Corey studied Alyssa for a moment without speaking.

"Yeah, you can stay here in the back room. Just pile the clothes off to one side, and clean it up a little, but if anyone asks. I don't know you're here! Harboring a minor! Right! That's all I need!"

"Thank you Corey," said Alyssa humbly.

"Yeah thanks Core. We'll be no problem. Promise. You won't regret it!"

"Just be careful out there. She's a beauty. All fresh and sweet. She won't last on the Strip."

"Sure thing!"

Finhead and Alyssa quickly moved into the room slightly embarrassed of their half asleep homeless situation. There were two twin beds. Both beds were unmade and dirty. Clothing littered the floor. The room smelled of body odor and stagnant air. They opened the window, and Finhead quickly raked the clothes into one pile. They pulled the bed spread over each bed, and laid down on top leaving their jackets on. Finhead fell back asleep right away, but Alyssa lay awake disgusted by the lack of cleanliness and bothered by the muffled sound of voices in the kitchen. Her mind raced over what her next move should be, and for the first time in her life, she felt lost. Finally she drifted back to sleep numb from the anxiety of her situation.

When they awoke, Corey and his friends were gone. There was no one in the apartment, and the front door was unlocked and

8

ajar. Finhead opened the door and looked around. There was no one to be seen. He went back inside, and shut the door completely.

"I'm uncomfortable here," said Alyssa. "The place is dirty, but it's more than that. I get a creepy feeling here."

"We can go over to my Dad's house for a while. He probably just left for work," said Finhead. "We can get some cereal, and head back to the beach before he gets back."

They worked together to make the beds. The sheets and blankets were dirty and wrinkled, but they weren't disgusting. They picked up the trash, put it in an empty grocery bag, and threw the bag in the dumpster outside. The room actually looked clean. Alyssa felt funny about leaving Corey's place unlocked when no one was there, but Finhead assured her it was alright.

"Corey never locks," said Finhead. "People would just damage the door breaking in. He's better off letting people come and go as they please. If anything happens, it'll happen on the street. What are we doing now?"

"If you don't mind, take me to Wilshire to the Miracle Mile area. I can spend the day in museums, and I won't look out of place. They'll be a lot of kids my age around on field trips. It'll give me the opportunity to think about what I'm going to do," said Alyssa.

"I'm not feeling so good about just dumping you off somewhere. I'm supposed to work later, but I could blow it off."

"You've done enough, and this is my problem not yours. I want you to go about your day. I need time to think. If you want, you can pick me up at Hancock Park at 6th and Fairfax at about 9 PM when you get off work."

"Okay, I can live with that, but if you have any problems, leave me a message at my Dad's house. I'll check before I come over."

Alyssa walked through the Los Angeles County Museum of Art and the Page Museum at the La Brea Tar Pits. She tried to blend in as best she could because she knew that by society's

9

standards she was a truant child, and could be turned in by any adult of authority that questioned her. She had an uneasy feeling throughout the day. She wanted to be in school, but just couldn't get herself to call home or go home. She felt like she was on the run, a fugitive from expectations. She was disillusioned with life and the people in control of her.

She was burning through money. She paid entrance fees at the museums and bought herself dinner at Marie Callender's. The $60 that she took out the night before was nearly gone. As the time approached for Finhead John to pick her up, she had nowhere left to go, and walked the streets to keep warm. She was tired and starting to despair about her situation.

Fortunately, Finhead arrived early. They went to Corey's right away so that they could get settled and relaxed. It was noisy, and Usher was playing on the stereo. The apartment was full of people, and it was crowded in the kitchen. They all stared at Alyssa when they entered, looked at Finhead, and then back to Alyssa, but the noise continued. It was obvious that most were gay.

"Wohoo, hot momma!" someone finally spoke.

They were referring to Finn not Alyssa.

"You too young lady! We can take you both on! Muy caliente!"

"Okay guys mind your manners," said Corey loudly, "these are my guests. They're straight and off limits. Are you with me? We're going to give them refuge from the streets for a few nights."

"That's a shame, Holmes. Could be fun."

"Just mind your manners!"

Corey waved them in without speaking further. They were all drinking, and it appeared as though they were also doing drugs with a big mirror lying on the table with white powder on it.

They went straight to the bedroom that Corey had given them. To their relief it was clean, and organized the way they left it, but the pile of dirty clothes was gone. They arranged their things and adjusted themselves while lying on the bed. They talked for a few minutes and turned out the light looking forward to sleep.

"I'm going to get in trouble for not being home for three nights in a row," Finhead said in the dark while staring up at the ceiling. "I want to ask if you would go with me to explain to my Dad. If I go on my own he may not believe me based on my past. I wouldn't blame him. If you're with me, he may actually believe me."

"I'll talk to your Dad, and I'm sorry for putting you through all this," said Alyssa without looking at him in the darkened room. "I was wrong to leave, and then I wasn't sure of how to go back. I was independent over the summer. I made a point, and proved to everyone that I can fend for myself. I didn't want to throw away everything I worked for. At first I couldn't admit that I was wrong. Once I did admit it, I couldn't face my family. I felt stupid and ashamed, and those aren't feelings I've experienced often. I've learned to trust my instincts, but this time, I just sort of went off like a whistling tea kettle. I'm ready to go back now, and face up to what I've done."

"We better do that first thing tomorrow," said Finhead. "It's not going to get any easier with time. We can talk to my Dad in the evening. I'd like to ask your Grandpa to go too."

"Okay, yes we'll go back tomorrow, and grovel to the right people. I doubt I'll sleep much tonight."

She was wrong. They both slept soundly through the night, but Alyssa was woken by the sound of loud noises coming from the kitchen. She heard yelling, breaking glass, commotion, and objects falling over. It all stopped almost as suddenly as it had started. She wanted to use the bathroom, but waited for what seemed to be a long time. She could hear muffled voices, but thought it was safe. She cracked the door, and peaked out. She saw nothing, and slipped across the hall to the bathroom. Without thinking she flushed, and somehow knew that she shouldn't have. As she

11

watched the water swirl down and disappear, fear welled up within her.

When she stepped out, someone grabbed her, and quickly bent both arms behind her back, and gripped them tightly. They pushed her toward the living room. Another man went into the room, woke Finhead, and muscled him into the living room too. Alyssa protested.

"You're hurting me," she yelled. "I can walk on my own. There's no need to push."

Finhead, still half asleep, kept quiet guessing what was happening, and not wanting to make things worse.

"Shut up," said the man forcing Alyssa into the living room. "Sit down and shut up!"

The people that were in the kitchen earlier were now lined up on the couch. Two men were holding them at gunpoint with a large caliber pistol. There was only one gun in plain view, but Finhead whispered to Alyssa.

"Keep your mouth shut and just do what they say," said Finhead. "You can only see one gun, but their could be more. They don't want to use the guns. They want money."

"Shut up," said the same man kicking Finhead in the thigh.

"Leave 'em alone they're kids. They have nothing to do with this," said Corey.

"Is there anyone else here that you haven't told me about?"

"No."

Corey and his friends looked like they had been beaten.

"They want money," said Corey looking at Finhead. "I owe them money, and they want it now!"

"Shut up!"

"You know I won't have any money until the first of the month. You'll get your money then."

"We'll see if you have any money. Give me the girl," he said.

"Leave her alone," protested Corey struggling. "She's a baby. I have no money today! You'll get your money!"

12

"Sit her down here!"

They sat her on a kitchen chair in the middle of the living room. He started to pace back and forth near Alyssa. He looked over at Finhead.

"One of your boys?" he said smiling nodding at Finhead. "Isn't he a little old for you!"

"I said you'll get your cake this Friday. These two just happen to be here. They have nothing to do with this place."

"I could extract one nut," he said while looking at Finhead and unsheathing a long shiny knife.

His attention turned back to Alyssa. He rested the point of the knife on her throat for a few seconds, and then walked back in forth in front of her. He stared at the knife and then at her. He put his face in close to hers and put pressure on the knife. Alyssa was glaring at him.

"You don't have the balls," Alyssa said to him as if seeing through him.

He spit on her.

"Ho! Don't speak! I'll tell you when to speak."

"Alyssa! Shut up!" said Finhead. "You'll only make it worse."

He walked over to Finhead, stuck the blade of the knife up against his neck, and got in his face.

"Shall I cut you little boy?"

He pulled the knife away, and after a moment, blood appeared where the blade had been. It was very minor cut.

"You coward," said Alyssa quietly starring at him.

"This one's peculiar!" he said re-sheathing his knife. "Some sort of a nasty little ho. There's no innocence in her voice!"

"I may only be 13, but I'm a thousand years old!" she said.

"Only 13," he said laughing.

"Leave her alone," said Corey. "She's just a runaway. I told her she could stay until she had the courage to call home!"

"Courage! She's not lacking courage," he replied. "Her brazen attitude is very appealing . . . almost seductive!"

13

The room was quiet.

"Leave her alone!" said Corey. "She's not courageous. She's naïve. I'll give you you're money Friday! Now leave us alone!"

"Last chance to come up with it," he said pulling his knife again.

"I don't have it!"

The man picked up Alyssa, and slung her over his shoulder. She screamed, and beat him on the back with her fists. The man found humor in her feeble attempt at protest, and smiled slightly for a second, then returned to his glum expression. Finhead stood and dashed toward the man, but he was hit with a bottle, and thrown to the floor by another man. His back hit with a loud thud, and his head cracked against the floor so loudly that everyone in the room grimaced except the man carrying Alyssa. He laughed.

He took Alyssa into the room that she was in with Finhead just minutes earlier, threw Alyssa to the floor, and held her down with one hand while attempting to remove her clothes with the other. Alyssa screamed. He grew impatient, and ripped at what remained in the way of what he wanted. Finally, he dropped his own pants, and Alyssa planted one solid kick, but it missed to the side, and he laughed again. He fumbled with himself for a moment temporarily incapable of committing the act he intended.

In that moment Alyssa came to the realization of what was happening to her. As she did so, time slowed, movements were slow, and she became clear. She stopped struggling sensing that it was useless to fight, and in her mind, she separated herself from her own body. She was very aware of the struggle, but felt as though she was viewing the scene as a spectator from above. Her inner awareness seemed to reach out to her, and for the first time since she left home days ago, she felt empowered. She connected to an unknown source of energy, and waited for her next move to become clear.

"You've succeeded in getting to where you wanted," Alyssa said feeling his hardness against her. "Now take me with love

14

rather than heated anger. This is my first time, and I don't want the memory to be one of pure pain."

Alyssa's words had the tone and depth of another world. She spoke as if the ancient ghost within her was taking control, and she was a mere vehicle of expression. She spoke with calm and authority. Her request was void of emotion, and seemed to carry so much weight that everything in the room was still.

The rhythmic nature of her words made her aggressor take pause. In an instant, he realized the depth of what he was doing. He flinched, and briefly scanned Alyssa, the room, and finally himself.

"What better way to be taken your first time without feeling, and without emotion. Just pure need is driving me. We're all prostitutes in some way. You're fortunate to be learning young. Now you know how the world works."

As soon as he began to speak, the feeling in the room changed. Light seemed to creep in, and the focus transformed from one of pure sexual rage to philosophical bantering. In that instant, Alyssa knew she was safe. She succeeded in shifting the energy, and her aggressor's attention changed from the physical to the intellectual.

"Yes, there's some truth in the words you speak," Alyssa replied, "but I also sense the love in your heart. You haven't fully become what you think you've become. There remains an innocent child within you, and in the back of your mind you have concern for someone like me in your life. It could be a sister, a niece, or a past love, but you wouldn't want to happen to them what you're about to do to me."

Alyssa spoke forcefully, and with authority, but as she spoke, her words became tender and understanding. She could feel him soften and hesitate. She watched as the range of emotions ran across his face ending with the sudden desire to flee. He separated from her, and even in the dim light she could sense shame and then self loathing. He turned on the light ignoring her vulnerable position. She quickly covered herself with what was available and retreated to the corner.

15

At first he hastily rummaged through the room ignoring her. He went through her backpack, found the rest of her money, and pocketed it. Then he went through Finhead's pack finding nothing of value but a debit card. He flung the card on the floor, left the room leaving the door ajar. Tears welled up in Alyssa's eyes, but she wasn't crying. She was relieved.

Moments later Finhead came in, and comforted her.

"He didn't take me," she said to his eyes in a pleading tone. "He wanted to, but somehow I talked him out of it. I can't even remember what I said."

"I would say you're lucky, but somehow I know that your retained virginity wasn't luck," said Finhead holding her. "Now let's get you dressed and get out of here."

Corey helped them pull their things together. Corey's friends stayed in the kitchen and talked about what transpired with excitement and enthusiasm.

"I'm sorry this happened while you were here," said Corey. "It's never happened before. I'm very sorry. I really mean that. I hope you don't report this, but I will understand if you do. It was outrageous, wrong, and potentially tragic. I hope that one day you'll forgive me for what happened in my home."

Alyssa thanked him, and she and Finhead nodded to the others as they left.

Chapter 2

It was nearly six in the morning when they arrived at her Grandparent's in Monterey Park. Grandpa Jack was getting ready for work. When he saw her he was expressionless. He stopped and stood with feet planted waiting for one of them to speak, but when they couldn't, he took the opportunity.

"Are you okay?" he asked without emotion.

16

"Yes," Alyssa responded looking at the ground.

"Nothing bad happened?"

"Yes, something bad happened, but I'm okay. I retained my innocence. I'm frightened but not shattered."

Grandpa Jack turned to Finhead and looked at him for a moment before he spoke again.

"I assume you took care of her?"

"I did my best sir. I learned that some things are bigger than me," Finhead said looking at Grandpa Jack but bowing his head toward the ground as he completed his sentence.

Grandpa Jack looked back at Alyssa, walked over to her, and took her into his arms. She melted into Grandpa holding on to his forearm.

"Are you home now?" he asked.

"Yes," Alyssa replied with tears running down her face.

"If you want to live here, you have to promise me that you'll never do this again. I've been worried sick for three days, and this time, we asked the police for help. You never called, and never told us you were safe. We didn't know what to do. I've made mistakes in my own life. I understand mistakes, but I can't live like this."

"I'm sorry Grandpa!" she said breaking down into sobs.

"Do you promise?"

"Yes," she said.

"Do you promise John?"

"Yes Mr. Daingerfield, I promise," said Finhead.

"Okay, well you get on home John, and you get inside. Grandma Lin took the day off to look for you. Since you're here, you can talk through what happened with her. I'll try getting something done. I may not be very useful today, but I'm going to work anyway."

Grandpa Jack took her by the hand, and they both walked together to her room. It was all there just as she had left it, and it made her breakdown in sobs again. She realized for the first time that she had something to lose.

Alyssa explained to the police, Grandpa Jack and Grandma Lin everything that had happened. She described her experience on Sunset, her night in the homeless shelter, Corey's apartment, and the attempted rape. Alyssa didn't want to pursue her attacker. Corey had been kind to them, and she didn't want to upset his life with police investigations, court time, and scandal. In the end, nothing had happened, and she wanted it left that way. Grandma Lin agreed.

When Alyssa first saw her Mom, the meeting was very different than it had ever been in the past. They both had a big scare, and Daisy was just happy to get her daughter back safely. She was surprisingly calm, and allowed Alyssa time to explain without interruption. She observed her daughter's situation from a new point of view. During Alyssa's absence, Daisy realized that she too had something to lose, that her daughter was growing up, and that she might not always know what's best for her. She explained her thinking to Alyssa, and suggested that they work together as a team.

"From now on anything I do that impacts you we'll discuss," Daisy told her. "I want your buy-in, and I want your teenage years to be as carefree as possible. I don't want a miserable runaway."

Alyssa was surprised by the change, and was touched by her mother's openness. She apologized for what she had done, and was surprised again by Daisy's reaction.

"Thank you for apologizing honey. I was hoping you would, and you did," Daisy said with understanding while holding Alyssa's hands. "This time, however, it went beyond me. The police were involved. You were a missing person. We're going to have to get some counseling. We'll get counseling each on our own, and we'll have a few sessions together. I know that you probably don't want to do that, and neither do I, but we must. I owe you that much. I also owe you an apology for drinking to

18

excess around you, and to make you come over when I intend to get drunk. I know you don't want to be around me when I get like that. I'm drinking too much, and hung over a lot. I need to change, and won't force you to come over anymore. I'm sorry."

"I realized something too while I was gone Mom. There are always going to be drinkers around me. Drinking and drunkenness are a part of life. I can't change that, and I can't change you. I'm not going to force you to be something you're not. I would appreciate it if you wouldn't drink around me, but if you do, I can handle it now. I won't overreact. I don't want you to be uncomfortable around me either. I realize that I'm lucky to have a Mom. We may not see things the same way, but I do appreciate you. I love you Mom."

"Oh honey! That's so sweet, but I have some growing up to do too. I need to make more of an effort to focus on us when we're together. It took me a long time to realize that we're not clones of each other. In fact, our interests are on opposite ends of the spectrum. Manicures, massages, shopping, and clothes aren't your interests. We need to find some common ground, and do things that we both like."

With Grandpa Jack it wasn't as easy for Alyssa to come back. He had been on her side all along, and had given her everything she ever wanted her whole life. He was hurt by her actions, and needed time for the wound to heal. At first he was very standoffish with her, but as time passed he came to understand.

She understood too. He wanted things the way they were when she was a little girl. Time had caught up with him, and he wasn't quite ready to be the wise old man. Soon they fell back to their old habits, and he would come up to read to her before bed.

Chapter 3

Only a year earlier, at twelve years old, Alyssa's life was very different, she was in a world of her own, and had her own space. She considered herself a misfit publicly, but was content with her private surroundings. With the arrival of adolescence, she could feel other big changes coming, and it worried her how people would judge.

She mistrusted adults, and thought of them as overgrown children. Because of the way adults ran things, the whole world seemed upside down to her. What she saw as important, they saw as insignificant. She had a vision of how the world could be, and if adults would only wake up from their catatonic state, that vision could be realized.

She was always rebellious, but in her mind, she was just thinking freely. She defiantly went forward with her truth no matter what obstacles were in her way. Sometimes her thoughts became so abstract that few people could relate to her.

She was comfortable living at her Grandparents, her days were full, and she had a routine. In many ways, it was no different than other kids her age, but in most ways she was very different than many of the kids she knew.

There were solid reasons she found herself out of place. Her Mom was only 32, whereas, most kid's parents were older. Her mom was very beautiful, and acted like a teenager herself. That was unusual. In her memory, she had never met her Dad, and didn't live with either parent! She didn't know anyone that didn't live with at least one parent. She spent most of her time outside or on the streets while most other kids were watching TV or playing video games. She was the opposite of the current urban child, but did things that others had a growing interest in.

As much as she felt like a misfit, there were many things she liked, and she focused on those things that helped her fit in. One of her favorite activities was soccer. She played as much soccer as she could, but her love of soccer had been changing too. The farther she went with it, the more competitive it became, and the less attractive it was for her. She saw it as a game, and wanted to have fun and meet other kids. She liked to win, but winning wasn't everything to her.

At an earlier age she loved soccer, but now, at twelve, she was almost done with it, and ready to move on. Her current team was outstanding, so there was no sign of the season ending. Playoffs could press on through the holidays. The drive to win increasingly bothered her due to the brutality it could generate. Competition divided her own teammates, and the game wasn't nearly as enjoyable as it once was. Slowly she drifted away from soccer, lost touch with her team, and began to resent her coach. Her coach was extremely competitive, and had received a yellow card several times due to his temper. Alyssa was skeptical of people with flaring tempers, and refused to respect him as a leader. Her values were harmony, peaceful interaction, and higher level thinking. Her mind was far beyond her physical years and was yet another factor in her struggle to relate to people.

She had always been tall for her age with large brown eyes and reddish brown hair. The slight curl in her thick hair gave it a wave that added volume. Her friends said she had big hair. She had so much volume she often tied it back in a pony tail to keep it out of the way, but when she let it out, it gave her an unusual exotic look, and people really took notice. Her unusual combination of features was one of the keys to her allure. She was aware of it; but it troubled her. Her subtle beauty was yet another factor that made her stand out when she wanted to fit in. The girls envied her. Some were openly jealous, but all of them seemed to be drawn to her.

A lot of boys wanted to meet her, and stumbled all over each other for the privilege of talking to her. Their infatuation didn't help Alyssa fit in with her female friends. They never seemed to get noticed by boys, and wondered why Alyssa was always the center of attention. It wasn't Alyssa's fault, but they punished her for it socially. They treated her as a boyfriend stealer, or worse yet, a promiscuous bad girl, and reluctantly forced her out of many social circles. They loved her and hated her at the same time. The conflict and ridicule only served to make Alyssa stronger. She developed strategies and a sense of humor. She made friends in a broad based fashion without getting too close to anyone. She focused on individual relationships, and stayed low key in groups.

It wasn't just young people that were attracted to Alyssa, all people were. She blamed her looks for that, but never considered that the attraction could be something deeper. People would stop her in the street, and approach her like a long lost friend. She handled it the best she could, but it was impossible to keep up with all the names and the many social events. Her unusual popularity intruded on her alone time, and that frustrated her too. She craved alone time and originally viewed socializing as a nuisance; but as with other things, teenage changes impacted her opinion of her situation. She was beginning to see the advantage of being attractive, and her desire to avoid people and social events subsided.

She had realized that it wasn't so bad to use her attractiveness to her advantage like some other girls. In a way, it leveled the playing field for her, and she could deal with people better.

Her new attitude softened her piercing gaze that startled people. She could see right through people with one quick glance. It was especially odd for someone so young and seasoned adults were thrown off by it. She tried to avoid looking at people intensely, and learned to offset her look by turning on the charm. She had no mastery of it, and would revert back to intense staring especially when angered. When she was younger, she didn't realize she was so intense, but now it was obvious. She desperately wanted to tone it down, and worked hard at disguising her emotions.

People sensed an element of danger in her. She couldn't quite understand why, but it was there. They would sense it right away, but it took them a few minutes to put their finger on it.

She reasoned that it was her decisiveness that was striking. She drove right to the point in conversations, and was very candid with her opinions. People expected political correctness, and were surprised by her frank responses. She couldn't see the danger in it, but people were often cautious with her. Many adults assumed she was always in trouble, and would isolate her almost immediately as a preventative measure. In fact, her personality was quite the opposite: helpful, kind, gentle, and caring. It pleased her to help others. Her benevolence hinted at her softer inner self, but the softness was well guarded by an esoteric exterior. She thought it was better to be careful in exposing her true softer side, and found it easier to let people think what they will.

One person she opened up to was Grandpa Jack, and he called to her so that they wouldn't be late to the game.

"I'm coming!"

"Well don't let the moss grow under your feet."

She strapped on her shin guards, and pulled her red knee sox up and over while wishing the season was finished and wondered if her team would continue on through Christmas.

Grandpa Jack was her grandfather, but in a figurative sense, he was also her father, mother, her best friend, confidant, and protector. He was the most important person in her life. He was everything to her. Grandma Lin was important too, but Jack was her rock, and she built her life upon his gentle nurturing ways.

It was Saturday morning, and early enough to be a warm autumn day, but the on-shore flow was already picking up, and by the time the game was over there would be cool wind blowing off the ocean.

23

"Bring your jacket," said Grandpa Jack, 'it will be cold time we're done."

"I've got it," she said bounding down the stairs.

Grandpa Jack loaded his old folding chair into the back of his 1989 Volvo station wagon. The chair had been repaired several times, and had duct tape holding one of the arms together. Alyssa stuffed her duffle bag through the door to the back seat. The seat was always folded down so that Grandpa Jack could haul materials around for his weekend handyman work.

"Why don't you get a new car Grandpa?" asked Alyssa.

"This one is fine," he replied surprised by the question, "still has the original paint!"

"Mom says it's the color of baby poop," said Alyssa, "faded yellow with a slight greenish cast to it."

"She would say something like that! This is the most reliable car I've ever owned, and it's paid for. That's a very attractive feature."

"You deserve a new one. You work hard," said Alyssa.

"It's not about how much you work," he replied and fell silent.

They rode along in content anticipation toward Manhattan Beach driving down the Harbor Freeway to Artesia Boulevard and underneath the 405. The game was at Mira Costa High School at 10:00 AM, but the coach wanted his players there by 9:30. The breeze was already picking up when they arrived. The smell of the ocean hung on it, and that lifted their spirits as Alyssa joined the other girls tapping her FIFA approved ball along with her feet as she ran. Grandpa Jack set up camp opening his lawn chair on the sidelines, and far enough away from the other parents so as not to intentionally stir up a conversation. He put on his face of age and slight disinterest, but it didn't mask him well because he looked young for his 52 years. He could have easily passed for Alyssa's father.

Grandpa Jack was from Springfield, Virginia and was distantly related to one of the original inhabitants of the area

24

named Henry Daingerfield. John Daingerfield was born February 12th, 1948 in a house on Backlick Road. His father didn't believe in hospitals, and considered them a place where people go to die. So he was bound and determined that none his children would be born in a death trap hospital. Grandpa Jack was the third Daingerfield to be called John, and since his father had the same name, they immediately began to call him Jack to avoid confusion.

Jack's brothers and sisters joked with him that they called him Jack because he was all jacked up all the time. He was so jacked up that he was crushed when LSD was made illegal in 1966, and he made up his mind to drop out and move to San Francisco with his girlfriend Linda. He was only 18, and never drank alcohol, but he smoked pot, ate magic mushrooms, and occasionally took LSD. His rationalization was based on the proverbial theory of the times.

"If it grew out of the ground it was profound. If it came out of the lab, it was probably bad."

With processed LSD his theory didn't hold up, but because it was derived from seeds, he claimed it was natural too.

Now in his fifties, however, he had given up substances. His granddaughter was the focus of his life, and his worst vice was his obsession with Starburst fruit chews. He left a trail of wrappers wherever he went, and his 1989 Volvo was littered with them. He drank a lot of coffee, and Starbucks was a treat for him.

"Anything with the word "star" in its name is good enough for me!" he told his granddaughter.

The theory justified his love of Star Trek and Star Wars.

Jack and Linda left Virginia in December 1966 in a used Chevy Van with all their worldly belongings inside. Their parents strongly disapproved, and treated them as runaways, but there was little they could do to stop them. They had some money, more than most kids, but beyond that they had hope and each other. Their goal was to make the Human-Be-In set for Golden Gate Park on January 14th, 1967, and stay through the summer. They watched Jerry Garcia and Ron "Pig Pen" Mc Kernan play music in Golden

Gate Park in April. It was the beginnings of the Grateful Dead, but for Jack it was the period where he really "tuned in and turned on". They ended up at Monterey Pop Festival in June by accident when driving down to Big Sur for a love-in. They never left California again, but eventually, ended up moving to Monterey Park in Southern California to find work. Jack became an electronics technician and accepted a position with TEAC.

Alyssa's usual soccer position was fullback. She was comfortable as a fullback because she could anticipate what people would do, and could run anywhere on the field. She was effective at holding her end while working together with the goal keeper. Forward wasn't her position, not that she couldn't dribble and shoot the ball well, but being aggressive, particularly toward others, was not something she could do easily. In order to be competitive she had to focus and work against strong inner instincts. Even as a fullback, the coach would often yell at her for her compassion and lack of aggression.

The coach was yelling now. The ball rolled right past her because her attention shifted to helping a forward on the opposing team who appeared injured. When the referee noticed her, he blew the whistle and everyone on both teams went down on one knee. Suddenly Alyssa was praised for her concern rather than criticized for her lack of competitiveness; but she knew that the acknowledgement was temporary, and soon the collective emotion would shift back to winning.

Alyssa was inexplicably drawn toward helping others. She was always first on the scene.

When the quarter ended, she rotated out, and sat on the ground next to Grandpa Jack while he poured coffee from his stainless steel thermos.

"Why doesn't Mom come to any of my games?" she asked her Grandpa.

"Because you're Mother is still a child herself, and doesn't comprehend the precious moments that are passing her by. You

26

may have been brought into the world to take care of her. Some people call it a role reversal. You're the Mom, and she's the child even though you're 12 and she's 32."

"But I don't really take care of her."

"You take care of everyone whether you know it or not," replied Grandpa Jack.

"I just wish Flower would notice me when she doesn't need something," said Alyssa.

"She will, she will."

Alyssa called her Mom "Flower" occasionally to her Grandpa because her Mom's real name was Daisy, and she related so well to the "Flower Child" movement of the 1960s. Grandpa Jack played a part in the 60s revolution in both the California Bay Area culture and in civil rights demonstrations. He made sure that his daughter Daisy was immersed in his belief system.

Daisy Daingerfield was born seven days after the death of Martin Luther King Jr. April 21st, 1968. Her mother, Linda Daingerfield, claimed it was a sign and a bad omen, but she prayed that Daisy was protected by another seemingly coincidental factor. She was conceived in Golden Gate Park the day that John Coltrane died July 17th, 1967. She and Jack were so devastated by the news of Coltrane's death that they got high in the Park with their friends and had sex that night near Mallard Lake before flopping in a house on Cole Street after being invited in by Dealer Bob. They found out the next morning that Dealer Bob didn't actually live there, but they were invited to stay anyway. They stayed for a month in a room with a bean bag chair, two blankets, and about two hundred National Geographic magazines that previous tenant had saved.

"What's even more coincidental," Linda says, "is that they later changed the name of the street by Mallard Lake to Martin Luther King Jr. Memorial Drive. Truly Daisy is blessed, and the timing of her birth wasn't a negative thing."

Alyssa wasn't so sure her mother was blessed in a divine way, but was truly blessed when it came to looks. She was stunningly beautiful, and had a perfect body. Men came flocking to her with dazed looks and attitudes the screamed "take advantage of me," and Daisy did take advantage. She learned to work every angle, became aloof, and did everything in her power to drain men dry before dumping them back out on the street penniless and lovesick. Although Alyssa tried not to judge her mother, it was extremely frustrating to watch the parade of men come calling, showering her with gifts and begging her to go out with them. She chose the worst ones to be with, bad boys, substance abusers, gamblers, or black market salesman. Nearly every relationship was passionate, dramatic, and would end in disaster. There was an endless circle of meeting, dating, infatuation, moving in, fighting, prowling, finding someone new, and moving out. She was never without a man, and never with one for long. Alyssa was moved from home to home ultimately returning each time to Grandpa Jack's and Grandma Lin's. Grandpa and Grandma's house quickly became the stability in her life. She considered that permanent, and where Mom lived was always temporary. This time was no exception.

Daisy was dating Franklin Kennedy who liked to bet on horse racing. He frequented all the Southern California tracks during their respective seasons, and had particular affection for Santa Anita and Del Mar. Combining his first and last name, Alyssa called him Franken for short, but it made her think of Frankenstein. She thought that Frankenstein fit better due to his Jewish decent and since he was born and raised in Eastern Europe. She anticipated that soon her Mom would want to move into his house in Rosemead.

Alyssa played the third quarter as goal keeper, but returned to fullback in the forth performing brilliantly and keeping the faith. She was happy, however, because they were losing by a wide margin, and it appeared that the season would finally be over. The parents were sitting in stunned silence, and would occasionally stare at Grandpa Jack who was oblivious to the score, and would applaud for good plays on both sides. At the end of the game, the parents formed a human tunnel by standing across from each other and abreast and touching hands above their heads. Grandpa Jack never participated in this ritual, but watched intently from the sidelines with a curious look on his face.

"I'd rather not play next year," Alyssa stated as a matter of fact as they were driving home.

"That's okay with me sweetheart. You know this has always been something you loved to do. Maybe you've just outgrown it," said Grandpa Jack.

"I don't see the point anymore," said Alyssa, "it's not fun, and everyone seems like they're out to get each other. Even on my own team!"

"Sports can get very competitive the higher you go," said Grandpa, "people start to take it very seriously."

"I guess that's what I don't like," said Alyssa, "it's just a game. Why would anyone take it seriously? It's all for fun!"

"I don't know honey."

Chapter 4

Alyssa experienced a lot of dreams. Her dreams were vivid to the point of being unsettling. It didn't matter if it was night or day or whether she was awake or asleep. She never knew when a dream would arrive. Some dreams were pleasant, some hard to understand, and some very disturbing, but all were very real and memorable. Most dreams she could recall at will, and a few required no recollection at all because they were so repetitive in nature that she had them memorized. Some aspects of every dream, however, were always new, and she couldn't decide if she had noticed any particular detail before. She was sure that once she fixed her attention on something, she usually noticed it again.

One of her repetitive dreams took place in Hawaii on the island of Kauai. The dream was almost identical every time she had it, but she wasn't sure if it took place in the future or in the past. Her physical surroundings gave no hints of date, time or era. She lived in a very small building designed for one person. The building was on stilts so that the waves could pass underneath, but it was several blocks from the shoreline. Only a rogue wave could possibly make it to her house, but if it did, her house would be safe. Some of the other houses near the shoreline may be washed away if a wave actually made it to her doorstep.

She lived by herself in a little town called Kekaha. The people in Kekaha called her "Huna". They honored her as an elder, but she didn't appear to herself to be old. Kekaha was near a bigger town called Waimea, but she avoided this town because some people in Waimea disliked her and called her names like "Witch" or "Crazy Witch". They would make fun of her unkempt hair and the clothes she wore. Sometimes they threw things at her. In Kekaha, however, they loved her, and would seek her out for help and advice. Some would ask her for medical attention, and others would ask her for a blessing. Many fishermen lived in the town, and they would ask her to bless their boats before heading out to sea. The most interesting people came for her lessons. She taught personal development, healing, holistic medicine, meditation, and how to honor the earth and the heavens. Once a week people would gather outside her front door and sit on mats waiting for her to speak. She didn't know why they came, but they came every week, and she made sure she had something interesting and helpful to say about their spiritual development. She had a group of core followers that would come every time, and help her with her presentation. After the talk she would hike up the Waimea Canyon ridge to Kokee to pray, meditate, give thanks, and be tranquil.

Only her faithful followers would climb the canyon with her, and she would teach the seven principles that she knew by heart:

1. The world is what you think it is
2. There are no limits
3. Energy flows where attention goes
4. Now is the moment of power
5. To love is to be happy with
6. All power comes from within
7. Effectiveness is a measure of truth

When walking back down the canyon trail, she would suddenly wake from her dream startled and sweating. It was similar each time.

In another dream sequence she was in the Carapathian Mountains of Romania during ancient times. It's seemingly just after the time of Jesus Christ dating 20 or 30 AD. The Roman Empire is in full swing, and the first vivid memory of this dream is the crucifixions being held outside the city walls. There were many crucifixions, and she distinctly remembers the soldiers breaking the victim's legs in order to hasten death once the body was mounted on the cross. Corpses were left for many days, and if the wind blew in the right direction, the smell of death would drift into the city. The bodies were only removed if the post was needed for someone else. In this dream Alyssa worked in a hospital. At times she's not sure it's a hospital. It could be some other public building or ancient hotel for the wealthy. She remembers changing bed linens. Changing bed linens is a reoccurring theme. There are many beds and people of various ages in the beds. Some people appeared to be insane, but she reasons that the twisted faces may just be those of torment. The lower classes lead lives of despair and anguish. They serve in back breaking jobs for wealthy landowners that mistreat them. Most of the time this dream transforms, and suddenly, she's in the Southeastern United States in what appears to be the Civil War. Again she's changing bed linens in a hospital or similar public building. She's serving as a

31

physician, nurse, or some combination of the two. She speculates that she's a trained doctor, but that she's discriminated against for being female, and relegated to the duties of a nurse. This dream usually ends abruptly, but if it plays out, she recalls going out to the battlefield with a group of people after the fighting has ended looking for living bodies among the dead. They tag the bodies that are certainly dead, and estimate the chances for survival of those they find breathing. The sights and smells are horrific, and she operates in an automatic mode with her emotional mind turned off. For those that have a chance, she treats them, and her helpers load them onto wagons to be hauled back to town by horses. Several horses mill around nearby. They've been released from service due to the death of their riders. They are also collected together, and brought back into town as a herd. In the hospital, everything appears grey and drab, and the only thing that stands out are the faces of people with no expression existing beyond despair without hope, feelings, or willingness to live.

In Alyssa's rarest dream, but the most enjoyable, she lives in Alaska in the city of Sitka on Branaf Island. In this dream she's obviously some sort of priest or spiritual leader. At times she is a Christian priest among Russian men, at other times she's a shaman priest among the local inhabitants. She's not sure why she's both, but she's sure of very high spiritual status, and held in regard by everyone who lives in the town whether they're Russian or native. What is interesting to Alyssa about this dream is that no one knows what sex she is. They're not sure if she's male or female, but speculate that she's male. Alyssa is quite sure she's female, but outwardly acts and dresses male so that she's not disrespected by the male dominated culture of Sitka. The village people subsist on a diet of seafood, and as she does in the Hawaiian dream, she blesses the fishing boats and tools before they go out, and when they return, she leads them in prayer thanking the Great Spirit for their good fortune, and acknowledging their prey for giving their lives to provide sustenance to the people.

32

For a long time Alyssa kept quiet about her dreams. She was afraid that something might be wrong with her, and that people would use her unusual experiences against her. It seemed to her that many people were out to get each other in this life, and it didn't make any sense to expose a weakness. It never occurred to her that her visions may be an asset rather than a liability. She didn't know anyone else who had vivid waking dreams and to her, that was a bad sign. She speculated that the dreams would get worse, and that her sanity would soon slip away. Eventually, she wouldn't know the difference between dreams and reality, and would be consumed by madness. With time she decided that this was not the case. Her dreams weren't getting any worse, and not all of them were bad. She decided to approach Grandpa Jack about her dreams. She started with her Civil War dream, but carefully explained all the dreams in detail, and how she felt about them. Grandpa Jack listened patiently and intently to the whole revelation occasionally raising an eyebrow, widening his eyes, or furrowing his forehead. After she finished, his eyes moved toward the ground, and he remained silent for what seemed like minutes. He let out a long sigh and began.

"You know it could mean anything, and it could mean nothing," he began with a look of concern. "Certainly it's nothing to worry about, but we should consider what it could mean so that we're not ignoring something important."

"Do you think the dreams actually mean something?"

"Well of course they do," Grandpa Jack replied, "These are no ordinary dreams. Repetitive dreams are rare, and waking dreams are even more so. They're important, but nothing to worry about. Something within you is sending a message to your conscious being that is functioning in the daily world. Based on experiences in a past life, it seems that you're destined to do great things in this life. You're telling yourself so, and trying to give yourself some guidance. The secret to these things is to not overreact. When they happen, just casually review and decide what may apply to now.

Apply what you learn as you see fit, but don't ignore it. The life you're living now is precious. Use everything at your disposal to make this life more fulfilling."

"Then you don't think I'm crazy?"

"I think your less crazy than most, but your question has a Yin and Yang aspect to it as all questions do. If you think you're crazy, then you're probably not crazy. Then again, if you think you're not crazy, then you probably are crazy. The answer lies somewhere in between and changes from day to day. Nothing is fixed. What we perceive to be reality is but a manifestation of what we think and believe. What we think and believe changes all the time."

"Grandpa, you're talking in circles."

"Life is circular, darling. I can't help it. We always end up back where we started."

"I'm not sure if I understand," stated Alyssa.

"That's probably good, dear. If we understood everything there would be no wonder or mystery in life. Our non-understanding can often lead to good things by acting in ways that, to most people, appear illogical. What we do is up to us and no one else," Grandpa Jack said with fading interest.

"What do the dreams mean then?" asked Alyssa.

"If I were to guess, it sounds like you're a healer. I don't mean a doctor necessarily although you could be one. I mean a healer of souls. You heal people physically, and you heal them emotionally. You must be good at it because you've been elevated on more than one occasion to a spiritual leader, a chief, or a high priest. You're a very advanced soul, and very powerful. I've always sensed that in you, but you can't just take my word for it. You should sense it within yourself. It's the same thing with your dreams. It's up to you to interpret your own dreams. It can't be done for you, but there's nothing wrong in asking for opinions. If you ask me, you're an accomplished healer and perhaps more."

Alyssa decided to break from the conversation since it appeared that Grandpa was done with the discussion. She

34

understood that she was not crazy, and that there may be something to learn from her day dreams. These were the nuggets she was looking for, and she wished she had the conversation with Grandpa Jack sooner. The discussion was good. He always calmed her and made her feel safe. She was at peace with herself.

The rest of the discussion was very intriguing to her, but it didn't make a lot of sense, and didn't fit the model of the world she knew. She witnessed the repetitive cycle of birth and death with a melancholy material existence in between. It was few people that seemed truly happy. She could admit that there were some people that recognized the joy and beauty in day to day living. Whether rich, poor, weak, or strong they were happy. Perhaps this small population sample was what Grandpa was talking about. Spirituality, higher planes of existence, reincarnation, self-actualization were just big words to her that he would endlessly talk about, but now she realized there may be something more to it.

She had already judged him as an old hippie from the 60s, and had missed everything about him. This image was shattered now that she saw him from a new perspective. Just because he was an old hippie from Golden Gate Park, it didn't mean he had nothing left to offer.

Chapter 5

Alyssa didn't have a problem distinguishing dreams from reality. Although her dreams were very vivid and similar to what she experienced in the waking world, day to day to living was very predictable, surreal, and even macabre. The more peculiar life was the more real it seemed to her. Daisy was one of Alyssa's peculiar realities. Her Mom was different than any other Moms that Alyssa knew. Her Mom was young and beautiful, and acted like a kid herself. She was into fashion, and loved shopping. Being sexy was important to her, and she practiced it. She liked men, and men went crazy over her. She was irresistible, and her hypnotic voice drew men like rats to the piper. Women were instantly on the defensive around Daisy, whispering to their friends about what a slut she was, that her butt was too big, or her jeans too tight. They didn't know whether to love her or hate her.

Meeting Daisy for the first time was unusually exciting. Like Alyssa, there was something special about her, and people were attracted to her at first; but unlike Alyssa, what was special was superficial, and the bright glow of a new relationship would quickly fade, and Daisy's interest would soon follow. Beneath the choice veneer, Daisy was a bit shallow and insecure, particularly when it came to holding onto a friend. She played hard to get with everyone regardless of gender, and with the ladies, she tended to overdo. She was over the top, and it made everything worse. She used men like toothpicks and went through female friends like water.

She lived in the future always looking for the bigger better deal that would propel her to social queen status and restore the young adult life that was denied when she became pregnant at 19. Anything that was appealing to a broad spectrum of people was unappealing to her. Her greatest desire was to be with overly charming people sipping Mimosas and Martinis while looking bored and indifferent.

To Daisy it was a chore getting out of bed in the morning, but she deemed it quite necessary to make the next social event. Although life seemed a bore, she didn't want to miss anything, and this was her motivation to dress. She worked behind the fragrance counter at Macy's not because she needed the money. She could easily soak men for money, but people were expected to work, and she was no exception. As a consequence, she worked where she wanted, and in this job, she was paid to stand and look beautiful. It suited her. She needed to be seen, and she was. She enjoyed the

36

second take glance and the subtle deniable stares from customers and passers by. It made the annoyance of working tolerable.

Daisy had a serious need to socialize and be the life of the party. She had missed years of childhood when she became pregnant with Alyssa. She needed to make up for lost time, and was fully engaged in doing so. Alyssa was second priority, but when convenient, Daisy showed her off like a prize. She was a prize, and this was obvious to all including astute parents who immediately sized up the situation knowing that Alyssa was put back on the shelf as soon as the attention was over. Without Alyssa's grandparents, it would have been shameful. No one really cared whose eyes, nose, and mouth Alyssa had, or where she got her high cheekbones, they just wanted to fix things. They wanted to take Alyssa home if necessary, and make things right for her. As her Grandpa had pointed out so many times, Alyssa was more mature than her mother, and took care of her as well as taking care of herself.

When Alyssa arrived home in the early afternoon, her mother was laying on the couch in a robe eating popsicles and watching the movie "Drop Dead Gorgeous" on the television. Although she had seen the movie at the theater a year earlier with Alyssa, she seemed to be enjoying it more. Alyssa reasoned that she was very likely hung over from the night before, and was doing her best to recover so she could be in good shape for Saturday night. Eating popsicles was Daisy's secret to re-hydrate, and was a telltale sign of a hangover. Alyssa knew all the signs, but had a burning question for her Mom anyway. She perched on the arm of the couch by her Mom's feet and waited for the commercial before asking.

"Mom why don't you ever go to my soccer games?"

"You know I wanted to Baby. I just got up late," Daisy replied.

"Well you don't need to worry about it any more. We lost the game. We're out of the playoffs. The season is over," said Alyssa.

"I'm sorry you lost honey. You know I wanted to be there!"

"You've been promising all season Mom, and you didn't make a single game."

"It wasn't intentional honey. You know I usually work on Saturdays. This is the first Saturday I've had off in a month."

"It's okay Mom. I just wish you would do some things that I like sometimes."

"I'll make some games next year hun! I promise."

"I don't think I'm going to play next year. It's not that fun anymore. Do you think we can make some Christmas cookies? It's the perfect time for that!"

"That would be great! Sure we can do that. Are the Pillsbury kind okay that you cut off the roll? We could form those into shapes!" Daisy said wide-eyed.

"No Mom. We want the homemade taste. Grandma Lin will help us make them. She knows how! She probably even has all the ingredients. You won't have to go to the store."

"Not today honey. Okay? I'm going out again tonight, and I need to start getting ready soon."

"Well how about tomorrow?" Alyssa asked. "It's Sunday, you won't work until three."

"Okay honey sure! We'll skip church, and whip up a batch in the morning. Okay?"

"Okay Mom," said Alyssa knowing her Mom always skipped church, and that it would never happen.

Alyssa retreated to her room that was really a converted attic that Grandpa Jack had built for her because she had spent so much time there as a little girl playing with Tinker Toys and reading books. Back then, she was sharing a room with her Mother, and Jack thought it would be better for Alyssa if she had a room of her own. He removed all the clutter, finished the walls with reclaimed barn wood, and built her a little dormer with a window. The dormer was more for safety than it was for function. In case there was a fire, she could escape down a ladder to the second floor porch above the living room. The porch had a regular staircase down to the backyard. The window in the dormer was just large enough for her to get out. She had her bed arranged just right so she could look up at the stars while lying down. She felt like she was the football headed cartoon character "Hey Arnold". She imagined she was living in a boarding house, and her Grandpa Jack was the equivalent Arnold's Grandpa Phil. Arnold's Mom was conspicuously missing most of the time just like Daisy, and Daisy's boyfriend Franken was just like the tenant Mr. Kokoshka in "Hey Arnold". Even their Eastern European accents were similar.

Grandpa Jack came up every night to read Alyssa a bedtime story, and she never tired of hearing them even now as she approached her teens. Her favorite story was biblical, and Grandpa Jack knew it by heart. The story was about a little girl who served the wife of a reputable Syrian Army Captain named Naoman. Although very great, Naoman had leprosy, and the little girl convinced him that the Israelites could cure him. After several inquiries, Naoman ended up at the house of Elisha, but Elisha didn't go out to greet the great Captain. He sent his servant to provide instructions. Naoman was told to bathe in the Jordan River seven times. No matter how many times Grandpa Jack tells Alyssa the story, she always stops him to ask why Elisha didn't greet the Captain himself. Grandpa Jack, of course, doesn't know why, and continues the story. The Captain is at first outraged with his treatment and the seemingly simplistic advice, but eventually heeds what Elisha's says, bathes in the Jordan River seven times, and is cured. Very happy, he returns to Elisha and offers gifts of silver. Elisha refuses the gifts, but Elisha's servant Gehazi sneaks off later to find Naoman's departed caravan. Gehazi takes the gifts, but Elisha finds out. This is Alyssa's favorite part of the story. When Gehazi asks Elisha how he found out about his improper behavior. Elisha responds: "Did not my heart go with you?" When Alyssa first heard the story, she thought about Elisha's response

39

for several days, and finally decided it was the best response he could have given. It made her very happy, but most of all she liked the way Grandpa Jack told the story - from the heart.

Chapter 6

Alyssa never made Christmas cookies with her Mom, but she did make a few batches with Grandma Lin, and decorated a batch with Dylan and his Mom that lived down the block. Dylan was Alyssa's best friend. They had been together since they were young growing up on the same block and spending time in each other's homes just like Daisy and Dylan's Mom had. Like Daisy, Dylan's Mom had also been pregnant early in life, but unlike Daisy, Dylan's Mom got married, had more children, and lived the typical lifestyle of a middle class American with the only diversity provided by the experience of living in Southern California.

This Christmas was no different than others. Alyssa spent most of her time at Dylan's house, and the rest at Grandpa Jack and Grandma Lin's. Daisy managed to show up for Christmas Day with Franken in tow complaining how hungry he was. They arrived mid-morning long after Alyssa had opened presents and the glow of Christmas morning was long past. The mood in the house changed from carefree to awkward with their arrival, and although Daisy officially lived there, in recent weeks she had been conspicuously absent.

There was no excitement in their visit. Daisy's gifts of clothing were well received by Alyssa, but very practical, and something she should have received anyway. Franken gave her a toy that was more appropriate for someone much younger. The toy was obviously an afterthought, and purchased at the Thrifty drug store that morning. Everyone except Grandpa Jack seemed unwilling to engage them in conversation, but Grandpa boldly

40

questioned them about their plans, and seemed dissatisfied with the answers. They left quickly after Christmas dinner with everyone breathing a sigh of relief.

The New Year came, and Alyssa was actually grateful for Franken because he kept her Mom busy. She was much happier doing her own thing at her grandparent's. For interaction with people she relied on Dylan. She spent other times doing things enjoyed by past generations that were now forgotten by kids her age. She lingered in the schoolyard, on the block, or in front of the Circle K. She cased the Mall, and lounged by herself at Starbucks. She was alone most of the time surrounded by people in crowded situations. She felt like she belonged among strangers. It made her feel good to blend in. Watching people in public kept her from boredom, but occasionally she would interact, and felt compelled to talk to strangers who appeared troubled. It reinforced, in her mind, the suggestion from Grandpa Jack that she may have been a healer in past lives.

She knew she shouldn't be out on the street as much as she was, and that it may be dangerous. So to be on the safe side, she deliberately dressed down and wore loose clothing. She tied her hair back, and wore a Dodgers cap. She did what she wanted because no one kept tabs on her anyway. She was a latch key kid, and kept her house key on a chain around her neck under her shirt. After walking home from school each day, she made herself comfortable at home, had a snack, and went back out. Grandpa Jack and Grandma Lin both worked, and Daisy was no where to be found. She was home alone, and she liked it that way. Sometimes she stayed in her room reading books, but she preferred to be on the street. When she got lonely, she would visit Dylan. This was the life she enjoyed, but she knew in her heart that it wouldn't last long.

Daisy appeared one day during dinner with Grandpa and Grandma. Alyssa remembered it quite distinctly because it was Tuesday, February 13th. The day before Valentines Day, and

41

Dylan's Dad's birthday. Franken and Daisy walked into the dining room.

"Frank and I are getting married," Daisy stated very mater of fact, "and we're moving into Frank's house in Rosemead in the Spring."

Everyone stared in stunned silence, but after a moment resumed eating without saying a word in reply.

"Did you here me?" Daisy asked, "Franky and I are getting married!"

"Well congratulations," Grandpa Jack replied nonchalantly, "I hope you'll be very happy. Frank if you're going to be married, you're going to need to lay off playing the ponies."

"Well Daisy, she loves me," Frank replied, "she does anything for me, no?" he said turning to look at Daisy. "She'll let me do everything I want. I take care of the little one too," he finished in his eastern European accent.

Grandma Lin continued to stare. Alyssa was clearly upset with the last remark.

"No one needs to take care of me," Alyssa stated flatly, "I take care of myself."

"You've considered Alyssa in this?" Grandpa Jack asked.

"Yes," Daisy said cutting off Franken, "She'll move in with us after the school year is over."

"No I'm not," Alyssa replied in a stalwart tone.

"Why don't you let Alyssa stay here?" Grandpa Jack asked before Daisy could respond to her daughter, "This is really her home now. You're always working anyway, or out with Franken . . . I mean Frank. She could spend weekends with you."

"I don't know Daddy," replied Daisy, "kids should be with their mother."

"I don't see why not, yes," Franken said, "the girl she love her granny-parents. Should she not? She love Jack. Maybe that work – no?"

42

Daisy was surprised that Franken was so easy to give in to her Dad, and Alyssa was surprised by the whole affair. Grandpa Jack had never interfered with Daisy's whims before, but he seemingly disliked Franken, and he definitely loved his granddaughter. He wanted Alyssa to stay put, but he also wanted Daisy to feel okay about it.

"I'm not moving to Rosemead," Alyssa said with defiance. "I'm not leaving my Dylan, and I've always dreamed of going to Mark Keppel High School. That's where most of my friends are going. That's where Dylan is going. This is the neighborhood where I belong. This is more like Los Angeles. Rosemead is a boring suburb. I'm not moving to Rosemead."

"You'll stay with your Mom, and you'll love it in Rosemead," Daisy said. "They have a great football team."

"Mom you know I don't care about football," Alyssa replied. "It's a brutal game for egotistical macho guys who need to demonstrate their primordial warrior instinct. I'm not moving to Rosemead."

Everyone but Franken turned to look at Alyssa surprised by the adult words and her understanding of advanced social concepts.

"The girl is right, yes?" said Franken. "She be of teen age soon. Is not good for us to fight her. No? She need to be her own thing."

Now everyone turned to Franken surprised that wisdom existed within.

"We'll see," said Grandpa Jack. "You two make your wedding plans, and when school let's out we'll address it then."

"That's a good idea," said Grandma Lin entering the conversation. "I'm sure we can work something out where everyone will be happy. When is the wedding?"

"We want to get married in South Lake Tahoe. We want you and Dad, Alyssa, and a few friends to come. We're thinking of doing it during spring break so it doesn't interfere with Alyssa's school."

"That sounds like a great plan Daisy," said Grandpa Jack. "We'll mark it on our calendars when you get a date together."

"I knew you would understand Daddy," said Daisy.

"Yes, and before we go, we want your blessing, No?" Franken said looking at Daisy.

"Yes, do we have your blessing?" asked Daisy.

"Yes dear," said Grandma Lin while Grandpa Jack nodded without speaking.

"Thank you then we go!" said Franken.

"Thanks Daddy," said Daisy as she kissed him on the cheek.

With that they left, and it seemed like a whirlwind left the house, and shut the door. The next day Alyssa came down with the flu, and missed Valentines Day. Daisy was nowhere to be found, but Grandma Lin stayed late before work, and Grandpa Jack came home from work early to care for her. Dylan stopped by after school to drop off her Valentines. She thought that she may be too old for Valentines being an eighth grader, but she had a whole stack. The best valentine was from Dylan. She was touched and surprised, and then felt bad that she didn't have one for him. They sat and talked while she opened the envelopes, and Dylan kissed her on the cheek and went home.

Grandpa Jack thought that Daisy's announcement the night before drained Alyssa's energy, and that's what caused her to get sick. In the past, Alyssa would have considered the statement one of Grandpa Jack's leftover flashbacks to the 60s, but ever since he provided his opinions on her dream sequences she had a new respect for whatever Grandpa said.

"What do you mean drain my energy Grandpa?" Alyssa asked.

"It's hard to put into words, but you've been very happy for the last few months. Your Mom has been busy with Franken and leaving you alone. The threat of moving you out of your refuge pulled the plug on your energy. Losing that much energy at once left you vulnerable. You may have been carrying that virus for a long time, but you were so drained it seized the opportunity. Think of pulling the plug on a swimming pool raft, that's how your energy left last night. You need to protect yourself from predators and the unrelated drive-by energy drain. Your Mom and Franken were a drive-by. You can feel them coming like an ill wind. When you feel that, you want to shield up immediately and keep your energy tight. Don't let them get to you. Think positive. Whatever they say or do let it bounce off, and go about your business like they don't faze you."

"Is that what you did last night?" Alyssa asked.

"Maybe so, but if I did, I was unaware of it. Like a lot of things you practice in life, after awhile it becomes second nature and you don't even realize you're doing it."

Chapter 7

Weeks passed and life drifted back to how it was before Daisy's big engagement announcement. Alyssa didn't see much of Grandma Lin, less of her Mom, and Grandpa Jack only at night before bed. Her home was the neighborhood streets. That's where she liked to be, and where she felt a sense of belonging.

She was oddly attracted to the homeless, found many homeless intelligent and articulate, and reasoned that they were just misunderstood. What she found odd was that many had piercing looks like she did, and that made her curious. She found alcoholics, druggies, and some junkies, but all were definitely misfits living on the fringes of society. For reasons she couldn't explain, she felt an attachment to them. After some study, she decided that many homeless were self-medicating. They couldn't cope with the boredom and absurdity of daily life, and eventually just stayed gone in a substance fueled alter-reality, not wanting to come back, and accepting the trade-off of a life devoid of creature comforts, safety and self dignity.

She liked to talk to a woman in her thirties named Merle who lived in a cardboard box on the side of the local Blockbuster. She slept in dirty blankets, and complained of the smell of urine nearby. Other homeless relieved themselves too close to her home.

"Things are bad," said Merle one day.

"My Grandpa says that these are boom times! It's 2001 and a new century!" replied Alyssa.

"I didn't say times were bad! I said things are bad," Merle remarked while glancing back and forth nervously. "If people had fewer things they would be a lot better off."

"How do you mean?" asked Alyssa.

"Simple," said Merle, "without things you don't need a place to store them. You don't have to worry about having them stolen or losing them, and you don't have to worry about cleaning them or maintaining them. Life is much easier without things. People get attached to things. It's not right I tell you! Give up your things and within a day or two you'll feel wonderfully free."

"What about a toothbrush?" Alyssa asked, "You look like you could use one of those."

"You're twisting my words, but yes I could use a toothbrush," Merle said. "When you live on the street, it's hard to keep track of things. A tooth brush is a valuable tool. It's different than other things. It's very empowering to have clean teeth, but all things can weigh you down including toothbrushes."

"I'll bring you one, and some toothpaste," stated Alyssa while walking away backwards.

If Alyssa was found indoors during the day it was at Dylan's house. Although they were too old, they occasionally played the board game Candyland, used the cards like fortunes, and joked about what they said. They liked to watch VHS tapes, and Dylan's Dad had one of the newer DVD players. They watched old Shirley Temple movies, "The Mask" with Jim Carrey, "Big" with Tom Hanks over and over again while they were doing other things, and had the dialog mostly memorized. They played Mario Kart on

Dylan's Game Cube, but would quickly tire of it and end up back out on the street.

One of their outdoor pastimes was to try and kick the football high enough to hit the street light. This went on for years until Dylan actually hit it one night and broke it.

More time passed, and before she knew it, Alyssa's 13th birthday arrived. She was born Tuesday, April 12th 1988. It was the same day Sonny Bono was elected Mayor of Palm Springs. Daisy reminded Alyssa of the circumstances of that day every year. Daisy claimed that Alyssa was conceived the day the world population reached five billion on July 11th, 1987. One more person in the world wouldn't make a difference Daisy thought when she found out she was pregnant the day after a big argument with her current boyfriend. The cyclical nature of Daisy's relationships had already started. Alyssa's father was but one of the first in a long line of failed relationships.

According to Daisy, labor was only the beginning of the pain of child rearing, but Alyssa never really understood this claim since Grandpa and Grandma seemed to have done most of the work in taking care of her.

Even in 2001, Grandma Lin had made her a birthday dinner, and Grandpa Jack made her the cake. They invited Dylan and his parents to dinner. They were all having a wonderful time laughing and joking about the recent past while clearing away the dishes. Daisy and Franken blew in like a chilling winter breeze.

Both of them were drinking, and Daisy's speech was slightly slurred. In spite of the intrusion, the mood at the impromptu party remained light through cake, ice cream and presents. It changed abruptly, however, when Daisy mentioned moving Alyssa to Rosemead as soon as the school year ended. Dylan's parents sensed the tension, quickly said goodnight, and exited with Dylan in tow.

"Why can't I just stay here with Grandpa and Grandma Lin?" asked Alyssa pleadingly.

"Yes Daisy, why can't she stay where she wants to be? She can spend weekends and holidays with you when you have time off work," added Grandpa Jack.

"A child should be with her Mom," Daisy firmly stated.

"But it's her birthday!" Grandpa Jack responded. "Give her a real gift, and let her stay here. You can be together whenever you want."

In a moment of clarity, Daisy seemed to react to the fact that it was Alyssa's birthday, and that she actually should give her daughter something meaningful even if it was a small sacrifice on her part and a blow to her motherly instinct. In a moment of tense silence, everyone present stared at Daisy while she processed the information within her own head.

"Alright," said Daisy in a trancelike stare, "we'll see how it works out."

Everyone breathed a sigh of relief including Franken.

"Thanks Mom," said Alyssa, "that's the greatest gift you could have given me."

"I'm glad you're happy honey," said Daisy, "come on Franky. Let's go. It's getting late."

With Daisy's comment, the whirlwind couple left the house once more, and life returned to normal with Alyssa spending most of her time on the street or at Dylan's house. She would have her evening meal with her Grandparents, and Grandpa Jack would read her a story each night at bedtime. That was her routine. Beyond that, she was on her own, independent, and liked it that way. She woke herself up each morning, and got herself to school. She was on a meal program for low income kids, so she had a hot breakfast and lunch each day at school for free. On weekends she ate cereal in the morning at home, and had lunch with Dylan. Dylan usually had money, or they would raid his kitchen with his mother's blessing making their own macaroni and cheese, sandwiches, or quesadillas.

48

Alyssa always carried a jacket, an extra set of clothes, toothbrush, and other necessities in her backpack. She was prepared to stay wherever she was. She did all her own laundry, sometimes washed the clothes right off her back sitting on top of the washer in her underwear like in the old movies. Dylan was accustomed to this, and took little notice. They were both entering puberty, however, and their brother-sister type relationship couldn't go on forever.

The last few weeks of the school year were so blissful that Alyssa could feel the impending doom, and it reminded her of Grandpa Jack's music that started:

"Well the first days are the hardest days, don't you worry anymore, 'cause when life looks like easy street there is danger at your door."

The last day of school happened to coincide with the Bush Tax Cuts being signed into law on June 7th, 2001. Alyssa's class discussed the new tax cuts because books were turned in, grades were done, and there was nothing else to do. Most of the people in the class didn't understand how tax cuts could really improve the economy, but they all agreed that it was a good thing. If nothing else, their parents would be happy, and it may improve their mood through summer vacation. Alyssa knew, however, that her only vacation would be a trip to Rosemead.

Her suspicions were confirmed when Daisy and Franken showed up early in the morning on Saturday with a borrowed pick up truck to move Alyssa's things. Grandpa Jack and Grandma Lin were out for the morning and unable to help her cause.

Chapter 8

"I thought you were going to let me stay here with Grandpa?" Alyssa asked.

"We need to be a family darling. We need to make a fresh start together. We need to give Frank a chance. Besides I don't want to be there alone without you," Daisy replied.

"Sure," said Franken, "we be a good family, yes? You learn to be a good cook, and keep you Momma company, no?"

"I really hope this works for you, but I don't think it's going to work for me. I want to stay with Grandpa and Grandma! This is home to me!"

"You just try it honey. You'll love it there," said Daisy.

"But I love it here!"

"Well a very wise person once said, "If you love someone, set them free. If they come back, then they're yours. If not, then they probably never were yours anyway. You need to let go of this place dear, and try a new life with your Mom and Frank in Rosemead."

"That's the dumbest thing I've ever heard," said Alyssa. "I'm talking about a place to live, not an animal! Animals are naturally free, and if they're not, there being held against their will. That's not love, that's oppression. If you love something it is free. That's what love is. Love is freedom. Love is giving freely and unconditionally, and also accepting freely and unconditionally. You already know love in your heart. You don't need to test yourself! That expression is absurd."

Both Daisy and Franken were a bit shocked with the confidence and stern tone of Alyssa's voice. It was as if she was teaching them, and they paused awkwardly before responding looking at each other nervously.

"If you say so dear," said Daisy sheepishly. "But you're going to attempt a new life with me and Franken, I mean Frank. There's a bed already there, and a chest of drawers, so you can leave most of your furniture. Just bring your clothes and your bike."

With that statement, Alyssa decided that she would never live with Franken. She may spend a few days there, but with her bed

50

and furniture at Grandpa's safely tucked away in her attic bedroom, this would always be home.

They went to the Rosemead house, and it wasn't as bad as Alyssa had envisioned. The furniture was cheap, but was in good condition. The walls were bare with the exception of Daisy's things that didn't really fit in with the house. Daisy's bedroom and bathroom were clean, but those were the only rooms acceptable to Alyssa. She spent the day cleaning while she watched Daisy and Franken drink all afternoon. Franken watched basketball playoffs with a green beer bottle in his hand continuously. Daisy drank her favorite drink called "Sea breeze" that was mostly Vodka and a little cranberry juice. Alyssa called the drink a "Shleebreeze" because that's how Daisy pronounced the word "Seabreeze" if she had more than two.

Franken managed to set up Alyssa's room and dusted off an old 19 inch color television from the garage with a piece of coaxial cable hanging from it. He plugged it in and turned it on before hooking up the cable. The picture popped in through the snow.

"You watch TV while you fix up room," said Franken as he walked away down the hall.

"I don't watch television," Alyssa called to him as he departed, "it limits your thinking."

"That's okay. You limit your thinking then. It's there for you if you want," said Franken.

She watched it despite her comment. There was no remote, but she was thankful for the noise. She decided to leave it on infomercials because they seemed to bother her least. She found clean sheets and made her bed, unpacked her clothes and arranged them in the chest of drawers. She was pleased when she found that her window had no screen, and was a straight shot out to the street with no bushes or fences blocking the way.

She arranged some towels under the covers of her bed so that it looked like she was lying there under the covers watching TV. In a few minutes she was out the window and into the street with her

51

backpack. She managed to find a convenience store that had once been a seven-eleven, but had dropped out of the franchise, and was now just called 'Lucky Seven'. She bought already shelled sunflower seeds and a drink with a screw top that she could reseal. Just to get the feel of it, she hung out in front for ten minutes, but there was no action, and she decided to walk the neighborhood. There were few people out besides Hispanics cutting lawns who waved and smiled while finding amusement in their leaf blowers. There was a lot of traffic on the streets, but she wondered where everyone was going because there were very few businesses.

She noticed a black cat with big green eyes that wasn't much more than a kitten. It came out to her mewing, but then changed its mind, and returned the way it had come without crossing her path.

She ended up walking beside a dry river bed with a bike trail on top of a flood control dam next to it, and found a place to sit underneath an overpass for a major street. There was evidence of homeless. Bunched up dirty blankets, and an array of mostly worthless articles littered the area. There was an empty grocery cart at the bottom of the dam on the riverside.

"Here I am with the homeless again," she thought, "I might as well live here myself."

The thought filled her with energy and gave her courage. She felt empowered and declared herself independent. At 13 years of age, she concluded that she was a grown woman of the streets. She was a drifter, but wasn't lost. Her mission was to find new meaning in what was a mostly empty life. Her medium would be the street, and her color palette would be the personalities she found there. She was a self proclaimed outcast from established Southern California society.

She stayed in that spot overlooking the dry riverbed for over an hour caught up in the moment and letting the energy flow through her. The evening sky turned red, and then various shades of blue and violet. So close to summer solstice, she decided it was getting late, and walked back to Franken's.

No one had noticed her absence, and an episode of "Cops" was playing on the television that she had left on. When she turned it off, she could hear people in the living room. Not wanting to go there she shut and locked the window and went to bed.

The next day both Daisy and Franken were obviously hung over, and Daisy asked Alyssa to go to the store with Franken to buy her some popsicles and handed her a ten dollar bill.

"Why did you bring me here?" Alyssa asked with a confrontational look of disdain.

"What do you mean baby girl?" Daisy replied with a startled look.

"You obviously didn't bring me here to spend time together," Alyssa said. "Did you bring me here to cook, clean, and take care of you?"

Daisy paused for a moment. The look of surprise faded from her face, and she was at a loss for words. In her state she couldn't rally her mind or body. She couldn't think, and even her scalp seemed to hurt.

"I brought you here because I love you," Daisy said looking for the reaction. She looked nervously down at the ground.

"To use your quote Flower, "if you love someone, set them free," Alyssa said while seemingly rising up above her mother.

It wasn't the reaction Daisy was looking for, and she had never been called 'Flower' to her face by her own daughter before. Daisy was suddenly aware that she was being challenged, but couldn't rise to the occasion. Her mind was cloudy, and her body was in pain. She couldn't muster any reaction let alone one of parental authority. Instead, her expression turned to one of shock. She felt assaulted, and went on the defense. Alyssa had overwhelmed her and won the argument before it started. Franken came to her rescue to defuse the situation.

"We will go out to the store, no?" he said glancing back and forth at each of them. His expression suggested that neither of them should reply to his question.

"When you came home you two talk. We go!" he said forcefully.

Alyssa reluctantly accepted the offer and walked out with Franken following close behind.

She brought back the popsicles, but refused to have any sort of conversation, and stayed in her room all day with the television on. She made occasional appearances in the living room and kitchen but didn't speak. It appeared as though she had given in, but when Daisy and Franken started drinking again, she decided to leave. She made up her bed once more to appear as if she was in it, left the TV on, and slipped out the window with her backpack. She left a note that said if she couldn't live with her grandparents; she would rather live in the street, and would be better off without Daisy to care for.

She had taken what cash she had available. She had saved $48.00, and with the change from earlier in the day she had well over $50.00. She also had grabbed a box of pop tarts and two bottles of water to stuff in her pack.

Chapter 9

She moved quickly down the street with a lump in her stomach, unsure of where to go, but certain she was doing the right thing. She was completely on her own for the first time in her life, and although in one way it was very uplifting, in another way it was unsettling. She was already lonely, and was worried that she wouldn't make it on her own. The unsettling feeling motivated her, and she quickened her pace to keep her mind off things. After walking over an hour, she found herself at an on ramp for the Santa Monica freeway. She suddenly had a strong desire to stop and stare. She stood studying the I-10 sign, the broken curb, the dirty street, and each of the various pieces of litter lying about on the grass and pavement. She wanted to move, but stood frozen in time. Her trance narrowed in on the west bound I-10 sign. It could have been hours or it could have been minutes. She didn't know.

Suddenly a car pulled up. It was a beat up Chrysler Lebaron with one primer gray fender. It was a convertible with the top up, but what was left of the top was in complete shreds. It was a sight to behold, but looked inviting in a strange way. The driver leaned across to unlatch and push open the passenger door. He was wearing sunglasses but it was dusk and getting dark.

"Going west? Get in!" was all he said.

The spell was broken; she got in without comment, and slammed the door shut.

The wind was blowing around in the car as they lobbed down the freeway in the slow lane. Their hair was blowing around and getting in their eyes, but they enjoyed it. The absurdity of it all combined with the excitement of the moment made them laugh. What remained of the convertible top was flapping around loudly in the wind, and it added to the craziness. As they approached the end of the freeway by Lincoln Boulevard, Alyssa looked over at her unknown driver.

"Where are we going?" she asked.

"I'm going to the Topanga Motel on highway one, but you're going to the Santa Monica Pier."

"I am?" she asked.

"Yes! That's as west as you can get around here." was all he said in reply with a slight smile.

He knew exactly where he was going, and wheeled around on highway one, and pulled up in front of the pier entrance by the bike path.

"Here's your stop," he said turning to her and smiling.

Instinctively, she opened the door, got out, slammed it shut, and leaned back inside the open window.

"What's your name?" she asked.

"They call me 'The Breeze'," he replied.

"Where do I go now?"

"Why walk out onto the pier of course! Follow the bubbles on the breeze."

"Okay," she said turning away and hustling off.

When she turned again he was gone.

She walked out on the pier and almost immediately noticed bubbles blowing in the breeze. There were hundreds of bubbles, and maybe even thousands blowing around in the night sky illuminated by all the lights on the pier. The bubbles got thicker and more concentrated after she passed the carnival rides. She found the source. It was coming from a machine clamped on to the pier's railing with a tube leading down to a gallon jug of bubble stuff sitting on the pier's decking. There was a man with a video camera filming, and as Alyssa approached, he started filming her.

"I've been waiting for you," he said.

"Why me?" she asked.

"I've been waiting for someone interesting to shoot, and you're the first one," he replied.

"What is that?" she said pointing at the source of the bubbles.

"That's a bubble machine. They use them in the movies and sometimes in modeling shoots."

"Why do you have one?"

"I'm a professional photographer. I come down here sometimes on Sundays to see if I can find anything interesting. I've had the machine for a long time. It attracts attention. It's actually a lot of fun."

"I love it!" said Alyssa.

"People like you usually do," he said returning the camera to his eye.

"What do you mean?" she asked.

"You'll find out," he said. "You're way ahead of me, and you're just beginning."

"What now?" she asked him.

56

"I would suggest doing what everyone else does. Continue walking to the end of the pier, turn around, and walk back! You never know what you're going to see on the Santa Monica pier."

"Okay!" she said and continued her excursion.

She walked to the end of the pier, paused for a moment to stare out at the cold black of the Pacific at night. The breeze was a little too cool for her, and she thought of her ride down the freeway with her unknown driver called 'The Breeze'. The cold made her turn and head back. When she got to where the bubble machine was, the photographer was gone as well as his gear. There was a pretty woman that appeared to be in her mid-twenties standing there instead. They locked eyes and were immediately drawn to each other.

"You look lost," said the woman.

"I'm definitely not lost," replied Alyssa. "I really don't know what I am yet, but I know I'm not lost."

"You look kind of young, are you out here alone?" the woman asked with a look of motherly concern.

Alyssa knew that her answer may leave her vulnerable, but the woman seemed trustworthy, and not much more than ten years older than herself. She felt she could trust her.

"Yes," Alyssa answered with a defiant look.

"Do you live near here?"

"No, I live in Monterey Park."

"Monterey Park! That's a long ways. Do your parents know you're gone?"

"I live with my grandparents, and no they don't know I'm gone. I left a note."

"How are you going to get home?"

"I'm not. I'm on my own now, and going to find my own way in life. My inner feelings are my guide, and the street is my classroom."

The women smiled wryly, and then took on a secondary expression as if sizing Alyssa up. A moment passed without words.

"I'm Sheryl Leoni," she said offering Alyssa her hand. "I live here in Santa Monica. Why don't you stay with me for the night? You can leave anytime you want, and I won't report you to anyone. I respect your decision to be on your own making your own choices."

Alyssa didn't know how to respond at first, and the reality of her situation suddenly hit her.

"I'm a runaway! I'm also well underage and that makes me vulnerable to the police. I'm also homeless!" Alyssa thought to herself before responding.

She studied Sheryl Leoni for a few seconds, and the hopelessness of her situation actually calmed her. She had little to lose, and she studied her new acquaintance as Sheryl patiently waited for Alyssa to respond.

"Happy to meet you Sheryl," said Alyssa. "My name is Alyssa Daingerfield, and I'd enjoy staying with you for the night."

"Well it's settled then. Why don't we head over there now? When we get there, don't be surprised. I have a boyfriend. His name is Bob Reech. He's harmless. In fact, he's very kind and gentle, but he drinks too much. I basically take care of him, so our friends call me Momma. My ethnic origins are Italian. That's another reason they call me Momma."

"I bet you're a great Momma," said Alyssa. "Is it alright if I call you Momma, or would you prefer Sheryl?"

"Either one is fine!" Momma replied, "But I think your going to lean toward Momma."

They started walking back toward the base of the pier, and straight up Colorado Avenue.

"Yes. I'm Momma to a lot of people, but especially Reech. No one calls him Bob. They call him by his last name. He's very tall and thin, and he hangs drywall for a living, and can reach way up high to drive nails and screws: consequently, everyone calls him Reech. There was an old macaroni commercial on TV that had a jingle, "They call it beefaroni, it's made from macaroni". Our

58

friends sing that jingle to us, but they modify the words slightly, "They call him Reecharoni, he lives with Momma Leoni".

"How silly," said Alyssa, "but I guess that makes it clever!"

"It gets much sillier, trust me."

"Silly is fine as long as it's clever." Alyssa stated.

"Sure! I guess that's what makes it funny!"

Sheryl Leoni looked like anything but a Momma. She was a very attractive young woman with long brownish-blonde hair that came down to the middle of her back. She kept it in a pony tail, but swung her head around a lot as if she was accustomed to free flowing hair that frequently needed to be moved out of her eyes. She wasn't beautiful. She was pretty in her own charming way; she had nice features and a curvy voluptuous body. What was most notable about her was a loose and carefree demeanor. She didn't have a care in the world, and assumed she would live forever. She seemed mischievous in a fun loving way. Her eyes sparkled with excitement, and Alyssa liked that about her.

"Where are your parents?" asked Alyssa.

"I have my Dad," answered Momma. "My Mom died of breast cancer when I was in college. My Dad just recently went through angioplasty surgery. He had heart problems that I attribute to his time as a Colonel in the Army. He had a stressful job, and smoked and drank. I managed to visit him in Virginia just before his surgery, so we had a nice visit."

"So you're all alone?"

"Well yes, but I have aunts and uncles and cousins in Virginia."

"My Grandparents are from Virginia," said Alyssa. "They're all from the Springfield area. I've never been there."

"Springfield is very nice," said Momma while glancing over at Alyssa. "I hope you make it there one day."

Momma Leoni and Alyssa made a left on 6th Street off of Colorado Avenue, and Momma and Reech's building was about halfway up the block on the right.

"You're close to the beach," said Alyssa. "How do you afford it?"

"It's not too bad actually. Santa Monica has rent control, and this apartment has been in the family for a lot of years. Both Reech and I work. So we manage."

They walked up the stairs of a building that looked to be 40 years old or so, and after Momma maneuvered a key into the door, what appeared to be a lush jungle opened up to Alyssa. The apartment was full to the brim with houseplants, and two rather large salt water aquariums with brightly colored fish swimming around inside. The other side of the apartment had a glass gliding door that was open. There was a small balcony that overlooked the alley, and you could see portions of Colorado Avenue.

"Who goes there?" called someone from within.

"Who do you think?" said Momma. "You better be dressed right because we have a visitor."

"Shorts and a T-shirt as always," said Reech standing up.

He was tall, and very thin. His height was so great; he looked like a giant in the little apartment. He appeared as though he may hit his head on the ceiling. His arms and legs were boney giving him an awkward appearance. He had a long full face that looked gaunt with hollow cheek bones, long straight brown hair with bangs that hung in his eyes. His face had minor pock marks as evidence that his youth had passed. Alyssa thought that Momma was far too pretty for him.

"What have you been doing?" said Momma while entering the kitchen.

"I've been working on my 30 minute abs right here in front of the TV," said Reech.

"Well now that you're all buff," said Momma, "I want you to meet a new friend of mine. She's staying the night. Alyssa this is Reech."

"Pleased to meet you little lady," said Reech trying to sound like John Wayne.

"Nice to meet you too," said Alyssa looking up in awe of the towering man.

"You're not one of these Hollywood wanabe runaway's are you?" said Reech smiling from ear to ear.

"Reech! She's my friend. Don't be rude. She's from Monterey Park, and more Californian than you are."

"Hey, take it easy!" said Reech. "I was just trying to be funny."

"Well knock it off, and move over to the chair. I'm going to make up the sofa for Alyssa to sleep."

Momma hustled off to retrieve the linens and had to scold Reech again to get out of her way.

"I guess in some ways we're all runnin' from something," said Reech standing and moving to the chair. "Some of us run away from home, some run from marriage, others run from feelings. Some people run away from death. I personally run from Bruce Springsteen fans. Deadheads are almost as bad, but they're not so obnoxious. Are you running away from family Alyssa?"

"No, I love my family, and I love my Mom. I just don't want to live with her. I want to live with my Grandparents. That's my home. I've lived there most of my life, and that's where I want to stay, but my Mom wants me to move to Rosemead with her soon to be husband."

"I wouldn't want to live in Rosemead either. It will eventually work itself out. You can count on it. It's hard for parents to realize that their kids are growing up, and you seem very mature for your age. Give her a chance. She'll come around. What you don't want to do is something stupid while you're waiting for the change. Be patient while each person adjusts. I've seen kids turn to drugs and alcohol to numb the pain of problems at home, and by the time they get help, it's too late."

"I'll be fine," said Alyssa. "I have no desire to drink."

"Good!" said Reech. "There's much more to life than Martinis, weed, and caffeine."

"Did you want to call your Grandparents?" asked Momma.

"No, I'll call them in the morning," said Alyssa.

"Well you use the phone anytime you want," said Momma. "How about some dinner? Reech and I like Spaghetti without sauce. We just put a little butter on it. We eat that a lot. We don't eat much meat."

"Yes! That's the way I like it too!" said Alyssa.

Momma Leoni made up dinner, and they ate on TV trays while watching the end of the Laker game and then Nova on PBS. Reech switched from a beer to a big glass of water, and Momma had a small glass of Crème de Menthe after dinner while Reech washed dishes. She sipped it ever so slightly, and savored ever bit. Reech sat back down in the chair when he finished.

"Why don't you go to bed Reech? It's your bedtime anyway," said Momma.

"I'm not ready yet," complained Reech.

"Well alright. Alyssa, why don't you come out to the balcony for a minute? I want to talk to you," said Momma.

Alyssa walked out on the balcony that overlooked the alley. It was dark now, but the lights from the windows of the many apartments illuminated the stucco buildings. It was warm; everyone had their windows open, and the sound of televisions echoed around making the street seem lively.

"You didn't leave because you're unwanted did you?" asked Momma.

"No, probably the opposite. I'm wanted in two households, but I should be staying with my grandparents while my Mom attempts this new life. I don't want to be caught up in it again. I've been through one of her marriages before, and it didn't go well. I was too young to realize what was going on. I didn't know what marriage was really supposed to be like. My grandparents do their own thing. They don't really hang out with each other too much, but when they do, they seem to enjoy it. My Mom just seems to want everyone to serve her. It always seems to be about her, and I think that's why she wants me there. She wants a maid and a cook not a daughter. She's needy too. Whenever she has problems with her boyfriend, she comes to me to talk it through. I talk her through it, and in a few days, she's back for more. She never asks about what I'm going through."

"You must be good at helping or she wouldn't come back," said Momma. "You're successfully filling a need. That's actually quite impressive."

"My Grandpa says I'm a healer, and that I may have even been a doctor or a highly regarded spiritual leader in past lives. I always thought he was crazy, but lately, it seems to make sense."

"The shoe seems to fit. There's a fire in you that burns very brightly. I could sense it on the pier tonight even before we spoke. There's something special about you, and you need to find out what that is. If it's healing, then become a healer, but you're meant to do something great."

"I think I already know something. The knowing comes naturally to me. I mean, how did I end up here? It was no accident."

"I agree," said Momma, "it was no accident. I knew that I could relate to you directly on some level when we met. I take care of people too. I don't think I'm a healer, but I take care of people. When my Mom died, I took care of my Dad much the same way you take care of your Mom. He became a drinker, and the relationship got unhealthy as I got older. I was an enabler, and enabled him to drink when he got home. He never abused me, but abused the situation, and took me for granted. That's when I left much like you. I was on my own for a long time, but I eventually patched it up, and he lets me live here. This place is actually a condo that he owns, and he lets me live here for free. He has plenty of money, so he doesn't need the rent that this place would draw. We can't spend too much time together or else we fall back into the same rut. I do love him though. He's my Dad."

"We're caregivers I guess," said Alyssa, "people want us. We're in demand."

"That's good in a way," said Momma Leoni. "There's nothing worse for the spirit than being unwanted and unloved. All creatures know this. Humans know it more than the rest. Children know it even in the womb. They can detect if they're unwanted even as a fetus, and sometimes wonder why they weren't aborted if they survive, but they come to understand a greater purpose if their parents aren't capable of loving them, and quickly move on."

"Even though I have nothing, I feel very good," Alyssa said. "I feel strong, empowered, and in control of my own destiny. It's as it should be. I didn't eat much today except with you and Reech, but I never felt weak. I never felt hunger. I felt excitement."

"That's very likely because you're on purpose," said Momma. "You're doing exactly what you're supposed to be doing whatever that is. You're in touch with your inner voice."

"What do you mean my inner voice?" asked Alyssa.

"Well that's one way of describing it. Some call it gut feel. Others call it instinct. Deep within yourself you know exactly what to do from moment to moment. Getting in touch with that essence and trusting it is one of the secrets to life. I think it's the connection between the spirit world and the material world of incarnate souls."

"I get it," said Alyssa, "but what do you mean by incarnate souls?"

"People that have been born and are living here on earth," replied Momma Leoni. "You've heard of the term reincarnated. Well incarnated just means the first time I guess. I don't really know for sure. It's just my opinion on how things work."

"I agree that I'm on purpose. I'm doing exactly what I'm supposed to be doing for the first time in my life. You've captured it well. I'm finally waking up."

"Let's go inside," said Momma.

When they went inside Reech was fast asleep in the chair holding his big water glass without spilling any. Momma took the glass from his hand, woke him up, and scooted him off to bed.

"Reech and I have to work in the morning," said Momma when she returned. "You can come and go as you please, but leave a note if you're going to go home so I don't worry. Come back any time. Someone is usually here or the door is open. We lock at night, but just knock loudly and I'll let you in. We're friends now, so you must stay in touch."

Chapter 10

Alyssa was aroused by shuffling in the morning, but never fully woke up. When she did wake up it was mid-morning, and she decided to call Grandpa Jack. She was surprised when he answered. He should have been at work, but he was going in late for a doctor's appointment. He was very concerned, and talked her into letting him pick her up on the way back from his appointment. They met at Denny's at the corner of Lincoln and Colorado Avenue. Alyssa didn't want to get Momma Leoni in trouble by divulging where she slept the night before.

"Did either Flower or Franken know I was gone?" Alyssa asked Grandpa Jack after a long period of silence in the car.

"I haven't spoken to Daisy, but I doubt it because I haven't heard anything from them. I'll take you home, and you can call Franken's from there and let her know where you are. I think this is something between you and your Mom. Just remember that I'm always here for you if you need me."

"I didn't think they would miss me because I basically take care of myself and they didn't need me for anything. That's why I should be living with you and Grandma. You actually care about me, and we enjoy each other's company. I don't live there just to serve your needs and prop up your ego. I want to live at your house near Dylan and my school."

"Where did you sleep last night? Not on the street I hope. It may be summer, but you'll catch cold in the damp ocean air and June gloom."

"I met a real nice lady on the Santa Monica pier. She's in her mid-twenties, and she's a lot like me. Her Mom died when she was in college. She took care of her Dad for many years, and now she takes care of her boyfriend. I guess you have to take care of someone in this life. You can't just take care of yourself. That's kind of rare."

"You should be careful. There are a lot of predators out there that would love to take advantage of a beautiful 13 year old girl like you. You could end up kidnapped, sexually assaulted, or even dead. People can put on a good front to get what they want. You're young, inexperienced, and a fairly easy mark. Don't get drawn into a trap," said Grandpa Jack with a distant look on his face.

"My dear Grandfather! I think I'm a better judge of character than you. If you recall, you and Grandma Lin left Virginia for San Francisco with nothing more than a Chevy Van and a packet of money. You had more than most kids that hung out in Golden Gate Park, but not much. You trusted people, and you lived with people you didn't know!"

"I was 18 when I left for California, and so was Grandma. You're only 13, and you're female. You're at a physical disadvantage when you're on the street. There are also people out there that prey on children. I'm not talking about strictly sexual predators either. You don't know what you're going to find out there. Some people are sick, and don't know how to get help."

"You're giving me good advice Grandpa, but it's nothing that I don't know already. I can't make any promises besides promising that I'll never live in Rosemead. I have a friend in Santa Monica now. I trust her. If I leave again, I'll give you a call every day so that you know I'm safe. I was wondering if you might get one of those cell phones that everyone is getting?"

"We'll see how you do, but yes, I'll get one if you really want me to, but please don't run away again! You may not see it right now, but you're only a child."

"I've decided I'm on my own now. I'm starting my life as an adult as of yesterday, and I'll do what seems best at the time. I want to live at your house, and there's no reason to leave there, but I won't live with Daisy and Franken in Rosemead."

"I understand! I don't blame you, but I'm not your mother, and you need to work it out with her. You always have a bedroom with me and Grandma Lin. You better call me if you need me."

"Get a cell phone. Please!" said Alyssa. "Pretty soon everyone will have one anyway."

"You're probably right honey. Okay, I'll get a cell phone."

With that they both fell silent. Grandpa went to work, and Alyssa went home to her Grandparent's in Monterey Park. She called her Mom and left a message where she was, and spent the rest of the day at Dylan's where she knew that Daisy wouldn't look for her. Dylan was very happy to see her, and they spent the time in the usual way playing game cube, hanging out on the block, and walking down to the corner store. Alyssa stayed the night without incident at her grandparent's house, but in the morning, Daisy was there to take her to Rosemead.

First they had lunch together, and Daisy lectured Alyssa about leaving without permission, how she needed her at home, and that she should respect her mother. Alyssa wanted to leave the entire time, but she liked being with her Mom. She thought that she was on her own now, and was starting her own life, but she knew better than to say anything. She let her Mom continue the lecture until she was tired of talking.

"Mom, I want to live with Grandpa and Grandma. Dylan is there. That's my neighborhood, and my school is there," said Alyssa after her Mom was done talking.

67

"I know honey. We'll see how things turn out," said Daisy with slight irritation.

When they got to Franken's house, Daisy went to work, and Alyssa left a note and bolted out the window of her room. She took a bus as far as it would go, but missed her transfer. She stood on Valley Boulevard not really knowing where to go, and noticed a laundry van that delivered clean uniforms and picked up dirty ones. The young driver said "excuse me" as he rolled his cart past her.

"Where are you going?" Alyssa asked.

"UCLA," he said without looking at her.

"Can I ride along?" she said. "I need to go to the library."

"Do you have a ride home?" he asked.

"Sure. My Grandpa will pick me up when he gets off work," she replied.

"Hop in, and put on your seat belt. I'm behind schedule."

The driver continued down Valley Boulevard, and eventually ended up on Sunset Drive. He didn't speak to Alyssa, and seemed very preoccupied.

"Why didn't you take the freeway?" asked Alyssa.

"I like the drive down Sunset," he said while keeping his eyes on the road.

"It is a very interesting drive," said Alyssa. "What's on your mind?"

"I'm not supposed to have anyone in the van, but I felt like I should give you a ride. It's against the rules, but I did it anyway."

"Thank you," said Alyssa.

"No need to thank me. I know I did the right thing."

The driver pulled into campus, and backed up to a loading dock.

"This is it!" he said. "Good luck to you."

"Thank you," she said. "Best wishes to you too because we both know there's no such thing as luck."

Alyssa's comment made the driver pause.

"Bye!" she said slinging her backpack.

The driver smiled, paused, and waved after a moment. He went back to his work shaking his head and smiling.

Alyssa walked across the large campus watching people and taking in the sites. She liked the feeling of the university, and decided she would like to spend some time at one, but she knew that UCLA wasn't quite right for her. The people seemed too well cared for and either came from money, or were on a scholarship. She didn't want to be a part of the extremes when she already felt like she didn't fit into society as a whole. She ended up stumbling across Powell Library, and spent some time there looking up eastern religions trying to find a common thread that ran through her own beliefs. She could relate to Buddhism the best, but couldn't quite come to terms with the concept of reincarnation. She found it interesting, however, that Momma Leoni was talking about reincarnation the other night, and here it was again. It was no coincidence.

After a time, she grew tired of reading, and walked across the courtyard to the student activities center. There were lots of people working out. Some were running on treadmills, and she noted the similarity to caged rodents with a wheel that they can run on.

"People voluntarily cage themselves," she thought, "and run on a treadmill for diversion."

She walked over to the Ackerman Student Union, but before she stepped in, she noticed a young man waiting outside. He was wearing a Dishwalla T-shirt that said "98 Tour" on it. His jeans were ripped and torn but very clean and faded. His flip-flops were leather and worn, and his sun glasses were cheap. He had black hair that was combed into one wave that peaked in the middle front to back, and he was obviously anticipating some event.

"What are you waiting for?" asked Alyssa.

"Lunch," said the man looking interrupted by the question.

"Is someone bringing you lunch?" asked Alyssa.

"I guess you could say that," he answered without offering more.

Just then a cook came through a security screen door on the back of the building, and opened the dumpster. The cook looked at the man, and went back inside. He reemerged with a box, and gently set it into the dumpster. The cook went back inside and locked the door.

"I'll be right back," the man said to Alyssa.

He went over to the dumpster, retrieved the box, and came back to where Alyssa stood.

"See, Lunch!" he said with a smile.

"You're eating out of the dumpster?" asked Alyssa.

"If you want to put a negative spin on it, yes. You saw how long it was in there. I know the cook, and the food is good, but he can't sell it because it's a day old. He also can't hand it to me because his boss doesn't want him feeding potential customers for free. So he sets it in the dumpster, and I retrieve it! Lunch!"

"What's your name?" asked Alyssa.

"Finhead John," said the man.

"No, what's your real name?" said Alyssa.

"My name is John Finn, but people call me Finhead because I have a wave of hair on my head that looks like a fin.

"Can I call you Finhead?"

"Of course, Finhead John is my name! What's yours?"

"Alyssa, Alyssa Daingerfield."

"Any relation to Rodney Dangerfield the comedian?"

"Not that I know of."

"Would you like some lunch?" asked Finhead.

"What is it? Let's see it," Alyssa replied.

"It's Mexican food, and it's always good!"

"Wow that does look good," said Alyssa. "It looks like a carry out. Did he make it up just for you?"

"Not just for me," said Finhead. "It's for anyone who's hungry to take, but I know him. He doesn't like food to go to waste. He says that there are too many starving people in the world."

So Alyssa and Finhead John sat down to leftover Mexican food at UCLA. Neither of them, had much to say. Finhead John didn't have time to speak because he was eating so fast. Alyssa marveled at the speed.

"Are you homeless?" Alyssa asked.

"Homeless by choice," responded Finhead. "My parents are divorced. My Mom kicked me out because I'm 19, and wasn't working or going to school. My Dad said I can live with him in Laurel Canyon, but I have to work at his business. I can't do that so I'm out on the street. I haven't spoken to either one of them recently, but I'm making new friends, and I can find a place to sleep almost every night."

"That sounds similar to my situation," explained Alyssa, "but I'm only 13. By the time I'm your age I'll definitely be on my own, have my own place, and be doing something that I enjoy for money."

"Don't get me wrong," said Finn, "I'm having fun. I basically work to find food, and have a place to sleep. The rest of the time I hang out at the beach and surf. The trouble is I know it won't last. People are understanding with me now because I'm young and free, and in their eyes, dumb, but it won't last. If people start to perceive me as a lazy freeloader they'll stop helping me out."

"I could sense that when I saw you," said Alyssa. "You're in a self-made school learning how to survive, relate to people, and find a place where you can fit in and do your own work peacefully and in balance with nature."

"Nice words!" said Finhead John. "That's exactly it! Now I know what I'm doing. If I could only repeat what you just said in my own words, then maybe I could talk to my Dad again."

"You will," said Alyssa. "Just give it time."

"What are you doing?" asked Finhead.

"I'm headed to the Santa Monica pier," said Alyssa. "I have a friend that lives near there that will put me up for a while."

"Well that too," said Finhead, "but what are you doing with your life."

"I'm a healer and a priest," said Alyssa, "so I want to go into a profession where I help people. I could be a spiritual leader, but I'm not thrilled with the negative side of that. The persecution, controversy, and fanaticism are difficult to deal with over time, and if you're good, you're always in the public eye. I don't want that, so I'm going to move toward counseling."

"I've never met someone who speaks with such confidence and understanding of themselves," said Finhead John. "It's exciting and contagious. It makes me want to get to work on my own life, but how can you be a priest at 13?"

"I just know it in my heart. That's really all I can say. I've always known it."

"That's deep. That's really deep. I can give you a ride to Santa Monica if you want. I have a car."

"You don't work, but you have a car?"

"Yes, my Mom gave it to me when she kicked me out. I think it helped ease her conscience."

"I don't think so," said Alyssa. "You just needed one so she gave it to you."

"Well you're the priest. You should know," said Finhead. "Let's go."

Finhead John gave Alyssa a ride to the beach in Santa Monica. He left the car in metered parking, but didn't deposit coins, and walked to the pier with Alyssa. They stood by the carnival section for a while without speaking and glancing at passers by. There was a brisk on-shore flow, and they were both getting cold, Alyssa excused her self to walk to Momma Leoni's.

"When will I see you again?" asked Finhead John.

"I don't know," said Alyssa staring at him.

"Do you have a phone?"

"No," said Alyssa and looked down. "I'm going to go now."

"Well I hope to see you again here on the Santa Monica pier or at UCLA for a free lunch."

"Okay Finhead. I hope to see you again too."

Chapter 11

Alyssa turned and walked away without looking back. She stopped in the Denny's at the corner of Lincoln and Colorado Avenue until she was sure that Finhead John didn't follow her. She wasn't afraid of him. She just didn't want to show up at Momma Leoni's with a stray in tow. After an hour had passed, she walked back down to the pier taking a different route, walked out to the end to stare out at the horizon, turned when she couldn't take the cold breeze any longer, and started back toward Momma Leoni's. The door was locked and there was no one home, so Alyssa left a note that she was at the Denny's, but by the time she got there, Momma Leoni was waiting for her.

"I got your note," said Momma. "I came right away and had Reech drop me off."

"I'm happy to see you," said Alyssa. "It didn't go well at home, and I was going to ask if I could stay with you for a few weeks."

"That may work out well!" said Momma. "I've decided to leave Reech and I just discussed it with him. He's going to come for his things this weekend."

"Why?" asked Alyssa.

"I have a whole lot of little reasons that add up to one big reason," said Momma. "He's not ambitious, he's not going anywhere, and I'm not taking care of him anymore. I'm not his mother. I feel like I'm living with a child."

"Yes I know," said Alyssa. "I feel that way around my Mom."

"I bet you love your Mom too, but you're leaving her."

"No, I'm not leaving her. I just don't want to live with her. I love her, but we're not good room mates. I'm compatible with my Grandpa, and my Grandma understands me and lets me be. That's where I want to live at least for awhile."

"I love Reech, but I'm not raising a child. I'm not really done growing myself, and I can't be concerned with raising someone else. There's a saying by a writer named Richard Bach: 'If you love someone, set them free. If they come back, they're yours, if they don't come back they never were.' That's what I'm kind of doing with Reech. I'm setting him free."

"I've heard that saying before Momma, and I don't agree with it. You can never own another living thing in the first place. In that sense, they're not yours to let go. Your happiness can never depend on someone else. It always depends on you, and comes from within. You can love someone, but you must always be prepared for that person to leave because they're free. The saying should be: "Love freely not caring what comes in return or if that person loves you. If you truly love, and give love freely, everyone will be attracted to you."

"You're very wise for someone so young. Yes, you're statement is more reflective of the reality, but I think Richard was making a point. You only can do so much before you gotta let go. After that, let the cards fall where they will. That person may come back, or they may not. That's what I want to do. I think I'll be back with Reech one day when he matures and gets his beer drinking under control."

"You're very wise too Momma. My Mom drinks a lot. So we're both doing the same thing."

Momma Leoni and Alyssa both fell silent smiling. Moments passed before they spoke again inside the 6th Street condo. Alyssa told Momma Leoni about meeting Finhead John at UCLA, the lunch they had together, how he gave her a ride to Santa Monica, and how he didn't want to leave her.

74

"He likes you!" said Momma.

"He's 19ish, and he's still trying to find himself. I'm more mature than he is," said Alyssa.

"That may be true, but it doesn't change the fact that he likes you."

"A lot of people like me. In fact everyone seems to like me."

"Is that a problem?" asked Momma.

"No. I guess not."

"Has your Mom or Grandparents explained anything to you about guys?" asked Momma.

"I'm sure my Grandparents have said something, but not much from my Mom."

"Well listen closely. If a guy is talking to you, he's thinking about sex at least once or twice during the conversation, and more often for younger guys," said Momma Leoni. "You can see it in their eyes. With younger guys their thoughts may stray, and then their eyes. They'll try to bring it back, but they're not all successful. They can't really help themselves. It's a powerful primordial instinct that ensures survival of the species. They may think that their thoughts are pure, but subconsciously, they still stray. There's always a sexual angle to anything they do. A few guys may be pure at heart, but I haven't met one yet."

"You have a low opinion of the male. The female could be just as bad."

"I'm not saying men are bad. I'm just trying to enlighten you as to the nature of men. I'm not saying anything that isn't understood at the instinctual level. Just be aware that sex drive is a very powerful force within every man."

"So what are you suggesting I do about Finhead John?" asked Alyssa.

"Nothing," said Momma. He sounds harmless, and he probably is. If you run into him again, I would be straight with him. Tell him you're only 13, and you just want to be friends. If he wants more, tell him to come back in five years when you're of

75

age. He should understand that. On the other hand, don't underestimate him. He may sense the same thing in you that I did, and you may have something to offer each other on a different level. See what comes of the relationship, set boundaries, and enforce the boundaries if he encroaches on them."

"What about my best friend Dylan? We've been together as long as I can remember. Do I need to set boundaries with him now that we're getting older?"

"Perhaps, but you probably already have. I wouldn't worry about it yet. If he tries to take it a step further, then yes, update the boundaries, but for now, let it go. When you're young, and entering the change from childhood to adulthood, a lot of guys are going to be interested in you. Spend time with all of them. Learn about what they're like, what upsets them, and what motivates them. Think about the type of person you would like to be with, and then let the right person come along. Don't latch up too tight on the first one that matches your desires. It may be the second or third person that's right for you. If they ask you to marry them say no once or twice. If they're serious, they'll ask again."

"Is Reech right for you?" asked Alyssa.

"I don't think so, but I'm not sure yet."

Over the next two weeks, Alyssa took the place of Reech in Momma Leoni's life. They adopted each other as the sister they never had, and lived as if they'd been together their whole lives. They ate together, helped each other with chores, but mostly talked about life. They slept in the same bed since there was only one, but it was king size with plenty of room for the both. They both hogged the covers, and finally decided they should each have their own to prevent a fight. Momma Leoni snored but it didn't bother Alyssa.

Alyssa called her Grandpa each morning before he went to work, and every time he would plead with her to come home. Alyssa assured him that her room mate was taking care of her, and that she was safe.

Living in Santa Monica in the summer time was an education for Alyssa, and she explored everywhere she could. She made sure she walked out on the pier at least once a day, and she met a lot of interesting people on the pier from all over the United States.

There was a waitress that worked in the restaurant at the end of the pier. She said that everyone in the world passed through Santa Monica at least once, although Alyssa knew that wasn't true. She did see people from all walks of life as well as the stereotypical California eccentric.

There was another woman who set up a jewelry stand on the pier. Her name was Carol, and her husband Charlie made the jewelry right at the stand while Carol worked the crowd for sales. The jewelry was high quality and ranged in a style to suit various tastes and price ranges. Alyssa stopped by each day to browse, talk to Carol, and say hello to Charlie. Alyssa found both Charlie and Carol interesting because they were very gentle people, but on the other hand, they were hardcore bikers that rode Harleys and wore leathers. They sold their goods all around the Western United States, but their favorite spot was Santa Monica in the spring and early summer. Charlie didn't talk much, but when he did Alyssa seemed to remember it.

"Money and friends will come and go," Charlie said one day.

Then he fell silent. The next day he had another short comment.

"Money is not the root of all evil as they try to tell you," he said. "Misunderstanding, ignorance, greed, and lack of communication are the roots of all evil."

Charlie was a big man with the biker beard and the clothes and tattoos. He was a bit intimidating at first glance. Carol would sometimes speak defensively for him.

"Don't mind Charlie," said Carol, "he pipes up now and then, but he's just a big teddy bear. He'd do anything for you."

Carol had words of wisdom for Alyssa too.

"Cars are just money pits and ego advertisements. You need to get yourself a low cost reliable car and stick with it. Harleys are nice, but they're expensive. A young gal like you needs a car," said Carol when Alyssa showed up on a beach cruiser bicycle.

On another day Carol was talking about what men want, and her last few sentences stuck in Alyssa's mind.

"Men want food and sex in that order," Carol said. "Guns are in third place, but not required. They've gotta have food and sex. Guns are somewhat optional. Some men want knives. They're fascinated with knives. Watch out for the one's that are obsessed with knives."

When Alyssa had finished exploring in Santa Monica, she started riding her beach cruiser down to Venice Beach, and found the area a lot more interesting. Street entertainers and the vendors lined the sidewalk; there were also body builders, and peculiar people hanging out daily. She met the famous Harry Perry who wore rollerblades and skated up and down the beach sidewalk playing guitar in a white lab coat.

"You have a voice. Talk to the people," Harry told her.

She met King Solomon the snake man who rides a unicycle wearing only a swim suit and large snakes.

Tony Vera asked her to sit in a chair, and he would balance her on his chin. She spoke to a contortionist, and a man who dances with large steel balls wearing only shorts and sandals.

The contortionist asked her, "What are you doing out on the street everyday?"

Alyssa told him, "Staying away from home."

"Just remember," he said, "it never gets that bad. Life is always good. If you get the feeling that things are bad, or you're depressed or sad, you've misunderstood your own situation and complicated your life unnecessarily. Un-complicate your life if you need to. Talk to people. They will give you the help you need. Look at me. I'm a contortionist at Venice Beach, I don't make much money, but I'm very happy, and I'm my own boss."

Alyssa became a regular at Venice Beach, and became friends with Sara whose father ran an art store on the beach walk. They sold framed posters, pictures of Hollywood celebrities, matted pictures that you could frame yourself, souvenirs, and some beach paraphernalia. Occasionally, he would buy art from the starving sidewalk vendors and sell it in his shop for a slight profit. He did well, but he needed aggressive sales people, and he enlisted Sara and Alyssa for the task.

He taught them how to read people by the expressions on their face. He knew if they were just browsing, ready to buy, or waiting to be sold just by looking at them. Once he started talking to someone, he could estimate how much they were ready to spend by their attitude and appearance. He explained to Alyssa and Sara about a confidence man, also called a con man, and what methods they used to build a customer's confidence in order to sell something. The product could be valuable or worthless. What was important was the relationship they built with the customer within a few short minutes. They would roll play with Sara's father practicing their newly discovered art. Sara and Alyssa would take turns being the 'Mark', and the other would be the 'Con'.

The girls thought it was great fun, and looked forward to learning something new each day. They weren't actually taking people. They were selling people. They used the con man's methods to sell.

They learned how to bring customers into the store by showing them magic tricks out on the sidewalk. They made coins disappear in their hand, reappear somewhere out of the customer's clothes, and then offered the coin as discount inside the store. They learned the shell and pea game with three shells and one pea on a table. The customer had to pick which shell the pea was under. They didn't accept money, but learned how to read people's expressions while mixing the shells. They could remove the pea completely, leave the pea under one shell but fool the observer, or let the observer win depending on how they wanted to play their

'Mark'. Sara and Alyssa enjoyed working together. They were charming, and very effective at what they did.

Alyssa had become talented at sales, and Sara's father paid her in cash under the table. She earned 5% for items under $50.00 and 15% for items over. Soon she had substantial spending money, and she had hardly spent any of the $50.00 she brought with her when she first left Rosemead. She estimated that she now had over $300.

Chapter 12

The he weeks started to slowly drift by, and before long it was the second week of August, and Alyssa knew that school would be starting soon. One night she voiced her concern to Momma Leoni.

"Well you need to go to school," Momma said, "but you don't want to live in Rosemead. I would suggest secretly starting school in Monterey Park if you could pull it off. Then when you approach your Mom, you would have another arrow in your quiver to aim at staying with your Grandparents."

"I guess you're right," said Alyssa. "I need to stack the deck toward staying with Grandpa Jack. I don't want to leave you and Sara and all the crazy people at the beach. My life here with you has become like home."

"Sara will go back to school too, and Reech could come back here at any time. Tourist season will end, and the beach will get cold over autumn and winter. Enjoy your time here while you can, and treat your experience in Santa Monica and Venice for the street education that you desired when we first met. We're friends now and sisters and we'll always be together."

Tears welled up in Alyssa's eyes as she realized that Momma Leoni was telling her to go home for the school year. This was the most interesting and fun summer she had ever had, and she didn't want it to end, but she knew that Momma was right.

"Okay Momma," said Alyssa, "your insight and advice are appreciated. I'll start working toward that goal."

From that point on in the summer of 2001, Momma Leoni stepped up the frequency and length of her snippets of advice for Alyssa. She explained sexual relations between a man and a woman one night. Alyssa had sex education in school, but that version was based on high ideals. Momma gave the real world version, and Alyssa thought that Momma's version somewhat humorous. Some of Momma's advice was a bit shocking, but Alyssa knew that she was just trying to drive home her point.

"Always make a man wear a condom. There's too much risk in both pregnancy and disease not to wear one. When you become sexually active, have them on hand. Don't depend on the fumbling male to have one. All they think of is sex. If you trust a person, be even more cautious. They could be cheating on you. Your husband could be cheating on you. If you suspect your husband, make him wear a condom. It will upset him, but it will serve him right."

"What about the pill?" asked Alyssa.

"It's not a bad idea to prevent accidents, but never tell them that you're on the pill. That's like an invitation to leave the condoms at home, and before you know it, you're HIV positive. Also remember that guys will try to get you drunk to make it easier to get you into bed for sex. If they start buying you too many drinks watch out, and watch out for strong drinks. Let the drinks sit untouched, and always remember that you have what they want. You're in control, but once you give in, they're in control. It's your body, and you need to protect it. You only get one."

"My Mom would never have told me these things," said Alyssa. "Thanks for cluing me in. I already have guys interested in me. I'm not nearly ready for sex, but I want to know the truth."

"In a way, men are very stupid. They want their basic needs satisfied now. They're impatient. Food, sex, alcohol, sports, recreational drugs, nice cars, and macho trucks are very important to them. You can use these desires to your advantage. In another

81

way, they're very smart. They invest well, they're afraid of commitment, they're logical, long- term planners, and they want to be good providers for their family. You can use these ideas to remain in control too. Remember, if you've got them by the balls, their hearts and minds will follow."

This was a lot for Alyssa to take in. Some of it was crude, and some of it seemed far- fetched, but she knew it was good advice. She was sure that Momma had her best interest at heart.

Another week passed, and Sara went on vacation with her Mom, and it wasn't much fun working in the store without her. Alyssa told Sara's Dad that she was going back home, and thanked him for the training and all the good times. He paid her, gave her a bit extra, and offered her some advice.

"A bright young lady like yourself should be with her family, but you have a gift with people. You understand their nature as well as your own. Use that talent wisely. Once you're of age, you should get out on your own as soon as you can, but for now, you're making the right decision to go home," he said.

The statement stuck in Alyssa's mind as she peddled her beach cruiser back up toward Santa Monica. In her dreams she had received the same message to get out on her own as soon as she could, and recently, she had dreams of finishing both high school and college early. She stopped at the end of Rose Avenue to complete her thoughts, catch her breath, and sip from her water bottle. She glanced up ahead, and she did a double take on a man standing at the corner. It was Finhead John.

"What are you up to?" asked Alyssa as she peddled up to Finhead on her beach cruiser.

It took Finhead John a moment to recognize Alyssa. She had matured over the summer. She looked mysterious, shrewd, and wise. Her look had always been penetrating, but it was even more so now, and it was mildly shocking.

"Alyssa! I didn't recognize you. I haven't seen you all summer," said Finhead. "A better question would be what are you up to?"

"I've been in Santa Monica all summer. I'm thinking about going back home soon."

"Yeah, I was forced to move back in with my Dad. I had worn out my welcome everywhere else. He agreed to not make me work in his business for now, but I have to find a job. That's what I'm supposed to be doing here," he said while staring out at the ocean.

"There's a restaurant in Venice looking for a delivery person. I saw a sign in the window."

"Thanks, I'll check that out."

"Well I'm going to get moving Finn. It was good to see you," said Alyssa getting ready to peddle.

"Likewise," said Finhead. "When are we going to hang out?"

"Meet me at the Denny's at Lincoln and Colorado at about noon one week from today. I'll buy you lunch, and you can give me a ride to my Grandparents. Deal?"

"Deal!"

"We're just friends, so don't get any ideas."

"We'll always be friends," said Finhead. "If I thought I could get you by waiting, I would, but I think you're destined for someone else. I'm happy to be just friends. Somewhere in the future, I think I have a part to play in your life."

"We'll see about that," she said peddling away on her bicycle.

Alyssa found it peculiar how the tide suddenly turned. The anger she felt about moving to Rosemead turned into rebellion, and resulted in her leaving and declaring herself independent. She dove head first into the unknown. She became a homeless minor on the run. Her daring blossomed into the most exciting and fulfilling summer of her life. In the blink of an eye it all shifted. Her thoughts turned, and so did her world. People and things quickly fell into place around her thought. It had all started with a feeling. The summer was fading and it was time for school. The new

83

people in her life seemed to confirm her decision, and momentum quickly shifted toward that result. She was headed home.

Grandpa Jack was further confirmation of the change. When she called him, he told her it was past time to come home and face her Mom. She had made a bold statement, and demonstrated her resolve, but her task was complete. It was now time to be with her family. Pushing the point any further would reflect poorly on her. People would assume that she was physically or verbally abused during her upbringing. This was just not the case, and if she loved her Mother and Grandparents, it was time to return. He had worried about her all summer, and although he understood her plight, his patience was wearing thin.

When she walked into Momma Leoni's condo, Reech was sitting at the kitchen table. He smiled at her, but Momma spoke first.

"Reech is back. I felt that it may happen the past few days, and now he's here," said Momma.

"How's our cosmic crusader?" said Reech referring to Alyssa.

"I'm well," Alyssa said in a trancelike state wondering if there was such a thing as coincidence.

"We're going to dinner," said Momma Leoni. "I know you're headed home, and Reech is moving back in. I want to celebrate!"

They went to dinner at Momma's favorite Italian place called Luichi's. They were early, and when they walked in, there were hardly any customers. Everyone noticed Momma, and they rang out in song.

"They call him Reech-a-roni, he lives with Momma Leoni!"

The hostess showed them to their table while the staff repeated the song twice, and everyone clapped and cheered. Dinner was somewhat awkward because Momma was the only connection between Reech and Alyssa. They didn't know what to say to each other, and they wouldn't be seeing each other very much. After dinner the waiter brought out a cupcake with a single candle. They set it in front of Momma Leoni, and she said a prayer.

"I pray that Alyssa's move back into her Grandparents' home is very successful, and that she finds peace with her Mother and Franken. I also hope and pray that this fresh start with Reech works out for us both, that he controls his beer drinking, and helps around the house. Amen," Momma finished with her head bowed and eyes closed.

Everyone replied, "Amen."

Momma took a bite of the cupcake, then Alyssa, and Reech finished it off grinning and chewing.

Chapter 13

Alyssa spent the next few days cruising the beach, and stopping by to see her friends at the Santa Monica Pier, Venice, and at Denny's at Lincoln and Colorado Avenue. She had become a local icon with her classic beach cruiser bicycle that was older than she was and too big for her. She spent her time saying goodbye to people. While she was saying goodbye, she did manage to meet someone new. A chance meeting was 17 year old Luan near Muscle Beach in Venice. Alyssa took Luan with her on her rounds, and introduced her to her friends in the beach community. They took turns riding on the handlebars.

Luan loved to surf, and she was so grateful for all her new friends that she gave Alyssa an old surf board. They spent Alyssa's last few days in the surf until she could stand on the board while riding a wave.

Soon it was time to go back to Monterey Park, but Alyssa's beach cruiser and surf board wouldn't fit in Finhead's car. So they left late in the day hoping Grandpa Jack would be off work. If things went well, they could double back with the Volvo Wagon to get the rest. They were anxious about how the homecoming would go, and unsure whether they should divulge where Momma Leoni lived.

Grandpa Jack was very excited to see her when they arrived. He gave Alyssa a big hug, and shook Finhead's hand. They all came in for dinner with Grandma Lin, and after introductions, they ate quietly. In order to ease the awkwardness, and save Alyssa from too many questions, Finhead rattled off his entire life story to the Daingerfields. While he went on, Alyssa thought of the parallels between Finhead's life and hers. They were both growing up with one parent that didn't have a lot of interest in them, and both spent a lot of time on the street. They were both smart, and both capable. She decided that she may have misjudged Finhead, and after hearing his story, Alyssa was appreciative of having Grandparents that cared about her and loved her. Finhead had much less.

Grandpa Jack took Alyssa back to Santa Monica to pick up the rest of her things. Finhead rode along wanting to meet Momma Leoni and Reech. Unfortunately Reech wasn't there, but Grandpa Jack had a short conversation with Momma Leoni, and at the end, thanked her for taking care of his Granddaughter for the summer. As they said their goodbyes, Grandpa Jack went to shake Momma's hand, but she went by it to give him a big hug. While she was hugging him, she winked at Alyssa and silently spoke to her by moving her mouth.

"He's a wonderful man!" Momma gestured.

Alyssa didn't reply she just smiled, and giggled. Finhead watched the whole process with amusement.

Grandpa Jack wasted no time. He and Finhead loaded up the beach cruiser and surfboard in the back, and they rode three in the front to Monterey Park.

When they returned home, Daisy and Franken were there. Daisy started to cry when Alyssa walked in the door. They both said I love you at the same time, and started sobbing on each others shoulders. Once the tears slowed, Daisy promised that they would start anew, and make things easier for everyone. Alyssa would stay with her Grandparents for the most part, and visit at Mom's and Franken's on weekends on Daisy's off day. Franken looked as though he wanted to protest but remained quiet. Alyssa also proposed that when she's with her Mom, that she and Franken don't drink, and that she and her Mom should do things together. Daisy agreed, and there seemed to be an accord. Daisy and Franken headed home, and Finhead went to his Dad's, but in departing, asked for the Daingerfields' phone number.

"May I have your number Mr. Daingerfield?" Finhead asked very politely.

"Aren't you a bit old to be friends with Alyssa?" Grandpa Jack asked.

"Alyssa is very mature for her age sir, and I think we have something to offer each other. There'll be no trouble from me."

Alyssa was surprised at Finhead's attitude. He was like a little soldier in her unknown cause asking the big boss if he can join the ranks.

"Is that alright with you Alyssa?"

"Sure, but don't call too much Finhead. I like to do my own thing, and don't want to be beholden to anyone. I do appreciate the ride. Thank you very much!"

"My pleasure!"

They exchanged numbers, and Finhead left skipping to his car as if he had just won a prize.

"I worry about him," Alyssa said to Grandpa Jack, "he's infatuated with me."

Earthly existence was much improved for Alyssa in the days that followed. She missed her free wheeling beach life, Momma Leoni, and her friends, but there was peace and harmony at home, and that made her very happy. Daisy actually helped her get started in school, and she got reacquainted with Dylan. Dylan's Mom promised that she would speak to Daisy about letting Alyssa spend the night sometimes, and that she would make sure they were well taken care of, but she made Alyssa promise to contact her if she ever had any problems at home again.

"We love you too darling," said Dylan's Mom. "We wouldn't want anything bad to happen to you."

The first weekend, Alyssa didn't go over to Franken's. Daisy picked her up, and took her out for the day. They each chose something they wanted to do. For Daisy it was shopping, and for Alyssa it was a movie. Daisy was sure Alyssa would want to see "Harry Potter and the Sorcerer's Stone", but was surprised when she asked to see "A Beautiful Mind" instead.

They were getting along better than ever, but a month after their first outing together, Alyssa came over to Franken's for the first time. She suspected they were hung over from the night before. Things were fine at first, but in the early afternoon both Franken and Daisy started to drink. Daisy started with a Seabreeze, but it wasn't long before she started asking Franken for a Schleebreezsh, and Alyssa new that it was time to go. She went to her room, lay on the bed, and contemplated her situation. Her first inclination was to call Grandpa Jack. In her heart, she knew this was the right thing to do, but her motivation suddenly vanished. She continued laying on her back and staring at the ceiling. Thoughts of her summer of independence in Venice and Santa Monica continued to replay in her head. Her rebellion was completely successful. She remembered how welcoming arms were waiting for her when she returned. She could do what she wanted, but now she was stuck at Franken's and it aggravated her. Continuous thoughts of her situation allowed her emotions to build to the point of eruption. With anger she stood and rationalized her proposed actions. She loaded her back pack and headed for the window once more.

As she moved down the street with the exhilaration of being free. She felt a sudden pang of anxiety. A strong feeling quickly welled up within her. She was doing something wrong. She shrugged it off. Minutes later the feeling was back again. Once again, she rationalized her feelings to suit the outcome she desired. She decided that she was just worried about heading off into the unknown.

She had taken half of the $300 that she had accumulated over her successful summer, and had few small bills to use discretely. She took three twenties out, and stashed the rest in her backpack.

She tried to call Finhead John, but it was picked up by an answering machine. The greeting on the answering machine was an unfamiliar voice, but she left a message anyway, and said she would call back later. She caught the same bus that took her down Valley Boulevard; then she ended up on a laundry truck and dropped at UCLA. This time, she took a transfer, and ended up in downtown Los Angeles. Not knowing what to do, she hailed a cab, and went to West Hollywood because she knew that Finhead lived somewhere near there. The cab driver asked where in West Hollywood she wanted to go. The only place she new of was Mel's Drive-In on Sunset in West Hollywood. Everything was going wrong.

The anger she felt before leaving the house was now replaced with worry, and the exhilaration she felt upon leaving was replaced by fear.

"It's a short walk from the alleluia to the hoot," she thought to herself.

The expression was one she had heard her Grandpa say, but now she understood it. When sitting at home, she was overconfident when contemplating her next move. The lingering taste of success from her carefree summer in Santa Monica had played on her ego, and she had become slightly arrogant. She realized it now, but was stuck on the streets of Hollywood miles from home, and she couldn't get herself to call no matter how much she tried to convince herself. After her struggle, she decided to continue on with her foray into the streets. Even though she knew she was making a mistake, she didn't realize how quickly things could degrade. Trouble comes in bunches, and she continued on with the biggest mistake of her life.

She spent the first night in a homeless shelter with John Birch unwilling to call home and unable to contact anyone she trusted for help. The next morning, contacting someone gave her a false confidence, and she wanted to continue. She could sense in her heart that her situation continued to get worse, but she accepted help from Finhead, and stubbornly continued her breakout. Although their afternoon together was dismal, she enjoyed Finn's company, and the comfort of his protection egged her on. After securing a place to sleep at Corey's apartment, false confidence filled her again, and she continued sliding downhill while all along thinking she was going to make it on her own once more.

"It was a close call, but I may pull it off after all," she thought midway through.

In the morning she and Finn plotted a course, and Alyssa spent the day at a museum in the Wilshire District and fending for herself and blending in with the crowd. She thought she was going to make it, but as the day wore on, despair began to creep back in. She recognized the opportunity to stop, but for a third time, she failed to call home and break off her fumbled rebellion. At this point she was resolute and beyond redemption. Only after hitting bottom would she ever quit, and that bottom arrived quickly that night in Corey's Hollywood apartment with the rape attempt. The extreme nature of her experience was what finally broke her loose. She surrendered to her situation, and went home.

Her first attempt at leaving home was a great success. The second time was a great failure. After it was all over, she wondered if she actually needed both experiences to learn, and after a lot of thought, she decided that she did. When all was said and done, she ended up getting what she wanted. She would live with her Grandparents, but her victory had come at a cost. She had hurt the person she loved most. Her Grandpa Jack had changed toward her. She was no longer his little girl.

One night, after he read to her, Alyssa asked him why things had gone so well with Momma Leoni, but so horrible with Finhead John on Sunset Strip.

"It depends on your outlook on life to some extent," said Grandpa Jack. "I'm not a person who believes in coincidence. I think there's a reason that things happen. In your case, I think you became overconfident after spending the summer in Santa Monica. You learned a lot living with Momma and the regulars on the beach. You learned working for the vendors in Venice. It was a great life lesson, and through it all, you made your point with your Mom. You weren't going to be jerked around anymore. It was a bold statement. You refused to move to another house depending on the boyfriend or husband of the month. You proved that you can take care of yourself and live on your own. That was great, and I think you were in touch with your deepest sense of self as well as a source of energy and learning. You were doing what you believed in, and that is something we've spoken about before. That's what we all should be doing.

"On the other hand, when you left your Mom's because she was drinking with Franken you were frustrated. Your motivation was self-centered, and you fueled it with pride. You could have easily put up with her for one night. You put yourself in much greater danger by going out on the street. You know as well as I of all the strange goings on in Hollywood.

"You disconnected from your deepest instincts, and you separated from source. You experienced the result almost immediately, and your situation became progressively worse. It was a bigger lesson for you than what you learned last summer, and it was a much more important point.

"In your life, you've always found it easy to know the right thing to do, and not to mistake that knowing for short-sighted emotional desires. That is the key. Not everyone has that ability. It is quite rare. You already have what most people work a lifetime to achieve. So what happened? Well, the lesson in it for you is to stay

91

connected to source, and stick with your deepest instincts. They come natural to you, and will never steer you wrong. Once your thoughts turn solely to your own personal well being, without consideration for others, your purpose will change. Instead of serving the greater good you're serving yourself."

"I know what you mean Grandpa. I've never felt that way before. It was like I was lost for a time, but not really lost. It was more like being adrift in the sea in a rowboat without any oars," said Alyssa.

"Exactly right and I don't think you've ever experienced that before. Maybe you needed to see how most of us live everyday. It's not easy. It's much better to live like you do trusting your instincts and knowing when you're just emotional."

"How do I keep from doing that again?" she asked.

"That's a tough question, and it's not one I can answer. I think you're better at it than I am. I may be older than you, but I don't think it's related to age."

"I thought that you get older and wiser," said Alyssa, "not just older."

"You're born with some wisdom," said Grandpa Jack, "but from there, I'm not sure how much you gain. For what we're talking about, I think it's a matter of practice. You may be getting to the point where you need to meditate. Some people call it prayer. In a way they're all the same thing. People like you who are very advanced usually meditate a lot."

"I sometimes dream about meditation! How do I do it?"

"Go to a quiet place where you know you won't be bothered. For you that's probably your room. Don't put any music on or your mind will drift. Sit quietly and comfortably. Close your eyes and relax. Quiet your thoughts. Try not to think at first, and then simply sit without thought. You'll feel very peaceful. Let the energy flow from inside to outside rather than outside to inside. Feel yourself breathing –in and out, in and out. Your mind will naturally slow down and go into what they call alpha. It's a type of low-level brain activity. When you're ready, slowly bring yourself back out of it. Give yourself a minute or two to come back, and go about your day. You should feel very relaxed and refreshed when you finish. The first few times you try, it may not work, or you may fall asleep. Give it several tries before you give up."

"It sounds complicated," said Alyssa.

"It's not. It's like riding a bike. It might take you a while to get started, but once you learn, you never forget. You better get to sleep now. You can try it tomorrow."

Life seemed to go back to normal after that night. Alyssa and Grandpa Jack spoke nightly about life and the mysteries associated with day-to-day living. Peace and harmony took over Alyssa for the first time in many years. The mundane became normal, and excitement was rare.

Alyssa went to counseling for a few sessions with Daisy, but it ended quickly. Daisy made an effort not to drink around Alyssa, but Franken drank, and she could sense that they were often hung over when she arrived for her weekend. She suspected Daisy of having a nip or two in the closet to relieve her hangover. Hair of the dog was what her Mom called it. Alyssa could smell it on her, but it no longer bothered her, and she ignored it.

She planned her reading for her weekend at her Mom's. She read everything she could get her hands on that was religious, philosophical, or had something to do with understanding the human condition. Her favorite books were sales and business. She understood business naturally, and selling things seemed to be an important skill. Soon she grew tired of business books. She wanted to know how people worked on the inside, how their thought patterns worked, how to change their opinion, and how to manipulate their actions. She discovered Dale Carnegie books and quickly read through them all. Then she went through Tony Robbins.

She investigated what motivated people, what their desires were, and why people lost interest once they obtained something.

93

The thrill of the chase she found fascinating, but why only the chase was thrilling she didn't understand.

She moved on to classic philosophy: Socrates, Plato, and Plutarch. When these no longer satisfied her, she switched to the more modern writings of Kant, Hegel, and Nietzsche. She read the Bible cover to cover. She started with King James, but found the Old English difficult and switched to the New American version. When she completed that, she enjoyed reading the Tao and Confucius. She read both Hindu and Buddhist Sutras, and anything classic and Eastern. She read until she was exhausted, and eventually found some sort of underlying pattern that she could use as a reference for her own life.

Chapter 14

Alyssa's first few attempts at meditation mostly involved falling asleep, but the practice intrigued her. Calming her mind became easier, and she found herself meditating for short periods of time. She considered that a success. Falling asleep remained a problem so she practiced daily in the morning when she was rested and awake. She made progress in bits. It was invigorating, and helped in ways she couldn't explain.

She began to have more recurring dreams. There was an underlying message that she should finish school early, and that high school was a waste of time. Her dreams suggested that everything worthwhile learning in high school could be done in a year, but in California it took four years. She reasoned that the system was designed to keep young rebellious people off the street. She agreed with her dreams, and viewed high school as a jail, but beyond its physical constraints, she saw it as a limitation to thought.

"Impressionable students are conditioned to accept 100 to 200 year old ways," Alyssa thought. "Conventional thinking is rewarded, and original thinking punished. The innovative thinkers are definitely persecuted or bullied. We're exposed daily to petty and often cruel social circles that force us to shut off and keep to ourselves! We're labeled as nerds! Teachers and administrators are powerless to make changes. They're up against the same limited thinking. They fear the system and prefer to stay low key and hope for status quo. Our most important social institutions are, in effect, stifling creativity and free speech!"

Beyond her new activities, Alyssa had a need to be with Dylan, and once or twice a week after school they would climb a tree together that they climbed as kids. They sat on some aging boards that were crudely nailed to the limbs, and talked about life. Alyssa preferred to talk about what she read in her philosophy books, but Dylan liked to talk about the world, politics, government, 9/11, and whether George W. Bush would invade Iraq. Dylan liked philosophy too, but preferred the Greeks. Alyssa favored the 19th century philosophers. Their belief systems were somewhat similar. They were best friends, but Dylan's point of view had a traditional flavor that reflected current conservative American society. Alyssa's was more open minded, and in some ways, radical. She considered positive change more important than outdated moral values. She thought that the morality would work itself out after a better system was in place. Dylan worried about the fairness of change, and thought that the system should be equal across the board and well thought out before being implemented. They were of opposite points of view.

"I'd like to drop out of high school and take the GED," Alyssa told Dylan as if it was a real option. "It's such a waste of time. I can't really pin it on anyone, teachers, students, government, bullies, or social circles. There all just there. It just seems so inefficient."

"You're Mom and Grandparents would never let you quit," Dylan fired back with a scornful look. "It's a right of passage more than an education. People like you are forced to interface with people like me! After that, you're done, and you can have your life in the ivory tower."

"Yikes!" Alyssa responded. "What a mean thing to say! What do you mean people like me?"

"You know damned well," said Dylan. "People that get it right away, and people that don't. I'm not referring to smart people either, and I'm sure you know that too. There are a lot of smart people living in the river bottom that don't get it. I don't get it, but you do. You seem to get everything right away."

"I may "get it" as you say, but I hardly fit in! That's why I want to drop out. I don't fit in, and probably never will. I want to get on with my life. High school is a waste. I'd rather be in college."

"Yes, but you're different than us, and that's why you're forced to be around us so that you understand before you run off and take charge. You'll be taking charge of us."

"Wow, you're in a mood today! I'll talk to you tomorrow," Alyssa replied as she jumped out of the tree.

There were many similar discussions in the tree, and they would each jump out, and run home angry and frustrated. The next day they would be cool toward each other at first, but when they realized they were both being stubborn, they would break out laughing about their behavior. Sometimes they would hug each other and say they were sorry. Other times they would hold hands.

As the months passed the hugs became more frequent and longer. They enjoyed it, looked forward to hugging, and held on until they felt each others presence deep inside. One evening after an uplifting discussion in the tree, they hugged each other hard before going home. They lingered with Alyssa's ear against Dylan's chest listening. Something unusual stirred deep within. They looked into each others eyes while holding tight, and in a moment of spontaneity, their lips met in a gentle touch. The touch inspired passion, and they both continued more intensely. They kissed with excitement and gentle movements. Finally they stopped, but continued hugging. On a nearby street a car horn and the sound of traffic entered their experience. Reality crept in, and they both realized what just transpired. It shocked them, and they separated. They were momentarily embarrassed. Alyssa raised her hand to cover her mouth, turned, and ran home without saying goodbye.

Alyssa avoided Dylan for what seemed like a long time, but was only a few days. She was unsure of what they had together, and wondered of they were just friends, or if they should be more. Her body was going through changes, and although she was aware of the physical changes, she wondered if emotional changes had led them to kiss. She worried that their innocent friendship could no longer continue because they were of the opposite sex and becoming adults. She was angered that she couldn't always control her feelings when she was physically close to him. To her Grandparent's surprise, her frustration drove her to her Mother. They began to spend more time together. Daisy was eager to provide her advice on emotions and relationships.

"You loved each other as children," said Daisy. "That part is simple. The love was already there. Beyond that, you know that you're now changing. You're not only becoming adults physically, but your evolving into what you want to become in this life. That's really the hard part, and what you have together after that change occurs will dictate whether your relationship can continue."

"I don't intend to lead him on in that way," Alyssa pleaded. "When I get close to him it just seems to happen, and the feeling is somewhat mutual. It doesn't start out that way, but once we're close, it ends up that way."

"You need to learn the basics of controlling a man," Daisy said. "Touch is a big one. Touch in many ways shines a green light. Use touch sparingly until you're ready. Another trigger is how you dress. Dress according to what reaction you want out of a man. Provocative dressing can almost always get you what you want in an intimate social setting. Clothing that allows the option to show skin at the appropriate moment is particularly useful. It drives men crazy and some women too. When you're out in the city or in a crowded nightclub, dress more strategically. You want to be sexy, but not too sexy. Too much will get you assaulted or killed. As with the weather, dress in layers so that you can take it off if the need arises, but always be aware, because they're always watching you!"

"Mom, I don't want to dress like a ho."

"We're not talking about dressing like a street corner girl. Always dress tastefully, but use it as a tool, and don't ever use that kind of language. Never! It's obvious evidence of your social class. The word "ho" came from the lower classes, and you're not low class. Even if you don't see it that way, others will, and from then on you're labeled. Provocateur is the harshest word you'd want to use."

"I would never use that word, but I see what you mean."

"Yes, and you can be provocative and tasteful at the same time. Think classy. Classy doesn't need to be snooty. Classy and warm is the way to go."

The advice came from a point of view that Alyssa was not familiar with: Daisy's point of view. This was a lesson on looking good, men, and getting what you want. These were subjects Alyssa had purposely avoided for so long, but she now found interesting. Daisy may have had many failed relationships, but this was her area of expertise. Alyssa was ready to hear it, and Daisy was excited to give it to her. The daughter she had hoped for had finally arrived.

They went shopping together, and Daisy tastefully dressed her as discussed, but subtly accented her beauty in many ways Alyssa hadn't thought of. The change was brazenly apparent, and the radically independent misfit transformed into a refined young lady.

Inwardly, the radical remained, but Alyssa already had a deep awareness of self, and had delved into the mysteries of life at a young age. She was practiced with expression, and could now use her sexual energy as well. She transformed her penetrating stare. It became more mysterious and alluring, and she could turn it on and off at will. Her internal knowing combined with her external beauty to give her a tantalizing appearance. Men immediately wanted her, and felt challenged to obtain her.

Her early education on the streets and the shops of Venice made her unique. She was brimming with energy, and had a subtle glow about her. After meeting her, people realized that she was friendly and well grounded. All people were attracted to her and excited to be around her.

Dylan and Alyssa's relationship had bounced back with the passage of time after their first real kiss. The subject had never come up, but the experience lingered in the back of both of their minds. Dylan thought of it frequently, but for Alyssa, it was a one time natural occurrence that was unlikely to repeat itself. It was in the past and didn't warrant much attention. In Dylan's mind, however, it was much different. He was intrigued by Alyssa's enhanced beauty at the hands of Daisy. She was turning into a woman, and she was no ordinary woman. He looked for opportunities to show his intentions, but few if any of his subtle hints went noticed. If given the opportunity, he planned to take the next step.

The recent changes were welcomed by Franken who was feeling smothered, and happy to have some time on his own. Daisy and Alyssa were temporarily inseparable. They became best friends. Daisy spent more time at Grandpa and Grandma Lin's. Their house converted to the social center for both the family and the neighborhood. People came and left regularly. It was always interesting to find out who would be there.

Grandpa Jack, who had recently turned 54, wanted to get reacquainted with his own rebellious youth, and had been getting in touch with old friends from the bay area from the late 1960s. Grey haired people balding with a pony tail wearing tie-dye clothing would often be in the living room waiting for Jack to get home when Alyssa arrived from school. Sometimes her Mom would already be there talking to them. They would call her little Daisy or Flower, and would say how they knew her Dad when he was a Hippie in Golden Gate Park and Monterey. It was a happy time, and all the things that the Daingerfields were came together in a positive way that was very relevant to what was currently happening in the world.

When Alyssa's 14th birthday came along, the entire family looked forward to the celebration. There were no longer worries of drama or awkward moments, and with warmer feelings in the household, everyone agreed that Alyssa was a good cause for celebration.

Daisy's reinvented relationship with her daughter was a major factor in the new family harmony. They had much more in common and Alyssa was no longer hard to buy for. Her anti-materialistic views had softened, and she was neutral on simple vanities like perfume, make up, and purses. So Daisy loaded it on. Alyssa stopped by her work at the fragrance counter for just a few samples each day being careful not to burn out her nose.

"A woman's scent is her signature, and it can't be cheap," Daisy explained to her.

Alyssa finally settled on three that her mother approved of, and that became an early birthday present.

When April 12th rolled around, Daisy showed up early without Franken to bake Alyssa's birthday cake with Grandma Lin. Daisy had actually made box cakes before, but it wasn't her thing. For birthdays past, she had just bought a cake at Albertson's or Vons, and had the lady behind the counter write "Happy Birthday Alyssa Love Mom" on the top. To Daisy, that was a homemade cake, but today she and Grandma Lin were going to make a special cake in the shape of a house made with both yellow and chocolate cakes and a real fruit filling.

That year, Alyssa's Birthday was on a Friday, so everyone was in a good mood when they arrived. The work week was over, and a Birthday was a good excuse to get together. Surprisingly, neither Daisy nor Franken drank during the festivities. Dylan and his parents were surprised when they arrived to a house full of merriment with odd and peculiar looking people from the Daingerfield's past that they didn't know.

The Grateful Dead was playing on the stereo, and everyone over 30 seemed to know all the words. Most guests would intermittently sing along. Their singing was off, but the band sounded off too, and it all seemed to fit together.

There wasn't room at the dining room table for all to eat, and several people ate with their plate on their knees in the living room. Alyssa blew out the candles after the loudest rendition of "Happy Birthday" she ever heard.

She received numerous small presents from guests she really didn't know. Some of them were odd like sewing kits for repairing clothes, God's eyes, water filters for hiking in the mountains, and thermal socks and underwear. Her Mom gave her more clothing on top of what she received at the mall. Franken gave her a $20 dollar bill scotch taped to a beginning Tai Chi VHS tape, and a book on meditation. Of all the things she received, she found it interesting that Franken gave her the gift that she was most interested in. Grandpa Jack and Grandma Lin gave her antique collectible books on Eastern philosophy and religion. All of the books were very old with leather covers. Alyssa felt each cover and observed the wear on each before she opened them. One book was primarily in Chinese characters, but had English translations. Grandpa Jack told her that he had a Buddhist priest examine them, and that they all had good energy, and good previous owners.

Chapter 15

In the weeks that followed Alyssa immersed herself in meditation, and found some of the new techniques she learned in her book very useful. She was now accomplished at clearing her mind of thought. The practice had transformed from an experiment to a daily ritual. She found it becoming an essential part of her day.

What she found even more curious was her interest in Tai Chi. Of all her Birthday gifts, the Tai Chi tape became the most used. She practiced during all her free time, and found it a good excuse to spend time with Dylan again. They learned the moves together, and critiqued each other as they practiced. They quickly outgrew the tape. Their interests expanded to martial arts and various forms of Chinese meditation that Alyssa had read about.

Alyssa remembered a man from Muscle Beach that everyone called Frenchy. He had immigrated to the United States from Brest, France, and had a French accent. His real name was Wang Diang. He attracted an audience when he practiced Tai Chi daily at the beach, and some of the body builders were envious that he took all the attention. Unlike the body builders, he was very thin and lean, but very muscular.

Frenchy was an officer in the South Vietnamese Navy, and when Saigon fell in the mid-1970s, he fled the country to avoid execution by the new government. He was an illegal alien for many years in France. He survived by teaching martial arts and Tai Chi in the streets and parks for donations. During the day, he would watch French soap operas to learn the language. Eventually, he ended up meeting a Canadian who offered him a job in his studio in Montreal. From there he applied for citizenship in the U.S. landing in Los Angeles and hoping to be the next Bruce Lee, but stardom never called for Frenchy.

Frenchy liked Alyssa in a fatherly way, and marveled at the spirit within her clamoring to get out. When she and Dylan found him at Venice Beach one day, he agreed to give lessons, but there was a catch. They were to accept life lessons not strictly martial arts or Tai Chi. They agreed to learn Vietnamese culture, honor, respect, community service, and spiritual meditation. Frenchy promised to explain all types of Chi including Jing (essence), Shen (spirit), and Ying (nutritive). Frenchy held his classes at Grandpa Jack's on Tuesdays and Thursdays. Alyssa was allowed to invite friends. The classes turned out to be very popular, and before long, between 10 and 15 kids would show up for every class. Dylan and Alyssa put up a donation jar, and collected about $80 for each class. They gave 50% to Frenchy for the class, and 20% to Grandpa Jack for use of the house and yard. The remainder was kept in reserve.

It turned out that Frenchy loved becoming a role model and a teacher of Los Angeles teenagers. He taught them balance of mind, body, and spirit. The various forms of Chi were reviewed frequently. He taught them that each individual is born with a certain amount of life Chi, and that you must preserve, nurture, and replenish that life Chi because once your life Chi is depleted, you die. Murmurs resounded throughout the class on that note, everyone paid particular attention to the attainment of Chi, what types of Chi were to be given away freely, and what types should be conserved.

He taught the kids that most people consider Chi to be energy, but that was wrong.

"Chi is not matter and not energy specifically. It is the transitional state between matter and energy. In the material incarnate world," he taught, "this is an unknown state, but in the parallel world of timeless spirits, Chi is well known and familiar.

"You'll notice that ancient Christian paintings are often depicted with a halo above the head of the subject," Frenchy continued. "This is a method of denoting Chi. The halo was symbolic of enlightenment and advanced spiritual awareness. These people were brimming with Chi of all sorts, and Chi can extend beyond their bodies. There's no way of depicting the glow of Chi in the master's painting; consequently, artists of the day adapted a halo to denote the radiance of the subject's Chi.

"Tai Chi is primarily nonaggressive. If you need to defend yourself, use your opponent's energy. As your opponent attacks, the direction of his energy is readily apparent, and you have a small opportunity to assess and react. Their energy can work for you instead of working against you. To deflect them or avoid them all together is the best strategy. To strike first puts you at a disadvantage."

Alyssa, Dylan and a few of their classmates practiced tirelessly. They practiced until their movements were second nature. There was no reaction time because their moves became automatic. They performed without thought. Dylan was pleased with the amount of time he was spending with Alyssa, and what was even more encouraging was that they were bonding at an even higher level. They were spiritual partners, and had advanced together on that level. Dylan felt intimacy.

"It's only a matter of time," he thought to himself, "until our relationship transcends into something more."

Alyssa's thoughts were much different.

"I wonder what's up with Dylan. He seems to stare, and has that weird look. I don't know if it's boyish look or just plain goofy, but it's definitely bothersome."

At this point in their development, Alyssa and Dylan took different paths. Alyssa easily processed everything Frenchy taught and excelled in her own interpretation of what she learned. Dylan, on the other hand, didn't take well to the cultural and spiritual aspects of the training, and focused on the physical moves. It was obvious that it was purely exercise for him. In particular, he struggled with the explanation of Chi and the Yin and Yang.

"Success with Tai Chi will depend on your understanding of all Chi," Frenchy explained. "In order to understand Chi you must understand the Yin-Yang relationship, and how that affects Chi. Yin and Yang are two opposite and opposing forces. It is important to understand the reflective properties of nature. If there's a thesis, then there also must be an anti-thesis. If there's a black, then there must be a white. If there's male, then there must be female. If there's Yin, then there must be Yang, and the struggle between the two causes change. The two parts make up the whole, and one is dependent on the other.

"Yin-Yang represents the struggle. The Tao represents the how.

"The I-ching and the Tao are not the same thing as commonly believed in western cultures! The I-ching is the book of change, and that action precedes change. The Yin and Yang represent action. The Tao represents a path or a method and suggests how this can be done. The only thing common between the Tao and the I-ching is change.

"No matter," he began to summarize. "This is not important to the beginner. Focus on understanding the Yin-Yang relationships throughout life.

"Change can be hard, but change may also be welcome and comforting. Couples often struggle because the female represents Yin and the male represents Yang. It is the way of things, or the Tao, and can't be avoided.

"When Yin becomes stronger than Yang, Yin loses energy and the balance may shift. Yang becomes stronger than Yin, change occurs, and the energy balance shifts again. External forces may also randomly strengthen or weaken the Yin or Yang causing more or less change while adding a layer of complexity to the natural processes. They become unpredictable, but change is always occurring in and endless eternal struggle between Yin and Yang.

"Westerners some times refer to these phenomena as the ups and downs of life, but Yin and Yang apply to everything:

individuals, families, societies, countries, the world, and the universe. The rules apply to all, and Chi flows between them. Western philosophy, such as Sir Isaac Newton's laws of motion from the 15th century, is nothing more than the Tao. Newton claimed that 'For every action there is an equal and opposite reaction,' and this is simply the Yin and Yang. A lot of what is considered original western thought is actually ancient scripture."

Dylan and Alyssa took Frenchy's word, and worked hard to meet his expectations. They took notes, compared, and made sure they knew the material before the next class. For Dylan it was of no use. Frenchy donated a lot of his time to help his struggling student. Alyssa would often sit in, as a result, Frenchy's attention migrated to her, and they would discuss advanced concepts. Dylan was unintentionally left out while Frenchy encouraged Alyssa to get in touch with her inner self.

Alyssa asked bluntly about her dreams but Frenchy declined comment. He told her that her dreams were very personal, and that she should decide the meaning for herself.

The summer of 2002 passed quickly for Alyssa with her energies focused on meditation, Tai Chi and Frenchy's teachings. Every week she improved, and Frenchy was very pleased with his prodigy student.

Dylan, on the other hand had progressed in Tai Chi, but didn't practice meditation at all. He lost interest in the cultural aspect of what Frenchy was teaching. They started spending less time together, and it began to worry Dylan that they might be slipping apart.

In an attempt to mix it up a little bit, Dylan arranged a beach day near the Santa Monica pier with his parents, Alyssa, Daisy, Grandpa Jack and Grandma Lin. It provided an opportunity for Franken to get away to the Del Mar race track without being missed. The beach goers planned to spend the whole day if the on-shore flow didn't stir up the sand. Dylan and Alyssa brought their beach cruiser bicycles in the back of Dylan's Dad's pickup so they could cruise up and down the strip at Santa Monica and Venice beach looking for old friends.

They ate lunch early before the winds kicked up, and talked awhile about baseball and whether Barry Bonds would break the home run record. He had recently hit his 600th homer, and Dylan's Dad felt strongly that he would break Hank Aaron's all time record of 755.

Dylan and Alyssa played beach smashball for a while, and enjoyed occasionally hitting the ball off into the adults. While both were wearing their swim suits, Dylan couldn't keep his eyes off Alyssa. He was obviously doing his best to keep from staring, but the tension made him appear goofy. In a feeble attempt to cover up his feelings, he paddled Alyssa on the bottom playfully, but with one swift martial arts move she instinctively knocked him to the sand. She surprised herself, worried about his feelings, and fell on top of him playfully. They both started laughing, but when the adults asked them to move farther away, they lost interest in smashball and got on their beach cruisers.

First they went out on the pier and met Carol and Charlie making and selling jewelry at their stand. Carol recognized Alyssa right away, but it took Charlie a moment or two to place her. He claimed that she had grown and matured so much he didn't recognize her.

"You're a young lady now!" said Charlie, "and very beautiful. When we knew you before, you were still a little girl. You've done good for yourself!"

Charlie went back to his jewelry making, and Carol said goodbye before they rode off to Momma Leoni's.

There was no answer at Mamma Leoni's. Alyssa was disappointed, and had wanted to introduce Dylan and show off her Tai Chi moves, but there would be no catching up. Alyssa had sent her a postcard every month, but Momma only wrote back the first few times. Alyssa wondered what happened to her.

107

They peddled down to Venice, and Alyssa realized that very few of her old pals on the pedestrian walk recognized her. She had changed. Sara's Dad was one of the people that did, and was very excited to see her. He was impressed with her new look, and how it enhanced the depth of personality that had already been present when he knew her. She was street smart good looking and radiant. It was perfect for her and he marveled at the change. He wanted her to start working the crowd right away to sell his store, and began to point out marks. Alyssa reacted quickly as in past times, but caught herself. She smiled at her former employer and declined. It was a great memory despite being troubled times for her. She had learned from the experience and moved on. It was in the past and now she understood what people meant by 'the good old days'.

They peddled their beach cruisers back to the Santa Monica pier, and were about to carry them down to their beach camp to avoid sand in the bearings when Alyssa heard someone calling her.

"Alyssa! Hey Alyssa! Hey wait up. I want to talk to you," said a young man with long hair and mirrored aviator sunglasses.

Alyssa didn't recognize him. He wasn't wearing a shirt. He wore only shorts that came down to his knees. They hung on his hips exposing most of his boxers, no shoes, and an ankle bracelet made out of many tiny colorful beads strung together. He was thin, and had a tattoo on his right shoulder of a bulldog with a spiked collar.

"Alyssa, I'm so happy to see you. What a coincidence," he said.

"I don't believe in coincidences," said Alyssa recognizing the voice but not the person.

"Oh that's right. There's no such thing as a coincidence. You're probably right. I was meant to run into you down here," he said smiling and trailing off with his enthusiasm.

"What's with the sunglasses?" Alyssa said looking at him with suspicion.

"Oh their just cheap things," he replied. "I always lose sunglasses, so I can't have anything nice."

He removed the sunglasses, and Alyssa immediately recognized him as Finhead John, but didn't let on.

"What's up with the ugly tat?" asked Alyssa without expression. "Do you feel the need to mark yourself now? You should know better."

"I knew you would hate it," said Finhead.

"I didn't say I hated it. I said it was ugly, and you should think twice before permanently marking your body."

Finhead laughed, but Alyssa kept a straight face. Dylan wondered how she could be so void of emotion in a situation that was mildly humorous.

"You hate it, and I knew you would!" Finhead replied jovially. "What I wanted to ask you is if you want a job at the Whittier Narrows Golf Course? I'm working there cleaning golf carts and doing maintenance. They have a few openings."

"Why haven't you called me or stopped by!" said Alyssa with a tone. "I thought you were my friend? What about all the things you said? Were those idle words?"

"I've been busy," said Finhead laughing, "and so have you. I know all about your martial arts training, and bringing in kids from the neighborhood to pay for the classes. Very clever! Do you think you're the only one who knows Frenchy? Every local in Venice knows Frenchy, and he talks about you all the time. You'd think you were a rock star or something. Good thing we all know you already, or we'd hate you."

"Very funny," said Alyssa furrowing her nose and brow. "You should have been in those classes."

"Maybe so, but I haven't been slouching either," said Finn.

"What happened to your fin?" asked Alyssa.

"I needed a change, so I grew out my hair so that the fin went away. I may cut it off soon. It's a bother. I have to wash it and comb it. That takes time."

109

Alyssa studied him up and down without expression.

"I think you should lose the mirrored sunglasses. You can't see your eyes at all, and that's suspicious. You have nothing to hide."

"You're right as always, but I like the look. It makes me look bad!"

"It makes you look like a druggie. Like you burn weed all the time. You know, a stoner."

"A stoner! Where you born in the 60s? Nobody uses that word anymore."

"My Grandpa does! He lived in San Francisco and Monterey in '67. He's met the Grateful Dead, and he went to the Human-Be-In in Golden Gate Park. He knows everything. He's my walking encyclopedia of social phenomena."

"You're killing me," said Finhead laughing. "So how about applying at Whittier Narrows?"

"I have no transportation other than a bike," said Alyssa. "I have no way of getting there."

"It's really not that far from you. I can give you rides, and you can mooch rides from your family. You can do it!"

"I'll think about it," said Alyssa. "We'll see you Finhead. We have to get back to our group."

Alyssa and Dylan walked away on the sand carrying their bicycles and left Finn standing and grinning.

"You're not thinking of actually doing it?" Dylan whispered.

"Why not?" stated Alyssa at full volume.

"What about our classes with Frenchy?"

"Well. I can do both!"

Chapter 16

After a ten minute interview, Alyssa accepted a job at the Whittier narrows Golf Course working at the snack bar. She liked the job because she entered into a different world. It was an unfamiliar world of leisure, and she encountered people that she would never have met otherwise. What was even more interesting was that her customers considered her unusual. She found it humorous how they behaved around her – skeptical and inquisitive. She wasn't radical or gothic. She had no piercings or tattoos. She was different in other ways that were subtle and difficult for her customers to put their finger on. She spoke to retirees, pampered wives, spoiled children, dapper business people, and clueless guests. Every member had the look of money, but she wasn't sure how many actually had money. One thing she was sure of was that they all had a story to tell. They were eager to tell it, and she was eager to hear it. Whenever the conversation stalled, she would pump them for more information by asking questions that they couldn't resist.

She wanted to know what went on in their heads, and whether she could fit into their lifestyle. They took things for granted, and she found that odd. She never dreamed that there were people that didn't worry about money, working, or making bills at the end of the month. She had been told of their existence, but had never met any before. She had been happy living in her own minimal world.

Most people enjoyed talking to Alyssa. Besides being attractive, she was up-beat and full of energy. She beamed when she spoke, and seemed generally interested. A lot of young men returned to the snack bar numerous times when she worked, but seemed reluctant to ask her out. Alyssa looked mature for her age, and those that did have the courage to ask her were generally older.

"A year ago I couldn't have done this," she confessed to Dylan one night.

"Why not?" asked Dylan.

"I would have thought these people shallow, materialistic, and not interesting enough to talk to. Now I realize I was mistaken. I was closed minded and judgmental while egotistically thinking I was the opposite."

"Why do you do it now?" Dylan replied. "You don't need to."

"I like it," said Alyssa. "Talking seems to help them. They trust me and open up to me. They're more energized when they walk away.

"I also have money for the first time in my life. You're right in that I don't really need the money, but I have it. Money opens up new doors for me. For the first time I have enough money that I no longer worry about spending a little.

"Another thing I like is talking to Finhead. He's interesting and funny, and he thinks I'm some sort of magician or spiritual guru like the Dali Lama, but I'm quick to assure him that I'm not."

Dylan looked annoyed.

"Do you like him?" he asked.

"Well of course I like him! We're friends, and we had a traumatic experience together. I like Finhead a lot, and I think he's important in my life for some unknown reason. I feel it, and I like having him around. He quite often gives me a ride to work, and we enjoy the time together. Grandpa Jack trusts him, and that's important to me. He calls him John. Finhead doesn't let anyone call him John accept Grandpa Jack. It's either Finn or Finhead, but never John."

"Is he interested in you, or are you interested in him?" asked Dylan.

"It started out that he was interested in me. He saw something in me that intrigued him, and he wanted to be a part of it. He became my first follower although I found it strange because he was older than me."

112

"I find that strange too," Dylan added. "More than strange!"

"His interests were beyond sexuality at first if that's what you're thinking. He's changed recently. He's interested now, but his original interest is more important to him. He was always attracted to me, but attraction of any sort between a man and a woman can lead to other places."

"You sound like the Dr. Phil authority! Are you interested in him?" Dylan asked bluntly.

"Yes, and for the same reasons he's interested in me, and it's beyond words," Alyssa said in calm yet forceful manner that had a hypnotic tone. "Are you interested in me Dylan?"

"Of course," said Dylan blushing and feeling suddenly uncomfortable. "I thought you knew. I've always been interested since the day we met all those years ago. The feelings have only grown."

"I guess I did know it, but we've grown up together, and our love for each other was more simplistic, but now it's different. Sometimes when we're close I'm attracted to you in a way I've never felt before. It doesn't scare me, but it's unsettling. Part of me wants to leave things alone, and we can stay fast friends like we've always been. Another part of me wants more. It's a part of me deep inside, and it's hard to explain."

"Part of me wants more," said Dylan, "No, all of me wants more. Did it surprise you when we kissed?" asked Dylan.

"No, it startled me after we kissed. It felt good and right, but when I realized what we were doing, it shook me up. It took me a while to sort out. Now, I wouldn't have any problem kissing you, but I'm not sure it would be the same. That first kiss was innocent and spontaneous. Now it would be purposeful and deliberate. Beyond that, we've both changed, and we understand where we're at with each other."

"Would you kiss me now?" Dylan asked.

Without answering him, Alyssa walked over and kissed him on the lips with delicacy and a simple purity that overwhelmed

113

Dylan. When he recovered, he leaned in, and Alyssa responded, but after another moment she pulled away."

"You see, said Alyssa, "not the same, but still good!"

After a split second they both started to crack a smile, and then they laughed.

"I'm not really ready for that yet," said Alyssa, "I have important things that I want to do, but I don't want to lose you either. You're my best friend!"

"You needn't worry about that," said Dylan, "we'll always be friends even if I don't end up with you. I was just wondering about Finhead John."

"Finhead John is just a friend," said Alyssa with sincerity.

Alyssa knew in her heart that Finhead was much more than a friend, and that he had some cosmic connection to her that she couldn't quite grasp. She met him bumming for food on the UCLA campus, they ran the Sunset Strip together, and they got in trouble together. To Alyssa, these occurrences were significant. One thing that she was absolutely sure of, she would know Finhead John for a long time to come.

"You've missed a lot of Thursday's with Frenchy," said Dylan looking concerned.

"I know. I'm going to tell Frenchy I can't make Thursdays anymore. Besides, I think I'm where I want to be with Tai Chi, and I sense that he knows it's time to cut the umbilical chord. He's given us almost everything freely, and it's satisfied beyond measure. We've helped him fulfill some inner need he had, and he's complete. He's given freely of himself to us, and we need to give back by allowing him to finish up in his own way. He's ready to let go now, and he's very happy to have had the experience."

"I think you're right. Frenchy is winding down. We can cut back to just Tuesday's, and that would reduce his need to commute. It would be very respectful if we let him choose when to end the class completely. We could have some sort of graduation ceremony in the Vietnamese tradition. Perhaps somewhere around Chinese New Year. It's already almost Halloween."

"Yes, let's talk to him about it. He's our Sensei, he should decide," Alyssa added.

When they spoke to Frenchy, they were surprised to find out that he already knew most of what they discussed without him, and there was a further surprise for Alyssa.

"You've been ready," Frenchy said looking at Alyssa. "You've journeyed far," he said turning to Dylan, "but there's a pattern in the snowflakes that you have not yet noticed. It's important to see from this experience that people can communicate without words. In fact, deep thoughts to another person are more important than words. That's how I know that you want to have a graduation ceremony on the Chinese New Year. I think that's a good idea, you've earned it, and I accept."

Dylan and Alyssa gave each other a confused look.

"Alyssa, I suggest you continue with the class as the teacher. You're the Master Sensei now. You recruit students with physical and spiritual potential, and bring them to your class. It is important, however, to teach what you feel is right in your own style. You don't necessarily need to teach as I have taught you. You're a great leader. That will show, and your teaching style will manifest itself. Let it develop on its own."

Frenchy's words were driven home when at the next Tuesday class the Master announced that Alyssa would be taking over. The class averaged five regulars, and about five more random shows for a total of ten students. All had seen the change coming, and welcomed Alyssa as their new Master Sensei. Frenchy continued on for every other class until the Christmas break taking questions but sitting with the students. The transition occurred naturally, and Wang Diang was very impressed with the growth of his gifted student.

They had their graduation ceremony in Little Saigon at the entrance to the Asian Garden Mall on Bolsa Avenue in

Westminster a few days before the Chinese New Year. Frenchy gave a speech about Vietnam as a French colony, the invasion of Japan during World War II, the French war with the Viet Minh, and the American occupation of South Vietnam in the late sixties and early seventies.

"Vietnam was not a super power," Frenchy said, "nor even a strong military country, but despite its lack of strength, it survived all of those wars and foreign occupations to become a united independent nation once more. "Strength and aggression aren't nearly as important as united wills of a committed human spirit. Vietnam is a great example of that concept.

"The behavior of an individual is similar to the behavior of a nation," he continued while looking intently at various individuals in the group. "People will try to own you and have power over you, but eventually you will prevail and take yourself back. These are examples of non-aggressive emotions and thought patterns that win lopsided wars for both nations and individuals. Thought and emotion, therefore, are much more powerful than money, weapons and tactics.

"Lastly, look to the rubber tree, indigenous to Vietnam. It was a highly desired by the foreigners, but when synthetic rubber was invented, the whims related to the desires of foreigners no longer focused on Vietnam, and the dynamic changed once again. By controlling or reducing your desires, your emotions are much less vulnerable to control by outside forces."

To conclude the ceremony, Frenchy handed the Tai Chi training book to Alyssa. It was a symbol of his passing the class to her. She accepted and bowed, and then turned and bowed to the audience.

Chapter 17

Alyssa was a natural at teaching Tai Chi, but struggled with the cultural lessons that Frenchy was so adept at providing. The mystical nature of the class was blatantly missing, and it became more of a workout session. Frenchy's persona and control of the ambiance could not be replicated. Although there was a mysterious knowing deep within Alyssa, she simply didn't have the life experiences necessary to express it. As a result, she focused on the physical, and they practiced more as a group during the class instead of sitting for lectures. Some students liked the new class better, others wanted to listen to Frenchy, and drifted away. There was turnover, and Alyssa and Dylan had to recruit new students as Frenchy had suggested. The new class was more energetic, and after a few weeks they added fitness exercises to replace cultural studies. Tai Chi blended well with the meditation techniques that Alyssa had always practiced; as a result, the class was balanced. It was a natural fit. They brought back the donation jar, but most of the money went into a bank account that Grandpa Jack setup to pay for materials and field trips.

Her new status as a teacher, as informal as it was, gave her renewed confidence. Dylan began to take direction from her. It was a change in their relationship that mainly applied to class time, but often carried into the afterhours. It didn't bother him that she was in charge, but the fact remained that they were no longer equals, and he made mental notes of his subservient status. He pushed to become an instructor too, and they often worked together so that eventually, he could teach the class on his own. When he did finally take a class, Dylan taught his own style of martial arts. His style was much more aggressive. When demonstrating moves, it appeared as though he had something to prove. He went overboard, and his behavior struck Alyssa as inappropriate. Her

117

interest was dwindling anyway, and she saw it as an opportunity to slip out. He saw it as an opportunity to dominate. He took over scheduling, management, and accounting. His efforts allowed Alyssa to pursue her personal interests.

In an effort to take over teaching completely, Dylan asked Alyssa to cover only spiritual lessons. Looking to bow out, she agreed. The class desired snippets of Eastern philosophy mingled with their workouts. She developed thought provoking scripts to recite when appropriate, and she also recorded drum beats to aid in meditation. In doing so, she became more like Frenchy, but in becoming like Frenchy, she decided that her contributions were complete, and she passed the torch to Dylan.

Outside of the class she saw very little of Dylan. Her life was now at the golf course, and she immensely enjoyed meeting the people of the middle and upper classes that she had been unfamiliar with for so long. She was changing again, and her early life of hanging out on the streets became a childhood memory. She was exploring American society, and formulating her plan to chart a path through it.

While working in the snack bar at the golf course, Alyssa always wore clothing that advertised martial arts. It served as a conversation starter, and she recruited several new students through her efforts. With her help, Dylan was making money and gaining notoriety. He located a space to rent, and set up the classroom. With the change in venue, there was almost an overnight transition. Their craft quickly turned into a business rather than an art, and everything changed rather quickly. Dylan was consumed with managing the enterprise, and Alyssa completely transitioned to the golf course. As a result, she spent most of her time with Finhead.

Dylan was proud of himself for converting the business. The success went to his head, and he subconsciously resented Alyssa for abandoning him. He knew that it was partially his fault. For all intents and purposes he had asked her to phase out, but he didn't expect her to disappear completely. What really bothered him was that he had made his intentions clear. He wanted to be more than friends, and had told her so point blank, but there was no change in her behavior. He felt ignored.

Alyssa's absence left a gap. Dylan brought in another teacher. Her name was Karen Vanhayden. She paid attention to Dylan when he spoke. More than that, she was the opposite of Alyssa. She was a tae kwon do third degree black belt, and very competitive. Dylan liked her because her techniques were aggressive. It was a refreshing departure from the peaceful defensive moves taught by Frenchy and Alyssa. Dylan had wanted to go on the offensive, and he became enthralled with Karen. He substituted Karen for the void left by Alyssa, and he worshipped her. Karen was egocentric to begin with, but Dylan's infatuation with her made it worse. She was good-looking, tough, and cut throat. Alyssa disliked her upon meeting her, and warned Dylan about her lack of humility. Dylan ignored her. He had found the partner that was aggressive and that appreciated him. He had no intention of going back.

Now that she no longer had teaching responsibility, Alyssa had more free time, and spent it almost exclusively with Finhead, but she didn't share her thoughts or passions with him. She was his sounding board. They had one sided discussions about his personal life, and dealing with his boss. He continued to have ups and downs with his father, and her suggestions always helped.

"I think my Dad is delusional," Finhead told Alyssa while driving her home.

"Aren't we all?" she replied.

"No really! He's paranoid. He thinks we're all being controlled by a handful of very wealthy people mostly in New York, and that even fewer people control the media!"

"That doesn't sound too far-fetched," Alyssa replied. "What does it matter?"

119

"It matters!" Finn said. "He thinks that subliminal messages are controlling our thoughts. He even thinks that others can hear your thoughts."

"I doubt that!" Alyssa replied; "but you can read their body language!"

"Sometimes I hear him having a conversation with himself. I think he hears voices in his head."

"Haven't you every talked to yourself audibly?" Alyssa asked.

"Do you think he's schizophrenic?"

"No," Alyssa replied calmly, "but you may want to check your own head. Do you hear voices?"

"Okay," replied Finn, "I'll stop now, but I'm telling you, parents, they're all nuts."

"No, we're all nuts," Alyssa stated.

The next day while working at the snack bar, Alyssa's theory that we're all nuts was put to a test. She met a man that she had seen several times before. He looked like a woman, but his manner of dress was neither male nor female. He wasn't tall, but Alyssa could tell he was a man. He had the vibe of a man, and slight mannerisms of a man. He was very fine featured and impeccably groomed. Not one hair on his head was out of place. He ordered the fish tacos, and paid with an Amex Card.

"Our reader is not taking your card," Alyssa stated. "Would you have cash?"

"I never carry cash," he replied, "cash is dirty."

"Let me try wrapping your card in a plastic bag," Alyssa said. "I've seen them do that in the stores. It worked! I'm sorry for the trouble."

"No trouble," he said.

He appeared to be in his late twenties. His voice had a genuine feminine quality to it. He didn't sound contrived or put on.

"Yes I'm male, and no I'm not homosexual or bi," he said looking at Alyssa.

120

"Okay," said Alyssa in a subdued tone without looking up, "that's what I thought, but thanks for confirming it for me."

"My name is Matt," he said. "I could tell that you could tell, but I didn't want to leave you guessing. People call me Metro Matt."

"Because you're metro-sexual?" asked Alyssa.

"That could be," he replied, "but I lived in Washington D.C., and took the Metro everywhere. Here in LA, I have a car, but the name stuck. I guess you could say I'm metro-sexual. Perhaps I'll use that explanation from now on."

"Not that we need to use labels," Alyssa suggested. "Metro, bi, gay, homo, they're all just labels. We're all people."

"Agree! Do you have a name?" he asked.

"I'm sorry, Alyssa Daingerfield, thanks for asking."

"Pleased to meet you Alyssa!"

"Likewise."

Metro Matt sat down and ate his tacos with a knife and fork while looking out the window.

"When do you get off?" Matt asked when he was ready to leave.

"At five."

"In 35 minutes?" he asked.

"About."

"I'll see you then. We'll talk.

"Are you asking for a date?"

"That's not what I had in mind, I just wanted to speak to you. Is that okay?"

"Yes that's okay. We'll just talk. Can you give me a ride to my Grandparents?"

"Sounds good, I'll see you in a half hour!" he said walking out with his back turned.

The last few minutes of Alyssa's shift passed slowly. There weren't many customers, and her mind kept drifting to Metro Matt. He showed up right at 5 PM. They didn't speak much as they

121

approached his car. He drove a Land Rover. It was a few years old, but was impeccably clean. Alyssa thought that it looked and smelled brand new.

"Can I ask you a personal question that I'm sure you get all the time?" Alyssa asked.

"Yes, I get mistaken for gay all the time."

"That's what I thought."

"It has its advantages though. Women think I'm gay because I act and appear gay. Because of that, they feel non-threatened. They trust me and confide in me. It makes it easy to get to know them, and once I get to know them, I can ask them out. They like it that I'm clean and well groomed. I smell good, and don't drink too much. When they find out I'm hetero they're always shocked."

"I bet you were abused in school."

"I was at first, but in High School I just hung out with the girls. They liked me, and because they liked me, their boyfriends felt obligated to like me and back me up. It all worked out, but I was never really afraid of other men anyway. I'm okay one on one. I can fight, but if they gang up, then I'm in trouble!"

"Do you have gay friends?"

"Yes. Doesn't everybody these days? I was okay with gay people before it was popular to be okay with gay people, and I supported gay marriage before it was popular to support gay marriage. To me people are people. It's a lonely world, and if they find love, that's a good thing whether it's the same sex or not. By the way, are you gay?"

"No, but I have this dream where people can't tell if I'm a man or a woman."

"So then you know what it's like."

"Like what's like?"

"You know, what it's like for your sexual preference to be judged by the way you look or the way you act."

122

"Yes, and beyond that, I've always been somewhat of a misfit. People definitely judge me for aspects of my personality," Alyssa responded.

"I could sense that in you," Metro replied. "I have dreams too. We're a lot alike!"

"I guess we are. Why did you want to talk to me?"

"You're a good worker, and you're good with people. I've seen you work the snack bar before."

"Yes, so, and then?"

"I was wondering if you would consider taking a part time job at an alcohol and drug rehabilitation center. It's not dangerous. The people are all there voluntarily. They're also screened to make sure they're free of violent infractions. Many have drunk driving arrests, but they're not violent. You would need permission from your parents."

"I don't have a Dad," replied Alyssa.

"That's pretty hard to do!" Metro said jokingly.

"I mean, I have a Dad, but I've never met him, but I could ask my Mom and Grandparents. Why are you asking me?"

"I think you'd be very well suited for it. You have abilities that bring people up. You provide them with an upbeat energy. Everyone walks away from your snack bar energized. It's crazy. I've never seen anything like it! It's as if you have crazy good healing abilities. I'm not talking about just physical healing, I'm talkin' bout emotional healing! Most people in rehab are damaged emotionally, and that's where they need help. Normal medicine can't deal with that."

He paused and there was an awkward moment of silence. He started again.

"You'll find out over time that when you approach someone that you've never met before you can tell a lot about them. Everything they are and everything they've been projects from them. I'm not talking strictly about obvious visible clues, but visual clues do play a part. Their energy, their expression, their

123

body language, and even their karma are evident, and you quickly sense a lot about their being before they even say a word."

"Yes, and after they speak," Alyssa added "the aura that you've already experienced is usually reinforced. It's rare when you sense incorrectly. It's easy to judge incorrectly, but not sense incorrectly. Their inner spirit handshakes with your inner spirit before you're conscious of it. It's the way of things."

"And that's how you know what they need?" Metro asked.

"Yes, do you have a dog?" Alyssa queried.

"No. Dogs smell, they leave hair. You have to walk them, and carry around a bag of poop. That's not on my list of things to do."

"That may be, but animals are great at sensing your inner spirit. Dogs are a common example. They may come to you or they may shy away, but when they first meet you they have a keen sense of what type of person you are. People can do this too, but we've separated ourselves from nature for so long that we've forgotten how. There may be a reason why we've forgotten," said Alyssa.

"I may be done at the snack bar," Alyssa continued, "and you're right, I have these abilities you're speaking of. My Grandfather claims I do. He said that I could have been more than a healer, a doctor, a nurse or even a priest in past lives, but I just didn't expect this. I'm only fifteen. How am I going to get to work?"

"Let me worry about that," said Metro. "You worry about permission. Tell your Mom it's the Hollywood Recovery Treatment Center on Wilton Place in Los Angeles. It's on the internet if you need the details."

"Okay, I'll ask," said Alyssa.

Chapter 18

Grandpa Jack thought it would be a great opportunity, and encouraged Alyssa to apply. Grandma Lin agreed, but was concerned that she was entering an adult world at a very young age.

"Children don't have much time to be children," said Grandma Lin. "There's nothing to be gained by rushing into things, but you've always been ahead of your yourself, so I would suggest doing what you feel is right."

Grandpa Jack and Alyssa looked at each other after Grandma spoke surprised that she would consider the importance of enjoying childhood.

"She has a point," said Grandpa Jack. "There's no need to hurry. Life passes by rather quickly. These are things you already know in your heart and from your training with Frenchy. Choose a course, stick to the course, and work toward your goal at a nice easy pace."

"Well I've already decided I want to do it," Alyssa responded. "This is obviously my type of thing. Metro Matt requested that I ask my parents, and I consider you my parents. Daisy is more like a sister, but she's my Mom. I want her opinion, and then I want her blessing. If she doesn't approve, I'll just stay working at the snack bar for the summer."

The position in question was for a student aid that was willing to work at the center through high school. If job performance and high GPA warranted at the end of the program, they could receive a scholarship for a degree in substance abuse counseling at California State University Los Angeles campus. It was a great opportunity. A carpool was also available from Monterey Park and Rosemead at East Los Angeles Community College. It was a great match.

Alyssa had passed the interview process with flying colors, obtained an endorsement from Metro Matt, and had a letter of recommendation from Whittier Narrows Golf Course. She wasn't selected, and there was no explanation. The rejection left everyone feeling flat, and the excitement around the house quickly passed. After another week went by, however, the phone rang with an offer for Alyssa. The center's first choice had declined the position.

After Alyssa started, she had little time for socializing. Her life became a monotonous routine of work and school. Her relationship with Finhead suffered because of it. She had no time for friends. The most exciting part of the summer was taking driver's training at the community college during the 2nd summer track. Her 1st track class on medical terminology was over, and she had just enough time to fit driver's training in. She wanted to get it over with. The class was full, but she was put on the waiting list and showed up the first day with cash. There were openings, but she needed parent's permission. She was frustrated with the unanticipated requirement, but she met someone else on the waiting list. Her name was Kaylee, and she suggested signing each others forms as parents.

"My Mom would just sign anyway, she reasoned out loud to Alyssa. "I'm just saving her the hassle. Besides, it's a dumb rule, and rules are made to be broken."

"My Mom would too," Alyssa agreed. "Let's try it."

Their paperwork was accepted without question.

"See," said Kaylee, "they didn't even look."

That wasn't the only rule Kaylee broke. She was only 15 yet she smoked cigarettes.

"Why do you smoke those nasty things?" Alyssa asked.

"I don't know. I just like them. They're bad for you, but I never smoke more than three a day."

"You smoke three a day!" Alyssa said frowning.

"Sure, I steal them from my Mom," said Kaylee, "and if I take more than three she'll notice. I should really quit, but I like it too much. Only the bad people smoke, and I seem to fit in with the bad people. I like hanging out in the smoking area sucking and blowing smoke neurotically as if I'm in a hurry to get back somewhere."

Kaylee and Alyssa became driver's training buddies, teamed together in one of the instructors cars, and sometimes hung out after class.

"You're too good," Kaylee said to Alyssa one day. "Have you ever been in trouble?"

"Yes, I've left home twice."

"Do you mean you ran away?" asked Kaylee. "How old were you?"

"I didn't run. I walked. I could be gone right now. I was fine on my own at 13, but I missed my family. I wanted to be with them."

"Is that what made you come back?"

"No, it was a feeling deep inside that made me come back. I missed my grandparents, and I love my Mom, but that's not what made me come back. It's hard to put into words."

"Was it fun?"

"The first time it was fun. The second time it was a disaster. The whole experience was just awful. The second time I came close to being raped."

"Isn't it just like me to hit on a tender subject," said Kaylee. "Open mouth and insert foot. I'll never question you again. I promise."

"That's okay. How could you know? It's not that I'm bad or good anymore," said Alyssa. "I just know what I want, and I know what I want to do. I'm in a great place, and I'm on the right path. It just took me a while to find it. Now I just work, but I enjoy my work."

"I have absolutely no idea what I want to do with my life!" Kaylee stated while staring. "I'm surprised you do! Most people I talk to don't know what to do with themselves. You're an odd duck."

127

"What a great compliment!" Alyssa said. "I hate being like everyone else!"

"I guess it is a compliment," Kaylee replied. "Yes, you're right. I should have said refreshingly unusual."

Just before school started, Daisy and Kaylee's Mom took them both to the Department of Motor Vehicles on the same day, and both passed their tests. Alyssa had her driver's permit.

Chapter 19

Metro Matt was a manager and administrator at the rehab center where Alyssa worked. He was several layers above her in the management hierarchy. He called Alyssa into his office a few times a week to talk about how she was doing. Occasionally, he gave her a ride home. What Alyssa found interesting was that they never talked about work. Their true interests were religion and philosophy, and would query each other on their belief system and argue about who was right. They enjoyed arguing. Metro Matt was Christian, but he didn't go to church for fear of being judged for his feminine appearance. Matt enjoyed money, and struggled with fitting money into his religious beliefs.

"Why did you call me to your office?" Alyssa asked.

"I just wanted to see how things were going and how you're doing," Metro Matt gestured by waving his hands.

"There's nothing to report," Alyssa answered, "I work and I go to school. There's not much else."

"There must be something," Metro said smiling. "There's no man in your life – no drama, family problems?"

"Not really, no," Alyssa replied blankly. "I have male friends, but they're just friends. My family is fine. We're better than ever. My life is enjoyably routine."

"What about work and school?"

misunderstood misfits. They can't cope and they self-medicate because of it."

"A lot of the people that pass through rehab will be homeless someday," Metro Matt stated distantly. "I think I see what you mean."

"First of all, I would suggest that you stop obsessing over your discontent," Alyssa suggested. "You know how you want to be but let it happen naturally. Remember the old saying. The prostitute wants to find God, yet the priest is ravenous for sex. Just let go and live how you want to be."

"Easy for you to say, you don't have expensive tastes. I'm Christian, but I have a love of money and the fine things it can buy. I can't be enlightened and rich at the same time. You can't serve God and mammon!"

"I wouldn't get too hung up on words either! There are a lot of people these days that are hung up on the word "enlightenment". They read a Deepak Chopra book, ditch their PC in favor of a Mac, and buy a yellow Livestrong bracelet, and they think they're enlightened! I would say that luxuries are only mildly important. They're not dragging you down. Relationships with people and with nature are where you'll progress. Relating well to people can bring contentment."

"I have a Mac and a Livestrong bracelet. What are you trying to say?" said Matt smiling.

Alyssa's lips thinned. She was done talking.

"Nothing! Absolutely nothing!" said Alyssa. "I'm going back to work now, anything else?"

"I'd like to hang out now and then and talk like we did today. Would that be okay with you?"

"Are you asking me out?" she responded halfway through the door.

"Not really! Of course not! You're too young for me remember?"

"Okay, sure then, we'll hang out. Now get back to work!"

Alyssa walked down the hall without saying goodbye.

Over the next few weeks Metro Matt made an effort to finagle his way into Alyssa's life. He gave her rides home whenever he could. Occasionally, he took her out to dinner, and at other times he would drive her down to Venice Beach or Santa Monica to walk along the shoreline and talk. The discussion was always philosophy, religion, and enlightenment, but beyond that, Metro sought to be like Alyssa, and wanted to know everything about her.

Overall, Alyssa trusted Metro, but she was skeptical of one aspect of him. She couldn't shake the feeling that he wanted her. He wanted to be intimate, and looked at her in that way. By his own admission, he played off his semi-gay personality to lure women into his web, and she waited for the moment when he would make that move on her. It never happened. As time passed, she was confident that he was just another lost soul looking for direction in a world devoid of meaning. At times she felt sorry for him. He was a good person, and had everything with the exception of someone to share his life. For the time being, she filled that void, but there was an unspoken understanding that their relationship would never pass beyond friends. He was, in effect, her student, and although he was 12 years older than she was, he was a beginner in comparison. He craved the understanding that came naturally to her.

"I want to try some of the things that you practice regularly," Metro said while they walked past Muscle Beach. "Doesn't one of your old mentors live down here?"

"Yes, Frenchy, but I haven't seen him for a long time, and I don't see him here today. What did you have in mind?"

"You know, some of the moves and exercises. I want to sit in the lotus position and chant "Hummm" and things like that."

"Do you want to meditate?"

"Yes, didn't you tell me that your Grandfather meditates?" Metro asked quizzically.

132

"Yes he does," she replied. "Some people do it differently than others. I'm not sure what his methods are. He learned in San Francisco in the late 1960s. He was part of the whole communal anti-establishment awareness movement. He claims he's met several famous people like Janis Joplin, Pig Pen Mckernan, and Ken Kesey."

"How interesting," said Metro. "That is so tuned in! I want to try it!"

"I can teach you Eastern style, but like I said, I don't know what his methods are. He may just say prayers."

"Saying prayers is like meditating?"

"It can be," Alyssa replied. "Repetitive prayers like multiple 'Hail Mary's' help clear your mind of thought and connect you to source."

"I'd like to pick up some of that vibe from the '60s. That was such a hip era. They were so cool!"

"Metro, that whole trip is in the past! It's difficult to go back. You weren't even born yet!"

"I know. I was born in '76 when it was mostly over. I'm a bicentennial baby. It was the beginning of glam rock and punk. The Ramones were just getting started. The late '60s were so much more of a cultural revolution. It was inspired change rather than angry teenage angst. Can you put me in touch with your Grandfather?"

"How can you pick up that kind of vibe in the new century?" Alyssa asked. "It's in the past, and it's so done. Take a look at yourself! You're not gay, but you're so, you know, . . . gay. You're a heterosexual gay man, and that's completely new. You're relevant to what's going on today! We're not required to fill the mold of yesterday."

"You're Grandfather is so crazy though in a calming sort of way. It's as if he's all knowing, and nothing bothers him."

"It's important that you can even notice that. Most people don't. You have awareness. His peaceful knowing, however, may be due to other factors. He's in his 50s. He's been on the planet a long time. He has wisdom. He experimented with new things and practiced the ones that he found interesting. It may just be blind faith. You can do it too but in a modern way."

"Some people are naturally good at things," Matt stated. "Like you. You're naturally in tune, and your Grandfather is the same way. You see things and feel things."

"I do," Alyssa responded, "but it doesn't mean you can't. I'll teach you Tai Chi and meditation, and we'll see what that brings."

"Good!" said Metro, "I'm ready to try new things, definitely!"

"You're studies are a little lopsided to the western ways," Alyssa stated randomly. "I suggest you read up on Chinese philosophy and Buddhism. Read everything Chinese that you can get your hands on. Have you ever heard of the eightfold path?"

"What is the eight fold path?" Metro asked. "I remember reading it, but eight things are a lot to remember."

"They won't be hard to remember once you study them enough:

Right View
Right Intention
Right Speech
Right Action
Right Livelihood
Right Effort
Right Mindfulness
Right Concentration

I study them one at a time, and take several days on each. I know them all by heart."

"I'll get started reading," Metro replied, "but I'm very interested in the meditation and Tai Chi. I want to get started right away."

Rather quickly, Alyssa was teaching again. She may have only had one student, but she was back at it with her first older student. She was fulfilling her dreams, but in a new life.

Chapter 20

Kaylee and Alyssa spent increasing amounts of time together until they were inseparable. Alyssa taught Kaylee meditation techniques too, and she made fast progress. Before long, she took an interest in everything Alyssa did, but it was from a new angle. Kaylee was a socialite, and wanted to use what she learned from Alyssa to improve her social status, and it was working. Although she would never admit it, she was Alyssa's next new follower after Metro Matt. She marveled at Alyssa's ability to instinctively know exactly what to do. She desired to have the same outstanding self-confidence. She wanted to know how to decide whether someone was trustworthy just by meeting them. Kaylee had always trusted the wrong people. She had been burned by it many times, and it had hardened her. Since she had met Alyssa, her life had drastically improved. She was trusting again, and sensitive to the feelings of others without attempting to discern their angle. She had found new excitement, and at the center of it all was Alyssa.

"Have you ever made out with a guy," Kaylee asked Alyssa while walking through the mall.

"No, how bout you?" Alyssa asked.

"No not even once?" Kaylee asked ignoring the question.

"No I haven't made out with anyone," Alyssa responded as if it was no big deal. "Laying down and kissing while caressing each other in an endless embrace. Breathing heavy. No, I haven't done it."

"Wow," Kaylee replied, "well how about kissing a guy then?"

"Yes!"

"Okay, now we're getting somewhere!" Kaylee said with satisfaction. "Do I know him?"

"You've seen pictures."

"Finhead?"

135

"No, Dylan. I think Finhead's afraid to touch me because he's older. I would have to seduce him, but it wouldn't be hard."

"Oh my God Dylan," Kaylee said with horror. "Your nerdy little playmate. Were you playing doctor?"

Alyssa laughed.

"No it was recently, we would talk after school about philosophy, religion, and the meaning of life. It just sort of happened. It was a real kiss, long and sensual. It startled both of us afterwards. How about you?"

"Oh yeah, I've made out with several guys. I have yet to find a good kisser. They need to brush their teeth too. If they're clean and well groomed at our age, then they're gay. What a waste. I like the guys that are vain. They need to work out and dress nice. It helps if they wear cologne."

"You can still make out with a gay guy," Alyssa stated casually. I bet they're good kissers. I bet Metro Matt is a good kisser."

"Have you kissed him?"

"No, I see him a lot but we just talk. He's never so much as hinted, and he's so old! He may be 28 or so."

"Well, I think we're ready for boyfriends," Kaylee stated as if it were a forgone conclusion. "I'll find you a good one."

Alyssa smiled and dropped the subject.

Kaylee was a girl's girl, and for that, she was immediately embraced by Daisy. Clothes, manicures, stylish shoes, Coach purses, "People" magazine, and sexy lingerie where all important subjects between the two. They spoke of them at length. These things were a part of their being. Mostly due to Kaylee, Alyssa had come to enjoy clothes and shoes too, and that had been a very welcomed change for Daisy; but Alyssa's interests were mild in comparison to Kaylee. Kaylee delighted in it. She wanted to be beautiful, and she wanted to be girly. It worked well for the three of them. Kaylee and Daisy would talk beauty, fashion, and celebrity gossip while Alyssa remained in her own world

136

fascinated with the goings on around her. The new relationship allowed the three to spend more time together, and Daisy, still being young herself, became one of the girls.

"How many pairs of shoes do you have now?" Alyssa asked Kaylee after work.

"Not enough!" Kaylee replied. "More than ten and I know what you may be thinking, but as long as I'm not attached to them, and as long as my happiness doesn't depend on them, I'm okay. Isn't that right? I can have as many pairs of shoes as I want."

They both looked at each other and laughed.

"I could give them up at any time!" Kaylee stated smiling.

"Are you going to give them up?" Alyssa asked. "Donate them to the homeless shelter?"

"Not in your life!" said Kaylee with a sudden look of concern. "I've worked hard for that collection! I'm just not attached to them."

"Do you have a pair of boots?" Alyssa asked

"One pair," Kaylee replied. "I need more."

"I love boots," said Alyssa. "Those early 20th century styles were great. I'd like a really tall pair."

"You've been holding out on me," Kaylee replied. "We better make that happen for you soon!"

Another thing that Kaylee never did, despite all the encouragement from Alyssa, and all her meditating, was quit smoking. Smoking was a part of her look, and she felt awkward in a social setting without a cigarette in her hand. She would chain smoke if allowed, but since she couldn't smoke inside, she would stand with an unlit cigarette in her hand, and occasionally place it in her mouth while she was talking so that it would bounce up and down with her words.

"It's an act," she would say indifferently to those close to her. "I enjoy actual smoking far less than using the cigarette as a prop. I'm not as good as May West was, but I'm getting there. 'When I'm good, I'm good, but when I'm bad, I'm really good,' she would say. I can completely relate to that quote although it was coined many years before I was born."

Sometimes when standing with her unlit cigarette in public places she would get warned about smoking.

"There's no smoking allowed in here!" someone would say.

"Does it look like I'm smoking?" was her curt reply.

Kaylee was a Californian born and raised. She was from Los Angeles, but spoke with a New Jersey accent as if she grew up across the water from New York City. She picked it up watching old movies, and she practiced it so much that it became her normal speaking pattern. She loved Marisa Tomei as Lisa in "My Cousin Vinny", and knew most of her dialog by heart. Kaylee loved the accent, and thought it was just right for her. It was brash but not too tough. She very much wanted her accent to be authentic, and would test it when she met people from the New York area.

"Where are you from?" they would ask.

"Hoboken," she would always reply not knowing anything about Hoboken, and without further comment from them.

When it became time for Kaylee to get her license, Kaylee's Dad leased her a new BMW 325si and paid for her insurance. Her Dad was a film editor, single, and divorced from Kaylee's Mom. Much like Alyssa, Kaylee had grown up without a Dad, and although she had spent some time with him, she didn't really know him well. Instead of spending time with her, he would occasionally throw money her way or gifts. It soothed his guilt for abandoning her as a baby, and leaving her Mom without much income. He failed to show up himself. The dealership delivered the car on Kaylee's 16th birthday, and explained the terms of the three year lease that had already been paid in full. All Kaylee had to do was turn in the car when the lease was over.

The girls became dangerous in Kaylee's new car. They were beautiful, innocent, sultry, and neatly packaged. The combination made them extremely attractive, and guys were mesmerized by them.

Kaylee's BMW may have been part of the reason that Alyssa did so well when her birthday finally arrived in April. There were odd cars in Grandpa Jack's driveway when she arrived home from school that evening, but she thought nothing of it because it was her birthday, and some of her Grandparents' friends were likely to be on hand for some sort of celebration. When she walked in the door, everyone yelled "surprise", and Daisy was dangling a set of keys in the air.

The whole family had pooled their money together to buy her a 2002 Honda CRV. It was a mini-SUV that was only two years old with low miles and lots of good options. It was the perfect vehicle for her. It was feminine but not too girly, and she couldn't believe her eyes. Her family didn't have money, and she fully expected to work for whatever she received. This gift was totally unexpected.

"The car is yours, but you'll have to pay for your own insurance," Daisy stated loudly so that everyone could hear.

Alyssa hugged her still in a state of shock while Daisy started tears of happiness. Everyone in the room applauded and made comments on Alyssa's look of surprise. Her expression was usually one of all knowing, so a look of surprise was very unusual for her.

Her shock subsided and turned to a smile of disbelief as everyone filed out of the house and into the driveway to look at the vehicle. It was just a little sky blue Honda, but it was her little Honda. The men popped the hood and kicked the tires while the ladies peered inside and out with their arms folded. Kaylee checked to see if there were lighted mirrors on the back of the visors.

"I like your car better than mine," she said with humble sincerity. "Your car came from the heart."

Alyssa was touched by the comment and felt a tear well up.

"This is truly a wonderful thing for me," said Alyssa, "but it doesn't compare to your car Kaylee."

"My car was for my Dad not me," Kaylee responded. "It was obligatory but in a big way, and that's my Dad. He didn't have the courtesy to stop by or even call to see how I liked it. It was so nice, he knew that I would have to like it. He didn't send a card with hugs and kisses in it, and I had to leave a message at his office to thank him. I'm not complaining at all! Please don't think I'm ungrateful and spoiled. It's a great car! I know that you know what I mean, but it's a lease vehicle and a tax write-off against his business. It must go back to the dealer in three years. Your car is for keeps, and from the heart. It came full of love!"

Alyssa looked at her differently than before and could sense the mild hurt in her words, but when they both realized they were being watched, they started to laugh.

"What you're saying may be true," said Alyssa, "but the fact remains that you have a very nice car to drive for three years."

As they glanced over at the guests staring at them, they began to crack up, and turning back to each other broke out in full laughter. Daisy walked over and touched Alyssa on the upper arm with her hand and looked at her straight-faced through the laughter.

"It's important to me that you know that Frank covered the majority of the cost of your car," said Daisy. "Now please don't take that wrong. He's not trying to buy your affection, and I know how independent you've always been. You could have done this on your own. We know that, but he wanted to do that for you. He does love you."

"It was nothing, yes?" said Franken looking at Alyssa and smiling. "One good day at track pay for it."

Franken paused, looked around at the people, and started speaking again.

"We make the girl feel, how you say, awkward, No? Forget about the money," he said looking around again, "let her enjoy it. We not kids very long!"

140

Alyssa understood what he meant, and although she never disliked Franken, he was just there. He was someone who was about but never a part of things. For the first time she felt his human side, she understood his gift, and felt close to him. She felt compelled to hug him.

"Thank you Franken," she said suddenly hugging him tightly around the waist.

"I told you. It was nothing," he said slightly amused by the sudden affection and blushing.

"My turn," said Kaylee.

She hugged Franken big too. His face flushed beet red, and he looked around at the people happy yet slightly embarrassed.

"Very nice, but you going to ruin my reputation as a two bit gambler."

Everyone laughed including Grandpa Jack, but Grandma Lin walked over with only a gentle smile.

"We did what we could honey," she said looking at Alyssa. "You know we don't have much. We live a simple life, but we did what we could, and we're very happy for you."

"You've turned into a fine young lady, said Grandpa Jack joining them and putting his arm around Grandma Lin's waist. "We're very proud of you."

Her Grandpa's words overwhelmed her, and she broke down suddenly into happy tears.

"Okay," said Kaylee loudly to the group. "We girls must cry when we're happy, but that's enough. We're going to sing, blow out candles, and eat cake!"

Chapter 21

Driving made Alyssa's life much easier. She found a new level of freedom, and could do much more without the worry of transportation. The job at the Rehab Center became much easier as a result. They liked her work, gave her a raise, and asked her to work more hours. Although school came easy to her, there was no longer enough time left in the day. She hadn't seen Dylan or Finhead, and decided she should stop by before her schedule got worse. Dylan was nowhere to be found. She ended up discussing his whereabouts with his partner Karen Vanhayden.

"We found someone to pick up your class no problem," she said looking down at her papers without making eye contact.

"That's good," Alyssa replied, "but I'm just here to speak to Dylan."

"We've been switching over to 8 to 12 year olds. It will allow us to organize another class."

Karen looked up at Alyssa with her last statement, and Alyssa found herself deciding whether she was being insulted. When their eyes met, Alyssa sensed envy and decided to end the conversation quickly.

"Please let him know I stopped by," Alyssa said turning her eyes away and getting up to leave. "Good day."

For the months that followed Alyssa welcomed the boredom of a monotonous schedule of school and work. Every day was full, and almost every day was the same, there was little time for play. In her heart she knew she was building up to something that would be very rewarding, and that all the hard work was a necessary preparation.

She wasn't sure what was to come next, but she knew that it would be a bigger challenge than what she had already done, and wanted to get out of what she was currently doing. Foremost on her mind was graduating from high school early.

So Alyssa walked the high school campus alone with her look of purpose and determination so common in college life but so lacking in high school. As soon as her last class was over, she was off to work. She had a small table where she could study and complete her schoolwork before her official hours started, and if she had no homework, she would help out anyway. Work was now a part of her. She had chosen this as her career.

She made time for Metro Matt, Kaylee, and Grandpa Jack, but those times were her only diversions, and some of that related to work. Whenever Metro called she went with him sensing some bigger purpose to their relationship.

Kaylee, on the other hand, was different. Their time together was completely enjoyable and never work related. Their relationship grew stronger daily. Kaylee was devoted to the same studies of Tai Chi, martial arts, meditation, philosophy, and religion, but it manifested in different ways with Kaylee. It made her more girly, more tantalizing, and more attractive. She was becoming very social and seemed to know everyone. Her knowledge and connections made her powerful, and her many friends came to her for help and advice. Her status could have easily gone to her head, but her spiritual training kept her grounded. In her own way, Kaylee was becoming the celebrity that she read about in magazines but on a smaller scale. Her influence was growing in every aspect of her life.

Kaylee and Alyssa were at opposite ends of the spectrum. Kaylee was the outgoing socialite finding her place in life through contacts based on deep-rooted philosophical beliefs, while Alyssa the more reserved healer and priest helping people and going about it in mysterious ways. They became a team playing off each others strengths, and backing each other up. When they went out, they took Kaylee's BMW, dressed up, and put on the bad girl front. They were a sight to behold bouncing between friends houses or hanging out at the local Starbucks. They practiced their indifferent attitudes while casually stirring their iced coffees. They had found their place together socially, and they were both very happy with it.

Since expanding her social horizons, Alyssa found it oddly irritating how guys wanted to latch on to her as soon as they met her. What was worse was that they didn't know what to say or how

143

to act when they did break through. They stammered and nervously stared at the ground. She did her best to soothe their nerves, but it was a useless endeavor. They preferred to be unnoticed in her presence staring and whispering to each other. They were outwardly bored, but inwardly excited, and unwilling to speak. They sat near her in a circle like house pets around a dying man.

Finhead John had been absent from her life since she left the snack bar at the golf course, but recently, he had been trying to get reacquainted with her. In social settings, he acted the same way as others, outwardly bored, inwardly excited, and unwilling to speak. Whenever she moved he seemed to get in her way. He was forcing her to notice him and communicate. He obviously wanted her to speak first. For awhile, she ignored him, but it continued until she was forced to confront him.

"Hi Finn. Is there something you wanted to say?"

"No."

"Why do you always seem to try and get in my way?" she asked.

"If I did, it wasn't intentional."

"It is intentional. What do you want?"

"Why have you been ignoring me?" he asked.

"I haven't been ignoring you."

"I never hear from you."

"Well I never hear from you." she responded.

His tone was terse, and he obviously felt neglected.

"I thought we had something together."

"What did we have together Finn?" she asked.

"We were friends. We were good friends. We were going to do something big."

"Yes, Finn, we were friends, and we're still friends and that's all. Are you interested in being more than friends?"

"Well I don't know. It didn't start out that way, but maybe I do. I hadn't really thought about it. I just miss you."

"Finn, you're five years older than me. I'm sixteen and you're 21. If you want me you're going to have to wait a few years. I'm not ready for that yet. Furthermore, you need to take charge and be a little bit more aggressive. I'm not just going to lie down for you."

"Well like I said, it didn't start out that way. I don't know what I'm feeling. I don't know what I want. I just don't want to lose you."

"Finn you're not losing me. What's gotten into you?"

"Well you're always hanging out with the gay guy, and you never call. He's much older than me."

"Metro Matt," she laughed, "he's no threat to you, and he's not gay. He just looks and acts gay. He's as hetero as you are."

"I don't know what's worse, a gay guy, or a hetero that acts gay!"

"Stop it now. He's my friend, and he's a good person. We have similar spiritual interests. He likes to talk, and I'm helping him learn martial arts."

"A gay guy learning martial arts?"

"I told you, he's not gay, but even if he was, anyone can learn! Why don't you learn?"

Finhead stood.

"Are you calling me gay?"

"Certainly not, but I wouldn't care if you were. You're my friend, and who you choose to be close to is your business."

Finhead walked up and got in Alyssa's face.

"Why don't you just dump Metro Matt and that dumb rehab job and come back to the golf course? You're wanted there. Why be surrounded by drunks and drug addicts?"

Finhead was raising his voice, and spit flew from his mouth when he spoke. Alyssa took two steps back.

"Finn, you're scaring me. I don't judge others and I like Metro Matt. He's easy going and fun, but most of all, I love my job. I think you need to sort things out in your own head. When you do, call me."

Alyssa turned and walked away.

With Alyssa's promotion, she had her first opportunities to work with people directly in therapy. These were people that had been off drugs or alcohol for two or more weeks and beginning to feel stronger. For them it was the start of a new phase of preparing themselves to re-enter their worlds. Alyssa was determined to give them the tools they needed to avoid the substances, and substitute meaningful activities in their place. In her mind, the substitute activities would be exercise, meditation, and martial arts. If they were open to it, she also helped them dabble into philosophical and religious studies. She had the luxury of targeting people as they came into the center just as she did long ago while selling at the Venice Beach shops. She considered who had the will and determination to get clean, who would be open to therapy, and who would have resolve when released back to their addicted friends. She chose people that she thought would be willing to work. Beyond that she looked for deep thinkers who she could relate to on a philosophical level. She started the interview process from day one, and subtly extracted the information she needed to determine who to work with.

As much as the professionals preached against it, her thought was that will power had a lot to do with success in the beginning, and would also come to play later on during moments of temptation. Her approach was to provide the spiritual training that's required to carry the person through the long months of transition from addiction to sobriety. She thought that spiritual strength should take over as they progressed to fill the void left by the substance and address the deeper lying issues that may have caused the abusive patterns to begin with. They also needed replacement activities to fill the time that was once consumed by using. It was the ideal time to learn exercise and martial arts. That was her new goal, and these were her new students.

Her methods proved to be very effective, and had some early successes. What her patients enjoyed most was feeling much better. They were energetic and in improving physical condition. They realized that there was a payoff involved in beating addiction, and that realization reinforced their recovery. Physical fitness drastically improved their outlook. They had fresh new lives, and their substance was no longer required to fill the void.

Her success at work cemented her relationship with Metro Matt. They saw each other daily, but instead of philosophical discussions, their focus shifted to work. They spoke of potential new methods of recovery including spiritual based physical exercise derived from the martial arts. Metro had caught on quickly with his martial arts training, and wanted to make the training available to patients at the rehab center. Like Dylan, Metro had started with Tai Chi, but soon wanted to press forward with a more aggressive style. He inquired into tae kwon do. The concept of striking with foot and fist was intriguing to him, but since Alyssa's focus was meditation and Tai Chi, she referred him to the only tae kwon do instructor she knew, Karen Vanhayden.

Karen was unusually receptive to teaching Metro Matt, but since her focus was children, she offered him individual lessons only until he could find something more permanent for his age group. Alyssa found it unusual how receptive Karen was to teaching Metro. It seemed uncharacteristic of her to do anything that wasn't self-serving, but since she remained cool in her dealings with Alyssa and yet warm toward Matt, she decided that Karen was slightly resentful of her relationship with Dylan, and that the plan to train Metro could continue forward with no hidden agenda. What Alyssa found more unusual was the lack of Dylan's presence at his own studio. Alyssa was hoping to run into him there, and showed up with Metro Matt for every lesson hoping for a chance to talk to him, but he never showed.

As the months progressed, Alyssa's training techniques at the rehab center improved, and she took on patients that were a greater challenge. With the volume of patients a few failures came, and some patients returned to the Center using, strung out, and in

147

worse shape then when they first arrived. She didn't dwell on her failures, but concentrated on what she did right with her successes. She started a new program where a patient could return once a week for counseling to reinforce their training and talk about the problems they were having. Alyssa covered the training portion, and a counselor explored their problems.

Unbeknownst to her, she had treated some high profile patients from the West Los Angeles area, and patients began to request her when checking in or when calling for information. She not only had developed a reputation for success, but she had something else to offer in meditation and martial arts. The Center's patient load increased to the amazement of the staff, and they were forced to establish a waiting list for the first time in their history.

One day a rock star named Nikki checked in for alcohol abuse and requested Alyssa. He had been a heroin addict, rehabbed for heroin earlier, and his alcohol problems increased as a result. It was time to clean up, and he wanted intense therapy. When Alyssa met him she refused claiming he had no resolve, he was weak, and had numerous deep-rooted issues. He had tattoos covering most of his body, and she found that not only repulsive, but further evidence of weakness. What she disliked the most was his cavalier attitude always joking and using profane language as if it was okay. Nikki pestered her every time he saw her. Although very successful, Alyssa remained a student aid intent on obtaining the scholarship to Cal State Los Angeles. She couldn't completely avoid Nikki's room.

"With one check I could pay for your complete college education including room, board and tuition. We could call it Nikki's Rehab Scholarship. I want you to work with me," Nikki said smiling.

"I can tell you're a creative person," said Alyssa, "the problem is you repulse me. I find you foul and offensive. I'm usually not so harsh and judgmental, so I've decided I should avoid you."

148

"I admire your logic, and I'm not offended. I think that I'm part of your development," Nikki replied. "You can't just pick and choose your clients. You're running a business. You must take the good with the bad. I'm the bad, and it's about time you stepped up. Why don't you ask Metro Matt?"

"How do you know Metro Matt?" Alyssa asked with a skeptical look.

"I did some research before I checked in here. They have this thing called the internet now-a-days! I also know a lot of people. I've asked around. I need real help this time. I may act pompous on the outside, but on the inside I'm worried. I have children, and I don't want to end up just another dead rock star."

Alyssa was taken back by his words. She acted the same outwardly as if he wasn't worth her time, but his words made sense, and she changed toward him.

"I'll ask Metro Matt about it, if he approves, I'll help you," she stated flatly before exiting the room.

Alyssa never intended to ask Metro Matt about Nikki. She was stalling to buy time in order to devise a path forward with her persistent rock star. She had decided to accept the challenge, but wanted to establish some boundaries when she did so, and needed a few days to think about it. In the mean time, she sought out Metro Matt to discuss other issues, but she couldn't find him at the Rehab Center, and couldn't reach him by phone. She knew that this was his day for tae kwon do training, so she dropped by the studio. It looked closed, and Metro's car wasn't there, but the door was open so she went in. She couldn't find anyone, and was about to leave when she ran into Dylan.

"What are you doing here?" he asked.

"Hi Dylan, nice to see you! How have you been?" she said ignoring the question and opening her arms for a hug.

Dylan's expression changed. He was caught with an attitude, and he felt embarrassed.

"I'm okay," he replied accepting the hug, "how are you?"

"I'm fine," she said while scanning the room. "I was looking for Metro Matt, but I've been meaning to talk to you too."

"What about?" he asked staring her down.

"Well, I don't see you anymore. I've been wondering what you've been up to and how the studio has been going?"

"I've been kind of busy," he said looking to the ground and pausing. "Things are going okay I guess."

"Dylan we've been friends a long time. I can tell when something is bothering you. You're not telling me what's been up with you!"

"You blew me off," he said staring.

There was an awkward pause, but Alyssa didn't immediately reply. She could see anger building in Dylan's eyes.

"Yeah, you blew me off," he said more forcefully than before.

"What are you talking about?"

"We had our own business. It may not have been much, but it was something, and you abandoned it to work in a snack bar."

"If you're talking about our Tai Chi class, we had a group of friends. It was played out and you know it. Frenchy knew it. You took it to the next level not me. I was ready for a change."

"You went off to the snack bar job at the golf course with Finhead," he replied to her squinting one eye and raising the other eyebrow. "We were friends for years, but you left me flapping in the breeze."

"Is this about Finn?" she asked.

"I don't think so," he said looking to the side and back to her feet. "I think it's about you and how you take me for granted. Now you've blown Finhead off in favor of this pompous queen. He gives you a job at a rehab center, and then you start dating him. He's pushing thirty. How do you think that looks?"

"You also have a problem with Matt," she said. "I wasn't even sure that you knew Matt, and no we're not dating. We're just friends, and I don't like what you're implying! If I hang out with you as a friend does that make me something?"

150

"At least we're the same age. We're both minors, and we grew up together. Matt is just weird. How could I not know him, he's in here once a week. He comes in early before he starts with Karen to wipe things down with disinfectant. He's a freak!"

"With all we've been through together, you could at least respect me enough not to cap on my friends. We're all weird, all six billion of us. We're all freaky, not just Matt. What makes Matt so different?"

"It's because you like him and admire him. You think he's interesting, and you suck up to him. It's nauseating."

Alyssa laughed and then paused.

"I . . . . , I always wondered how you really felt about me," she said quietly looking in his eyes. "In one way I knew, and in another I didn't."

"What are you talking about? If you don't know then you're blind!"

"I just went through this the other day with Finn," she said with intensity. "I don't need this. I'm being judged for being myself. Coming from you it's painful."

Her eyes revealed hurt but her look was cold.

"If you're interested in me the way I think you are, then you must act on it. I can't do it for you. What you want I can't do for you. You must do it for yourself. You're going to have to fight for it like everything else in life. I'm not going to fill out a special invitation, and then make it easy for you."

"I'm not interested," said Dylan breaking eye contact. "I would appreciate it if you would leave, and one more thing, tell Matt that his tae kwon do lessons are over. He can find another instructor."

Alyssa didn't move until Dylan made eye contact with her again.

"If that's the way you feel. I'll go."

Just as Alyssa turned to leave, Karen Vanhayden walked into the room. She had a smirk on her face. She had the same look as

151

when she took someone down in a match. There was no way of knowing how long she had been standing there.

"Is there a problem here?" she asked.

"I was just telling Alyssa that we'll no longer be giving lessons to adults, and that she'll need to find an instructor for Matt. She was just leaving.

"That manipulative bitch," Alyssa thought. "She had this planned all along. She knew that bringing Matt in here would get Dylan all riled up and out of sorts. She took him on purpose to get at me. She wanted to drive a stake between us."

"Just remember that you can always count on me Dylan," Alyssa said concealing her anger. "That's what friends are for."

Alyssa turned and left the studio.

Alyssa never spoke to Metro Matt about what happened in the tae kwon do studio, and never asked about Nikki either. She let a week pass while she sorted things out in her head, and then confronted Nikki.

"I'll work with you, but you need to clean up your language. They'll be no use of the "F" word, and you'll cover up your tattoos with a shirt when you're around me. You'll have homework. You'll need to study, and I'll ask questions so that I'll know whether you've been working."

"Yes Maam!" said Nikki chuckling and saluting. "I shall do my best. You'll be happy you did this. You'll see!"

"You'll do what I say or else we're done!"

"Why didn't you ask Metro Matt?" Nikki asked innocently.

"You don't know whether I asked or not. You're attempting to play me, and it won't work."

Nikki laughed, and Alyssa ended up laughing too. She already had sensed that Nikki was very creative, and she had felt other good things as well, but with a little probing, she found out a lot more.

He was very intelligent, and was a born writer capable of transforming his feelings into words on the first try. He had written

152

most of the songs for his band, and worked on most of the melodies as well. He was logical and mathematical, and could work large numbers in his head very quickly. This sometimes worked against him in his religious studies. If what he read wasn't logical, he had a hard time accepting it. He never took anything at face value. He liked children, and he liked people in general. His family was very important to him, but his traveling profession and substance abuse had damaged those relationships many times.

As she had guessed from the start, he had deep-rooted issues in childhood. He was abandoned by his real father, and had an abusive relationship with more than one step Dad. Like herself, he had never met his real Dad, but he had gotten in touch with him later in life after achieving some success in his music career. He had been bitterly disappointed with the response.

Like Alyssa's Mom, Nikki's Mom was very beautiful, and he had experienced the same parade of men through their home when he was young. According to him, his Mom still looked good at 60 years old, but she had finally settled down with a man that treated her decently. His family was from Anthony, New Mexico near El Paso, Texas. When he was young they were poor most of the time, and Nikki had to hustle for everything he had. Like Alyssa, he spent a lot of time on the streets in the early days. He bartered for what he wanted, worked odd jobs, and hid his money. Nikki liked attention when he was young, and dressed flashy at school. He sometimes wore makeup, and took intense criticism for how he looked. Standing up for himself, he was involved in a lot of fights, and was expelled several times. Like Alyssa, he grew tired of high school and wanted to drop out, but found it easier to finish up and get out.

Alyssa could relate to him on several levels, and softened to him slightly, but on the other hand, she was very wary of him. He was crafty, highly skilled socially, and could actually be charming if he wanted to be. She wasn't about to let on that she was starting to grow fond of him.

153

"We have a lot in common you and me," he said one day after meditating.

"We have absolutely nothing in common," Alyssa responded. "You're addicted to everything including sex, you dress like a freak, and you're tattooed from head to toe. What would make you think that we have anything in common?"

"We grew up without natural fathers or enough money to get by. We're both very driven, and we like what we do. We're both smart, but not just book smart, savvy smart. We know how to work things our way. We're good you and I. We're very good!"

"Just the thought of being like you makes me sick. One thing I'll give you is that we're both driven, but in opposite directions thank you very much, and stay away from me. You're old enough to be my father."

"Maybe I am your father. What did you say your Mom's name was? Daisy? Did she ever hang out at the Roxxy or on the Strip? I seem to recall a groupie named Daisy."

"Oh please you're achieving new lows, and for you, that's saying a lot," said Alyssa cracking a smile. "I've been to the Strip. It's like fly paper for lowlifes. It figures that someone like you would hang out there."

"I may be a lowlife, but I'm king of the lowlifes," Nikki said laughing. "You're a lot of fun, and smart. Who ever taught you, taught you well!"

"Most of my training came from Frenchy," Alyssa replied nonchalantly.

"A Frenchman? That doesn't seem right," said Nikki.

"He's Vietnamese," said Alyssa, "We just call him Frenchy!"

Despite all the caution flags, they were becoming friends. As Nikki had said, they did have a lot in common, and they liked each other for that. They were self-made, and that was admirable.

Nikki was making great progress with exercise. He practiced the moves she had taught him, worked out every day, and had some of the basics memorized. He had lost weight and a lot of the

154

bloat that came with chronic alcoholism. He was starting to look good. His health was returning. The meditation hadn't worked so well for him. He had a hard time slowing down his mind and calming his thoughts. These were the same problems that Alyssa had starting out, and she explained that to him, but he was too impatient. He was ready to give it up.

"I'm getting out of here in a week," said Nikki one day. "I'm really going to miss you. You're really out there. I've never met anyone quite like you. I want you to come by the house and give me Tai Chi training."

"How do you put it, wish in one hand?" replied Alyssa.

Nikki laughed.

"No really, all kidding aside. Would you come by the house, and give these lessons to my family? I can pay you!"

"Since you're leaving, I'll admit that I like you. You're clever and genuine. I like you a lot actually, but between work and school I'm too busy."

"Well how about once a month then, on a Saturday morning."

"You don't get up until noon," Alyssa said with a wry look, "how is that going to work?"

"If you're coming I'll be up. Think about it. Here's my number and address. This number is unlisted and rings right through to the house. Leave a message. If you don't get through, then definitely stop by. I've told the kids about you and they're very interested."

Alyssa took the card staring at it.

"I'll think about it, but don't hold your breath. I have big plans. I want success in my career like you've had. I may not be a rock star, but I'm good."

"Big plans for what?" Nikki said smiling.

"I don't know yet, and that's the beauty of it," replied Alyssa smiling.

155

"I know you're good," said Nikki. "I would be thrilled if my kids turned out as well balanced as you. Please drop by. We'd love to have you."

Alyssa had told Nikki the truth. She was too busy to teach a class on Saturdays, but she kept his card. She would have time during the summer, and she thought she might call him then. In the meantime, Nikki kept referring his numerous alcoholic friends to Alyssa at the Rehab Center if they needed to get dried out. She had a following again.

Part II Big Sur

Chapter 22

When summer arrived there was no break for Alyssa. She signed up for two classes at Los Angeles Community College to complete her history and English credits to stay on track for a June 2005 high school graduation. Daisy thought she was overworked, and should take some time off to enjoy her youth, but to Alyssa, her work was what she liked to do. School she could live without, but her work was her life, and she knew deep inside that she was working her ultimate job.

It proved fortunate that she arranged to take both classes during track one of summer. This left her about six weeks to take time off before school started again, and Metro Matt suggested that she attend a retreat at the San Francisco Zen Center at Big Sur. The retreat was for promising students in metaphysics. Metro Matt was forced to cancel, and he couldn't think of anyone more promising in the spiritual realm than Alyssa, so he suggested she take his place. Her fees would already be paid.

Daisy was worried about Alyssa attending a retreat at the San Francisco Zen Center wondering what type of people would be there, and she wasn't sure about Metro Matt. She thought he was gay, and she didn't know how to react to gay people.

"She's only sixteen," Daisy said to Grandpa Jack. "It's sometimes shocking to me how mature she seems. She's more mature than I am, but San Francisco, Monterey, and Big Sur have some strange people."

"Yes I know. I'm one of them," said Grandpa Jack.

"That was a long time ago before AIDS and other things. I've seen stark naked people walking around in the Castro district as if it was nothing," Daisy said with a look of shock.

"I've seen stark naked people walking around in Golden Gate Park. Nudity is nothing new. They take their tops off at Lake Havasu all the time. People think nothing of it. I think she should have the opportunity to go," said Grandpa Jack.

"If you go up there with her, and see what its like before you leave her for two weeks, then I'll be okay with it."

"Done," Grandpa Jack replied. "I've wanted to go up there anyway with your Mom. We'll follow her up, spend the weekend in Monterey, and check in on her before we drive home."

The retreat turned out to be nothing like Alyssa expected. The majority of the people were college students in pre-med or nursing. Alyssa was the only high school student, the only one who worked rehabilitation, and the only one who knew anything about Buddhism. She was ignored at first because she was so young, but when they saw her bowing respectfully to her elders, they realized that she knew something, and then she became an assistant.

She spent the first three days helping to explain the eightfold path, the 10,000 things, reincarnation, and the different forms of Chi. They were open-minded, and that's why they were chosen to attend the retreat. Some saw it as a free trip to Monterey and Big Sur, others just wanted to get away for awhile, but a few were generally interested. These few were the ones that Alyssa

157

concentrated on. The remainder she kept within earshot so that they might pick something up on the periphery.

Daisy had been correct in her vision of the Zen Center. There were a wide array of people studying Buddhism and Zen. Many of the Masters were actual Buddhist monks with shaved heads and orange robes. Others looked like unkempt refugees from the 1960s walking barefoot with books in their hands and looking intellectual. They wore loose drab clothing that looked worn but very comfortable. There were guest speakers from all over California, and some from out of state. Most of them were from the medical profession. The speakers wore very casual western clothes for tennis or golf. There were also guest speakers on Zen and Buddhism. The group was honored to have a Shaolin Priest, but he spoke little English and was impossible to talk to without an interpreter. Alyssa tried to talk to him. He looked at the palms of her hands and nodded approvingly.

Few people knew that Zen was a form of Buddhism based on meditation. Alyssa knew this, but she was a student of the martial arts, and would not claim to be Zen if questioned. She liked the words and the philosophical points of view of more traditional forms of Buddhism. She found that very intriguing, and it pulled the whole package together for her.

Some of the students at the retreat had never meditated before. Alyssa held a crash course after hours. This impressed the monks, but like most Westerners, the students found it difficult to calm their mind and rid themselves of thought. They often fell asleep. Alyssa assured them that it was a common problem, and something that could be overcome with practice. She impressed on them that there's much to be gained by learning to meditate.

As the days clicked by, Alyssa found the medical lectures too technical for her, and ended up going out to sit with the monks. They didn't seem to notice that she was there, and she sat with them during meditation. She found that her meditation was more intensely calming when she was with the monks. She enjoyed being with them, and seemed to feel their presence. They appreciated her too. On the Friday of the first week, when everyone was about to start their weekend off, one monk approached Alyssa. He spoke English.

"We are all honored to have you with us. We are thankful that you are taking time here."

He bowed to her and walked away.

A man from San Francisco walked up and introduced himself as Pastor Dave.

"I've been coming here for five years and I've never seen that happen before," he said. "You must have something about you that is very special."

"Thank you," Alyssa responded. "You're very kind. I think that they sense how peaceful I've been since arriving. I don't think I've ever meditated on such a deep level before. I feel very fortunate."

The glow of that experience stayed with Alyssa for the rest of that afternoon. She was smiling as she drove into Big Sur, and was excited to finally see the famous rocky blue coastline. A few of the students at the retreat had spoken of a place called Fernwood with a restaurant, a bar, a little convenience store, and a gigantic fireplace that was as tall as she was. Fernwood became her first stop, and she planted herself in an overstuffed easy chair by the big fireplace. Even though it was August, there was a misty overcast in Big Sur. The mist provided a feeling of enchantment, and lent a chill to the air. Alyssa was appreciative of the fire, and pulled her body tightly together within the easy chair. When she adjusted, she noticed a Japanese man in his late 60s staring at her. His sudden appearance startled her, but she decided that she just hadn't noticed him when she sat down.

"It seems as though you've taken a long time to get here," he said to Alyssa, "but I realize in truth that it was neither long nor short. It just was. Do you know why you've come here?"

159

"You're obviously talking to me, but why? Do I know you?" asked Alyssa.

"In your heart you know the answer to your questions, but let me make it clear. You know me, and you know why I'm talking to you. Now, why are you here?"

"I've heard about Fernwood from my friends at a retreat in Carmel Valley. I wanted to see it for myself."

"Did you want to see it or did you want to feel it?" asked the man.

"Now it's my turn to say that you already know the answer to that question," said Alyssa. "Yes, I wanted to feel it. I should have chosen my words better."

"It seems as though our egos are at work," the man said with a subtle smile. "We think we're so clever when we're only egotistical. We could be attempting humor, but in another way we could be attempting egoism."

"My battle with the ego seems ever present," said Alyssa. "That's a big battle for me. I've heard that there's some sort of energy spot here in Fernwood. It's rumored that it's near the big fireplace, but that sounds too simple. It can't be here. It must be elsewhere, and it may not be an energy spot. It must be a point of transformation. It's a place where Chi can be static-neither energy nor matter, and stuck at that in-between point. It could be an inflection point between dimensions."

"I would venture to say you're correct," the man said looking slightly amused. It must be here and it cannot be here!"

"Good point," Alyssa said, "I hadn't considered the Yin Yang aspect of it."

"It may not be a static point geographically at all," the man continued. "It may move around, but for some reason, it frequently appears at the fireplace at Fernwood in Big Sur. It may be here now. How would we know?"

160

"We may not know," Alyssa agreed. "If you and I exist in more than three dimensions at one time, it may seem very normal to us.

The man chuckled.

"I've heard it's near the Point Sur Lighthouse, that the concentration of Chi causes things to move randomly, and that's why so many people consider the lighthouse to be haunted."

"I've heard that too," Alyssa stated. "The Point Sur Lighthouse is haunted. You may be onto something."

"The Point Sur Lighthouse is worth visiting if for no other reason than to just see it. It is beautiful, and there is abundant wildlife. You can often see dolphins swimming off the coast, and sometimes whales. It's a very delightful place. I recommend that you go there. I try to visit as often as I can," said the man.

"What's your name?" asked Alyssa.

"My name is Youki," the man said smiling.

"That name sounds familiar. I've heard it before! What's your last name?"

"We've known each other through many lives," said Youki. "You know me by just one name. I don't have a last name."

"You must have a last name," said Alyssa. "What's on your birth certificate, or how about your social security number, or maybe a driver's license?"

Youki laughed, "I don't have any of those things. I have no need for them. I may have had other names, but they are forgotten. I am Youki."

Youki stood and bowed to Alyssa. This gesture surprised her. She stood, and bowed to him too.

"I'm very pleased to meet you, and if you're correct, then I'm very pleased to meet you again!"

"We'll meet many more times," said Youki. "Our paths are intertwined. Please excuse me, and I will see you again soon!"

Youki walked from the fireplace to the convenience store that was attached to the building. Alyssa was warming her hands on the fire.

"Wait, where will I meet you?" she asked.

"At the lighthouse," he replied and was gone out the door.

Alyssa stood for a minute in subdued excitement evaluating what had just transpired. She quickly went outside to the front of Fernwood where Youki had walked, but when she looked, he was already gone.

Chapter 23

The next day Alyssa decided to go to Point Sur Light house where Youki had said that there was a power spot. She spent a few hours there, but didn't notice anything unusual as she browsed through the tourist information and absorbed the beauty and feel of the location. She wanted to talk to Youki, and decided that was the reason she was really there. After another hour, she grew tired of it, gave up and decided to leave.

"Did you find what you were looking for?" asked Youki.

The voice made her jump. Youki seemed to appear suddenly in the parking area as Alyssa walked out. She turned to the voice, and there he was.

"It was fascinating," said Alyssa smiling and relieved to see him, "but no, I didn't see what I was looking for. At least, I don't think I did."

"That may have been because you were looking for it. Let go of the desire, and you may find it. It could be waiting for you."

"I'm right here," said Alyssa, "why would it wait for me?"

"Because you want to see it, you're being held from seeing it. You're on a mission with a preconceived notion of success. Your mind is closed to a new experience," Youki responded.

"What would you suggest I do?" Alyssa asked skeptically.

"Give up," said Youki.

"Give up what?"

"Give up everything. Give up the whole idea. Give up your thoughts on it. Give up trying to make sense of it. Give up looking."

"Give up trying to make sense of it?"

"Yes, most of all that. What is sense? Is it your preconceived ideas based on past experiences and things you've read in books? There is no sense to make. There is no sense. Give up! Let go!"

"My ambition, my sense of accomplishment," said Alyssa, "my drive. They all desensitize me. Yes, I see. I base my perceptions on the opinions of ghosts from the past. I get caught up in wanting to learn, and accept what I'm being told without question."

"Spend a few minutes here giving up and letting go," said Youki. "After a few minutes of that, clear your mind of thought, and walk around again. It's important to free your mind so you can accept new possibilities. I'll wait for you."

Alyssa sat by the cliff overlooking the ocean and meditated. When she finished, she walked around the lighthouse grounds, but she didn't notice anything unusual. She watched a bird glide in the updraft of the cliff. It looked like a hawk, and moved gently from side to side barely moving its wings, and scouting the beach area. She saw some chipmunks scurry around, hole up, then scurry some more. She saw a child reaching from her stroller trying to grab a tassel dangling from a zipper pull on her mother's purse. The tassel was very colorful. The baby smiled, laughed and reached as the tassel moved while the mother dug in her purse.

Alyssa walked back to where Youki was, but he was no longer there. She shrugged her shoulders, and decided to walk around the grounds one more time. A working dog lay on the ground in front of his partially blind master. The dog pricked his ears and raised his head as she walked by. As she passed, the dog laid his head

163

back down. Three brown pelicans flew by in formation. Alyssa noted the graceful flying of the large birds.

As she finished her walk, Youki was nowhere to be found; so she drove back to Fernwood with thoughts of buying an ice cream before going back to the retreat for the evening.

When she walked into Fernwood, she found Youki sitting by the fireplace nodding off.

"I thought you said that you were going to wait for me," Alyssa stated loudly as if intentionally waking him up.

"No need to raise your voice," said Youki with a jump. "My body may be old but my ears are working fine. I said that I would wait for you. I didn't say where!"

There was a very faint indication on his face that he found humor in the situation. Alyssa thought for a moment before she spoke.

"Very true, but how did you know I would come here."

"I didn't know for sure. No one knows anything for sure. I know that you know that I'm drawn to this fireplace. This is where we first met. I decided to wait for you here, and here you are!"

"Would you like an ice cream?" Alyssa asked. "I'm buying."

"I was waiting for you to ask," Youki replied. "Let's take a table over there."

He motioned using only his eyes without moving his head.

"Our conversation can be more private," he finished.

Alyssa walked up to the counter to buy the ice creams without asking Youki what flavor he wanted.

"I bought you vanilla," she said when she returned. "You seem like a vanilla person."

"Thank you," Youki said without further comment.

"Do you like vanilla?" asked Alyssa smiling.

"Yes," said Youki without looking at her.

She looked puzzled as if wondering why he didn't elaborate on his preferences.

"Did you find what you were looking for?" asked Youki.

"I did," said Alyssa. "After I took pause, my whole perspective changed. I saw a hawk gently gliding in the breeze. I concentrated on the hawk, and became part of his experience. I felt the wind against my skin and the smell of the sea. I saw far, and I noticed the tiniest movements on the beach below.

I didn't notice a power spot or an inflection point. I just walked accepting what came my way. What I found most interesting was a baby grabbing at a tassel that dangled from the pull tab of a zipper on her mother's purse. The baby was fascinated by the tassel, but the mother didn't notice any of it as she dug for something in her purse."

"Children delight in the small and inconspicuous," said Youki. "They don't reflect on the past, or what they previously thought. They're immersed in the moment and the joy of their fascination. The baby understands what we often fail to even notice. They have no attachments, no material desires, and no judgments. If you watch a baby with its first Christmas gift, you'll notice that they're not so interested in it's contents as the package itself. The unwrapping process becomes the joy, and the gift itself is discarded within minutes. The young child has it already, selfless, without ego, without desire, and confident in love."

"I had never thought about it before!" Alyssa stated. "A baby is very joyful in its fascination, and they don't make bias judgments because they have no memories to reference."

"As you've already noted, your experience with the baby may have been a far greater lesson than conditioning yourself to find some sort of power spot."

"I agree, but I've heard about this from many good sources. There's an important power spot somewhere in Big Sur. It's an inflection point in the continuum, or a place where the transition between matter and energy is slower. It could all be rumor, but that's what I've heard."

"What about the dog?" asked Youki.

"How did you know about the dog?" Alyssa replied.

165

"There's always a dog," said Youki with a very subtle smile slipping onto his face.

"Well the dog pricked up his ears," said Alyssa. "That was about all."

"He didn't just prick up his ears," said Youki. "He pricked up his ears when you walked by. There's a big difference. Sensitize yourself to the small inconspicuous details."

"I struggle with my ego," said Alyssa changing the subject.

"People in their late teens are often at the peak of their ego," said Youki. "They think they know everything because they've seen the cycle of life a few times by age eighteen. They become disrespectful to their elders because they consider them old, dumb, and out of it. They say disrespectful things like "duh", and they have insolent attitudes. Did I leave anything out?"

Alyssa laughed, "Yes, a lot of us do, but not all of us. You're painting with a broad brush."

"Since we were discussing ego, I thought that I would put on a show by being slightly sarcastic. Of course not all teenagers are egotistical. If you were, we wouldn't be having this conversation. You would have prejudged me as a homeless old man warming himself at the Fernwood fireplace because he has nowhere else to go. You would have laughed at me while I drooled on myself as I nodded off."

Youki laughed loudly and heartily at the thought. His laughter surprised Alyssa who had hardly seen an expression on his face before this point.

"I did laugh at your drool, said Alyssa smiling sarcastically, "I just didn't mention it."

"Ego is developed as a protection mechanism," Youki stated. "You've perhaps noticed already that insecure people usually have big egos. As we grow, we're trained to be safe, do the right thing, be honest, work hard, and honor our elders. Usually, this training is associated with an award system. Awarded are behaviors that are deemed correct. Praise, affection, and sometimes gifts are

166

bestowed upon us for so-called good behavior. Bad behaviors are discouraged. Negative attention or even punishment results from bad behavior. Children catch on quickly to this early conditioning, and the ego begins to be reinforced as a result. Eventually, we begin to compare ourselves to the other children around us. We notice what praise, rewards, and gifts they receive in comparison to ourselves. Jealousy and envy begin to enter our psyche, and for the first time, we have a reason for liking or disliking our neighbor based on how they're treated with respect to ourselves. Over time, resentment sets in. These are all elements that contribute to building the ego. As we learn to function and cope within this flawed system of an aggressive society, our ego grows."

Youki paused to lick his ice cream.

"Over time we become attached to the system. We come to expect the results. We rely on the results. With the attachment, we become desensitized. Our egos grow further. Our views become jaded. We become so sure of ourselves that we become cynical. We're right, and everyone else is wrong. Once we reach this point it can be hard to recover."

"It doesn't seem like it's pure learning as you're suggesting?" Alyssa interjected. "Some people just seem to be like that."

"Yes, you understand at a young age what so many don't. They may never understand before it's time to leave this world again."

"Children are so truthful," Alyssa stated with a questioning tone. "A lot of things are adding up for me right now. That's why Jesus said that you can find truth in the mouths of babes! They haven't been tainted yet. They haven't been forced to conform."

"You'll see that depicted in ancient art. Innocent truthful characters are painted as children or babies. Cupid is depicted as a baby. In the story of David and Goliath, David is a youth. David hasn't been infected with thoughts of failure or limitation. He doesn't see Goliath as having an advantage due to size."

"David didn't view things in light of how everyone had viewed things before him," said Alyssa. "His point of view was fresh. That's why you made me walk around the lighthouse grounds again today, and that's why you weren't there when I came back. You were demonstrating how we can get caught up in preconceived notions."

"That wasn't all," said Youki. "There are always the 10,000 things. There are many things to consider in any given set of circumstances. Our limited human minds can't comprehend them all, so we keep our minds open so that we absorb what's needed at the time."

"When do we begin to relearn what we already once knew," Alyssa asked finishing up her ice cream.

"Some of us never go too far in that direction. The realization comes early. Others who learn about maintaining balance in their lives, they're much better off. For many Westerners, particularly here in the United States, I would say the change comes at age 30. By that age, they've been out in the workforce for seven years or so. They've accumulated material goods until their houses are full, and found no meaning in them. They have many friends, and they've taken many vacations to help keep them from thinking about what's missing in their lives. The search for meaning begins. They want to know who they are, and why they're here. They read the Bible for the first time. They discover Emmet Fox, Joel Goldsmith, and Anthony De Mello. They explore other religions, and adapt bits and pieces that help their cause. They do this secretly, because if they expose their quest for meaning to others, they're looked at as freaks and malcontents. If they do expose themselves to anyone, they make that person uncomfortable. That person becomes insecure because they have the same issues brewing inside themselves and masked by the monotony of everyday survival. They despair, and resent you for exposing them, and bringing them face to face with what they've known all along. You've broken their facade, and they coldly hate you for it."

168

"That's a dim view of the middle age American," Alyssa said smiling.

"Not all people go through it, but some do, and it seems to be about age 30 when it starts. The world can be a wonderful place or an awful place depending on how you react to it."

"I know what you're saying," Alyssa said smiling. "I've already gone through it. Questioning and investigating can be exciting. It wasn't bad."

"And we're done with our ice cream," said Youki.

"Would you like more?" asked Alyssa.

"I abide by what Miss Piggy says, "Never eat more than you can lift."

"Well you could lift a lot more than that," said Alyssa.

"I was making a joke," Youki said without smiling.

"Very funny," said Alyssa giggling. "You need to work on your delivery. I'm going to head back now. I can tell you're done, but just one more question. Are we usually successful?"

"More and more each day," Youki answered. "There's a marvelous new awakening happening. We're no longer falsely rejecting material things and the establishment like we did in the 1960s. We're recognizing that these things are inevitable and part of incarnate life. We have drugs and material goods in perspective now. We know that we need a house to live in, transportation, and a few comforts. We're also smarter about spiritual study. We're finding the truth earlier in our development, seeking out teachers, and putting what we've learned into practice. The world is a better place for it already."

"Will you help me progress more?"

"Yes, but you'll need to buy me ice cream."

"When?" asked Alyssa.

"Soon," replied Youki.

Chapter 24

Alyssa went back to the Zen Center but couldn't get herself to socialize with the other students. All she could think about was what Youki had said, and how it was so true. The majority of people in society were walking around wondering what it all means.

"I'm not alone," she thought, "and it's getting better! People are waking up to the fulfilling side. There's hope; it won't be bourgeois forever."

As she thought more and more about what Youki had said, she realized that her vivid and unique dreams might not be bad, and that they might actually be good. She wasn't a freak. She was just a part of the new awakening. She was ahead of her time.

Alyssa skipped the Sunday morning social functions at the retreat, and drove into Fernwood again looking for Youki. She asked around about him, but no one knew who she was talking about.

"A short old Asian man with bad posture named Youki?" they asked with amusement. "That could be half of San Francisco!"

"But we're not in San Francisco," pleaded Alyssa. "We're in the enchanted mists of Big Sur. There can't be that many gurus here."

"Everyone is a guru in Big Sur Miss! You need to spend more time here. I would suggest looking at Phiffer-Burns State Park. A lot of the wandering monk types head up there during the day. They come here to sit by the fire at night, people watch, and look for potential students."

"So I'm just a potential student?" asked Alyssa.

"No, I didn't say that. They're good people. They mean well."

Phiffer-Burns State Park was like a place out of a story book for Alyssa. There were hiking trails, cottages, giant redwood trees, spectacular views, and plenty of wildlife. Alyssa was so impressed when she got there she forgot about Youki for a period of time. She stopped by the management office.

"Do you have any summer jobs for college students?" she asked.

"Yes, there are several, but this season is almost over. You need to apply during the January-February time frame for the following summer. We usually have many more applicants than jobs. You need to make your application stand out. For those who qualify, we handle it like a lottery. If you really want to work here, I recommend selecting housekeeping services as your first choice. Most students don't apply for those jobs, and it increases your chances. For housekeeping jobs, you clean the cottages, and change bed linens. It's the same sort of thing you would do working for a hotel."

"Yes, I know," Alyssa said sheepishly in a trancelike stare.

"Here's an application. Take it home, and mail it in after New Years."

"Thank you!" said Alyssa waking from the trance, taking the application, and walking out.

"Changing sheets," she thought to herself, "this job must be for me. I change sheets in all my dreams. I must be meant to spend some time here!"

The remainder of the retreat was more socializing than study and lecture. Alyssa was exposed to a lot of young people with thoughts and interests similar to her own. They studied philosophy and religion, and meditated in groups. Alyssa had never meditated using their methods, and found the energy different. She didn't find the methods as refreshing, but she felt a bond between her meditating classmates.

It bothered her that she never found Youki again, but when she finally arrived home in Monterey Park after the retreat, she was

171

very happy she participated. She was delighted with her new perspective, and it was a much needed break from her routine. Work was exciting again, and her energy level was high. Her excitement rubbed off on other patients. She was infectious, and the energy at the rehab center improved almost instantaneously upon her return.

The center awarded her a one year scholarship toward a four year degree in Rehabilitative Counseling. The scholarship was for tuition and books only, and she had to keep her GPA above 3.0 each semester. She was also required to work at the Center as long as she was going to school. She had already been accepted at California State University Los Angeles, but she had to change her major.

Grandpa Jack was excited about her decision, and Grandma Lin strongly approved. Daisy was excited about a college scholarship, but wasn't thrilled about her career choice.

"Are you sure you want to be around drunks and drug addicts for your whole life?" Daisy asked.

"Yes, they need me Mom," Alyssa replied. "After all, these people are often very successful. Their stories are part of what makes the job interesting, and they're asking for help! They've already admitted they have a problem. They're entering the next phase. Remember from the Bible that Jesus was criticized for spending so much time with prostitutes, politicians, tax collectors and lepers. Those were his clients. They needed the help."

"I understand," said Daisy. "I think you just made my point. I'm not saying don't do it. All I'm saying is to think about it. There are a lot of careers where you can help people without exposing yourself to addicts. Alcoholics can be so abusive."

"Yes, I understand your concern Mom. I'll think about it, but I'm also focusing on recovery not detox. The patient doesn't see me until the recovery phase."

"No need to explain honey. If that's what you really want to do, then I'm fine with it," said Daisy.

172

Alyssa had taken several Advanced Placement (AP) classes in high school. The classes qualified as credit toward some entry level requirements. She was essentially starting in her second semester, and could take 200 and 300 level classes starting out. Her desire was to load up with 21 units, but she was put on the waiting list for one class, and ended up with 18, but since she met her scholarship requirement of at least 15 units, she was satisfied.

College was more work than high school, but Alyssa was prepared. The schoolwork focused on what she was interested in, and that made it easier. Work, however, became more difficult. They expected her to be full of energy and eager to dig in. They had given her a scholarship, so naturally their expectations were high. She was their superstar, and they showed her off to both patients and sponsors. As their innovator, she was adept at targeting patients for certain activities that maximized success probability. Besides her analytical work, they still expected her to teach martial arts as she had always done.

The combination of the emotional demands and the workload took a toll on her. What was more, she felt obligated to maintain relationships with family and friends. She kept the pace for the first month, but when mid-terms hit, she broke down. A full time workload and staying up late to study caught up with her. She lost sleep, and could no longer bounce back. Her complexion paled, and dark circles appeared under her eyes. Despite the excessive workload, she did the best she could, and handled the stress without complaint. She became intolerant of people wasting her time and walked away from idle conversations. Something had to give, but she couldn't see an escape path.

One at a time, her friends and family confronted her: first Kaylee, then Grandpa Jack, Daisy, and finally Grandma Lin.

"You're the most intuitive and emotionally balanced person I know," said Grandma Lin catching her off guard. "You know better than anyone that, at the pace you're keeping, you'll soon do permanent damage to your health. Honey, you're the one who's always preached to me the importance of balance in your life. Now you're violating your own guidelines. This is your Grandma speaking! You know that I've rarely interfered. I'm asking you through genuine love and concern. I want to see change."

Alyssa looked at her as if she had been physically beaten. She looked void of energy and incapable of thought let alone words. She looked lost and alone. After a moment, however, of staring at her Grandma, her attitude softened, she smiled slightly, and began to speak.

"After this semester I'm making a change," she said firmly with a straight face.

The force of her response surprised her Grandma. She didn't think she had it left in her. Grandma Lin began to speak, but Alyssa beat her to words.

"I'm stuck with this scholarship Grandma. I need to work there because they're paying my tuition. I need to do school work because I must meet standards to maintain my scholarship. I can't quit or walk away because I just can't do that. I don't quit what I've started through painstaking assessment and careful planning, and I won't break down physically or mentally. I just won't! If I made a mistake it was taking on too much, but I've painted myself into a corner. I'm going to do the best I can to finish the semester with both work and school. During semester break I'll make a change. I promise."

As it turned out, Alyssa wasn't forced to make a change. When classes ended just before Christmas, her semester GPA was 2.94. The number was just below what was needed to maintain her scholarship. Alyssa wrote to the board for consideration based on her past job performance and heavy workload. When all things were considered, her accomplishments were quite impressive. Furthermore, she had brought many patients into the center. She thought that her contribution should mean something to management, and her friends and family agreed. Alyssa was dropped from the program despite the efforts, and the scholarship

174

was awarded to another student aide less ambitious and considerably less deserving then Alyssa. The decision was made by management several layers above Alyssa's supervisor at the national level. The evaluation panel screened the candidates strictly by the numbers first. Alyssa didn't make the cut.

Alyssa was hurt, and interpreted the rejection as a personal failure. She felt used and taken advantage of; but after the holiday season passed, her mind cleared, and the hurt and anger subsided. She took a fresh look at her situation, and to her, the path was clear.

Besides insurance and gas for her Honda, she had no expenses. She rarely ate out like some of her friends did, and made an effort to pack a lunch when leaving for school or work. Her bank account had grown to almost $10,000. Keeping in mind that money, in truth, wasn't tangible in and of itself, she decided to take a risk with her hard-earned savings.

She resigned from the Rehabilitation Center, and paid her own tuition for her second semester at Cal State L.A.; but what was most significant was her decision not to work while in school. She would be content to attend her classes, and would take no more than 18 units.

Daisy was shocked with her decision. It was so unlike her, but she was maturing, and had learned her lesson. Daisy offered to pay for her books.

Grandpa Jack was relieved more than pleased, and suggested that she ask him for spending money from time to time. He couldn't afford to help her with tuition, but he could help her with some normal living expenses. Grandma Lin's reaction was to smile and hug her about the shoulders.

"I knew you would do the right thing!" said Grandma Lin.

Kaylee was most pleased with her decision.

"Surprise! I'm going to Cal State L.A. too," Kaylee said evaluating Alyssa's expression. "After you started, I decided that I better get off my butt. So I applied for the next semester, and since

175

you're not working, we'll have time to go out more! This will be great! I knew that I was doing the right thing. You helped motivate me. You've been a good influence and a good friend!"

Before Alyssa could recover from the shock, the two hugged, and Alyssa spoke during their embrace.

"That's fantastic," said Alyssa. "I'm so happy to have a friend at school. It's been lonely not knowing anyone, and it's hard to make friends when you're commuting."

"Well, now we can do things together," said Kaylee as they ended their embrace. "I'm sure it can't be that hard, and you'll have more time to yourself."

"It's mostly a commuter college you know," said Alyssa. "People don't seem all that interested in meeting you. In fact, many look rather glum as if they don't really want to be there. How are you handling your tuition? Is your Mom helping?"

"No, my Mom doesn't have any money! My Dad is paying the whole thing. He sent the money directly to the school. My Mom offered to pay for books, but I told her I'd pay half."

"That is so great!" said Alyssa. "Now you're all set until June."

"He told me he would pay all four years if I would just stick with it and room and board too if I want it."

"Wow, that's crazy!" Alyssa said wide eyed. "I'm so happy for you! Have you seen him?"

"Hardly ever!" Kaylee responded, "but he keeps promising."

"I hope you see him again soon!" said Alyssa.

"I won't pretend," said Kaylee. "I would like to see him too, but I won't let on, and I keep pretending not to care, but I won't be fooling you."

Alyssa was truly happy that Kaylee would be going to school with her, but it struck her funny. She thought about how hard she had worked at the center for a scholarship, and how it had slipped away from her when she had done her best to handle everything. With Kaylee, it was just handed to her with no strings attached. All four years-bang. The same thing had happened with Kaylee's car. It was delivered to her on her birthday. No effort was required. It didn't seem fair, and Alyssa had a strange feeling that she had never experienced before.

"Is this jealousy?" Alyssa thought to herself. "Am I becoming the insensitive egotistical teenager that Youki was talking about? Will I become callous as I learn to survive in Southern California?"

She thought of Youki and what he would say to her.

"He would probably say "give up" trying to make sense of it," Alyssa thought with a laugh.

Thoughts of Youki reminded her of Phiffer-Burns State Park in Big Sur, and how she wanted a summer job there. She went home, filled out the application, and mailed it the next day. After a week she called them to make sure they received it. Several calls were required, but she wouldn't let it go, and finally they acknowledged that her application was on file, and that she would get first consideration. That was good enough for her, and she was finally done with it.

"I've done everything I can," she thought to herself. "If it's meant to be, then I'll get the position. If not, it won't be for lack of effort."

Chapter 25

As the semester pressed on, Alyssa found that she had the opposite problem of the previous semester. She had too much time on her hands. She had longed to meditate, and she practiced daily along with Tai Chi, but it didn't offer the same satisfaction. There was something missing in her life, but she couldn't put her finger on it. After weeks of meditating and self analysis, she decided that she wanted to meet her father. Other people have two parents, and why shouldn't she.

"It may be selfish," she thought, "but I'm going to find my father if he's still alive."

She went to visit her Mom when she knew that Franken wouldn't be there.

"Mom," she started with a grave expression as if what she had to say was very troubling, "I want to know about my Dad. Is he dead? Where is he?"

Daisy was shocked and surprised, "Oh baby, why would you want to overturn that rock? You're doing so well, and everything has been so good the last few years. There's peace in our household. We all get along. You have your Grandfather who loves you very much. Isn't that enough?"

"Yes, that's enough. I love my Grandpa! I'm not saying I want to invite him into my life. I just want to know about him. Where is he?"

"He's probably alive. Yes, I would say he's alive. Word of a death has a way of finding its way to your door no matter how long it's been. I haven't heard anything from him since you were a baby."

"What's his name?"

"His name is Brad Stone. When I knew him he sold cars at a Chevrolet dealership. He was very good at it. He had a slick tongue and a way with people. He liked people, and they liked him. They trusted him, and that charisma worked well for him in sales."

"Why did you break up?"

"You already know my patterns. Before I explain it to you, let me point out that I'm not the easiest person to get along with either, but with Brad, it was worse. He was a heavy drinker, and a womanizer. He was also into cocaine when it was available and he had enough money to pay for it. He didn't care about saving, or making a home, and spent money as if there were an endless supply. He wasn't ready to have a baby when I became pregnant with you. He was very happy about you when I told him I was pregnant, but he just wasn't ready for a family. When you finally arrived, he was delighted, but the responsibility scared him. His alcohol abuse increased along with his responsibility. He drank all the time. I think he drank at work too. Sobriety was the exception. I didn't know much about alcohol and addiction back then. I told him to cut down, and I probably nagged him about it. I really don't remember how much of a nag I was. He wanted you, but not the work. At one point he wanted me, but that went away before you were born. I was a pregnant woman and he was a con man. I was alone in a relationship and pregnant too, but what was really funny about my situation was that it didn't bother me. I was happy that you were coming, and happy not to have a drunk bothering me. A few months after you were born he left."

"Is that why I got your last name?" Alyssa asked.

"He wasn't there the day you were born darling, I'm sorry! While he was around, and while you were inside me, he loved you.

"I put our name, Grandpa's name, on the birth certificate. Grandpa Jack agreed. I don't think your Dad ever knew. He was too hung up on himself. He was a wheeler-dealer, and if he wasn't bringing down the next great deal, he wasn't happy."

"He never paid child support?"

"No, he disappeared. I could never find him, and then I gave up. I thought you were much better off without being legally tied to a heavy drinker. My Dad was willing to be a father figure and role model. Brad was alcoholic, and was probably living on the street. Your Grandpa is a good man. He made mistakes early too, but he's been a good Father and Grandfather."

"Do you mind if I try to find him?" Alyssa asked.

"If it's important to you, I would encourage you to do so. It's probably time to find out, meet him, and put the whole issue to bed. Since it's too late to pay child support, you'll probably find him. All I would ask is that you take Grandpa Jack with you the first time you meet him. Grandpa Jack is your real father; Brad is only your biological father. Your Grandpa has always been there for you. If you meet Brad, I want him to know that he has to deal with Grandpa Jack in order to get to know you. Brad always felt uncomfortable around Grandpa Jack. He could always see right through his clever front, and he knew how Brad could draw people in."

"It is interesting that he was sort of a con man and a car salesman too! I have a little of that in me. I can sell people. I can gain their confidence!" said Alyssa.

"Well he was the master dear. He could sell eyeglasses to the blind. He made friends with everyone. I'd be ready to leave the party, and he'd be off making friends. It was annoying at times."

"I'm going to find him. It's easy with the internet." Alyssa said with excitement.

"Just be careful honey. Please be careful. When you find him, you may not like what you find."

Alyssa was very curious after her discussion with her Mom, and went right to work to find her biological father. She had no problem finding Brad Stone born on equinox, September 21st, 1967. She discovered an internet service called "People Finder", that would provide most of the information you needed for $10. For $30, they could check criminal and civil records too. They gave out his address for free, so Alyssa already had an idea about where he lived. He wasn't dead. He lived in Agoura Hills.

She, of course, wanted to know everything about Brad, but she needed a credit card to pay the $30 on-line fee. Grandpa Jack and Grandma Lin didn't have any credit cards. They thought credit cards were a "rip-off", and refused to use one. Daisy had a Discover card, and agreed to help her, but Alyssa had to wait for her Mom to come over to use the card.

Days went by without hearing from Daisy. Alyssa worried that her request to investigate her Father may have hurt her Mom's feelings. After all, Daisy and her Grandparents had done everything for her without any help or interest from the father's side, but Daisy seemed to encourage Alyssa to investigate.

"It couldn't be that she never expected me to ask about him," Alyssa thought. "She's not hurt, but she might be feeling some guilt for not dealing with it sooner. It just doesn't make sense that she's upset."

Daisy's reaction had been clear. She knew the day would eventually come when her daughter would want to know about her Dad. Although it took longer than she thought, the day was here, and Daisy was prepared for it. She wanted to get it out in the open so that everyone could move on.

Although Daisy wasn't stalling, Alyssa decided to slow down. She wanted to let things happen naturally. She could sense within her that somehow she would meet her Dad soon, and being anxious about it wouldn't make it happen any faster. She let go of her desire, and let events transpire naturally. It was unusual not to hear from her Mom for more than a day at a time, but she was determined not to read anything into it.

Kaylee and Alyssa became inseparable as the semester progressed. They spent their entire days on campus leaving in the morning together at 7:30 AM, and returning after 6 PM. When they didn't have class, they had designated areas in the library or student union where they would meet. They spent time together and with their new friends as their class schedule permitted and organized activities for evenings and weekends. They became an item on campus. Wherever they went there was a whirlwind of excitement.

"There's a new band playing at a club on West Valley just off campus," said Kaylee as she plopped herself down in a chair in the student union. "Everyone is going. We have to go!"

"Do I need ear plugs?" asked Alyssa. "Since we're not 21, will they let us in?"

"We can go in the restaurant part," Kaylee replied, "plus I know the bouncer. He'll let us in after awhile. They want women there. It's a predominantly male audience."

"Who are they?" another girl asked.

"They're called +44," Kaylee replied, "and they're made up of remnants of other bands. Blink 182, Nervous Return, and The Transplants all have former members in +44. It's a pop-punk sound."

"Are they any good?"

"Who cares," Kaylee replied, "everyone's going, and since its punk, it'll be full of guys. We'll be the center of attention blowing guys off all night long. With our group we can dish out rejection better than any on campus. That makes the guys want you more. Treat 'em like dirt and they'll do anything for you."

"Sounds cold."

"It is, but its fun," Kaylee stated casually. "It keeps you in practice. It keeps you from being too sensitive. There's nothing worse than a sensitive guy gushing all over and smothering you. We need to learn to act like cold bitches outwardly. If the guys have the balls to break through to us, then they'll find out we're actually nice."

"Oh brother," said Alyssa, "it wouldn't hurt to be ourselves."

"It wouldn't," said Kaylee, "but that's boring. You know as well as I do that we're all forced to play the game. You really can't escape it."

"So do I need earplugs?" asked Alyssa.

"I have a bunch," Kaylee replied. "I'll bring them along."

"I'm leaving by 11:30," Alyssa stated emphatically. "I don't stay out past midnight."

"Heaven forbid you turn into a pumpkin," Kaylee said smiling.

It was the ideal partnership with Kaylee as the savvy provocateur and Alyssa the stout calming visionary. They understood their relationship and played off each other to a comedic degree. Students were initially attracted to them out of curiosity. They wanted to know what all the fuss was about. Word spread, and they became the subject of common campus chatter. The man who ran the student union café started to call them the twin flames. The name stuck, and it was soon shortened to The Flames. The Flames were high energy, low maintenance, and very alluring. They laughed, joked, and randomly talked to people that happened into their area. Kaylee was outgoing to begin with, but on campus she was aggressively bold. With Kaylee, The Flames made friends quickly, and before the end of the semester they had a large social circle.

They decided to use their contacts to become a part of the Santa Monica and Venice Beach communities once more; but times had changed, and most of the people Alyssa knew as a child were gone. Those that were left were a few years older and not so interested in socializing with teenage women in a BMW. Since Venice was no longer a fit, they explored up the coast past Malibu with their entourage from Cal State LA. They went as far as Trancas, and sampled every possible hangout they could find.

In the spring, after they turned 18, their explorations grew bolder. They drove up to the Ventura County line and stopped at Neptune's Net. On the way back, they would intermittently stop at beach spots hoping to meet people and watch surfers. They went to restaurant-bars where they could sit legally and order appetizers and soft drinks. They found beach grills in Trancas and Malibu that suited their needs. They gravitated toward places that sold beer and wine but catered to the younger crowd. Kaylee wanted to meet rich guys that were already 21.

"Why do they have to be rich?" Alyssa asked.

"They don't, but it doesn't hurt!" Kaylee replied.

They frequented the Starbucks at Trancas, and used that spot as their northern outpost. They usually had several other girls with them. Wherever they stopped, they had an instant party. They were young, energetic, and beautiful. The excitement surrounding them attracted business. The proprietors loved them.

"We need a better place to hang out," Kaylee stated one afternoon while on the pier in Malibu staring over at Duke's. "We can't get in a place like Duke's because we're minors, but that's where it's happening! These coffee shops and beach snack bars aren't cutting it for me anymore. Besides, Malibu is too far away."

"I like the coffee shops," said Alyssa. "They're not so noisy, and you don't have to worry about drinkers hitting on you or acting foolish. They play the music much lower. It's pleasant. I really like our Starbucks in Trancas. There are a lot of people from the entertainment industry that stop by there."

"I haven't really noticed," Kaylee replied. "If they are, they're older, and they play that awful classic rock."

"We should hang out at the beach to meet the younger people."

"These beach hangouts are getting old!" Kaylee complained. "The only people we ever seem to meet are surfers in wet suits. Their conversation is filled with words like dude, gnarly, wow-man, awesome, and stoked. They haven't invented a new adjective in 20 years. The New Yorkers, they're always evolving socially. Here we're stuck in the fifties."

"It can't be much different here than New York," Alyssa said while focusing in the distance. "People are people, and big cities are all the same. The culture's here is a little unusual, but beyond that, it's not much different. They spend most of their time inside. We spend most of our time outside. I prefer outside."

"I just like the way they speak. They get right to the point, and their accent is crazy and fun! I love it!"

"When you finish your degree you can move there."

"Well, I'm not going anywhere without you."

"I hope you like it here in California then. I have no plans to leave."

184

"I like it here; I'd just like to meet some different guys. It would be nice to meet someone from the entertainment industry. There's so much of that here, but we never seem to meet anyone."

"We're looking in the wrong places. We'll find it. Let's try to change things up!"

"You've got it. Let's go!"

Their new hangout became Gladstone's at the foot of Sunset Boulevard because a percentage of the people dressed formally during happy hour. They liked the atmosphere, and it was ideally located for most of their friends. At Gladstone's they could sit at the outside tables with their entire group and be loud without bothering anyone. It became their central meeting place. From there, they fanned out across the city looking for a place to meet the classy guys. Without much success, they often ended up near the university or in their own neighborhoods, but eventually; they ended up at Gladstone's.

Alyssa's busy life took a temporary turn toward socializing. It was the new pastime. What she found interesting was that she was no longer the leader. In this new game, Kaylee was usually at the point of the spear. She was a social queen, and Alyssa rather enjoyed being one step behind her. It gave her a break from being in the spotlight, and it suited Alyssa to be one layer deep within her group of cohorts. It was a relief not to always be the center of attention. Kaylee hadn't really noticed that she'd become the social leader. It came naturally to her. The Wu Wei (action without action) that she had picked up from Alyssa and Frenchy had instilled a refreshing sense of humility for someone so smart and outgoing. Her beauty and charismatic personality combined with her spiritual training to create something new: the enlightened party girl. Los Angeles was the perfect place to unleash the social hybrid to see what could be accomplished.

Kaylee was a rare combination of ingredients for a young woman. She was in tune with herself, her surroundings, and her purpose. She was metaphysical, yet she used guys and social

185

situations to her advantage. She was manipulative, and knew how to work a crowd. She was savvy, knew what she wanted, and usually got it. People were completely thrown off by her, and treated her like a curiosity. Kaylee used that to her advantage too.

Alyssa was impressed with the progress Kaylee had made in cultural studies related to martial arts; but what was more impressive was how she applied her knowledge in fashion, social politics, and career shaping. She was completely unique, and had taken charge in leading their little tribe. Alyssa was confident she could continue with their social goals while she departed for her summer job.

She hadn't received an offer from Phiffer-Burns State Park, but she remained relaxed and calm through finals and meditated. Her introspection resulted in accepting a job at Hot Dog On a Stick in the mall. Somehow she knew she would never work there, but she felt that her acceptance was important to stimulate other events. The very next day she received a letter from Phiffer-Burns State Park offering her a job in housekeeping, but she was required to start Monday of the following week. She had no time to delay.

She called them right away and accepted. She found out that she was the third person they had contacted on the waiting list. Two other girls had declined the offer.

As had happened the previous year, Grandpa Jack and Grandma Lin followed her up to Big Sur and took a mini-vacation in Monterey once Alyssa was situated. She stayed in a building at the State Park especially designed for boarding temporary employees. It was a duplex of sorts with male quarters on one side and female on the other and a shared kitchen in the center. Breakfast and dinner were served weekdays only, and bag lunches could be purchased during breakfast to carry to work. Since room and board was provided, the pay for summer aides was minimum wage.

Before she left for Big Sur, her Mom finally helped with her internet search for her Dad. The investigative service worked as anticipated. Brad Stone was born in 1967 and lived in Agoura Hills. He had several traffic tickets and two drunk driving convictions in 1989 and 1991. He divorced Patricia McDermott in 1995, and lost a small claims lawsuit in 2001. Other than that, his record was clean. They provided Alyssa with last known phone number and address. Both Alyssa and Daisy were reluctant to immediately call him, so Alyssa wrote a letter, and Daisy helped her craft it. The letter was simple and to the point. Alyssa wanted to meet him, but no strings would be attached for either party.

Arriving at Big Sur was a welcome change for Alyssa. The quiet and peacefulness consumed her, and she found herself quickly unwinding and adjusting to the slower pace. The enchantment of the mists and morning fog was tantalizing, and being surrounded each day by the natural beauty of the ancient forests invigorated her. She was comfortably at home.

Changing and washing sheets all day was grounding too. It was such a necessary task, and rooted in the human pursuit of cleanliness over millennia. It seemed very natural for her to do it. It was also hauntingly familiar, and strangely rooted in her own being. She knew that cleaning cabins was a very mundane job, but it was a needed task, and she embraced it. It gave her purpose.

Her work was solitary and methodic without problems, complications or drama. At the end of the day, she felt like she had accomplished something. The cabins were clean once more so that vacationing humans had a comfortable place to sleep. That was her reward.

In her free time she meditated in the woods, and took long walks on the hiking trails. She had time to reflect. She missed Kaylee and their friends but after a few days of texting, they adjusted.

Fernwood was just down the road a mile or two. She had dropped in a few times and walked through the convenience store to buy a few items that she didn't need. She walked by the big fireplace, lingered, and bought an ice cream, but never saw Youki as she had hoped. On her first full day off she visited the Point Sur Lighthouse. It was very foggy, cold, and difficult to see very far. She headed back disappointed that she hadn't found her friend.

Alyssa had never been obsessive about her cell phone use, and often times left her phone at home; but before this trip, Daisy insisted that she carry it. Daisy was uneasy about her being away for so long, and asked that she phone home once a day. Coverage was spotty in Big Sur, but when she was near the entrance to the State Park on Highway One, she could get three bars. One day in late June, when she had been at work almost two weeks, she received a call from her Grandpa.

"You have a letter from Brad Stone," he said. "I know it's important to you, so I thought I better call you."

Alyssa had a sinking feeling when he told her, but shrugged it off.

"Open it Grandpa would you?" she asked.

"Okay honey. Would you like me to read it aloud?"

"Yes Grandpa. Please."

"Dear Alyssa, I was very pleased to hear from you, and would very much like to meet you. I understand the concerns you may have, and realize we may not continue. In other words, I wouldn't blame you one bit if this is a one-time meeting. I don't really deserve your attention.

Yes, you have the right Brad Stone, and the right address and phone number here in Agoura Hills. I would be happy to meet you somewhere neutral near your home in Monterey Park. I hope to hear from you. Sincerely, Brad Stone."

"What should I do Grandpa?"

"I would send him a post card from Big Sur, and tell him you'll contact him at the end of August when you return from vacation."

"I guess you're right," said Alyssa. "Part of me wants to drive down there right now and get this over with, and the other part of me wants to forget the whole thing."

"Well you've gone this far," said Grandpa Jack. "You might as well finish it. After you meet him once, you can end it or continue. It's completely up to you. You're 18 now, and legal to make your own decisions."

"Yes you're right. I'll do this calmly and methodically on my own timetable. I'll suggest a date at the end of August when I get home."

"That sounds like a good plan. Now you take care of yourself up there and be safe. Okay?"

"Okay Grandpa. I'll see you in August."

It bothered Alyssa for several days that she was stuck in Big Sur when she would really like to meet her biological father; but after some time passed, she realized it was probably best that she was not there to rush to him. She wanted the timing to be just right.

When her first Saturday off arrived, Alyssa decided to spend it with a coworker touring the Big Sur art galleries, and taking pictures of the tourists. After they were done, they planned to drive up the coast, have lunch in Carmel, and take the 17 Mile Drive through Pebble Beach. It was Alyssa's first formal outing since she'd been back to Big Sur, and she was really looking forward to getting away.

When the day finally arrived, they were pleased that it was sunny. The overcast of Big Sur burnt off mid-morning and added to their excitement.

They went through two galleries thinking that the pieces were boring and overpriced, but when they arrived at the third they found much more variety in both subject matter and cost. They could actually afford something, and Alyssa's friend was debating on what piece to buy.

"I would suggest trusting your instincts," said a voice from behind them. "They may be visual pieces, but part of the draw is the energy of the artist who created them. Perhaps you could walk by without looking and feel which one is right."

189

The voice was very familiar to Alyssa, and she tried to place it before she turned. It was Youki. He stood behind them expressionless with his stooped posture and excessively wrinkled Japanese face probing at them.

"Youki!" Alyssa stated excitedly while she surprised him with a big hug. "I've been looking for you."

"That's precisely why you didn't find me," said Youki. "When you gave up on your desire then I appeared. You already know this."

"Yes I do. I already know this," repeated Alyssa smiling. "What else do I know?"

"That this is Hell," said Youki pausing.

"Okaaaay," Alyssa replied in a long drawn out word. "Yes! I do know. This is also Heaven. This is both Heaven and Hell. All places are absolute. I would also be correct in saying there is no such thing as Heaven and Hell. It essentially means the same thing."

"Whatever it means, it doesn't mean," said Youki finally smiling.

"Yes, your observations are very meaningful," said Alyssa agreeing and joking at the same time.

Alyssa's friend was observing the conversation with skepticism, and didn't quite know what to make of Youki. Each statement contradicted the last, and it made no sense. Furthermore, Youki's appearance was unkempt and unconventional. He wore robes, but didn't look like a priest or a monk. His head wasn't shaved, but it was very close to shaved, and he had more growth on his face that he obviously did shave, but hadn't done so for several days. He wore sandals that looked hand-made and laced up his legs, and he carried what appeared to be a bota bag or a canteen. She scanned him up and down, and didn't know whether to smile or run.

"Drop by the big fireplace at Fernwood tonight," said Youki sensing the discomfort. "If you don't expect me, I'll be there."

190

"Okay," said Alyssa laughing. "I won't see you there."

Youki walked away in his shuffling manner. Alyssa and her friend watched the door to the shop open, but couldn't really see him walk out.

"Who was that?" Alyssa's friend asked.

"A little old man I met last year when I was on a retreat at the Zen Center in Carmel Valley. He's a little eccentric, but he's very wise. I'm strangely attracted to him."

"Attracted to him? What do you mean?"

"Well not sexually of course! He's a hunched up old man, but other than that, I'm not sure. I guess because he's so different. He's pure essence, and he knows things. He knows things because he feels them. It's not just because he's old and experienced. He's all knowing."

"And a little weird too I might add."

"Weird in a good way," Alyssa said. "A very good way!"

Alyssa and her friend finished their road trip by driving all the way up Highway One into Monterey, back through Cannery Row, and finishing up in Pacific Grove. They had lunch at Latitudes across the street from Lover's Point Park, and drove back toward Big Sur through the Pebble Beach 17 Mile Drive. They couldn't believe the $12 charge to take the drive, and almost skipped it; but after seeing the majesty of the California Coastline, they were very happy that they spent the money. As they approached Big Sur, the fog had rolled in, and the first of the ancient redwood groves were poking through the fog like toothpicks as they drove down the hillside and across the famous white elliptical bridges. It seemed like they were driving into another planet, but it was only the mysterious forests of Big Sur.

The two Southern California girls had both seen the central coast before, but were awestruck and excited after seeing it again. They were filled with energy when they arrived at their destination.

"I wish we had some coastline like this in Los Angeles," her friend said as they pulled into the State Park.

"I like it how it is," said Alyssa. "I love it so much here, but Los Angeles is home."

Chapter 26

Alyssa skipped dinner and filled out a postcard to her newly discovered father as her Grandpa had suggested. She provided an address where she could get mail at the State Park, but mailed the postcard from Fernwood while looking for Youki.

The bar was noisy and full of tourists when she walked in. Most of them were on vacation from Southern California and already drunk. There was standing room only in the bar so that people were spilling over into the room with the huge fireplace where Youki usually sat. There were no seats available except in the snack bar. Alyssa milled about trying to look inconspicuous and hoping that Youki would show up. She walked through the convenience store and purchased a few more postcards. She walked back outside to the parking lot. After fidgeting with her clothes, she drifted back inside and slipped into a seat by the fire before someone else took it. Youki was nowhere to be seen. She waited an hour, and got up to go to the bathroom before giving up completely. She walked out of the bathroom, glanced around one more time, and headed for the door.

"Are you going to buy me an ice cream?" she heard the now familiar voice from behind her.

She turned to face him.

"You have a unique way of showing up!" she replied smiling from one side of her mouth.

"You must have finally given up on me," said Youki. "If you would have given up sooner, you wouldn't have had to wait so long."

"Very funny!" said Alyssa, "and yes I'll buy you an ice cream!"

"It was no joke," Youki said with a straight face. "What did the Buddhist Monk say to the hot dog vendor?"

"Make me one with everything!" replied Alyssa. "That's the oldest joke in the book. I heard it in Venice when I was 13."

"It is a very good joke!" said Youki. "It's old and funny."

They went to sit down in the booths by the snack bar.

"But we're not laughing!" said Alyssa while sitting down.

Youki looked at her with such a deadpan expression that Alyssa started laughing.

"See, it's funny!" said Youki.

"No you're funny," said Alyssa.

Now Youki laughed.

"I am not funny at all," said Youki. "Much too serious. Not funny."

Youki's comment made Alyssa laugh more.

"No, you're very funny," said Alyssa.

"What kind of ice cream do you want?" asked Alyssa.

"You said that I'm a vanilla person, so I'll have vanilla."

"You can have anything you want," Alyssa pressed.

"We all can have anything we want. We must only ask."

"Vanilla it is," said Alyssa smiling.

Alyssa went up to the counter and returned with two soft ice creams carefully spiraled into a cup with a curl at the very top. Alyssa set down the ice creams, handed Youki a spoon, and then sat down herself.

"Is this frozen yogurt or ice cream?" asked Youki.

"Ice cream!" Alyssa replied. "They don't have frozen yogurt."

"Good," said Youki without expression. "Ice cream is good and bad."

193

"How is that?" asked Alyssa.

"Good tasting and bad for you. That makes it better," Youki stated while looking at her through his brow."

"So what about work?" asked Alyssa.

"So what about it?" asked Youki while spooning.

"We sell ourselves for money. We kiss our boss's butt. It's not far from prostitution."

"We're selling our services not ourselves," said Youki. "There's a big difference."

"I guess you're right," said Alyssa. "At my old job it seemed like I was a purchase. They paid me, and gave me a scholarship, and as a result, they acted like they owned me. Some of my coworkers resented me because I got a scholarship. It didn't really amount to all that much money. They should have paid more. I was really good, and I was bringing in business."

"You may have been worth more, but the value of their service is relative to what they perceive is valuable; but what they perceive is valuable is often not you. Perception is a relative thing. What influences their perceptions is often key to their decision making process. It could be their own selfish motives, it may be the inflexible bureaucracy of their organization, or it could be that they just don't have the vision."

"They should at least understand that I need money like everyone else. It's very frustrating. I work very hard, and a lot of other people hardly work and get paid the same. It would be a lot easier if I was paid more."

"Eventually you'll be rewarded if you remain as interested and committed as you are. You're very valuable," said Youki, "but that may not manifest itself in money immediately. I would advise against using money as your measure of achievement. Money is very important, and can make a lot of things in life easier, but money won't buy success. Success is built up over a long period of time. You develop a reputation for success, and then the money starts to flow. Many of the world's successful people function

194

without money, and several human societies function without money."

"Here in the United States everything is money oriented," Alyssa replied. "It's the only measure of success here."

"On the surface, but you intuitively know that's not true. You're already ahead of the curve. You're motivation comes from a deep-rooted instinct to help people, provide a service, and make things better for all. These are the key tenets."

They both ate their ice cream without speaking for several moments.

"Instead of strictly money," Youki continued, "the secret is to have a well balanced life including money as part of that balance. Money has its part to play, but it's only a part."

"What would be wrong with having a whole bunch of money?" Alyssa asked. "It would be nice just to accumulate a big pile so you never need worry about it again! You know? Winning the lottery is a great example. You'd be set for life in one shot!"

"If you're ready to have that much money, then you'll have it. Whether you win the lotto or earn it, you're ready, and it will come to you. If you're not ready in your soul, you won't have money. Whether you win it or earn it, it's very likely it will leave you. As the saying goes, a fool and his money are soon parted. Have you noticed how many people are ruined by winning the lottery? Some people lose it all in a short amount of time. Others do fine."

"Well then that settles it for me. I plan on having a lot of money. I'll keep doing what I do, but I want a big pile of it handy just in case," said Alyssa.

"That may just work for you! Another thing I would suggest," Youki said distractedly, "is not to go overboard saving. Save a little for later years, but spend what you need in the present. In a society that's becoming more socialistic, you'll be taken care of when you get old only if you don't have money. If you get old with money, society will force you to use your own money until you're poor. Then they'll help you."

Youki wiped ice cream off his face with his napkin.

"Somehow I already knew I'd be working the rest of my life anyway," said Alyssa.

"Yes! We all work anyway," said Youki.

"I knew that I'd work in a profession that helps people. I just wondered what sort of helping profession I'd be in. I envisioned myself as more of priest, shaman, or even a doctor, but now that I'm working in substance abuse rehabilitation, I know this is it. I think I'm already doing what I'll be doing for the rest of my life!"

"I would agree with most of what you're saying," said Youki, "but one also must stay open-minded. Our calling in life can change based on what's needed in the world. As we've discussed before, part of living is to remain open-minded and unbiased. We must be capable of accepting things that may seem radical, and we must remain sensitive to all the beauty and natural joy that surrounds us every moment. These feelings of oneness with our surroundings will provide clues to our purpose, and guide us along our path. A balanced life is an important key to an enlightened existence."

"I'm in complete agreement with what you're saying although I couldn't have explained it as well as you did. Wealth, however, is a natural outcome of success."

"It's true the more powerful you get, the more difficult it is to control your ego and balance your life," Youki replied. "It's also difficult to be sensitized to the beauty and wonder of everyday life. People will say "power corrupts absolutely", and that may be true; but with the right training you can avoid corruption in the first place no matter how you become rich and powerful. The younger you learn, the more likely you'll be successful in controlling yourself. Be humble, and keep your ego in check. You'll be more successful that way."

"I don't worry about money," said Alyssa. "My thought is to have a lot of it. I need it to do my work. I don't think I'm very egotistical or corruptible, so I'll be fine with money. If I lose it, then I'll be the same as now."

"You're never the same as now, but yes, I would say you can do well with lots of money. That may be a good path for you. Now I'm going to go sit in the comfy chair by the fire that just opened up and dose off until closing time. I suggest you go home and get some sleep."

"I was just going to suggest that too before I buy another ice cream. I'll see you when I see you!"

"Yes. I'll see you when you're not wanting to see me."

They both laughed, and Alyssa headed home.

Chapter 27

Alyssa's life at Big Sur fell into routine. She worked during the day cleaning cabins and changing sheets. When she got off work, she would hike on the many trails through the ancient redwood trees in the State Park. While she was hiking she would stop somewhere sunny and insect free to meditate; and after dinner, she would sit by the big campfire with the tourists and listen to the lectures and stories provided by the park rangers.

Fernwood was only a few miles away, and she occasionally drove over looking for Youki. It was a rare day when she actually found him and it always made her think about whether she was really looking for him or if she had given up. When she found him, their conversations were short, and she wondered if he was tiring of her.

"You don't have much to say lately," Alyssa stated one evening.

"It's not that I don't have much to say. I remain here mostly for you. I was asked to stay for you. I just need to say the right things at the right time. I will say it then."

"Who asked you to stay for me?" asked Alyssa.

"I don't know."

"You don't know who asked you?"

"No."

"Where will you go?" she asked him.

"I don't know. I'm ready to leave this world. My body is very old, but something inside me is saying I need to stay. I'm not quite done here, and I think I'm here for you; but of course I can't be sure because that would be absurd."

"Yes, I know," said Alyssa, "to be unsure is to be uncomfortable, but to be sure is ridiculous. You told me that when we first met last year, but what do you mean leave this world?"

"I mean die," said Youki. "I'm ready to die."

"Now you're being absurd!" Alyssa responded. "We're friends. I need you here."

"I know," said Youki. "I'll stay for a while."

The conversation bothered Alyssa. She stayed away from Fernwood for several days, and spent the evenings by the campfire. She started writing in a journal. Her time was occupied, and the pain of her friend's bluntness started to subside.

One night at the campfire, a young man named Jim started to talk to her. He was handsome, and it made her uncomfortable being near him, but for some reason, she liked it. They talked for two more nights in a row, and he asked her if she wanted to ride trail bikes together with his family the next day when she got off work. She accepted, and he told her where to meet them.

The trail bikes turned out to be old Honda Trail 70s that Jim's Dad collected. He was an amateur driver at Laguna Seca Raceway near Monterey, and used the Trail 70s as pit bikes. Jim had been riding them as long as he could remember. He and Alyssa went off on a trail together that followed a dry river bed. Alyssa found the bike easy to ride, and after 10 minutes was riding with ease. It was exhilarating seeing the country side with the wind in her face. She and Jim stopped to talk and laugh, and then would ride on. He suddenly took a side trail that led to a small plateau where they stopped their bikes, shut down, and removed their helmets. They sat together on the edge over looking the river bed. The sun was partially blocked by a hill, but the light that did come through illuminated the colorful layered red rock of the hillside. It was a beautiful setting, but slightly awkward because they didn't have much to say. Words didn't fit into the peacefulness of the moment. Jim finally leaned over and kissed her on the lips. The kiss was short, but when he looked in her eyes, they kissed again and embraced. They went on for minutes in the quiet stillness. They didn't want it to end, but finally stopped, looked at each other and laughed.

"We better go back," said Jim. "They'll start to worry."

"Yes it's time," said Alyssa. "It was a very sweet ending to a great exploration!"

Without further word, they rode back to the day camp without stopping.

"Meet me at the campfire tomorrow," said Jim.

"I'll see you there!" said Alyssa and drove off.

The next day Alyssa thought a lot about Jim and the kiss on the plateau. It was spontaneous and exciting in the red waning hours of the afternoon, but her feelings for Jim were those of a friend. The kiss was playful more than passionate, but it had felt good, and stirred emotions within her that she had never felt before. She remembered her first kiss with Dylan years ago, and it wasn't nearly the same. She had loved Dylan, and her kiss back then was based on love, but they were young, inexperienced, and unsure of what they were doing. It hadn't evoked the same emotion. She was in new emotional territory with Jim. She was excited and intrigued. Her desire was to investigate further. She was unsure how Jim fit into the picture, but planned on kissing him again tonight anyway.

Her thoughts kept her busy while she went through her work day, and time passed quickly as the morning slipped by. She enjoyed her job, and there were moments when she wished she could do it the rest of her life. It was a peaceful, solitary and very systematic in nature. It was mildly therapeutic, and the natural environment and surrounding forests enhanced that feeling. She existed in her own private world devoid of problems communing with nature and observing the many ecosystems.

Her natural peacefulness continued as she finished her workday and headed back to her bunk. She contemplated how good she had it. She hiked in the hillsides and meditated daily. She socialized with interesting tourists. She cruised the beautiful central coastline, and visited Carmel and Monterey. Her expenses were covered by her employer, yet she was making a wage too. Her situation was ideal, and the traffic and problems at home in L.A. seemed nonsensical and remote. She wished she could stay, but the demands at home as well as the need for real income would end up driving her back to the city.

That evening she rested on her bunk rather than hiking or meditating, and ended up dozing off for an hour. She woke groggy, chilled, and late for dinner. She pulled on a hooded sweatshirt, and caught what was left of dinner. After checking the mail, she felt better, and meditated before heading down to the campfire. It was still light when she arrived, and she could see Jim already there with his younger brother when she approached. The remainder of his family wasn't there. Jim looked relieved, happy and anxious all at the same time when he saw her. Alyssa felt a little anxiety too, but smiled anyway.

"I didn't think you were coming," said Jim.

"You must be kidding. I've been looking forward to another kiss all day," Alyssa responded.

Jim looked surprised by her response that cut right to the point, and he glanced nervously to his brother, and then back to Alyssa.

"Me too," he said smiling. "Would you like to take a walk?"

"I'd love to!"

"Tell Mom and Dad I'll be back later," he called loudly to his brother as he stood up.

"Are you going to make out?" his brother replied.

Everyone at the fire looked over at Jim, and then turned back to the fire.

"Naw, we're headed to the snack bar," said Jim. "I'm craving a Red Bull."

Alyssa and Jim walked away, and Jim took her by the hand.

"Are we really going to the snack bar?" asked Alyssa.

"Of course not," Jim replied. "I just needed an excuse to ditch my brother."

"Good, I was hoping for a nice romantic walk under the stars," said Alyssa.

"I wanted to let you know that we're headed home some time in the morning," said Jim. "We live in Santa Cruz. I'm still a senior in High School. I won't be 18 until September. I know that you need to be 18 to work here. You're older than me. I thought it was important to tell you."

"I appreciate your honesty," said Alyssa. "I knew that you would be leaving and that I may not see you again. I thought about it most of the morning, and what it might mean."

"What did you decide?" asked Jim.

"I think we like each other, and neither of us ever kissed like that before. I felt it in you too. I don't think we have a future with you in Santa Cruz and me in Los Angeles, but we have tonight, and that's enough time for another kiss. I've never felt that way before. I liked it. It didn't feel wrong. It was only a kiss."

"I appreciate your honesty too! I think I felt the same way, and wanted to be up front about it. I was going to ask for your address

201

and phone number anyway. We wouldn't want to rule anything out!"

"Sure, you can have it, but my Mom's plan has limited text. I would prefer email to texting."

"You've got it!"

They walked together without speaking for several minutes. It wasn't completely dark yet, but the first few stronger stars were pushing through the remaining daylight.

As if mustering his courage, all at once Jim turned to her and went in for the kiss. She easily accepted kissing him gently at first, and then deeper as they embraced each other. They went on for several moments, and then stopped holding each other close while leaning against each other. She against his chest, and he with his cheek against the top if her head. She could feel him grow excited. It was startling at first, but after she accepted what was natural, she leaned into him harder feeling the curves beneath his clothes. They kissed again briefly and separated continuing to hold hands.

"That was intense," he said. "I've never felt so excited. I hope it was okay with you."

"I felt you against me, and didn't know how to react at first. I just accepted it as normal. We're fully clothed, and it's our first real kiss. It's not like we're doing anything wrong. Feeling you against me excited me too."

"I can see how people can get carried away. I didn't want to stop."

"Me either. Let's walk back now," said Alyssa. "You can walk me home and we'll say goodnight."

"Do you go to school?" Jim asked as they started walking.

"I go to Cal State LA," she said. "I'm studying substance abuse and rehabilitation."

"That's interesting," said Jim. "You don't hear about many people going into that."

"I've always wanted to help people. I thought of becoming a doctor, but I fell into this, and I like it."

"What do you do for fun?"

"That's a good question. This past year I've just hung out with my friends. Before that I mostly just worked. I had over $10,000 in the bank when I started college, but I've been slowly chipping away at that, and it looks like I'll be paying for my next year."

"You seem like a worker," said Jim. "I work too mostly helping my Dad, but I also work at a golf course doing odd jobs."

"That is so cool! I started at a golf course too. I worked at a snack bar. It was my first experience dealing with customers."

"You see! We do have something in common."

"We probably have a lot in common. I get a strong feeling about you. We could be great friends."

"So don't rule out more than friends."

"I know better than to rule out anything. I like you a lot, but I'm a Southern California girl, and you're from Santa Cruz."

Jim smiled, and looked at her with intensity and a slight smile.

"You never know," he said.

They walked silently the rest of the way holding hands. When they got to her door they embraced for several moments. She could feel his excitement against her once more. They kissed, but this time with more passion. When they separated Jim was speechless.

"Thank you so much for taking me with you on your trail bikes yesterday," said Alyssa. "You have a wonderful family, and thanks for meeting me again. I'll always remember this night."

"Me too. Good night Alyssa."

They kissed briefly one more time without embracing.

"Good night."

Alyssa turned and went inside without looking again.

Chapter 28

Alyssa woke feeling alone, and remained lying in her bunk staring at the ceiling while she reviewed the events of the past few days. It all seemed so surreal. She had sampled the comfort of companionship and the excitement of intimacy. It had changed her overnight, and she wasn't sure what was next. Her perspective had changed on everything that had been enjoyable only a day earlier, and her job was now a chore. She found it difficult to get out of bed.

There was no real attachment to Jim, but the anxious excitement of being with him was enticing. The thought of never seeing him again wasn't a comforting one. She tried not to dwell on it, and readied herself for the day.

Being at work wasn't nearly as bad as thinking about being at work, and Alyssa's mood improved. Moving and functioning took her mind off her situation, and performing familiar ritualistic tasks brought her around. Her pace quickened, the minutes began to pass, and before she knew it lunchtime had arrived. She walked by the visitor's center, and sat on a bench looking out at the coast highway and the entrance to the park.

"Why the long face?" asked a familiar voice from behind her.

"You always seem to approach from behind," she said without looking. "I never see where you come from. For all I know you materialize and dematerialize at will."

Youki walked up and sat down beside her.

"It took me over 20 years to master that skill," he said. "You haven't answered my question."

"My face is neither short nor long, it just is," Alyssa replied.

"Good answer!" said Youki chuckling.

"I was completely happy here. I was very content," said Alyssa. "I met a boy. Let me correct that. I met a young man. We rode trail bikes together along the dry river bed. We enjoyed each other's company, and we kissed. It was the first real serious kiss for me, and probably for both of us. Now everything seems different. The job I loved yesterday seems boring. I'm better now, but I wonder, why the change?"

"We're all constantly changing," Youki replied. "This was a big emotional event for you based on deep-rooted instincts. These instincts are almost impossible to fight."

"How can I shake this feeling?" Alyssa asked.

"I would suggest not shaking it. Accept the feeling. Let the feeling run its course. Allow time to pass."

"An interesting suggestion," Alyssa stated after a moment of thought, "and one I hadn't thought of. Just leave it be! Accept it and move on. How simple."

"An easy exercise that's particularly useful when you're having a difficult day, said Youki, "is to separate your conscious self from your body. Visualize yourself hovering above your physical body. Observe yourself, and note your emotions. Become the casual observer who has nothing at stake in the physical world that your body is working in. You may be surprised at what you find out about yourself. "

"I have already done that," said Alyssa. "Hasn't everyone done that?"

"Perhaps, but your observations from that vantage point are very powerful. You may find that many things seem silly. You'll have a new perspective, and your mental notes may change your behavior."

"Working seemed to help this morning!"

"Working is very good for the soul," said Youki. "Working will always help get you through difficult times."

"Speaking of work," said Alyssa, "I better head back!"

"Why don't you come down to the big fireplace tonight at Fernwood," suggested Youki. "We can talk some more, but don't look for me."

"Okay," said Alyssa turning to face him and walking away backward. "I won't look for you there."

While she worked through the afternoon, Alyssa's thoughts only briefly drifted back to her previous evening with Jim. She focused on Youki and how unusual he was. His body appeared old, but his thought processes seemed young. When she talked to him it was as if they were the same age. To her, Youki was so charming he didn't seem old. For an hour she contemplated the importance of charm and how to become charming. When her thoughts finished, she realized she hadn't thought of Jim in quite a while, and that made her smile.

"There are very few people that are naturally charming," she thought to herself. "Most people need to work at it, but some people seem to come by it naturally. That natural charm is what gives you an edge. I'm going to work on letting it come naturally!"

Fernwood was slow that night, and Alyssa sat by the fire while she waited for something to happen. She had a feeling she wouldn't run into Youki because she was eager to see him again. She had questions for him. After waiting an hour or more, she walked around outside, and then through the convenience store. She bought some fruit flavored Mentos.

"I see you in here a lot," said the checker in a probing manner.

"I like it here," said Alyssa. "This place has character, and I have a little Japanese friend who meets me here."

"A short old guy with no hair, wears robes, and walks with a stoop. Yeah, I've seen you with him."

"Well good! Now I know I'm not imagining him."

"You thought he was your imaginary friend?"

"You never know! I'm looking for him tonight."

"It could be we're both crazy."

"Could be."

"This may sound awkward and bold, but I was wondering if you'd go out with me?"

Alyssa studied his face momentarily without reply. She realized that they were about the same age. He was cute in an adolescent sort of way, mild acne, but with a piercing gaze similar to her own. There seemed to be more to him than what was readily apparent."

"What's your name," she finally said.

"Jim, Jim Nachman," he replied.

"You're kidding," she said smiling wide.

"Why would I kid about my name?" he said smiling too.

"I met another guy named Jim a few days ago, but he went back home to Santa Cruz with his family."

"Did you kiss him?"

"I did. He was nice, but that was as far as it went. Why?"

"Just wondered. Everyone calls me Nacho so that won't be a problem."

"Okay Nacho! Are you Hispanic?"

Nacho paused to ring up another customer, but Alyssa stood by while he finished.

"No, I'm Dutch," said Nacho. "I think our last name was Americanized when my great grandparents emigrated from the Netherlands."

"What if word gets out that I dated a Nacho?" Alyssa asked.

"They may ask if you had jalapenos on your Nacho?" he said holding back his own laughter. "What's your name?"

"Alyssa Daingerfield."

"Pleased to meet you Alyssa."

"Likewise."

"Any relation to Rodney," Nacho said smiling.

"Rodney's real name was Jacob Cohen who was the son of Jewish immigrants from New York's Long Island. No relation."

"You know a lot about Rodney Dangerfield."

"My family gets that all the time. So I researched him. His stage name was spelled differently too. I'm descended from English immigrants from Springfield, Virginia."

207

"Sweet. So will you go out with me Friday?"

"Yes."

"Meet me at the fireplace at 6:30."

"How do I dress?"

Nacho laughed.

"Dress like you are now. We'll eat here. I get a 10% discount."

"Well that seals it! I'll see you here Friday."

Alyssa quickly turned and walked out the door to avoid any awkward pauses, and headed straight to her Honda CRV to go back to the State Park. When she was unlocking the door she heard the familiar voice, but instead of standing behind her, he was standing next to her passenger door.

"Instead of an ice cream, can I have a ride?" Youki asked.

"Where are you going?"

"Same place as you, Phiffer-Burns."

"Sure! Hop in," Alyssa said smiling.

"Did you find another Jim?" asked Youki.

"How did you know that?" said Alyssa.

"I was making a joke," said Youki, "I meant Jim as another male friend. You know? If he was a dog he'd be another Fido. I take it that you actually met another young man who's name was Jim?"

"His last name is Nachman so everyone calls him Nacho."

"Things can change so fast, and now your emotions have changed too. You can observe your own emotional swings."

"I was just thinking that when you appeared out of the twilight and startled me," Alyssa replied.

"I wasn't standing behind you this time."

"Yes, you're improving."

"Are you going to spend time with him?"

"Yes, we're going out for dinner Friday. I don't know what day that is. That's one of the things I like about Big Sur. I lose track of the days."

208

"Time is somewhat irrelevant," said Youki. "We're given a set amount of years, and we set our watches, but what's important is what we do with our time. It's very important to take time to reflect and look within."

How do you mean?" asked Alyssa.

"We use many things available in everyday life to fill our moments and keep us busy to avoid thinking about who we are or why we're here. If we're busy, we don't have to think about anything. Our minds can be numb and idling. We're very comfortable idling. The last thing we want to do is reflect on ourselves. That could be painful. Thinking and feeling is hard, and there's risk involved. We avoid risk, and force ourselves to be busy without thought or reflection. We have a list of things to turn to in a panic such as sports, shopping, television, video games, gambling, internet, food, sex, drugs, and alcohol. If we have more than a minute, we grope for these things in a frenzy. We placate ourselves for moments at a time, but like an addict, when thoughts and feelings begin to creep back in, we're desperate for more diversion."

"I've learned that the hard way many times," Alyssa stated. "If I don't at least have some quiet time each day, then I get irritable. Same thing with exercise and meditation."

"From regular practice, you know that it's far better to reflect than not. You've never had the fear of seeing yourself in the first place. For most, our addictions protect us from dreaded thoughts about ourselves, what we've become, what we should be doing, or worst of all, our limited life spans. If we're lonely or bored we begin to think deep thoughts. We remember our connection to the spiritual world, and we realize how we've been neglecting it. We become uncomfortable, and that's why we hate it so much. The spiritual person purposely sets aside quiet reflection time. Each day they connect with the higher spirit, and look deeply into to corners of their soul. This exercise protects them from these worldly addictions, prevents stress, and keeps their head straight. There's no confusion or depression because they remain connected to source. They're happy and vibrant without television, booze or drugs. They're awake and alive."

"What about sex. That could be an addiction too, but it's necessary for the existence of the species. Lately, I seem so drawn to it as though I'm ready to lose my virginity! Then the other part of me wants to remain a little girl forever. I want to be my Grandpa's little girl!"

In a rare moment, Youki looked embarrassed.

"You're out of my area now. Consult your family on becoming a woman," said Youki. "All I can tell you is this: put your connection to God first, your human relations second and everything else comes third. Don't put too much value on material things, and put daily effort into developing yourself spiritually."

"You're not getting off that easy. What about sex?" Alyssa asked. "I think I'm ready, and I don't really know what to do."

"Take your time, and don't rush it. Choose wisely so that you can look back on the memory fondly. That's about all I can tell you!"

"My Mom has said similar things," said Alyssa. "She said to wait for the right guy. So you're off the hook. You passed!"

"Moms give good advice when it comes to sex, but your own advice is also very important. Trust your instincts. Your training and experience in dealing with people and emotions shows. Frenchy taught you well."

"I don't think I've ever mentioned Frenchy to you. How do you know about Frenchy?"

"Everyone's heard of Frenchy from Muscle Beach, but you have mentioned him."

"I don't think so, but I guess I'll never know for sure."

They had already pulled into the State Park, and were parked talking in the car.

"I'll see you after your date," said Youki. "Thank you for the ride."

"It was my pleasure!" said Alyssa. "Where are you going now?"

"I have some friends camping in the park. After that, I'll crawl into my Hobbit Hole and sleep. You shouldn't worry about hunched over old men. We'll be fine."

"Who said I was worried about you?"

Chapter 29

The next day Alyssa was thrown off by a surprise. Grandpa Jack and Grandma Lin had called and left a message during the day. They were in Monterey, and wanted to meet Alyssa at the Black Bear Café for dinner. She laughed when she listened to the message because the Black Bear was Grandpa Jack's type of place. It was upscale from a Denny's but not so nice that he would stand out if he was wearing jeans. She was excited about it when she got off work, and she knew that there must be some sort of news or they probably wouldn't have driven up.

Alyssa was thankful for the diversion as she drove up the beautiful central coast. It wasn't nearly dark yet, but the sky was already changing colors with various shades of red reflecting off the ocean. There were only three weeks left of her summer job in Big Sur, and she contemplated how she would make the best of it since she may never have this opportunity again.

Grandpa's old Volvo station wagon was already in the parking lot when she arrived. It warmed her heart to see the vehicle of her childhood, and hurried off inside with excitement. Grandpa and Grandma had a large corner booth, and stood when they saw her. After exchanging warm hugs and greetings, they sat down to catch up with each other.

"We just wanted to take a drive up and check in with you to see how you're getting along," Grandpa Jack started.

"Certainly honey," said Grandma Lin, "but what Grandpa didn't say is that he worries about you a lot being up here all by yourself. We want you to know that we love you very much, and we're always here for you."

Alyssa looked at them both as if being put on the spot. The waitress came and took their drink orders.

"I'm fine. Everything's fine. I was just thinking while driving to Monterey that I have only three weeks left."

"We can't wait until you come home," said Grandpa Jack.

"Is that the only thing you came up for?" Alyssa asked.

"Well not completely. We brought your mail, and there might be something important."

"You know something Grandpa, so you might as well spill it."

"You've always been very direct," Grandpa said smiling.

"I take after you Grandpa. Now what's up?"

"Your father has been in contact with us. You have a half sister in Cupertino, California. Her name is Sarah Stone. She's sixteen years old.

Alyssa wasn't prepared for the news, and sat in stunned silence. The waitress came with the beverages to break the tension. She took their dinner orders pleased that she helped break the discussion loose.

"Your father Brad got your postcard and came to visit me before he contacted you again. That was probably because the last time I saw him I told him that I'd kill him if he ever came near my daughter again. I probably meant it when I said it, but I doubt I could have actually killed him. I don't even like stepping on ants. It bothers me to eat animals, but I do anyway. The whole situation has been bothering me, so I wanted to let you know that there was a lot of bad blood between us."

212

"Brad was a drunk dear," said Grandma Lin. "We're not sure, but we also think he beat your Mom once. That's when Grandpa got involved. It was a long time ago."

"What does he want?" asked Alyssa.

"He wants to meet you, and he wants my blessing," said Grandpa Jack.

"Are you going to give it to him?"

"That depends. I wanted to talk to you first. I know you want to meet him, but I wanted to warn you that he's a skilled salesman. He's more or less a con man, and he could charm you into his web."

"So you're saying it's up to me whether you endorse the meeting."

"Not really honey, I guess my answer is yes, but I wanted to warn you first. He's a slippery one."

"But people can change," Alyssa stated looking at her Grandpa.

"Sometimes yes, but most of the time no," Grandpa replied.

"Well I want to meet him, but you're my Dad Grandpa. You'll always be my Dad, and Brad will be just Brad. If anything, we may just meet once and that's it."

"Okay then honey, I'll tell him it's okay with me. He claims to be sober and free of drugs, and I must admit that he didn't smell like booze when I saw him. He doesn't drive either. He took a cab from his house. That must have been a $200 cab ride."

"Well maybe he can afford it," said Grandma Lin. "Who knows what he's been up to. He may have money now."

"What about my half sister? Should I go to see her?" asked Alyssa.

"We don't know much about her yet," said Grandma Lin. "We better take our time on that one. I'm sure that she'll be curious about you too. You'll meet her one day."

"There's more," said Grandpa Jack.

"You're selling the house!" said Alyssa joking.

213

"No, but close," Grandpa Jack replied. "Dylan's parents are selling and moving to Idaho. Dylan came by to tell you he's staying here, and he's going to start at Cal State Northridge in the fall. I wasn't supposed to tell you the last part, but I'm not too good at holding back."

"Wow, all kind of changes," said Alyssa. "I haven't spoken to Dylan in two years. I assumed he started dating Karen Vanhayden."

"Who's that?"

"She's the girl that teamed up with Dylan to start a formal martial arts class. She basically pushed me out. I think there have been other women too, but I can't be sure. My lack of serious interest in him was frustrating, so he made an effort to separate himself. I wonder what spurred him to talk now. It can't be just because his parents are moving."

"Who knows honey, but he was your good friend. I suggest you give him another chance," said Grandma Lin.

"I promised him I would give you his phone number," said Grandpa Jack. "Here it is, and one more thing. Finhead John stopped by. He's going to UCLA, and he would like to speak to you too. Here's his number."

"I haven't heard from him in two years either."

"What a change Alyssa," said Grandpa. "He's a man now, and all dressed up. I didn't recognize him."

"I'll call Finhead when I get back. We're friends, and I always thought we had something left to do together. I'd like to find out what that is."

"I brought your mail," said Grandma Lin. "You have a few letters from Kaylee, and something that looks interesting from the Hillside-Zuma Recovery Center."

"I text Kaylee all the time. I don't know why she would send me a letter."

Alyssa opened the other letter, and it took a while for her to read it.

"It's a job offer," she said. They heard about my work at the Rehab Center, and they want to hire me. They have tuition reimbursement up to $2000 per semester, and I would only need to work weekends."

"Sounds too good to be true," said Grandma.

"Perhaps it is. It's up the coast further from Malibu. It would be a tough drive for me, but if it's only on weekends it may work out."

Their dinner order arrived, and they stopped talking momentarily while they were served.

"Is there anything else I can get you?" asked the waitress.

"No, I think we're all set," said Grandma Lin smiling.

"I wonder how they heard about you?" said Grandpa.

"I guess it could have been a coworker or a former patient. Maybe they felt bad about stopping my tuition payments."

"No, they didn't feel bad," said Grandpa, "maybe some of the people that worked with you felt bad, but I doubt your management felt bad. They're in business just like everyone else. If it's not their own family, they don't care."

"I think I've heard of this center," said Alyssa. "They cater to celebrities and wealthy L.A. people, and they charge a lot. I think they have a minimum fee too. The minimum stay is one week and they charge $15,000 up front. That's over $2,000 per day. If they have 500 beds, that's one million dollars a day gross income. With that income they can afford me easily."

"That makes a lot of sense. Your talents in teaching meditation and martial arts would blend well with their hoity-toity clientele," said Grandma. "You're a good fit."

"You're right Grandma," said Alyssa. "Since I have no interest in celebrities that makes me a good fit too. They're all just people to me."

When the news ended and the excitement based on anticipated change subsided, the conversation changed to stories of old times as they finished their meal. Subconsciously, their minds shifted to thoughts of sleep and ending their day. Light from the setting sun found a sneak path through the restaurant blinds and illuminated Grandpa Jack's face. Alyssa noticed how deep the laugh lines had grown, and how new wrinkles had become engrained where none had been before. She realized that not only was she growing up, but that the most important man in her life was growing older, and she had a limited amount of time to spend with him.

She felt a sense of gratitude as he spoke. He told her how difficult it had been to hold back when she ran off to Venice Beach for the summer, and how he couldn't have done it without the help of Momma Leoni. He spoke of the sleepless nights when she stayed in Hollywood near the Sunset Strip with Finhead, how it had ended badly, and how he had thanked God when she was alright. On the positive side, he spoke of how she took over the martial arts classes from Frenchy, how she didn't miss a beat, and what a great professional job she had done of managing the operation. She acted as though she had been teaching for years. He was very proud of her, and those were very happy times for him.

"What an impact I've had on his life," she thought to herself as she listened to him reminisce. "I really am like his daughter more than his grandchild."

As she drove back to Big Sur she saw a billboard in Monterey that said, "Family Counseling". She laughed, and her thoughts returned to Brad Stone. She treated the sign as a symbol that she should meet him, but her situation had changed, and now she wasn't sure of what she really wanted to do.

"Why am I doing this?" she thought. "Is it just for the tuition money? I don't need that anymore! I can accept the new job offer and I'll get tuition reimbursement. Is it money in general that I'm after? Am I just being selfish? Worse yet, am I just being jealous of Kaylee? She never sees her wealthy Dad. It can't be that great. It's not the love, it's the money. I must be hung up on the money! I'm like so many capitalists – driven by fear and greed."

Although she wanted to dismiss the entire matter from her own head, the thought patterns continued. One thought would sneak in, and that would lead to another and another until she went full circle again and again.

"It's only natural to want to meet my Dad, she thought while lying in her bed and staring at the ceiling in the dark. "For good or bad he's family, and I should meet him. I wonder if he'll look like me or if I'll have any of his mannerisms? I wonder if he's smart. They say he's sly, but is he smart? I know he'll be good looking or Mom would never have dated him, then again, look at Franken! I wonder if my half sister looks like me?"

She thought of Dylan and Finhead, and why they suddenly wanted to be back in her life.

"Why now? Why both of them?" she thought. "What is it that makes people attracted to me? Why am I always in the leadership role? I'm just doing my own thing, and not really all that interested in being out front, but I always seem to be there."

She was content to be on her own involved in a solo enterprise, and free to do as she pleased without being bothered by others. The subtle people attraction wasn't all that noticeable to most, but she lived with it daily. It was obvious to her. People surrounded her constantly; she rarely ever had time to herself. Because of this, she craved solitude, and slipped off to a quiet place whenever the opportunity presented itself.

After considerable thought, her reluctance to lead was overcome by need. In her experience, no matter what the endeavor, people that were willing to step up were in short supply, and she had the ability. People requested her, and staff willingly fell in behind her. Repeatedly she was drawn to the role. Like a siren out of Greek mythology, it called to her, she couldn't resist, and hypnotically she answered. She was destined to blaze some sort of mysterious trail, but for the time being, it was unknown what that trail would be.

217

"If I'm destined to be a leader," she thought, "I might as well embrace it and make it work for me too. I can serve the higher calling and take care of myself at the same time. I've changed while I've been away. Being isolated here among the ancient trees and the rocky shoreline has given me time to think. Now I'm ready to go back to L.A. and do whatever it is that I was meant to do!"

It was resolved for her. She would accept her leadership role without further resistance, but there were other bigger issues as well. The news from Grandpa and Grandma Jack was heavy upon her mind. In the morning, it wasn't long before her thoughts were racing about what transpired, and she began projecting probable outcomes based on her options. Possible interplay between her current situation, money, school and all the different people in her life played out in multiple hypothetical scenarios. Her thought patterns became like a television stuck on the same repetitive commercials. She forced herself to pause and organize her mental toolkit. It had taken her entire lifetime to acquire these tools, and she wanted them all at her disposal in the coming months. She was now confronted with decisions that would impact her for years, and she wanted to choose wisely.

Throughout the day she focused on work, and that helped keep her head clear. Her mind was comfortably idling while she performed her ritualistic cleaning tasks. While her mind idled, she was reminded of things Youki had spoken of:

"We use many things available in everyday life to fill our moments and keep us busy to avoid thinking about who we are or why we're here. If we're busy we don't have to think about anything. Our minds can be numb and idling. We're very comfortable idling."

It made her smile. After work, in order to continue her treatment, she hiked up into the hillsides and focused on the beauty of the forest and the ancient trees. The wonder and simplicity of nature helped her ratchet down even more, but when she returned home, the world outside came streaming in like light from the inevitable sunrise. When she checked her mail, a postcard had arrived from Brad Stone.

"Dear Alyssa,

Please forgive the delay in my response. I was on bad terms with your Mom's Dad, and I wanted to contact him before we progressed any further. I have spoken to him, and I expect him to approve. He won't endorse our meeting, but views it as an inevitable outcome, and thinks that this is as good of a time as any to proceed. That was important to me. He may already have told you about our discussion. Please meet me at you're Grandfather's house during the early afternoon on the Sunday of Labor Day weekend.

Sincerely,

Brad Stone"

The front of the postcard was from a restaurant called "The Melting Pot" in Agoura. Alyssa immediately envisioned smiling over a fondue pot in deep discussion with her long-lost father.

Friday arrived with heat and humidity. It was the first day that Alyssa had been uncomfortable at work. She was sweating and wiping her brow throughout the day, and was desperate for a way to cool off when she arrived home. She immediately put on the one piece swim suit that she had bought for the trip but never intended to use. When some of her coworkers saw her, they invited her to go tubing with them in the Big Sur River.

"It's a blast!" they said as they coaxed her. "We've gone two or three times this summer. The water is cold, but you get used to it. It's cheap too! The campground rents inner tubes to locals at half price."

Although she had stayed to herself for most of the summer, she was delighted to go with them this time, and they were happy that she had finally accepted their invitation.

She drove by herself so that she could stop by Fernwood and invite Nacho since she'd never make it back in time for their 6:30 date. Luckily, Nacho was still working, and agreed to meet her.

Tubing was a lot of fun. Alyssa hadn't laughed so much since she arrived in Big Sur. The water was very cold and made her feet a little numb, but with the excitement, she didn't seem to mind it. The late season water was swift but shallow. There was just enough for one person to ride a tube. If two people got on, the tube would drag on the rocky bottom. So they walked up river in pairs each carrying a tube. They rode separately, but held hands so they could ride the current together. Occasionally they would lose their grip, and letting go would sometimes spin one or both tubes. They spun each other accidentally at first, but after a few runs it became great fun. They started letting go with force in an attempt to purposely spin their partner. The guys would laugh and the girls would scream.

When Nacho arrived the group dynamic changed considerably. Most of Alyssa's coworkers had seen him at the store in Fernwood, but nobody really knew him well, and since it was obvious that the two were on a date, they began to give them space. Before long, Nacho and Alyssa were on their own tubing casually by themselves with the rest of the group occasionally throwing curious glances their way.

Alyssa and Nacho's interaction was awkward and muted at first, but as the pair grew comfortable with each other, they began to smile and talk more. They forgot that anyone else was watching.

Nacho was tall, thin, and somewhat gangly in appearance with brown hair and white skin that looked like it had never seen the sun. Alyssa found it interesting that he wasn't the least bit self-conscious about his stark appearance. He caught her staring, and his expression signaled that he understood her thoughts. He smiled and ignored her. She found his lack of caring interesting. She was attracted to him in a strange way, and wondered why.

He wasn't just a curiosity, he was a man, and she felt things stir within her that she had only recently experienced. She found herself doing things she wouldn't have considered an hour ago. Her actions were bordering on the absurd, but she continued. She watched his muscles flex as he moved his upper body, and she noticed the shape of his lean chest and abdominal muscles. He was scarecrow thin, strong, but not obviously powerful. She could tell that he was accustomed to physical labor, and enjoyed it. Standing all day to work the cash register at Fernwood was foreign to him.

She scanned the rest of his body being careful not to let on, and made mental notes about the curvature of his shoulder muscles, the definition of his arms, and the method with which he moved. He had an animal rhythm that made his gangly body appear somewhat graceful.

After a time, she noticed that he was inconspicuously staring too. His staring was lustful, and the unapologetic rawness of it surprisingly excited her. She wondered how much of their interplay was instinctive. Eyes, legs, buttocks, but mostly her breasts were the targets of his gaze. His glances became less concealed so that she would notice.

She suddenly became aware of her own body, and looked down at herself. The cold water had given her goose bumps and firm breasts. She realized how provocative she must look with the detail of her body showing through the thin swimsuit. She mischievously let her emotions flow with the feeling and exaggerated her sultry look. She was innocently aware of herself and her tantalizing beauty. The change in her drew him closer as if he had no will of his own. They frolicked and splashed each other in the water in anxious play as if trying to cool off inside. They chased each other up the river bank, and she screamed playfully as he caught her. They both laughed and embraced. Their wet outer skin was cool to the touch, but the warmth of their bodies quickly overcame the chill and became inviting. They clung to the warmth. His touch was electrifying. They loosened enough to adjust and hugged tightly again. She could feel his excitement grow against her. They stood transfixed for a moment in time. With just swim suits on, their embrace was very sensual and arousing. They adjusted several times as frustrated emotions demanded that they

221

go further, but their thoughts held them back. Finally, they kissed standing on the banks of the river. The kiss released tension. It was comforting, warm, and sensual. It was rewarding. Nacho wanted to continue, but Alyssa didn't feel the same. It was surprising to her that she didn't, and she wondered why.

"Why was it so good with Jim, but not with Nacho!" she thought to herself while still in his arms.

Her thoughts took her attention away, and their moment together ended.

"We better get going if we're still going to have dinner together," said Alyssa as she looked at him apologetically.

"Definitely," he agreed embarrassingly as his desire subsided. "Why don't we get rinsed off and changed, and meet back at Fernwood in an hour."

Alyssa smiled broadly, "Sounds good. Can't wait!"

Nacho was already waiting when Alyssa arrived back for dinner. She was 15 minutes late.

He looked very handsome dressed in beige shorts and a white collared shirt. He had a depth in his eyes that she hadn't noticed before. He stood when she walked up, and to her surprise, he embraced her, and kissed her on the top of her head. She liked this bold gesture, but avoided kissing him on the lips. They sat down at a corner booth away from everything else. The table was made from a single plank of a massive redwood tree.

There was no waitress, so Nacho took their orders up to the window and smiled at Alyssa as he returned. His yearning smile made her uncomfortable, but she shrugged it off and began to exchange information with him.

He was from Salinas, but had been living in Monterey and Big Sur since he graduated from High School. He wanted to go to college, and was saving his money. His parents had never had money, and couldn't help him. He planned to take community college classes at first, and eventually transfer to Cal State Chico.

She told him about her background in Monterey Park, and what she had done in and around the Los Angeles area. She explained her career motives in rehabilitative studies, and how she became a student at Cal State LA. She finished with her interests in meditation and Tai Chi.

"Are you Buddhist?" he asked.

"I'm a student of religion and philosophy. I believe in a common spirit and a higher purpose. I wasn't raised to be religious, but I guess I've become that way. I believe people should develop their spiritual side to provide purpose, balance, and find happiness. What about you?"

They were interrupted by their name being called to pick up their food. They both went up to the counter to carry their entrées back to the log plank corner table.

"I guess I'm more of a utilitarian," said Nacho after they sat down. "We should be performing activities that bring about a general form of good, and in doing so, our individual happiness comes about as a result."

"So you've thought about it?" she stated.

"Oh yes, many times."

"You settled on utilitarianism?"

"Well I'm not a purist. I started out having trouble with the God concept and the Jesus concept. Jesus said do unto others as you would do to yourself. I would say do to others before they do to you. That makes a lot more sense to me. The way others behave, it seems to be survival of the fittest that's important. It's a competitive world with scarce resources."

"To me the operative words are "seems to be"," Alyssa interrupted. "The way life seems to be and how it really is could be two very different things. What's obvious isn't necessarily truth. Things are not always what they seem."

"You need to grab your share of the pie and hold on before someone else wrestles it away from you," said Nacho in response.

"Being nice and spiritual might make you feel good, but it won't get you anywhere but to the end of the buffet line."

"So you believe in fighting for what you get and pleasures of the senses?" Alyssa asked with curiosity. "That's what you pursue in a logical and calculated matter. Unlike pure hedonism, you try not to hurt anyone in the process."

"You make it sound crude and self serving, but I guess it's so. I didn't start out that way. Like you, I started searching for meaning at a young age and never really found anything that made sense to me."

"A wise friend of mine says there is no such thing as sense," she responded. "What makes sense to you is a response based on society's conditioning and what people before you have done and thought. How do you know they were right? There is no sense!"

"What makes sense to me is what I need to survive in a cold world, but yes there is no right. There is only what I see in front of me, and that's about where I started. Existentialism first resonated with me. The individual is solely responsible for giving their life meaning in the face of difficulties and distractions such as money problems, family drama, despair, depression, and boredom. With existentialism, it really didn't matter if there was a God. You're responsible for yourself and your own happiness. That worked for me, but as I went on, I noticed how some people were living the good life and I wasn't. That bothered me. I had heard about hedonism. Hedonism was strict pursuit of pleasure, and that didn't really work for me either. I needed some middle ground. Blatant pursuit of pleasure would alienate your friends and eventually come to a bad end. So I combined the two. Existentialism and hedonism combined together where nobody gets hurt. That sounds idealistic, but that's as far as I've gotten. I found out that was utilitarianism. It really didn't describe me either, but it's the closest one. There are different approaches to the philosophy. There's a quantitative approach where the value of the pleasure is based on the intensity and the duration, and there's another approach where there are basically two levels of pleasure. Lower forms can be enjoyed by animals and humans alike. Eating is obviously the most basic. The higher level experiences like exotic sex are strictly human experiences."

"What do you think happens when you die?"

"Well then you're dead," said Nacho. "That's it. That's the end. What do you think?"

"I think the spirit continues in some way. I'm not sure how, but in some way we evolve. The Buddhists say we're reincarnated again and again until we're advanced enough to avoid birth. That may be true. Some of the newer religions say that we exist in a spiritual and material incarnate dimension at the same time. The spiritual one is more familiar to us, but when we're born, we quickly acclimate to the material world. What we can see outside of our material bodies becomes our reality. This is the world we live in filled with objects, spaces, animals, plants, natural beauty, money, and food. We cling to the familiar, and lose track of the eternal dimension that is, in truth, where we belong. That theory sounds very appealing and logical. I agree most with that theory, but the Buddhist one is interesting too."

"It could all just be wishful thinking to ease anxiety over our eventual deaths."

"It could be, but I don't think so," said Alyssa. "We can each believe what we want. I believe that all life is interconnected, and there's some basis for existence. It's all a mystery to us, and that's part of the beauty."

"That's where the ends meet," said Nacho. "We go about our daily lives doing the best that we can. We try to get along with one another no matter what our philosophies are, and try to enjoy life and each other while we're here. Wouldn't you agree?"

"Yes! I would agree. We have different philosophies of life, but that's where we have a very common understanding. That's why it all works!"

"Agree!"

225

Alyssa had never really met anyone before that didn't believe in the eternal nature of one's soul. At first she didn't know if it bothered her, but later she decided that it did. He didn't believe in anything! There was a fundamental difference, and the philosophy built on those fundamental beliefs could differ substantially. She couldn't understand his moral structure.

"In a way he couldn't logically have one," she thought, "but if he thinks death is the absolute end, then it does work."

The afternoon's tubing adventure had been a great distraction, but now her mind was racing again.

Nacho's childhood had been bleak. His parents both had low paying jobs in agriculture. He never had anything growing up. He felt fortunate to have a pair of shoes, food on the table, and heat in the winter. Their furnace burned fuel oil from a tank outside the house. Sometimes his parents couldn't afford the fuel oil, and they wore winter jackets in the house. Sometimes they wore jackets to bed. They always ate, but there were many days of no meat, and they survived on boiled cabbage and potatoes.

The conversation was startling to Alyssa who never had a lot but never lacked either. She thought about it while Nacho was explaining his background. Whatever she had wanted seemed to come to her. She always had what she needed.

"Don't get me wrong," Nacho said finishing up. "I like Salinas. I just don't want to live there ever again. My Dad says never say never, and I agree, so I'm careful with my words. I like what I'm doing now with summers in Big Sur and winters in Monterey. I don't have much money, but I'm happy."

After dinner, Nacho walked Alyssa to her car. She liked him, but the conversation still bothered her. She was eager to kiss him and see if there was more passion than that afternoon. She sensed his apprehension in kissing her at all, but she gestured as if waiting for him. He responded by going straight in. They kissed somewhat aggressively. Alyssa was accepting, and put effort into the kiss to try and make it good, but it ended leaving her flat. She couldn't tell

226

how he felt, but he looked excited. They said their goodnights and she headed home.

Chapter 30

Alyssa awoke feeling conflicted over the conversation of the previous day. She decided the discussion bothered her because Nacho might be right, and everything she had worked for in her life could be based on delusional thinking.

"God could be just a myth that helped us be civil with each other and happy while we're here on the planet and nothing more," she thought.

It was a repugnant concept, and it shook her up. Lifetimes of service told her otherwise. She didn't believe it, and had never believed it. The kiss bothered her too.

"Why was it so wonderful with Jim and so forbidding with Nacho," she thought to herself. "Was it because Jim was my first real kiss? Or was it because Nacho and I differed so much philosophically? Or was it just a compatibility thing? Jim and I were compatible, but not Nacho. Nacho would have been better as just a friend! Perhaps I shouldn't try to analyze things. Matters of the heart can be complicated!"

Her thoughts continued down that path throughout the morning despite many times wanting to stop thinking about it. It wasn't until her lunch break that she began to let go of the conflict. She walked to the nearest grove of ancient redwood trees and lunched under the thick forest canopy noting the comings and goings of the birds as they sang their songs in the branches.

"Being out in nature always has a calming affect," she thought to herself. "It's almost as good as meditation. No matter what is

227

happening in the political world of humans, it always seems silly when I'm a part of the harmony of the forest."

When she returned to work, her thoughts drifted back to Nacho. She went about her chores while attempting to sort it all out in her head. Now, instead of the kiss, the philosophical disagreements were the source of her consternation. She decided that this fundamental difference was at least partially responsible for their night ending on a down note, but that the physical compatibility difference had contributed too. The first was logical, and the second was instinctual, but both seemed necessary to have a relationship whether or not it was business, friends or lovers.

Late in the afternoon Alyssa's thoughts turned again. This time she stressed over her father, whether she really wanted to meet him. She thought of Kaylee, and beat herself up for being jealous of her.

She knew that she was going to accept the job offer, and would no longer need financial help. She could skip meeting her father. She knew very little about Brad Stone, and in most ways, didn't need him. It bothered her again that her motive for meeting him may be monetary, but there had to be something more to it or it wouldn't weigh so heavily on her mind.

Dinner and the bustle of the State Park on a late summer evening took her mind off her frustrations once more, and she walked down to the bonfire to sit among the tourists. She listened to the Park Ranger lecture on the nature of bears, and she peered into the flames in a mind numbing fashion. The Park Ranger's lecture took only twenty minutes, and most of the tourists returned to their campgrounds. Reluctant to drive up to Fernwood and run into Nacho, Alyssa decided to call it a night and read in her bed; but when she walked by the visitor center, there stood Youki under the parking lot street lamp staring at her intently as she walked up.

"Well this is a surprise, and I'm not even startled by your sudden appearance," Alyssa said smiling and happy to see him.

228

"I felt like I needed to talk to you," Youki replied without emotion.

"What about?" Alyssa asked.

"Nothing," replied Youki.

"Nothing!" said Alyssa, "how can we talk about nothing?"

"If we make it into something." Youki said smiling. "Let's go back to the Park Ranger's campfire. An old body like mine needs to sit."

"Were you at the campfire earlier?"

"No."

"Then why would you say return? How do you know I was?"

"What else is there to do around here?" Youki asked in his expressionless manner. "I guessed that you wouldn't drive to Fernwood tonight so what else?"

"Okay! Well I was just wondering. You always seem to know what I'm thinking."

"It may seem that way, but I know what I feel," said Youki. "I use what I feel to help me understand what I can do and what actions I can take. I can easily guess that things have been bothering you, and that these are things that I may be able to help with. You're already trained to handle them, but may need a little guidance from me. We all need help sometimes, and it's important to be open-minded enough to except when help is appropriately offered."

"Yes, you're right. It's sometimes easier to reject people that want to help for fear of having to open up to them. During these feeble attempts to keep our lives private, we can miss a lot. I need to be sensitive to what comes to me at all times. I can't be so focused that I desensitize myself to the things that bring help, learning, and understanding. These subtle nuances bring joy to living. That's an old lesson for me. That's a lesson I've had to relearn one thousand times."

"And perhaps one thousand more," said Youki.

"Perhaps!" said Alyssa smiling.

229

"What's been on your mind?" Youki asked.

"The biggest thing is my Dad, said Alyssa. "Something motivated me to want to meet him. I've never met him before. He may have been around a little when I was a baby, but I don't remember him. Recently, I contacted him, and it may have been out of jealousy over my best friend Kaylee's relationship with her Dad. What's more, he pays her college tuition without question. I've always had to work hard for everything I've gotten; whereas, it was just handed to her. So not only am I jealous for monetary reasons, I'm feeling sorry for myself too. I wonder why I've gone backwards. I've trained so hard not to be like that."

"Jealousy is not an emotion that you're familiar with," Youki started. "You know how to get what you want. What you want is mostly not self-serving, and if it is self-serving, it's a humble request. You've heard the expression be careful what you ask for because you might get it. Well the expression should be: be careful what you ask for because you will get it. You've asked for something, and whether it's consciously or subconsciously, there's something to it that's beyond money. You might as well let it play out."

"I would agree with you but there's more. Look, Kaylee goes to college and I go to college. We go to the same college! Somehow I've managed it, and so has she. I worked for it and she didn't, but we both go. We're both happy and we're friends. It all agrees with what you're saying. I got what I asked for, but why am I so torn up over this? I went to a lot of trouble to contact my Dad. I took risks with people that are important to me. I risked the relationship with my Mom that's been very stable the last few years. Why? Was it for easy money? What's even more curious is that just a few days ago, I got a job offer. It's a good offer that's compatible with college and has tuition reimbursement. So it turns out I don't even need the money. Now I don't want to contact him, but is it because I'm afraid? Is it because it will be very awkward and uncomfortable?"

230

"Look at what's at play here. It's a relationship that you've never had. It's one that's common to most people but unknown to you. Subconsciously, you desire it, and as we've already discussed, it's not a lot to ask, and not self-serving. You should have it. You were driven to contact your Dad. It could have been anything that triggered the action: money, tuition, jealousy of Kaylee, or a combination of all these factors, but the deep-rooted curiosity was already there waiting to surface. You've set the wheels in motion, let it play out, and follow your heart. He may have an important role in your life that's unknown to you at this point."

"In a round about way I came to that same conclusion," Alyssa responded to the advice. "I had planned to meet him once, and beyond that I didn't know. I speculated that he and my Mom broke up for a reason, and that reason may still be there. It's entirely possible that I wouldn't want to see him again, but I was anxious to meet him just once. I couldn't make it happen immediately. I came up here to work for summer, and the excitement cooled. Time passed, and I wanted to cancel, but then my Grandpa Jack came up for a visit. He told me he had recently met with my Dad, and that my Dad told him that I have a half sister. I would like to meet her, but I guess I should meet him first."

"What happened with your date?" Youki asked changing the subject.

"We had a great time riding on inner tubes in the Big Sur River. Then we kissed and it just wasn't the same, but I liked him, and I wanted to try again. He was manly and exciting."

"I wouldn't put too much emphasis on one kiss," said Youki. "If you like him, give him another chance."

"I did," Alyssa replied. "After tubing, we had dinner at Fernwood. We talked a lot and got to know each other. Everything was fine, but the conversation became philosophical, and things changed. We have completely different viewpoints. He believes that religion is basically a myth, and that people like me are

231

delusional. What you experience through the five senses is all there is. To me, that's a very bleak outlook, and it seemed like a left-handed slam. It wasn't intentional, but it felt that way. Oh, and one more thing. When you die, you're dead and that's it. That's the end. The soul does not continue on. So, as a result, he's somewhat hedonistic. Pleasures of the senses are what life is all about as long as you don't hurt anyone else. Oddly, I was somewhat repulsed by his point of view. I'm usually not critical of other people's belief systems. So, in short, the dinner was good, the conversation was lively, but the kiss fell flat. I wasn't sure why the kiss wasn't good at that point. It could have been that his outlook on life turned me off. I definitely didn't like it, or, it could have been that the chemistry just wasn't there between us."

"I would say the latter, but you're talking to a seasoned bachelor," Youki responded. "As for the philosophical differences, what he says, what he believes, and how he acts could all be different things. We all believe in one way or another. Many people may call it myth, but it's engrained in us. We subconsciously believe. What he thinks he believes works for him, and so be it. What we believe works for us, and more than that, we feel it down to the core of our existence. That's the important part. It matters not whether we're right or wrong. We simply exist, and our existence is no accident."

"We came to the same conclusion last night as you did tonight. We can exist together with different beliefs, and that's fine with me, but what you just said helps a lot. He may have the same belief system as we do, but he just thinks he's hedonistic."

"It's popular to be an atheist these days. Or even more radical, to be hedonistic. To believe in God, Buddha, Jesus, Krishna or whatever you want to call it carries risk. There's risk of being wrong, risk of rejection, and risk of ridicule. It's fashionable to be an atheist hedonic that's rich and famous. To be bad is good."

"Do you need a ride?" Alyssa asked.

232

"No, I'm staying here in the campground again. I'm sleeping in a real bed tonight, and not my usual thin mat."

"Well thank you for talking. You've been a great help."

"I've only reflected back to you what you've already learned. Use it wisely. I want to talk to you again before you go back to Los Angeles," Youki said.

"We'll run into each other at least one more time I'm sure" Alyssa stated smiling.

Chapter 31

Alyssa slept better than she had in days, and she realized when she woke how important it was to talk to someone from time to time. She had spent too much time alone, and through her short conversation with Youki, all her concerns had been sorted out. She would accept the new job and meet her father as planned. She knew what she wanted to do, and was ready to get on with it. There was a week left in her summer job, but she almost wished it could end that day.

She avoided Fernwood for days unsure of what to do about Nacho. She reasoned with herself that in time, her course of action would become clear. On one hand she really wanted to see him, but on the other hand, she didn't want to see him at all. She wondered what would win out.

After driving to Fernwood twice without locating him, she was about to give up, but decided to make one final attempt. She only had a few days left, and was running out of time to end it clean by telling him. If he wasn't there, she may get a chance to say goodbye to Youki. When she arrived at Fernwood, Nacho wasn't in the store. She asked around, but no one had seen him. Frustrated she settled into the easy chair by the big fire place. She was at the correct distance from the fire for the perfect temperature, and she dosed off momentarily.

"You may not be snoring, but you're drooling on yourself," Alyssa heard as if from a distance.

She snapped out of her sleep to see Youki looking at her.

"I'm not drooling," she said wiping the corners of her mouth with the back of her hand.

"You were getting close, but I saved you from embarrassment," Youki replied. "Since you weren't looking for me, I thought that I would show up."

"It's a good thing. I wanted to say goodbye. I'm leaving in a few days," Alyssa stated while yawning and stretching awake.

Just then Nacho walked by from the bar to the door. Alyssa looked at him, but he didn't seem to notice her.

"Nacho!" Alyssa called.

Nacho turned as he grabbed for the door handle, let go, and walked back to her.

"Hi," he said. "I hadn't heard from you. I thought that was it."

"Nacho this is Youki. Youki this is Nacho."

"Pleased to meet you young man," said Youki. "Please excuse me for not getting up."

"Pleased to meet you! I've heard a lot about you."

"I'm leaving for home in a few days," Alyssa said, "I was hoping we could hookup before we go."

Nacho looked at her and paused momentarily.

"Sure . . . . . I guess. How about tomorrow after work? Here at 6:30?"

"That will work fine," Alyssa confirmed.

"Great, I'll see you then. Pleased to meet you Mr. Youki," Nacho said while heading to the door.

"Likewise," said Youki. "So you actually came here to see him. Did you think you were going to get away without saying goodbye?"

"No, I would have definitely tried to find you," Alyssa responded.

"If you were looking, then you might not have found me!" Youki said with very little expression. "Give up first, and then I'll be easier to find."

"How could I forget?" Alyssa said. "I wanted you to know how much our time together has meant to me. I loved it. I hope to see you again."

"We've been friends for lifetimes," Youki replied.

"Well then the statement still applies," Alyssa said smiling. "Will I see you again?"

"If you love something, give it up, if it comes back, it was always yours, if it doesn't, it was never yours to begin with, Youki replied.

"Ughh, I hate that expression," said Alyssa. "You don't have it quite right either."

"Remember what I've said about being open minded, sensitive, and accepting. You may find new meanings in the old sayings that apply directly to you." said Youki.

"Does that mean no, I won't see you again?" Alyssa asked.

"We may meet again, we may not. That's the beauty of it, so we enjoy our time together while we can," Youki responded.

"Good answer!" said Alyssa. "I'm going to head back to camp. I love you. I hope to see you again."

"Farewell," said Youki. "I love you too."

Youki stood, Alyssa gave him a big bear hug, and she ran out of the room in tears.

On the way back to the State Park she found it difficult to hold back the tears, but then she remembered what Youki had said, and that made her stop to think.

"If you love something, give it up, if it comes back, it was always yours, if it doesn't, it was never yours to begin with," Alyssa thought. "What an odd thing for him to say."

235

The statement entered her mind occasionally throughout the next day. What bothered her was that the statement seemed so uncharacteristic of Youki. It came from out of the blue, and it didn't have anything to do with their conversation.

"He may have been referring to himself," she thought. "I have become attached to him. I guess I need to let him go. That must be what he meant."

Her explanation satisfied her at least temporarily. When she drove up to Fernwood for her date with Nacho, she was ready to let go. She was ready to transition to other thoughts. She wanted to say goodbye to Nacho, and let him down easy. She didn't think it could ever work out. He was already waiting for her when she arrived. He stood when she walked up. She immediately hugged him placing her head against his chest. She then looked up at him ready to kiss. He was surprised, and by his look, wasn't expecting affection at all, but kissed her anyway for as long as he could. Now Alyssa was surprised. She didn't expect anything so passionate, and she hadn't expected to enjoy it. She was totally thrown off and unable to speak. They sat in a booth across from each other.

"I wanted to let you know that I don't think we're compatible," Nacho started. "I think we can be good friends, but I don't think we have what it takes to be more than that."

Alyssa was stunned and surprised, and found it difficult to speak. She was going to say the same thing, but he had gotten to it first, and she didn't want to get into a competition to determine who was dumping who. They only had one date, and they lived 300 miles apart. They never had anything to begin with.

"What was it that made you decide?" asked Alyssa.

"I'm not sure exactly, but I would say that you were unsure of me. There was no emotion in our first kiss. I guess I got insecure, but I never could really recover from it. It's not you it's me," said Nacho with a serious look.

Alyssa almost choked on his last statement. She wanted to laugh, but held herself back.

"I respect your decision," Alyssa responded. "We gave it a shot and that's what's important. It was fun and we got to know each other. I must admit that I was taken aback with your philosophy of life. In other words, I disagree with your belief system. It's the opposite of mine. I don't think that would have made a difference if we really liked each other, but it appears that we don't like each other enough to continue. We're geographically challenged anyway."

"I could tell that you didn't like my borderline atheism," Nacho stated smiling. "I'm not blind. It was all over your face that you disapproved."

"Now it's my turn to say it's not you it's me!" said Alyssa. "What bothered me the most during our conversation was that my belief system could be wrong. I could be delusional and living in a mythical dream world. I was questioning everything I've worked toward. So it really wasn't your philosophy that was bothering me. It was my own. You've given me new perspective. I thank you for that!"

"I'm glad you clarified that," said Nacho. "You were looking at me as if I was the devil himself."

"You're an attractive man," said Alyssa. "I've never felt things before that I felt with you. I'm thankful for tubing on the river and the evening we had together. I've never met anyone like you before, and I hope you find someone you like."

"When you're up this way, be sure to look me up."

"I'll do that," said Alyssa standing up.

They kissed again, but this time it was just a smooch. Nacho drifted back to the bar. He was with a group of people. Most of them were female. Alyssa recognized some of them from working at the State Park.

Alyssa was ready to go home, but with just a few days left, it didn't bother her so much. She had resolved most of the things that were looming, and used her remaining free time wisely to meditate and hike in the forest among the ancient trees.

On Alyssa's last night, the State Park sponsored a barbeque by the visitor center near the Park Ranger's campfire for the summer hires that were leaving for home the next day. Since she had so much fun tubing on that hot afternoon, she decided to drop by to say goodbye to her friends, and exchange information with anyone that may be in her area. Most of her coworkers were from bay area schools, there was only one other person from the LA area. She worked in food services, and was gothic and creepy. Alyssa wasn't really interested, but introduced herself anyway. She was ignored by the girl that looked at her as of she were strange.

"That look means she likes you," said a girl standing near by.

"I'd hate to see the look if she didn't like me," Alyssa responded.

They both laughed and exchanged phone numbers. Her name was Misty.

"I mostly text," said Misty, "but I wrote down my San Jose State email address in case you don't text. Send me an email when you get back to Cal State LA."

"Will do, and nice to meet you," Alyssa replied.

After the barbeque, Alyssa packed up her car so she could leave right after work the next day. The experience was bittersweet for her since she loved the majestic beauty of the Big Sur and the central coast. She had found peace among the tourists, but she was ready to get back to Southern California to start her life again. She drove down to Fernwood on the off chance she would run into Youki, but hardly anyone was there. It was slow, and neither Nacho nor Youki were available.

"It's probably because I'm looking for him that I can't find him," Alyssa thought to herself smiling.

The next day was uneventful. The State Park was full for the upcoming Labor Day weekend, and some of the summer hires were staying over to help out, but the majority of them were already gone, and it was very quiet on the grounds. Alyssa took one last walk before starting her drive home, but when she stepped

238

out she saw Nacho peddle up on a bicycle with a concerned look on his face.

"I hate to be the bearer of bad tidings, but your Japanese friend died at Fernwood the night before last," Nacho said. "He fell asleep in that chair he liked by the fireplace and never woke up. Everyone thought he was just sitting there dozing all night like he always does. When closing time came, we tried to wake him, but he was gone. I'm sorry Alyssa."

"You mean Youki?" Alyssa asked in disbelief. "Are you sure it was Youki?"

Shock was registering on Alyssa's face.

"Yes, I'm sure. Yes, it was your Youki, the hunched over Japanese dude that looked a little like the Dali Lama. Yes, he died night before last. I thought you should know. I was hoping I could catch you before you left."

The realization of what actually had happened struck Alyssa, and she went into a blank stare momentarily recalling a month earlier when Youki told her he was ready to die. She broke down into tears, and Nacho took her in his arms. She sobbed in anguish against his chest. After a few moments the tears subsided, and Alyssa looked at Nacho with her grief-stricken face.

"Thank you. Thank you for telling me. Thank you for being here for me. You're a real gentleman," Alyssa said while sniveling.

"That's not all. There was a letter for you in his little satchel. It was stamped with your Monterey Park address on it, but he never got to mail it. I have it here for you."

"But I never gave him my address," said Alyssa sobering up and furrowing her brow.

"Well somehow he got it. He may have known it from the State Park," said Nacho.

"Or he could have gotten it last year. I was up here for a retreat. I don't remember."

"Well here it is. Are you going to open it?"

"Yes. Where is his body? What are they going to do for him?"

"Nothing," said Nacho, "He was homeless with no known relatives. The county took his body away for cremation."

Alyssa burst into tears again, and Nacho took her in his arms once more.

"All my life I've been drawn to the homeless," Alyssa said into Nacho's shirt while still crying. I wonder why that is?"

"I don't know. It may be because you can relate to them in some way. Why don't you open the letter? I'm curious what it says."

Alyssa reluctantly wiped her face on her sweatshirt sleeve for lack of a tissue, took the letter in her hand, and tore it open. The letter had a 1909 $5 Indian gold coin in it cellophane taped to a piece of cardboard and wrapped in a letter. Alyssa examined the coin through the clear tape, and read the letter to herself, and then handed the letter to Nacho for him to read while choking up and reexamining the coin.

"Dear Alyssa,

I wanted to give you this gold coin. It's the only money I ever carried, and obviously, I never spent it. As you can see, I've lived a very full and happy life without money. The coin has a face value of five dollars, but of course, it's worth much more. That's an important concept in itself. I'm ready to leave now. In my heart we've been friends for hundreds of years. I hope to see you in the next life. Please remember what we discussed the last time we spoke.

Your friend forever.

Love,

Youki"

After reading the letter Nacho started tearing up too. When Alyssa saw him, she started sobbing uncontrollably. Nacho took her in his arms once again to comfort her.

Too upset to drive or be alone, Alyssa spent the night in Nacho's rented room. Nacho gave her his bed while he slept on the floor on her sleeping bag. They both slept fitfully, and were wide awake at dawn. Saying goodbye to Nacho, Alyssa climbed into her Honda CRV for the long drive down Highway One toward Morro Bay. Just past Pfeiffer –Burns State Park, she thought she saw Youki waving goodbye on the side of the road as she passed. She smiled and waved back, but when she looked in her mirror, he was gone.

Part III Rehab

Chapter 32

Alyssa wasted no time upon returning to Grandpa Jack's. Nobody was home when she arrived. She pulled her car in the center of the drive and unloaded everything in a big circle around the vehicle. She was a whirlwind of efficiency. The camping articles went back in the garage, blankets in the laundry, and leftover food in the kitchen. Methodically, she carried the rest up to her converted attic room. It was hot. She turned on the window air conditioning unit. The space seemed smaller now that she'd been away for so long, but it was her space, and she loved it. Everything looked invitingly familiar. The smells were her smells, the colors were hers, and her precious philosophical and religious books were neatly arranged in the bookshelf by her bed. The comforting feeling of home relaxed her, and took her mind off the loss of Youki.

She was sweaty from carrying her things up the stairs in the late summer humidity. So she decided to take a shower, and lingered for a few minutes with the cool water flowing over her head and body. When she finished, she plopped down on her bed in just her underwear to relish the comfort of her own private space. She absorbed the sanctity and gazed out the window as if she was a little girl again. After a few minutes of lounging, she dressed as if going to work, ate a quick lunch, and drove up to the Hillside-Zuma Recovery Center to accept her job offer.

"We'd like you to start as soon as you can!" the Human Resources lady said as she handed her a package of paperwork to fill out. "You'll work weekends, but we want you to come in for a full week starting Monday to get to know the other instructors and get you integrated into the schedule. After that, you'll just work weekends. You won't deal directly with patients, and serve only as an instructor for meditation and martial arts classes. Is that all right with you?"

"That's fine!" Alyssa said flipping through the paperwork. Luckily, I have one week left before school starts. Do you know that I am studying recovery therapy in college? I'm starting my second year, and planning to make a career out of it."

"No we didn't know that, but that's good. That's very good," the lady said smiling. "We'll see how things go. I'm sure they could use you somewhere else at the center."

Alyssa completed the paperwork as best she could, and promised to finish the remainder that evening and drop it in the mail in the morning. She was required to take a urinalysis for drug use, and stopped by the collection center on her way home.

"Here I am starting work at a rehab center, and they're testing me for drug use," she laughed to herself. "How ironic! I guess we can't have instructors bringing in dope for the patients!"

Upon returning home, Daisy, Franken, Kaylee and her Grandparents were on hand to welcome her home with her favorite plain cheese pizza with sesame crust from Hungry Howie's. Daisy gave her big hugs smiling broadly and looking her up and down as if checking for marks. Franken hesitated when he first walked up and offered his hand, but Alyssa went by it surprising him with a big hug and kissing him on the cheek. He blushed, and smiled.

"If you love me so much you can make me a sandwich," he said joking as if he were Oskar Kokoshka from Hey Arnold.

242

Daisy laughed.

"How about a plain cheese pizza instead?" said Alyssa trying to sound like Mr. Hyunh.

"A sandwich would be better, but a pizza is okay yes!"

The impromptu family party commenced with paper plates and blue plastic cups. K-earth 101 was playing in the background from a high-fi console that Grandpa Jack drove back to Virginia to claim when his parents moved into assisted living. Grandpa Jack called it an antique, and Grandma Lin called it junk. The party went on as evening passed into night and Franken turned on the Dodger game because he had money riding on it. Just when it seemed that Kaylee was ready to leave, and Alyssa was ready to say good night, Dylan showed up.

Both Dylan and Alyssa were cautious at first, but they smiled and hugged.

"It's about time you two hooked back up," said Daisy. "You were practically raised together."

"Hello Alyssa," Dylan said calmly looking into her eyes.

"Hi Dylan" she replied. "I'll scold you later for blowing me off for two years, but right now I want you to meet Kaylee."

"Kaylee, Dylan, Dylan, Kaylee," she said pointing at each one respectively and smiling.

"Hi Dylan!" Kaylee replied. "I suggest we go over to my friend's house near Cal State L.A. so we can all get acquainted or reacquainted whatever the case may be. It's so hot, and they have air conditioning."

"Alyssa, are you up for it?" asked Dylan.

"Sure," said Alyssa shrugging her shoulders.

It was a short drive to Kaylee's friend's house that was halfway between Grandpa Jack's and Cal State L.A., and it turned out Alyssa knew her too from their exploits up the coast highway and hanging out at the student union.

They could hear music as they approached the house, and a shockwave of sound hit them when the door opened. Loud music

243

and many simultaneous conversations greeted them at the door. The smoke was a mixture of strange aromas, and Alyssa thought she could detect pot smoke mixed in with the smell of cigarettes and perfume. The door swung wide, and everyone cheered as Kaylee strutted into the room. Obviously things had changed while Alyssa had been away. Dylan shut the door as they entered to arrest the sound. It was much cooler inside than out. The air conditioning was on full blast.

The room was filled with mostly young women with a few guys sprinkled in. The guys looked glum and out of place. The young ladies were all talking excitedly, and the pace of the conversation increased as Kaylee stopped and greeted each one. There were ten people in the living room and another five in the kitchen all with drinks in their hand. Alyssa couldn't tell if they were drinking alcohol.

As they passed into the dining room, they could see a few people smoking a pot pipe with skeptical red eyes that seemed annoyed by their intrusion.

"Please don't mind the pot smoke," Kaylee said. "There are a few weed wackers in every crowd these days."

"I'm glad I took my drug test earlier today," said Alyssa. "I might fail after tonight just from breathing the air in the room."

"You can't fail by breathing the second-hand smoke," said Kaylee. "But why did you take a drug test?"

"I'm starting a new job next week at the Hillside-Zuma Recovery Center in Malibu. They're paying my tuition this semester, and they pay $18 an hour."

"That's great, but when are we going to have time to hang out?" asked Kaylee.

"We'll find time," Alyssa replied.

"What are you doing there?" asked Dylan.

"I'm teaching Tai Chi and meditation like I've always done! Just like the old days with Frenchy."

"Well you come by it very naturally; they couldn't do better!" said Dylan smiling.

"I missed you Dylan," said Alyssa looking at him lovingly.

Dylan looked nervous, and Kaylee lit a cigarette.

"You two are bringing me to tears," Kaylee said without facial expression. "So what are you doing Dylan?"

"I'm going to school at Cal State Northridge studying business. My parents just moved to Idaho. I didn't want to go with them, so I live at my Uncle's house in Van Nuys in the summer and in the dorms during the school year."

"Isn't it more of a commuter college?" Kaylee asked.

"It is, but there are some dorms too. I'm hoping to move off campus soon like everyone else."

"Were you two ever romantic?" asked Kaylee.

The question caught Dylan off guard, but Alyssa was accustomed to Kaylee's probing and took it in stride.

"We've always been romantic!" responded Alyssa taking Dylan in her arms around the waist. "We're childhood buddies. We love each other, and we always will. Right Dylan?"

"Oh….yes, of course, yes," said Dylan recovering and looking at Alyssa. "We're just two kids surviving in the hood!"

"Well you look like you belong together," Kaylee said as a matter of fact and walked away.

Dylan and Alyssa watched her walk away, looked back at each other, smiled, and started laughing.

"She's something else!" said Dylan.

"She uses shocking statements to test you. She likes to see raw emotional reaction. You passed. She's very bold. Don't be put off by her."

"She's also very beautiful in a dangerous sort of way. I'd be afraid to be close to her."

"Yes she plays off fear a little. With men she wants to see if they're brave enough to try for her. Very few are and that frustrates

245

her. The ones that do break through she doesn't like. She should lighten up but she likes the bad girl persona."

The conversation drifted off, and they moved into the living room to sit down. Kaylee was moving from one conversation to another, and dominating each as she purposefully mingled. Dylan watched in awe, and Alyssa remarked how much Kaylee had advanced socially since she had been gone. Alyssa may be a master in the spiritual realm, but Kaylee was a master in the social realm and well aware of it. She looked determined to use it to her advantage.

The next morning Alyssa awoke thinking about Kaylee and how she had changed. She was still the same old Kaylee, but she was older, wiser, and using her skill set to her advantage.

"That's what I want to do too," Alyssa thought to herself, "and that's the same conclusion I came to in Big Sur. I need to use my known talents to advance myself as best I can."

The other thing she thought about was how little Dylan had changed, and how their relationship just sort of picked up where it had left off without fanfare. It was the same old Dylan, and they just played quietly together as they had done for so many years.

"Whatever happened to Karen Vanhayden who helped you run the martial arts class for little kids," Alyssa asked Dylan the next time she saw him.

"She slowly took the whole thing over. She was very driven, and wanted it to herself. I was tired of it anyway, and not getting along with her, so she bought me out. She makes a lot of money now and really doesn't do any work besides watching over things, but I don't care. I wanted out. I was never really interested in teaching kids. I just wanted to be cool like Frenchy, but it didn't work for me."

"What about your romantic interests?"

"We dated," Dylan responded, "but the more I got to know her the less I liked her. I think I knew early on that it would never

246

work. We became romantic a few times, and she got rough. She hit me, slapped me, and talked dirty. She acted tough. It was weird."

"Well I'm very pleased you're done with her. I never could understand why, but she disliked me. She may have been jealous because of my teaching skills. She may have been jealous for other reasons, but I detected jealousy. Whenever I came around she bristled, and I could see her back arch like a hissing cat."

"How about the hair above her upper lip?" Dylan asked trying to be funny.

"That hair never stood up, but I did catch her bleaching it one day," Alyssa said pretending not to catch on.

They both looked at each other and started to laugh.

"She was jealous of you because of me," Dylan stated very boldly while straightening his posture. "She could never break the spell you had over me. That irritated her to no end. She wanted to be better than you, throw you out, and take me away. She failed on all counts."

"You may be right on that. I suspect that it bothered her that I left you alone to do as you pleased, yet your heart stayed with me. That may sound corny, but it may be true. Our friendship endured her."

The next few days drifted by slowly. It was hot, the streets appeared wavy with heat, and the passing cars whizzed by with their tires sticking to the hot pavement. There wasn't much going on in late summer. People seemed to walk around in circles. Alyssa was troubled with the thought of meeting her Dad; but finally, Labor Day weekend arrived, and the time slid by quickly. On Sunday morning she was very much on edge and wanted to cancel, but she remembered what Youki had suggested and resigned herself once more to go through with it. She dressed casually and waited in the living room. The minutes ticked by, and finally a cab pulled up. She remembered that he didn't drive. She watched him through the front window, but she stayed far enough away so that he couldn't easily see her. She could tell that he

247

sensed that he was being watched. Although she couldn't get a good look at him, she liked his walk. He held his head up high and took long strides. He was wearing white pants and a white sport jacket with a faded red shirt underneath with no tie. Although there was a doorbell, he knocked.

"Hello in there," he called peering through the screen.

Alyssa felt a pit growing in her stomach, but calmly walked over, opened the door and gestured for him to come through.

"You must be Alyssa. I'm Brad Stone," he said and held out his hand.

Alyssa shook his hand lightly and stared. He was very good looking as she suspected, but aged beyond his years and prematurely gray. His hair was all gray. There was no other color left anywhere. He was only 39 or 40, but he looked old. His attitude made up for his early aging. He seemed happy, energetic, and confident. He looked cunning.

"Are you going to invite me to sit down?" he said smiling.

"I'm sorry. Yes! Let's sit down. I had a vision of you that you just shattered, but all for the good I assure you."

"You're quite the beautiful young lady. I would expect as much. Your mother was very beautiful when we first met, and I bet she still is!"

"She's married," Alyssa blurted out.

"Yes, I know," Brad said grinning. "Your Grandpa told me when we met a few weeks ago."

Brad sat in Grandpa's chair, and Alyssa sat on the edge of Grandma's chair in anticipation.

"Why did you leave my Mom?" Alyssa started.

"The easy answer is that I didn't. She left me, and she was smart to do so. The more accurate answer is that I don't know if I left her or she left me. I was into myself and having a good time. All that really mattered was the next good party.

As you've probably heard, I was a slick talker, and could manipulate people into things. Because I could do this, I thought I was smarter than everyone else. I was young, egotistical, good looking, and in many ways stupid. Daisy and I fell in love, but I was too stupid to realize I was in love. I thought it was so great to have such a beautiful woman doting on me, but I just thought it came with the territory. It wasn't long before I just completely took her for granted."

"But why did you leave her?" Alyssa asked. "You've only really given me circumstances."

"Selfishness," Brad replied. "That's what it all comes down to, but again, I'm not sure if I actually had the courage and backbone to leave her. She may have left me. She probably left me, and I deserved it."

"Why did you deserve it?"

"I was a sociopathic drunk. I made a lot of money, and started getting into cocaine. When I started cocaine, my drinking increased. My drinking doubled or tripled when I was coked up. I looked at cocaine as a tool of the trade. When I was wired up on coke I could really deal, and the deal is what I loved. Money wasn't as important as making the deal. The deal was everything, and I was good at it. I was the best."

"Why did you stop?" Alyssa asked.

"I didn't really stop. I crashed. I had a complete physical breakdown."

"When?"

"Well, actually, that came later."

"When you came, I was no longer the center of attention in your Mom's life. That bothered me. More than that, she was concerned for your safety."

"Did you want me?"

"Yes, I wanted you. It's very important to me that you know that. I was very happy when you came, but I was still a child myself. Everything came easy to me. I had never really worked a day in my life. Selling wasn't work. Selling was fun. I loved it. When you came I didn't really know how to react. When you came, I looked in the mirror and saw a slime ball staring back at me. I didn't really know how to clean up, so I didn't. I just got worse until your Mom left for your safety, but I think it was your Grandpa that finally put an end to it."

"What happened then?"

"It scared me enough to clean up for a while. I managed my drinking, and lived a normal life. I met someone else, and we got married in 1992."

"Did you love her?" Alyssa asked.

"I loved the idea of her. I think I still loved Daisy, but I was so self-centered it didn't matter who I was with, but I don't really know. I may have loved her, but now, when I think back to the hate in her eyes, I wonder if there was ever love there at all."

"Is that when you had my sister?"

"Yes, when your sister came I panicked again. My drinking got worse and I started back into cocaine whenever I could afford some. I thought people wouldn't notice, but everyone noticed."

"So you got divorced?"

"Well yes, eventually. My wife hung on hoping I would change, but my drinking got worse, and eventually, she couldn't take it anymore either. She left me, and moved home thinking it would shock me into reform, but I really just pulled out the stops. I spiraled out of control. She served me divorce papers and I never responded, so it went into default."

"Did you ever think about getting help?"

"No, I didn't want any help. In my mind I was fine and everyone else was stupid."

"What made you finally turn around?"

"I lost my job. Then I lost my home. I started living on the streets."

"Then you finally got help?" Alyssa asked.

"No, not really. One day a woman who liked me had pity on me and let me move into her house. I had no money for booze so I actually sobered up for a while. She fed me, and I started getting

250

healthy. One night we went to a big party in Thousand Oaks. I lost track of her, and found the booze. She got pissed that I was drinking and left me there."

"What did you do then?"

"I blacked out. That's what I did. I blacked out and woke up on the floor of an apartment a few days later in Oxnard."

"Oxnard! How did you get to Oxnard?"

"To this day I don't know. I didn't know where I was or what I had done. I knew I had blacked out for at least a full day, but didn't know how many days. I had already lost everything. I was homeless and without any money. Red-eyed, bloated, and unkempt, I looked every bit of the mess I was. I had pissed off, screwed over, or stolen from every friend I had. Everyone had given up on me. I had abandoned two children. I deserved to die, and I wanted to die. I wanted to just crawl into a hole and lay there until I died. Thoughts of death became comforting, but I was too much of a coward. Death was too good for me, and the thought crushed me. I was utterly alone in the world, and too much of a wimp to end it all. Since death wasn't an option, the only alternative was to clean up. I went to a shelter in Oxnard where they let me lie down. When I started to detox, I had tremors, fits, mild hallucinations, and sweats. The people that ran the place knew what I was going through and isolated me. They let the process run its course, kept an eye on me, and offered me broth and soda crackers. They had seen it so many times before that their faces had absolutely no pity, amusement, or anger. Their only emotion was somber concern. Some of them had been through it themselves, and felt that it was their opportunity to give back. The sweats went away after a few days, and the tremors slowly dissipated with time. After I started to feel better the cravings set in. All I could think about was getting a drink, and since I had been sober for four days, I was "okay" in my own mind.

This time there was a change in me, and when I got a craving, I would substitute food for drink. Eating helped to both ease the cravings and assist my recovery. I was under weight from living on alcohol, and needed the food.

After a week went by I was well enough to work. Some people from the shelter went to Home Depot, and stood in the parking lot hoping for drive-by work. They offered to take me along. At first, no one would give me a chance, but one day, a man came by in a big truck and took all of us. We picked up the trash at a construction site, and did some preliminary work to prepare for landscaping. It was tough work, and I was still in bad shape physically, but I worked as hard as I possibly could. The boss seemed to understand what I was doing, and let me stay on. I became a regular, and as my health improved, so did my work.

I had no place to stay, so I slept on the job. It was illegal to stay on the job site, but no one said anything. As time passed, I learned everything I could about residential construction, and started to break out on my own. I learned from a coworker about assuming loans without the bank's knowledge. I took over several properties. I did the minimum remodeling required to convert the properties to rentals. Once I converted one, I would start searching for another. Life became endless days of working, dealing with tenants, and paying bills. I remained vulnerable to alcohol, so I didn't mind not having a life. I was afraid to be at a party or around anyone that drank. I wasn't sure that I could resist the temptation. Work became my life, and the only activity that felt safe.

I moved into a granny flat in an old woman's backyard, and life became much more tolerable. Now I had serious responsibilities of paying bills, collecting rents, doing maintenance work. Cash flow was a huge issue. My inflows barely covered my outflows, but I was doing most of the work myself. I managed to feed myself and pay my own rent. For the first time in years I had some stability, a warm place to sleep, and food to eat most nights."

"My Grandpa told me you don't drive. How did you get around?" Alyssa asked.

252

"I would hire people to work part time. They were mostly young kids that were interested in what I was doing and wanted to do it themselves. A few of them tried, but there was a big difference. I had had everything, lost it all, and was trying to survive and start over. I was hungry and determined. They wanted a get rich quick scheme."

"But why didn't you drive?"

"I had destroyed my driving record, and I couldn't afford the insurance. It was either drive or eat and I chose to eat. I needed to eat in order to stay off the booze."

"So how many properties did you accumulate?" Alyssa asked enthralled with the conversation.

"All told eleven properties. I ended up selling two properties early on for a substantial profit. At the time I thought I was a failure, but the cash I made on those properties kept the others afloat through major repairs and a few evictions. It also gave me enough of a slush fund to afford to spend on myself."

"How many properties do you have now?" Alyssa asked.

"I own one property. The one I live in. I have a three bedroom condo in Agoura. It's on Carell Ave near the intersection of Kanan Road and Thousand Oaks Boulevard."

"What happened to the other eight properties?"

"I sold them," Brad replied. "I witnessed the boom in the real estate market. I couldn't believe my eyes. Prices were skyrocketing through the roof. What's more is that I found it difficult to believe I owned nine properties during a boom. Although I didn't know it, my timing was perfect. When I started in 1995, no one wanted to get into real estate as an investment. I struggled with what I thought were dogs for eight years, but then the boom came. There was an overnight transition in attitude, and everyone started buying. In 2004 and 2005 there was frenzied buying. If you had a pulse you qualified for a loan. People were flipping houses or refinancing thousands of dollars out of their property within months of closing. These people were amateurs making big

253

money. It was pure insanity, and I knew that the free-for-all couldn't go on forever.

"What memory I had left from my days in sales told me that when amateurs start getting in the game that it's time to get out. After I sold, I thought I could do some consulting while it lasted. I started selling in 2005 and just finished this year. When I file my taxes for 2006, I'll pay all my capital gains tax, and I'll be free and clear. I've already paid off my condo and have enough money left in the bank to live off the interest. I could retire today but I don't want to. I have something left to do. I've set aside enough money to get started in a new venture once I figure out what that is."

"Amazing," said Alyssa. "So you're basically set for life. You went from the gutter to wealth in a matter of years."

"Those were some long years in the beginning. I struggled everyday. My only claim to success is sobriety. I'm alcohol and drug free. The rest of it was just luck if luck is what you call it."

"Well then what do you call it?" Alyssa asked.

"I don't know. I just don't believe in luck. Things happen for a reason, and I think I was meant to do something with my fortunate circumstances. It's time for me to pay back for my wrongs of the past. I don't think it was coincidence that you contacted me right when I'm ready."

"That's so weird," said Alyssa. "I don't believe in luck either. Perhaps that belief runs in the bloodlines."

"Perhaps it does."

"What do you want to do?" Alyssa asked.

"I want to start by apologizing to you. I've already talked to your Mom and Grandparents. I'm sorry for what I've done, and I want to make up for it although I know that I can never make up for it completely."

"Apology accepted. I'm very pleased to finally meet you. Just your story alone was worth the effort. That's some story! It's not rags to riches, its gutter to greatness. Did you know that I'm planning to go into drug and alcohol rehabilitation?"

254

"Yes, your Grandfather told me. I don't think that's a coincidence either."

"Well, where do we go from here?"

"I would suggest . . . well actually your Grandfather suggested a trial basis. We could start by trying to get together once a week for a meal."

"I'm very busy. I go to school full time, and I work weekends at the Hillside-Zuma Recovery Center."

"We can do the best we can. If you're too busy we can skip a week or two. I'm hoping later that Jack and Lin will accept me more, and I can join into normal family gatherings."

"Speaking of family, have you seen my half sister?"

"I saw her when she was a baby, but I haven't seen her since. Her mother won't speak to me."

"If things go well between you and me, then I'll talk to her."

"That would be great," Brad replied.

"There's just one more thing," Alyssa said. "I've thought about this for a long time. I would like to refer to you as Dad. You may not deserve it right now, but I think it's the least awkward way to go. If it works out, then it will be for the best. My Grandpa Jack is really my Dad, but I don't address him as Dad. So I'll give you that name and explain it to him that you're going to work toward deserving it. That way we'll get the name right from the start."

"I think that's generous of you, I would have asked that you just call me Brad, but what's most comfortable we'll use. I like it that your thinking long term because so am I."

"Good," said Alyssa, "this went well, and I'll see you next Sunday for dinner when I get off work."

"See you then," said her Dad.

Chapter 33

Afterwards, Alyssa was happy about her meeting with her Dad. There was anxiety relief. She was sure of that because she had been so nervous about meeting him her palms were sweating. She knew the relief was at least partially responsible for her upbeat mood, but there was something more to it. There was a reason they were put together. Her intuition was strong. He had an important role to play in her life. It just came later than everyone thought. She suspected that money had something to do with his role in her life, but the money wouldn't play the role that was obvious. They would collaborate on something that was bigger than both of them. She just didn't know what that was yet.

Regardless of her conclusions, she slept fitfully for several nights. She reasoned that she was subconsciously unsettled over her Dad, but it wasn't just that. Her vivid dreams returned. She was reminded of her childhood, and dreamed of changing sheets in some large room full of beds. She had dreams of being in Hawaii with a following of people. She dreamed of living in a fishing village in Alaska. She woke up in a sweat more than once; and in an effort to figure out what was going on, she started taking notes as soon as she awoke. There were no recurring themes. The only theme she could find in her notes was to finish school early. It was the same message she received in high school. She felt that she was needed for a larger assignment, but she needed her schooling first, and had to finish as soon as possible.

She signed up for another 20 unit workload for her first semester. She knew it would be tough, but she didn't need perfect grades. She needed a diploma, and at the rate she was going, she could easily finish up midway through her senior year.

Another meeting she had been postponing was to get reacquainted with Finhead. He had been very persistent in calling her, but with her introductory week at her new job, she hadn't had time. Finally she agreed to meet him at the Denny's on Lincoln Boulevard in Santa Monica for old time's sake. Grandpa Jack was right. He was clean-cut wearing a sport jacket and tie. He looked somewhat boring and uptight like someone who had been told what to do. He wore glasses now, looked to be too busy, and rather put out by having to make this rendezvous. She marveled at the change in him as he approached. She stood when he got to her booth, and like Franken, looked confused about whether to handshake or hug. Alyssa went for the hug straight away, and Finhead looked pleased and satisfied as she squeezed him tightly.

"I know what you're thinking, and it's true," Finhead started. "I look uptight and straight. I didn't sell out I assure you. I work for my Dad's company now. After two years in community college, I got accepted to UCLA to study business accounting. I'm working for my Dad while I prepare for my certification exams."

"That's fantastic! I'm so happy for you! My Grandpa told me a little about you," Alyssa mused. "I must say I'm not surprised. I always thought you were meant for something great. Certified what anyway? Certified nut?"

"Ha Ha very funny. I take the exam to become a Certified Public Accountant in January. I fully expect to pass, and then I'm freeing myself up for you."

"We're not compatible," Alyssa blurted. "We'll always be just friends!"

"I know that," Finhead stated with mild frustration. "I don't want to date you. I want to work with you."

"On what?"

"I don't know. That's for you to figure out," Finhead said while glancing around the room.

"Oh Finhead," Alyssa said with a sigh, "we don't have to work together. We said some things when we were younger. Things can change."

"Yes things can change but we're going to work together," he stated firmly and flatly looking her in the eye. "By the way, I would appreciate it if you don't call me Finhead anymore. That's too juvenile. I go by my last name now. Just call me Finn. It's one syllable and much easier."

They both fell silent but Finn stayed intent on her without wavering. At first she wanted to laugh, but she could tell he was dead serious, and didn't want to insult him. She studied his eyes a moment longer before finally speaking.

"Okay Finn, you take your CPA exam. If you pass the first time, then we'll work together, but if you don't pass, you sign up to take the exam again at first opportunity. Deal?"

"Deal," said Finn with satisfaction.

After her meeting with Finn, the weeks went by slowly while Alyssa immersed herself into her studies. She didn't get out much, and that seemed to make the days float by even slower. She knew that she could only take it for so long, so she worked hard to get ahead. She had completed most of the homework assignments listed on the syllabus, and she was already prepared for mid-terms.

As she anticipated, work did interfere with school. She had no time on the weekends to study, and when she got home she was too exhausted to go out. It made for a lonely existence, but on the bright side, she wasn't spending money on tuition, and her personal bank account was growing again.

She liked her job at the recovery center, but was forced to follow their instructor's manual, and wasn't allowed to deviate from the lesson plan. She was to avoid interacting too much with the patients; and when she did, she was only to discuss martial arts or meditation. Any psychological discussion was referred to the medical staff. For Alyssa, that took a lot of the fun out of work. She considered herself a healer and a shaman in training, and longed to talk to the patients to see what their deep-rooted problems were. She speculated from a distance what would help most, and planted bugs in the ears of people who could do things.

258

She was sure her methods would work, but there was never any feedback.

On a Thursday in mid-October she received a phone call from Kaylee while she was still on campus.

"Wassup? Hey, we haven't seen you in over a month," Kaylee stated nonchalantly. "We want you to come out to Gladstone's for the happy hour crowd. All of our pals are going this time, so you'll get to catch up with everyone. Are you down?"

"Pencil me in. I should easily finish here by four. I'll head over then."

"Why don't you meet me at your Grandpa's just after four? I'll drive."

"Okay, that works great. I'll see you at my house about four."

"Peace out!"

Alyssa's classes were over for the day, so for the first time in weeks, she left campus early, and finished her studies at home. It was unusual that both Dylan and Finn called her that same afternoon, and agreed to meet at Gladstone's.

When they arrived they were out of luck. Their normal place outside was taken. There was a medical work party wearing their green outfits and dancing around with drinks in hand. They looked like they had been there a long time. Kaylee's group went into the restaurant because they were too young for the bar. They took up three tables ordering sodas energy drinks and appetizers, but it was okay because the restaurant was nearly empty. The bar was packed.

For Alyssa, Dylan was wonderful as always. He sat next to her keeping her company through the loud and rowdy antics of Kaylee's female friends. Alyssa wasn't really a part of the regular crowd anymore, and she couldn't always relate to the campus gossip. Finn showed up for a while, but looked very uncomfortable in his sport jacket and tie. He was about to leave, but Alyssa asked him to stay.

259

"I'm curious about that guy at the bar. His look is interesting and mischievous. He has a sly smile and a twinkle in his eye. Needless to say he's also rather good looking, and he's been looking over this way," Alyssa said to Finn.

"Well of course he has! You're a table full of young beautiful college girls. Even if he was gay he couldn't ignore all this beauty," Finn responded.

Alyssa looked around and realized they were a spectacle. She smiled wryly and looked back at Finn.

"I'd like to talk to him," said Alyssa. "You're 21. You can go in there and tell him something for me."

"I'm not feeling the good vibe," Finn replied.

"What would that be," said Alyssa looking bored.

"He's interested in what all men are interested in. He wants either you or Kaylee because he senses you're the leaders. He's been checking you both out. I'll take care of him."

Finn stood and walked into the bar without further conversation. The music was loud. He leaned over and spoke into the guy's ear. Finn sat down, and the young man immediately stood and walked over to their table. He passed by Kaylee and went straight to Alyssa.

"Is there something you want to say to me?" he asked leaning over.

"Yes," Alyssa said. "What do you want?"

He looked back at her for a moment without replying.

"I would like to know why you have that mysterious look about you? It's mesmerizing," he finally replied.

"I've always had it. When I was a child it scared people. I've learned to control it. I'm sorry if it's bothering you."

"On the contrary, I love it! I can't even begin to describe it. It's very deep. It's a look of all knowing combined innocence. It's crazy in a way, and almost contradictory. It's very alluring."

"It's sort of a Yin Yang look?" Alyssa asked.

"What's a Yin Yang?" he replied.

260

"Never mind! What's your name?"

"Trevor, Trevor Granderson."

"Pleased to meet you Trevor," Alyssa said holding out her hand. "My name is Alyssa Daingerfield."

By now everyone at both tables was observing the pair. Trevor took Alyssa's hand, but instead of shaking, he kissed it. With anyone else the gesture would have been over the top, but his movements were fluid and second nature. He acted without thinking. It was artistic. She accepted his gesture with a slight blush, a gentle smile, and a profound connection with the eyes as she moved her line of sight to his face from their hands. Time stood still for a short moment. Everyone nearby was watching. A clink of glasses broke the spell and all returned to their conversations. Finn remained spellbound, and after Dylan realized what happened, he looked annoyed and agitated.

"What do you do?" asked Trevor.

"I'm a healer of souls," Alyssa said surprised by the words coming out of her mouth.

Both Trevor and Dylan stared at her for a few seconds. Finn walked back over and stood near by. The look on Trevor's face revealed that he couldn't muster a witty comeback. Alyssa was dead serious, and she looked at him point blank without revealing her emotions.

"Very good!" he said unsure of his words. "Where do you work?"

Alyssa's expression changed. She looked at Finn and back at Trevor.

"I work at the Hillside-Zuma Recovery Center in Malibu, but soon I'll be working with him."

She nodded in Finn's direction and looked back at Trevor. Again, she couldn't believe what she just said. Finn smiled broadly from ear to ear as if to say I told you so.

"What do you do?" Dylan asked of Trevor as if already part of the conversation.

Trevor looked over at Dylan and immediately evaluated him as he sat.

"I work for ServicePro," Trevor replied as if speaking to all. "They do fire and water damage restoration in your home or business. I work in the corporate offices. I don't do the work myself."

"Do you go to school?" Alyssa asked.

"Yes, I'm studying business at Pepperdine."

"That's great!" Alyssa said with interest. "I'm studying rehabilitation counseling at Cal State LA. John Finn here is a recent UCLA graduate in business accounting. He's taking his CPA exam in January."

Finn shook Trevor's hand.

"John Finn pleased to meet you," he said.

"That's great!" Trevor said. "Good accountants are hard to come by."

"Well I'm not there yet, but I'm working on it," Finn replied. "I'm going to head out Alyssa. I'll talk to you soon."

"Wait!" Alyssa replied.

She ran over to Finn and whispered in his ear.

"What did you say to him in the bar?" Alyssa asked.

Finn whispered back in Alyssa's ear.

"I said those two hot girls over there think you're checking them out. They want to talk to you. Simple and direct."

"See you Finn."

She gave him a hug about the shoulders. Finn waved bye to the rest of the group and made a quick exit.

"Do you guys meet here a lot as a group?" Trevor asked.

"We try to meet once a week. It's centrally located for us, and we like the action here at the corner of PCH and Sunset. We usually sit outside on the picnic tables by the short wood fence. Most of us are under age, so we can't legally sit in the bar," said Alyssa.

"I'm not of age either," said Trevor.

"But you were in the bar," Dylan interjected as an aside.

"I have a fake ID," said Trevor. "I'm 20, but I'll be 21 soon! I need to have access to bars and taverns to cut deals for my company," he explained defensively.

Dylan smiled as if he found the chink in the armor. Alyssa looked at Trevor without expression as if reappraising him.

"It's harmless," said Trevor. "I'm just trying to open some doors for myself."

"As long as you have a handle on it," said Dylan. "Just don't get caught."

"I'm not sure there is such a thing as having a handle on it," said Alyssa. "I've only worked rehab a few years, but I've seen some pretty awful cases. They all started out thinking they had a handle on it, and they held that thought until they woke up one day with their lives destroyed, homeless, and destitute."

"That won't happen to me," Trevor said smiling. "I only drink socially for business reasons."

"Some people control it for many years. It creeps up on you. It slowly slips into your life year after year secretly taking hold in the background. Then, after 20 years or so, it's dominating your life to the exclusion of everything else. Other people are hopelessly addicted after one drink. To some people it's like heroin."

"Have you seen heroin usage in your work?" Trevor asked.

"Yes, it's more prevalent than you might think. It's an affliction of the wealthy and the poor. The wealthy can afford it and keep it in the closet longer. The poor have nothing to lose and hustle it on the street. They'll do anything to get it."

"Sounds like interesting work and very rewarding if you can save lives," said Trevor.

"It can be depressing, but you're right, it's very rewarding to help people and watch them recover before your eyes. I feel very fortunate that I've already found what I want to do."

"How about you Dylan," Trevor asked. "What do you do?"

"I'm a full time student at Cal State Northridge studying business marketing. I'm not working right now. Unlike Alyssa, I haven't figured out what I should do with my life."

"You will!" said Trevor. "Have confidence. You'll fit right in somewhere."

"I hope so," Dylan replied looking at Alyssa.

"I'd like to take you out to dinner," said Trevor looking at Alyssa and relegating Dylan to the background.

"I've been waiting for you to ask!" Alyssa replied. "Weekends are better after work."

"How about Saturday? I'll pick you up at 7 PM."

"That sounds good!" said Alyssa. "Here's my Grandparents' address. Pick me up there, and be prepared for a grilling from my Grandpa on your intentions. He's very old-fashioned, and he'll want to talk to you before we go."

"All the better," said Trevor, "He should be confident that his granddaughter's safety is assured. If I was him I would do the same. I could meet him in advance if you'd like."

"No need," Alyssa said. "I'm young but he trusts my judgment."

"Okay then, I'll see you Saturday. I'm going to head home."

"See you Saturday!"

Alyssa thought Kaylee wouldn't approve of her date with Trevor. After all, Trevor was glancing at Kaylee as much as he was at her. He may have been interested in Kaylee too, but she was wrong. As Trevor walked away, Alyssa glanced over at Kaylee expecting a negative expression, but she was smiling, and had a look of anticipation on her face. She wanted the scoop that she couldn't hear sitting at the other end of the table.

She found a negative expression end up where she didn't expect one. Dylan had a sour look that he was trying to conceal. He obviously disapproved, and that made Alyssa wonder if he was interested in her as more than a friend. From her perspective, they were back to where they were before, but his perspective could be different, and she wondered what motivated him to come back. Did he want her? His presence was comforting, and very welcome. Alyssa was glad he was back, yet she wondered if she had been underestimating his intentions.

Chapter 34

Trevor arrived ten minutes early on Saturday. Alyssa wanted to answer the door, but Grandpa Jack asked her to wait in the kitchen with Grandma Lin.

"Let me answer and I'll call for you," Grandpa said. "You walk in first and Grandma will follow. We'll all sit down just for a minute while I ask a few questions. I know it sounds silly, but please honor my wishes. It's unlikely that you'll ever have to endure it again."

"Okay, Okay, answer the door Grandpa!" Alyssa said darting into the kitchen.

"Hello, my name is Trevor Granderson and I'm here to pick up Alyssa for a date."

"She mentioned you were coming. Come on in. My name is Jack Daingerfield. I'm her Grandfather."

"Yes, she's said a lot of good things about you. She says you're old-fashioned."

"She's more old-fashioned than I am," said Grandpa Jack chuckling. "Alyssa!" He called loudly, "your date is here."

Alyssa and Grandma Lin came walking in as planned. They each shook hands with Trevor. Alyssa was more taken by him than she was when they first met and it showed. He was dressed in a brown sport jacket and tie, and she was in a beige dress that Daisy had bought her and she had never worn. They simultaneously noticed that they were color coordinated, and laughed. They couldn't keep their eyes off each other. There was a feeling of excited awkwardness and anticipation in the room.

"Let's sit down just for a minute if you don't mind," said Grandpa Jack.

"I don't mind sir."

"Please call me Jack. Alyssa says that you're studying business at Pepperdine. What made you decide to go to a Christian school?"

Alyssa raised one eye brow upon hearing her Grandpa's question.

"I know that it is a Christian school started by George Pepperdine, but I must be honest, I'm not very religious. I went there because they have a unique Business school that focuses on managing the business as an enterprise. Basically, you learn how to be a CEO, and although you can't start at the top, at least you're prepared given the opportunity."

"I was just wondering if you really went to Pepperdine," said Grandpa Jack smiling. "It was a loaded question. What would you use a degree like that for?"

"I have a dream of targeting medium-sized businesses poised for rapid growth, and identifying them to investors. They can buy controlling interest, and I can make them wealthy by growing the medium business into a large enterprise. You can make a lot of money by taking their stock public."

"Sounds ambitious."

"It is ambitious, and it's fun," said Trevor smiling.

"Where are you headed tonight?" Grandpa asked.

"I thought we'd go down to Santa Monica to a fish restaurant I like. We'll be home at a decent hour."

"Take your time," said Grandpa Jack. "I have complete faith in my Granddaughter. She's been studying martial arts most of her life. She could probably take you!"

"Grandpa!" said Alyssa. "We're going out to dinner not to a kick-boxing tournament!"

266

Trevor and Grandma Lin were laughing. Grandpa Jack was grinning, but the grin faded.

"Okay kids," he said. "Go out and have fun while we doze in front of the TV."

"Have a good night!" said Trevor.

Alyssa thought he would take her to Big Dean's Oceanfront Café near the foot of the Santa Monica pier. Big Dean's had the younger crowd, and it was fun to watch the hustle and bustle of the Santa Monica beachfront through the window while eating. Trevor turned away from the pier parking lot and headed up Kinney Street.

"You probably thought I was taking you to Big Dean's," he said as if reading her mind. "We're headed to Enterprise Fish Restaurant. It's elegant and much more romantic."

"I like a man that knows how to take charge, and is not intimidated by a powerful woman."

"What makes you so powerful?"

"I can feel things inside. Some people call it gut feel. Call it what you will, but I can tell the difference between gut feel and simple desire. That makes me powerful."

"You're unbelievable," said Trevor. "The look in your eye and your various facial expressions just knock me out. You have the body of a young adult but the mind of wise old wizard."

"Is that a compliment?"

"Yes! You're amazing."

"From my perspective you have a similar look about you. You have a twinkle in your eye, but the twinkle is much more mischievous than Santa's. You know that you're good looking."

"Looks will last you for a couple years," Trevor said, "but it's what's behind the looks that will last much longer. Women will delight in a balding pudgy man if he's smart, exciting and has a sense of humor."

"Yes, but we don't look for them do we?"

Trevor laughed at the observation phrased as a question as they arrived at Enterprise Fish. It was quaint and lovely. Each table was illuminated by candlelight. The regular lighting was low level so that the many candles made a difference. Almost every table had its own enclave, but there were some larger tables in the center of the restaurant. The hostess acted as though she had known Trevor for many years.

"Mr. Granderson, we have your table waiting. It's the finest seat in the house for a couple."

"Thank you so much," they both replied at the same time as they sat down.

They both laughed about it as they accepted their menus. The hostess smiled. There was electricity in the air as they perused the menus, and there were occasional glances accompanied by smiles if the other noticed.

"Are you going to order a drink?" Trevor asked.

"No, I'm not interested."

"You're not 21 or you're not interested."

"Not interested, you know I'm 18. I'll be 19 in April.

"Do you mind if I have one."

"As long as you can drive home I'm okay with it."

Trevor ordered the Whitefish, and Alyssa the Halibut, and as they ate their meals, they were both caught up in the magic of the moment. There were periods of silence during their evening while they stared approvingly at each other through the candlelight. They were very compatible and strongly attracted to each other. When they realized they were finishing each other's sentences the evening was over, and the waiter brought them the receipt.

"I didn't see him bring the check," said Alyssa.

"I arranged to pay the bill before we sat down so that they would never bring it to the table."

"How thoughtful that was! Very classy."

"Only the best for you," Trevor said in a deep masculine voice as they stood. "We should come for the $29.99 Lobster Special on Monday nights. They have live lobsters."

When they approached Trevor's Acura TL, he opened the door for her, but instead of allowing her to climb in; he took her in his arms. Once she realized what he was doing she gladly accepted, melted into him, and absorbed the feeling as his arms tightened around her. She felt loved in a whole new way. She had sanctuary. She was safe in the world and yet free to leave his magical arms to go out exploring if she wanted to. While she leaned her face up against his chest, she thought briefly about how bold he was, how he took charge, and assumed control. She enjoyed the ride.

She drew her head back enough to look at him, and without thought, he smoothly moved his lips close to hers but paused before they touched. It seemed like sparks flew as the energy passed between them. He held purposely in the anticipation, then he gently touched her lips with his. They surrendered to each other and pressed closer. It was inviting, warm, and comforting. He was very graceful. It came naturally to him. They became passionate, and began to caress each other, but the sounds of the street bled through their moment. They realized where they were, and stopped. She smiled at him as she got in the car.

"That was wonderful," Alyssa said, "and very intense! I'm stunned. Give me a second to recover. I didn't expect that until the end of the night."

"It could have been the end, but since it was so fantastic, we'll continue on for a while longer. We'll do something straight out of a conventional love story and ride the carousel on the Santa Monica Pier."

"I was hoping we could walk out on the Pier. It's an old hangout of mine and I haven't been there in awhile."

Trevor pulled into $5 an hour or $20 a day parking lot near the end of the Pier. Alyssa watched him pay the fee, and thought about old times with her beach cruiser bicycle peddling up and down Venice Beach. Five dollars would have been a lot of money for her then. Now she was arriving in an expensive car and spending $5 just on parking.

There was no moon, but it looked like it was about to rise due to the brightening in the east. Despite all the city lights and the moon, a few stars managed to peak through the sky and the damp salty air of the ocean hit their noses as they joined hands for their walk.

Thinking of Youki, Alyssa noticed the little things. It was after 10 PM, but there was an eight year old on a bicycle who appeared to be alone. He was freely peddling anywhere he wanted. There was a scruffy looking dog that acted homeless but had a collar and tags. He was visiting the various trash containers on the beach. As they climbed the stairs to the Pier, Alyssa noticed a helium balloon escape someone and sail inland riding on the onshore breeze. Trevor and Alyssa looked at each other often and smiled, but seldom spoke.

As they got to the deck of the Pier and started their walk, Alyssa noticed hundreds of soap bubbles in the air. Her excitement grew as she reminisced about the first time she saw a bubble generating machine. It wasn't the same machine, but it was in the same place clamped to the railing of the Pier.

"Let's go by the source of the bubbles, and kiss me there," Alyssa said with excitement.

Trevor looked at her as if taken by surprise, "Sure let's go."

They kissed with the bubbles flowing around them as if putting on an act for all passers by. It was a touching sight, obviously heartfelt and authentic. A few people snapped pictures holding their cameras away from their body and watching the display as they clicked.

They laughed together holding hands as they continued on to the next thing. The carousel was almost empty, but in use when they arrived. They had to wait, and were giddy with the excitement of discovering each other as they did so. The operator detected what was happening.

"You two get a solo ride!" said the operator. You signal me when you want to stop. Walk around if you like."

They sat at first as the carousel began to turn glancing at each other with infatuation. After a few minutes the act continued as if she was Julie Andrews and he was Dick Van Dyke in Mary Poppins. They danced around, smooched, laughed, and made spectacles of themselves. After a few minutes they signaled the operator. He stopped the ride, and they exited laughing and breathing hard. Trevor slipped the man a tip and thanked him as they passed.

"You're such a smooth operator," Alyssa said. "How did you learn it?"

"I'm very observant," Trevor replied. "I use what works."

At that point they both knew that the evening was over, and they walked back to the car smiling and holding hands. They were quiet during the ride home occasionally glancing at one another to decipher what the other was thinking. They both knew what had just transpired, and they communicated without speaking. They were at the start of a relationship. They had found each other, and it was very exciting.

They kissed once more in front of Grandpa Jack's, and it was every bit as good as the first kiss. They went on for minutes. Alyssa didn't want to stop.

"I better go in," said Alyssa.

"Yes, I will call you tomorrow."

"Bye!"

"Until then, Bye!"

Trevor watched as Alyssa excitedly hustled inside.

Chapter 35

Being out to 11:30 PM wasn't routine for Alyssa since she had taken the job at Zuma-Hillside Recovery Center. Since she had accepted the job, it had been school all week and work all weekend for six straight weeks. This day was no exception. It was Sunday morning. She rolled out of bed at 8 AM to leave the house at 9 AM, and be at work by 10 AM. One good thing about Sunday morning was that she taught meditation in the morning and Tai Chi in the afternoon. Teaching meditation wasn't strenuous, and she could build up her energy for the Tai Chi later in the day.

This morning was different. She woke thinking about Trevor. The previous night replayed in her head over and over. All she could think about was the first kiss in front of the restaurant. She wanted to be with him right then. The wait was pure frustration, and she thought she was going to die. As much as she tried to focus on something else, her mind would drift back to him. She found herself daydreaming and staring at walls. She was almost late to work, and was often preoccupied while engaged in teaching. Her students noticed too. She was upset with herself. This was something she loved. It was important to her, but she just couldn't focus. It wasn't impossible to clear her mind of thought when every thought was about Trevor. She ran to her cell phone between sessions to see if he called, but there was nothing. Lunchtime came, and there were still no messages.

The afternoon sessions were much better. Physical movement kept her mind off him, and it felt good to move around and sweat, but when she finished there was no message on her phone. She got a pit in her stomach.

"Why am I like this?" she asked herself frowning, "We've only had one date!"

She turned off her phone and drove home with the music in the car on loud. She could finally let it go, and she had a peaceful ride, but when she walked in the house, it started again.

"How was your date?" asked Grandma Lin.

"Oh-humph!" Alyssa said in a sigh.

"That bad?"

"No, I couldn't stop thinking about him all day."

"Oh, that good!" Grandma Lin said smiling. "What did you do?"

Grandpa Jack walked in the room and sat down.

"We went to this cute little seafood restaurant that I'd never heard of. We ate by candlelight. It was very romantic. Then we walked out on the Pier and rode on the carousel. It sounds silly, but it was fun and dreamy. At the end of the night when he kissed me I thought I was going to melt. I didn't want it to end! He hasn't called!"

"He can't call dear," said Grandma. "Normal dating standards dictate that he can't call for a while or he'll look too eager. He's dying to call I guarantee it. He'll call sometime tonight."

"He'd better!"

"You don't want to be too eager either," Grandpa Jack added. "That's the way it works. It can't be avoided."

"I hate this," Alyssa responded pounding on her thighs with her fists. "Wait, no . . . oh, I don't know what I hate."

"It's hard at first dear," said Grandma. "It's almost painful, but you'll learn to handle it."

"Why do people do this?" Alyssa asked.

"Because we're all crazy," Grandpa Jack quickly replied. "There's no other explanation. Just take things one hour at a time. If that doesn't work, take things one minute at a time, but have faith. He'll call. You'll be together again soon."

"I hope so," Alyssa said dropping her head. "I'm going to go take a shower."

273

"Okay dear," Grandma Lin said, "just remember we love you and we're here for you."

After her shower there was still no call. Alyssa was concerned because she had class in the morning, she needed to study, and she couldn't concentrate. She phoned her Mom who already knew about her date. Daisy gave her the same advice as her Grandparents: work through it, take it easy, and don't be too eager. She agreed with Grandpa that he would phone soon. Hours clicked by yet she managed to study and prepare herself for school, and just as she was getting ready for bed, her cell phone rang.

"Hi, this is Trevor."

"Hi."

"I really enjoyed our time together last night. It really was great! I wanted to ask you if you would want to walk around in the museum at the La Brea Tar Pits. We could go during the day, and it's near your school. We both finish class early on Tuesday, could you meet me there at about 1 PM?"

Alyssa paused not knowing how to react. She wanted to see him tonight, but she thought about what her Mom and her Grandparents had said. Finally she considered how her mind had been on him all day and spoke.

"I'd love to meet you there, but I need to be home by about five. I have a lot of studying to do for class. I have a big paper due."

It had taken everything Alyssa had to keep from gushing all over him through the phone.

"Oh sure we can leave any time we want. In fact, for me it would be better to try and beat traffic. I just really want to see you. I've been thinking about you all day. The only time I could think of that would work was Tuesday, and the museum is about halfway between us. I know you're busy with school, but we could sneak this in."

"I'm glad you said that. I've been thinking about you all day too. I can't wait for Tuesday."

"That's a relief," said Trevor. "I might as well spill it all. I was feeling smitten and vulnerable, but I wasn't sure I should let on."

"I guess I was feeling the same," said Alyssa, "but I didn't have the words to describe it."

"Good! Well I'll let you sleep. We'll hang up for now, and look forward to Tuesday."

"So we're not going to speak tomorrow?"

"No, we'll give it a rest to focus on our duties. Talking might just make it worse. We'll see each other Tuesday. Let's just wait for that."

"Okay, it's the Page Museum. I've been there before. I'll meet you out front."

"See you out front at 1PM."

Sleeping and getting back to her routine helped her function the next day. She also had some resolution on her situation with Trevor and a time for them to get back together. That helped tremendously, but it didn't take away the feeling she had. It was a deep longing that she had never experienced before and a constant uneasiness. She agreed with her Grandparents that it was almost painful, but that she could live with the pain.

Besides attending class she stayed immersed in her studies throughout the day. Working hard helped occupy her mind and relieved her anxiety.

She was overworked. Taking 20 units of tough classes for the second semester in a row had taken its toll. She liked school, but had had enough of it, and was ready to do something with her life. She just had a hard time envisioning herself finishing up. She liked working much more than school, and wished she could get it over with and get to work. She had about a year's worth of classes to go. She cut back to 17 units for the next semester, and decided that she would cut back more after summer.

The next day proved almost as difficult as Sunday had been. She had classes, work to turn in, and had studying to do, but she couldn't concentrate. Her mind kept drifting back to Trevor. She found herself daydreaming about how good it felt when his arms were around her, his gentle kisses filled with energy and passion, the mischievous look and the twinkle in his eye. She started staring at walls again, and couldn't wait to be with him. It frustrated her. The saving grace was the thought of their rendezvous. It kept her going through her morning. She anchored her day with that thought.

As the hour approached she became giddy with excitement. She found it difficult to drive, and bounced up and down in her seat. The mid-day traffic on Wilshire was heavy, and she thought she was going to be late. It aggravated her. She didn't want to lose one minute of time with him.

After she parked, she walked by the fenced off tar pits on her way into the Page Museum. She stared at the tar and contemplated about the past while she waited.

"If those pits weren't fenced off," she thought, "humans would be falling into them today, and researchers thousands of years from now would be pulling us out and studying our bones! Perhaps we're not as interesting."

When she looked around, she spotted him, and they locked eyes. The question of whether they both felt the same way passed between them at a distance and was answered without a word being spoken. They rushed to each other and embraced in a passionate public display of affection. The few people that were nearby couldn't help but stare. They knew what was happening, and wanted to share in the intense feeling that all humans crave. They kissed frantically at first, clutched at each other, and then slowed to a more enjoyable pace. Alyssa was basking in the feeling of finally being held by him again. She was fulfilled. They took a moment to look at each other, kissed, and hugged once more. With a hug around her waist, Trevor lifted her up off of her feet, twirled her around, laughed, and smooched as if ready to proceed.

Trevor was first to speak, "It's only been two and a half days, but it feels like an eternity."

"I'm glad you feel the same way," said Alyssa. "It's been a disturbing feeling. I feel so alone in this, and wondering if I'm just another girl to you."

"Definitely not," said Trevor. "I've dated several girls but I never felt this way before. I'm completely taken, and it feels wrong being away from you. It goes against my instincts, and I'm not comfortable with that. I've spent my whole life learning to play off my instincts, and those instincts are what led me to you in the first place."

"I'm so happy your telling me this. It's been a long two days, and I was hoping it wasn't just me and all one-sided. What are your intentions with me," Alyssa said as they went into the museum.

"To date you of course!" Trevor replied. "I'm hoping we last a long time, and want to start off in the traditional manner so that no one can criticize us for acting impulsively or being out of sorts because we're infatuated with each other."

"Good! I would very much appreciate taking the traditional approach. People have already started telling me things like slow down, calm down, or don't fall for the first guy you meet."

"Am I the first guy you've met?"

"No."

"The things that your friends and family say to you are only natural; it's instinctual to want to protect members of your tribe. They mean you no harm."

"Just the same, let's take the right steps to protect what we have and get a strong start together," Alyssa replied smiling.

"Those were my thoughts exactly," Trevor said stopping her.

He hugged her, and they kissed again by the mammoth display. They kissed long and deep, and this time she felt his tongue against her teeth. She met his tongue with hers, and they stood transfixed in the museum. It didn't matter where they were, as long as they were together, no one else was there. Again they caught themselves remembering they were in public.

277

"That was my first French kiss," Alyssa admitted.

"It wasn't mine," Trevor reported, "but I wish it was. It felt like it was."

They continued to walk around the museum, but were obviously more interested in each other than the displays. They pranced around smiling, giggling, teasing each other, and kissing, but when they approached the display for the saber-toothed cats, Trevor got serious for a minute.

"These ancient cats knew how to survive. Survival was the guide to their day-to-day lives, and they lived off their instincts. These were the only things they knew, and as carnivores, they stalked and killed their pray relying on their instincts more than their training. Hunting was in their blood. You see cats today stalking in the backyard, and catching birds based on primordial instincts."

"Humans are much the same," he continued after a short pause. "Whether we know it or not, we live in a world that remains based on survival, and although we no longer have natural enemies, we're competing for the same limited resources. As the population grows, and the resources become even more limited, the competition will become fierce. We ourselves must be fierce to claim what's due us before someone else with huge fangs like the saber-toothed cat takes it away. We must be ferocious and very aware of what are instincts are telling us. There's no such thing as God or Karma or Voodoo or any of that mumbo-jumbo stuff. What we interpret as God is merely our own ancestors speaking to us through millions of lifetimes. Those interpretations are what we call instincts."

Trevor turned from the display to face Alyssa.

"If you want to be with me you must be aware of your instincts. You must be sensitive to your environment, quick on your feet, and ready to pounce. You must be ferocious, we must be ferocious together."

Trevor looked very serious as if deep in thought, but he was focused on Alyssa as if he was conveying the ultimate truth of existence on the planet.

"And you must be aware of your mate and her needs," Alyssa said laughing. "You must be ready for her to pounce."

Alyssa's laughing caught Trevor by surprise. It broke his trance. He smiled and kissed her.

"I'm ready for you to pounce anytime!" Trevor replied. "Let's go. We're done here."

"Surely you think there's more to it than survival instincts? Isn't that a little prehistoric."

"Prehistoric yes, but still relevant to today."

"I would add that today it's far more important to have good political instincts so that you can manipulate your fellow human."

"Do you mean con him?" Trevor asked.

"In it's most basic form, yes. You must be able to con someone so smoothly that you lift their wallet, remove their money, and put the wallet back without them being aware of it. That's the most powerful modern skill there is."

"What about the morality of it?" Trevor asked.

"You just stated that there is no God. There are only primordial instincts. If there is no God, then why do we have morals?"

"We changed subjects from survival instincts to politics. The political animal requires some form of moral guidelines, or the result will be jail or death."

"Okay, then we were just using different words for the same things. You call them instincts and I call them God, but our belief systems are one in the same."

"Perhaps you're right, but there sure is a lot of time and energy wasted on God and church."

"That depends too. You can never waste time on God. You could be wasting time on church, but church helps some people find God. They need the structure that the church offers them.

279

Other people don't know why they go to church. They're there to kill time or to be entertained by the stories or the choir. They may be there because their parents and grandparents told them to go. For them it may be a waste of time."

"I think you've managed to turn all of my animalistic theories into psychoanalytical theories," said Trevor. "That's not very nice of you!"

The statement made Alyssa laugh hard.

"I guess we just arrived back at the old Zen saying," Alyssa said controlling her laughter. "Everything just is!"

"Amen to that," said Trevor.

"So you do believe in God! You just said amen!"

"Amen to that," Trevor repeated smiling.

The afternoon ended with Trevor promising to meet Alyssa again within two days.

"If we made it two days once," Alyssa said, "we can do it again, but no longer than that. It seems to be easier if I have something to look forward to."

Trevor agreed, and it became the start if a hit and miss relationship between two very driven young people. They were so ambitious, they really didn't have time for a relationship, but hey pushed forward with it anyway, and saw each other in one or two hour blocks whenever they could.

The longing and pain of an intense relationship weighed on Alyssa. She didn't see him very often. Being overworked to begin with, not seeing him was just another new burden, but the thought of being without him was worse. The comfort of being in his arms kept her going. She knew she was working on something big. She just didn't know what it was, and she had to work hard in order to get things out of the way now for when that day came. She wasn't about to give up Trevor in the meantime. She could handle both.

When they were together, Alyssa became spellbound by Trevor. He was graceful, sly and reserved, but when he wanted something, he was attentive and focused. He acted like a wild animal graceful, nimble and ready to strike when the timing was right. There was no mistake about him. Every living thing that came near him sensed the danger. She sensed it too, and it excited her. When she came close, she could detect his scent. It transformed her, and she instinctively moved her body in synch with his. She could soothe the savage beast. Her power over him enthralled her, and she became aware of a new aspect of herself. She loved it, and yet, it drove her crazy. She could never rest.

At times she wondered why she was so bedazzled by him. Nacho was so much like him. He had the same instinctual moves, the same animal grace, and the same survival belief system, but it never worked with Nacho. It didn't click. His animalism fell flat on her, but with Trevor, it enticed her, and made her crave more.

"Thinking will get you killed in battle," Trevor stated abstractedly. "You must react instinctively without thought. You train to react instinctively. Like the military, train the way you fight, and fight the way you train. War requires humans to return to their instinctive roots."

Like an animal taken out of the wild, Trevor became more aggressive when Alyssa was around. He would snarl and act provocatively, but her reaction had a calming affect on him. She knew when to pull the right strings, what buttons to push, and what nerves were raw. She could always use his unharnessed energy to her advantage. She enjoyed doing this, and sought being in situations where he was emotionally worked up, so she could use different methods of managing him emotionally. It became a game to her. Trevor understood the game, and without letting on, he allowed her to continue.

"Sometimes I think our relationship is like that of the Silverback Gorilla," he said one day out of the blue. "I've asserted myself as leader of the group, and you've asserted yourself as the highest ranking female. All the other gorillas will manipulate themselves just for the privilege of picking fleas out of my hairy skin. Some get to pick out only a few fleas, and other's are favored flea pickers. Some are banished from the political circle completely. It sounds bonkers but it's true. Humans do the same thing, but instead of fleas, its money."

Alyssa disliked the analogy, and didn't agree. She hated fleas to begin with, and the visual of his statement bothered her, but more than that, she agreed with Youki. "You can have anything you want. You just have to ask for it. So be careful what you ask for," she remembered him saying.

Thinking of him, she took Youki's gold coin out of her purse. She flipped it in her fingers while contemplating how it had come to her, but then her thoughts drifted back to Trevor. Despite her occasional reservations, Trevor's animalistic style and grace enticed her. His world was brand new and fun. She had lived her whole life in a spiritual realm, and the foreign nature of the world she was entering was seductive beyond description. She desired him, and her raw desire made her feel alive. She slowly converted. He began to win her over to his way of thinking.

"You're too nicey nice," he said to her. "You must be fearless, and you must be aggressive in getting what you want. Eat some raw meat and throw away the rule book. The only reason rules exist are to protect the weak, and you're not the weak. You're not hungry enough. Go at things with reckless abandon. You may lose a few battles at first, but eventually you'll start to win! "

"I'm already a winner," she said as if it should be already understood. "I have you. I'm a junior in college and I'm not even 19 yet. I have a supportive family, and I have money in the bank. What else is there?"

"What do you have there? Is that a gold coin?" Trevor asked smiling broadly.

"It is, a friend left it to me when he died," Alyssa replied. "I think it's symbolic in several ways, but I haven't figured them all out yet. Its face value is $5 but it's worth over 100 times more than that. I know that's symbolic!"

"I find it curious that you would own something like that. Gold is symbolic of status and greed, and you have no greed or status!" said Trevor.

"I just like it because it was his," Alyssa replied.

"That's a $5 Indian," said Trevor. "It's very alluring, but I prefer the South African Krugerrand."

Chapter 36

Alyssa enjoyed working at the Hillside-Zuma Recovery Center, but wasn't really learning much. She was teaching the same classes she had been teaching since she took over Tai Chi from Frenchy years ago. The message was the same, and her style hadn't really changed. She wanted to work more within her field, and she requested to help out in rehab. They gave her 4 hours on Tuesday, and that consumed the only daytime hours that she had left. It would take time from Trevor, but she wanted to do it, and it was very fulfilling when she finally had the opportunity.

Just after Thanksgiving she was making her rounds on her Tuesday, and she noticed something written on an admitting clipboard.

"Ms. S. Leoni," it said. "Alcohol detox and 30 days rehab."

It caught her eye because it was a friend from the past; but she almost let it go thinking it was coincidence. She had forgotten Momma Leoni's first name. She rationalized her slip of memory reasoning that she had called her Sheryl so few times. She went to the room. There she was lying on her bed watching television. She was hardly recognizable. Her youthful appearance was clearly gone, she looked old and tired. Age lines had appeared on her face. She gained weight, appeared puffy and bloated, and looked unhealthy in general.

"Hi Momma I'm Alyssa Daingerfield. Do you remember me?" Alyssa asked.

"Alyssa Daingerfield! My adopted child! You're all grown up now! Look at you. So very impressive!"

Alyssa gave her a big hug and sat on the side of the bed.

"How's Reech?"

"Reech died almost a year ago now. He had an accident. He was painting and fell backwards off an extension ladder. The ladder fell backward with him and actually on top of him. He hung on for a few months, but couldn't quite make it."

"Oh dear! I'm so sorry. I'm so sorry that we lost him!"

Tears welled up in Alyssa's eyes but she brushed them away and pretended she wasn't crying.

"I am too, dear."

A few minutes passed while Alyssa composed herself.

"That was a great summer on the beach wasn't it?" Alyssa asked. "I think about it all the time. You and Reech, the street vendors, the homeless, and the muscle builders at Venice were all so wonderful."

"I don't remember it being perfect for you," Momma said. "You were a troubled teen trying to find your way. You were basically a runaway, but I worked with your Grandfather to help you. Did you know that we spoke at least once a day, and sometimes twice a day?"

"I had a feeling," Alyssa said. "I'm really good at understanding my feelings. That's why I was there in the first place. I was so young, and so naïve. I was very lucky nothing bad happened. My Grandpa recently told me how hard it was on him, and if it wasn't for you, he wouldn't have gotten through it."

"He's a good man your Grandfather," said Mamma Leoni. "He was basically a runaway too. He and his girlfriend left Virginia in a hippie van headed for California at age 18. That's a big deal. He was part of the great migration. All the head cases from all over the United States converged on San Francisco."

284

"Are you saying he's a head case?" Alyssa asked.

"The phrase had a different meaning then," Momma Leoni replied. "A head meant a young intellectual who renounced the dogma of materialism, and wanted a new way of life free of government oppression."

"Okay, yes I knew that, but my Grandma called them Flower Children."

"I think the meaning of Flower Child was a little different again, but similar. A Flower Child believed in communal living where everyone helped each other. Unlike hippies, they bathed frequently, and they liked things natural. Living off the land was fashionable."

"So how did you end up here?" Alyssa asked Momma. "You never drank when I knew you."

"I started drinking to relieve stress. That was a bad idea to begin with. I saw Reech drinking all the time, and one day I said give me one of those. Reech's work was never consistent. For long periods of time he wouldn't be working, but then he would work 10 hour days six days a week. The money was nice when he was working, but we didn't see each other much, and it wouldn't cover the long periods when he didn't work. I was basically supporting us. It seemed like all I did was work. I also wanted a baby, but I just couldn't see having one with Reech. He didn't seem responsible enough. He didn't fit my vision of a Dad. I wanted a balanced happy home for a child, but what I had was two overgrown teenagers acting like we had just moved out of our parent's house. On top of that, I've had friction with my Dad. He never liked Reech and wanted better for me. All of these things combined began to drag me down, and I used alcohol as a crutch. Finally when Reech had his accident, I spun out of control. I was managing work, hospital visits, doctors, and bills. I used alcohol as reward, and found any excuse to reward myself. When Reech died, I broke down. I couldn't handle it. I couldn't go on any longer. I wouldn't get out of bed in the morning, and I had a bottle handy wherever I went. Finally my Dad put me in here."

"I'm sorry that it hasn't gone well for you," Alyssa said. "You were always so positive. I thought you'd be happy whatever you did."

"I was happy when you were with me, and I stayed happy on the outside after that, but I was struggling on the inside. I've learned that I need to take care of myself first. I can't just give away all my energies to people in need. I'll drain myself out."

"What are you going to do now?" Alyssa asked.

"First I'm going to give up the booze and get back to how I was. I want to be a happy non-drinker like the olden days. Then I'm going to try and pay back my Dad for some of the $67,000 he paid for this place. I may end up working for him, but that no longer bothers me. I want a fresh start."

"This place charges $67,000 for a 30 day stay?" Alyssa asked.

"Oh yeah, this is considered luxury rehab," Momma Leoni said.

"No wonder they can afford to pay me $18 an hour and reimburse my tuition!"

"What do you do for them here?" Momma asked.

"I teach Tai Chi and meditation techniques."

"Well see! There you go," said Momma. "Meditation, yoga, Tai Chi, message therapy are all activities for the wealthy. They probably love it that a young beautiful girl like you is teaching them. It blankets their world with perfectness."

"They're using me!" Alyssa said.

"Aw, let them use you. You're so smart you'll be running this place some day. You'll be pulling down a half million a year," Momma replied. "What else have you been doing?"

"Going to college. I'm almost done with a degree in rehabilitation, and I have a boyfriend."

"That's great that you're going to college!" Momma said. "Tell me about the boyfriend!"

286

"He's tall, thin, and very handsome. He always has a mischievous look and a twinkle in his eye. He makes you think he has something up his sleeve. He's kind of a schemer. He's studying business, and intends to take over mid-sized privately owned businesses and take them public for a big profit. He acts like an animal, and he studies the behavior of animals, but he's not purely wild. He's classy and has good upbringing. He's cool and slinky like a cat, and he stalks his prey. Business opportunities are the prey he stalks."

"Why do you like him?"

"Mostly because he just makes me go crazy. It's very exciting to be with him. It's almost as if he's dangerous. The funny thing is, I crave the danger, and yet I expect him to protect me. He's a great kisser. On our first date he took me to Enterprise Fish in Santa Monica. After dinner we walked out on the Pier. Someone had one of those bubble generators going and we kissed with the bubbles flowing all around us. It was very romantic. I melted right into him. He had me from then on."

"Sounds like a typical bad boy hotty to me. You may be like me falling for the bad ones! Remember it's okay to date the nice ones too. They're not as exciting, but they're better long-term companions."

"Yes, he's a bad boy hotty! I've never thought of him like that but yes."

"You be careful with him. The wild ones will use you and toss you aside. They may be fine pets for a while, but one day they'll turn on you. Watch out for him."

"I'll be careful Momma!"

"You may not need to keep the first fish you net out of the barrel. At your age, a good policy is catch and release. There's always more fish in the barrel," Momma said.

"Yes Momma," Alyssa said as if speaking to her own mother. "That's good advice. I better get back to work now."

"Okay dear," drop back in to see me real soon."

287

"I will!"

"Promise?"

"Promise!"

Chapter 37

Although she had heard them before, Momma Leoni's words registered with Alyssa, but she wasn't sure what advice would come into play. There was one statement that continuously rang around in her head.

"You be careful with him. The wild ones will use you and toss you aside. They may be fine pets for a while, but one day they turn on you. Watch out for him."

The statement didn't apply to their current relationship but she could see that happening with him. He was wild, and he liked things his way.

Kaylee had been looking for a boyfriend since the end of August, but really couldn't find one that she liked. Her friends told her that she was too picky, but Alyssa claimed she wasn't picky enough.

"You need to feel the attraction deep inside you," Alyssa told her. "Don't flirt based on looks alone. You'll only attract a bunch of Ken dolls. When you meet someone, close your eyes when they're around you, and concentrate on how you feel. If that person moves you in some way, he may be worth dating."

"There's nothing wrong with Ken dolls, but I see what you're saying," Kaylee replied.

Shortly after this conversation, Kaylee found someone she liked. She was attracted to him even though he was very obedient. He did whatever she said. There was no challenge in it for her, but she liked that.

"I'm a control freak," she told Alyssa, "and this one is easy to control. Besides that he's good looking and has money. He may not be the one but he works for now."

When the semester ended Alyssa had a lot of free time, and they started to double date. They had great times together, and they expanded their stomping grounds to the entire Los Angeles basin. Trevor had turned 21, but got everyone else fake IDs so they could get into clubs if they wanted to. They clubbed up and down Sunset Strip for about a week. It was the first time Alyssa had been back. Alyssa never drank, and Kaylee only drank a little when it tasted good, but Trevor drank wherever they went. He was usually stiff, but loosened up considerably after a few drinks. Since he became much more agreeable, they accepted his drinking patterns without much thought. At a certain point in the night, he was the life of the party, and provided witty humor frequently for a short portion of the night. After that, he would retreat to the background. They had a blast together during this period. For a while, Alyssa forgot about being overworked. Toward the end of the night, when the drinks started to wear off, sometimes Trevor would become moody. When he did, they knew it was time to take him home and call it a night.

They bought season passes to Disneyland, and visited the park as often as they could. Kaylee's boyfriend was named Randall, but everyone called him Rusty because of the color of his hair. Rusty ended up with Trevor when they were at Disneyland. The girls went their own way. The guys hung out together in the less crowded areas of the park. Trevor's spirits always seemed to pick up when it was time to leave Disneyland.

On Christmas morning, Trevor came by Grandpa Jack's and Grandma Lin's for a waffle breakfast and opening presents. Daisy and Franken were there too. It was the best Christmas they had in many years with everyone having done well financially. There were mounds of presents around the tree, and a bigger pile of wrapping paper when they finished. Alyssa was very pleased because Trevor had a great time, and it seemed like he'd been part of the family forever. Everyone liked him except Franken who was skeptical of everyone until he got to know them.

Trevor bought Alyssa a gold necklace with a single emerald stone. Alyssa was very impressed that he remembered that she liked emeralds and simple designs. She bought him a gold watch with a black square face and a small solitary diamond in the 12 o'clock position. In the bottom of the watch box she placed a one once gold Krugerrand. The idea came to her from an earlier conversation they had when he stated that he preferred Krugerrands to American gold coins. He loved both gifts, but was obsessed with the Krugerrand looking at it from all angles, holding it in his hand, and playing with it all morning. Grandpa Jack thought the gift was a little extravagant, but Alyssa assured him that it wasn't.

"He spends a lot on me Grandpa! He always pays whenever we go out. He buys me things. He's very generous!" she told him.

Trevor managed to avoid every other family gathering through the holiday period, and he never invited Alyssa to any of his family functions. She was suspicious, and wondered if he was afraid of commitment. He claimed that his family didn't get along anymore, and that he'd rather not have the drama in his life. He promised to bring her to meet his Dad early in the New Year.

Alyssa hadn't managed to spend much time with her newly discovered Dad. Brad Stone had spent one Tuesday afternoon with her at the Getty Museum in Los Angeles, and he had met her for lunch a few times on campus. When New Years Eve approached, she and Trevor wanted to see the "All American Rejects" play at the Canyon in Agoura. They decided to invite Brad. He declined, but offered to let them stay at his place to avoid driving. Not wanting to jeopardize his new relationship with his daughter, he made sure it was okay with Daisy. They took him up on it never thinking they needed approval from anyone. After all, he was her Dad.

Kaylee, Rusty, Alyssa and Trevor spent most of New Year's Eve at Rusty's parent's house in Woodland Hills, but at 8 PM they drove to Brad Stone's place to get some privacy. They watched the ball drop in New York, and headed over to the Canyon to see the band. They had a great time, but when they arrived back at Brad's, the party really got rolling because more of Alyssa's friends had been waiting there. Brad's condo was very nice, modern, and well decorated. Alyssa's friends commented on why she had been hiding her rich Dad in Agoura Hills.

"Are you embarrassed by his wealth?" they asked knowing her disdain for people infatuated with money.

"No," she replied without further comment.

She never bothered to tell them that they had just met a few months earlier.

When Brad returned, he seemed to enjoy the spectacle, but was very concerned about what Daisy would think.

"There's alcohol here, and I'm a recovering alcoholic," Brad told Alyssa in a mild panic. "Your Mom will think I'm a bad influence! That's basically why she never wanted me around!"

"Don't worry Dad," Alyssa responded, "I'm not the one who's drinking. You're not influencing me. You're just trying to keep us safe. If Mom does find out, which she won't, she'll know that you were just trying to do the right thing."

Trevor and Rusty, who were both old enough to drink, were already drunk and singing Auld Lang Syne arm in arm, the girls were all talking about how they liked each other's dresses. Brad began to look annoyed at the length of the festivities, but was relieved when they all fell asleep about the place only minutes later.

"Now I know what it's like to be a parent of a teenager," he thought to himself.

The arrival of the New Year wasn't all that welcome for Alyssa. Classes started the third week of January, and the days clicked by swiftly while she caught up on her chores and other tasks that she had put off due to the previous semester. She managed to go snowboarding at Mountain High on Martin Luther King Jr's Birthday with Trevor, but the lift lines were long, they didn't get many runs in. Despite the crowds, they had a great time together on less crowded green runs, and keeping each other company while waiting in line for the chair lift. They had never been closer, but all the fun ended with the arrival of the new semester.

Now that she was an upperclassman the pressures of school were greater than ever, and even though it was the beginning of the semester, she was having a hard time keeping up. She wanted that time on the weekend to study rather than work, but she was making good money at Hillside-Zuma, and they were reimbursing her tuition. She didn't want to quit. The other thing that bothered her was that she had little time to spend with Trevor, and she worried that they would drift apart. She was sure she loved him, and felt very fortunate. The last thing she wanted was to lose him due to her workload.

"I'm ahead of the game, and I shouldn't let work and school interfere so much," she thought to herself.

One Friday the whole group decided to meet at Gladstone's because they hadn't been together since November. They had been having Santa Ana winds. It was the third day, so the gusts and blowing had died down considerably, but it was still hot. It seemed like the entire city had decided to go down to the beach. Highway one was packed, and so was Gladstone's.

Not surprisingly Dylan and Finn were there. They had caught word of the event too, and wanted to escape the heat. Alyssa hadn't seen either of them since last year. Trevor hadn't arrived yet.

"As soon as we got back together you got a boyfriend, and now I hardly see you," Dylan complained half joking.

"Dylan, you know we'll always be friends. I love you and I think about you a lot. It's not Trevor that takes up all my time. Its school and work," Alyssa responded.

"Yeah I know how that goes," Dylan said. "I'm not even working and yet I'm always stressed out about school."

"I like working much better than school," Alyssa said. If I could, I would quit school and just work, but I want my degree. I've gone this far. I'm going to finish. It just doesn't seem worth it sometimes, but after this semester, I'll be on easy street. I'll have light workloads from here on out."

"I would almost rather be back in school!" Finn said. "Work can really be a drag too. My Dad is motivated to buy this distressed property near Cedar Sinai Hospital. It's a luxury apartment building, and the owners are about to go under. He says he can buy it and make a killing. He wants me to manage it. I've already done the math. Principal, interest, taxes, and insurance would run me $41,000 a month, and there are 14 units. I would need to collect $3,000 a month per unit. I don't think I can make it. What if a unit goes vacant for a month or two? The math just doesn't quite work out, and he really wants to buy this thing. He's pushing me hard to take it on. He says it would be good for both of us. I don't know what to do!"

"What about maintenance?" asked Dylan.

"Actually, the $3000 includes $100 maintenance," said Finn. "In exact numbers it comes out to about $2,888 per unit per month to cover the mortgage, taxes and insurance. I just rounded it off to include a little maintenance."

"Where I work they charge $67,000 per month per room, and it's a room. It's not an apartment," Alyssa said. "I just found that out the other day."

"Wow, that's outrageous," said Dylan.

"Not if you're wealthy and you're going to die if you don't clean up your act," Alyssa said. "This is luxury rehab. These people can afford it."

Finn appeared as though he was about to burst. His eyes went wide, and his face turned red. He pulled out a pen and started frantically writing numbers on the back of a napkin. As usual, the

293

people in their group were mostly Kaylee's friends. They were discussing much more unimportant topics. They all stopped talking at the same time to stare at Finn. Without speaking, their stares questioned why Finn was working numbers when he should be socializing. They simultaneously shrugged their shoulders and returned to their conversations.

"Sounds like we should open a rehab center," said Dylan joking. "Instead of wasting our time in college we could be making some real money."

"That's it! That's exactly it!" said Finn standing suddenly.

His outburst interrupted their conversations once more.

"Dylan there's genius in your tongue in cheek humor!"

Finn's excitement was infectious. He sat back down, but both Alyssa and Dylan's eyes got big. They started smiling as they watched Finn's excited expressions, and looked around the room as if to check for the security of what Finn was about to say.

Finn scanned his napkins before speaking, "Instead of taking over a luxury apartment building, we can turn it into a luxury rehab center. Just using round numbers, let's suppose we had $50K in expenses and staff salaries of $150K each month. That's $200K a month outflow. If you divide $200K by 14 units, that's about $14.5K per month of expenses per unit. If we charge $20K per month per unit, we cover our expenses plus a nice profit. That's about 68% cheaper than what they're charging where Alyssa works."

"You might be on to something," said Dylan, "but a regular Rehab Center only charges about $10K per month. They would be our competition too."

"Great point! Even if you weren't wealthy, you may be willing to pay twice as much to get a nice apartment for 30 days rather than a cold hospital room and an obnoxious roommate. If you're wealthy, the sting of $20K is far less than $67K, plus you get your own apartment."

"What about medical insurance," said Dylan. "A lot of insurance companies pay for rehab. Our rehab center would be too expensive!"

"They pay what's customary and reasonable, and the patient pays the rest," said Finn. "That may actually work to our advantage. The patient is out of pocket ten grand. The insurance pays the rest!"

"Being close to Cedar Sinai has advantages too," said Alyssa. "That's the hospital of choice for the rich and famous. We could discretely transfer patients from their care to ours without the media finding out. That's a big selling point. Another thing that would interest these people is a work release program of sorts. It's difficult for them to be away from work for 30 days. That keeps them away from detox in the first place. After they detox for a few days to a week, if they had some opportunity to work, that would be a big selling point, and very beneficial to their long-term recovery. Slowly they learn to return to their normal environment without using. We could assign each person a full-time assistant, and have them travel around with them while they're away from the center. Every night for the first 30 days, they would return to the center rather than the temptations of home."

"We even have someone with experience in rehab," said Finn. "Alyssa has some actual experience helping people."

"We approach it from the other angle that Hillside-Zuma is using too. We need massage, manicure, pedicure, tanning beds, yoga, Tai Chi, meditation, and spiritual training," said Alyssa. "We fill up the time that the patients once spent using drugs or alcohol. That's another secret to success. They need uplifting fulfilling activities so that they don't have time to think about using. They must feel better about themselves and their health when they get out. It's their reward for not using, and it keeps them from wanting to go back to the pain and drama."

"How sweet," said Finn. "There's a warehouse that's for sale near the apartment building. I wanted to buy it for storage, but my

Dad doesn't want it. We could buy it and convert it into classrooms and a small gym. It's only a few blocks away. We could have a shuttle."

"That's what I was just thinking too," said Dylan. "A lot of these people will have lost their driver's licenses. If we could offer a shuttle during their recovery, they could get back to work slowly without a hassle. By the end of their stay they could have their license back."

"A lot of great ideas!" said Finn. I've been jotting a few down, but all I have are napkins to write on. So are we going to do it? Let's agree right now. I'll get the apartment building, and you guys get the gym! We'll create a partnership starting right now, and I'll incorporate us as soon as I can get the paperwork done."

"You'll have to bring your Dad on board," said Dylan. "We can't do it without him."

"You leave him to me. I'll put a business plan together. That'll give me an opportunity to use my UCLA education. If I show my Dad a nice comprehensive plan that makes money, he'll buy the building. Trust me! So do we have a deal?"

"Deal!" said Dylan.

"Deal!" said Alyssa.

"Let's shake on it then.

They shook hands all around smiling and proud of themselves. Although their project was far-fetched, they all looked as though it was a done deal. As if on cue, after they shook hands, Trevor walked up.

"What are you guys talking about?" he said. "You look like you just hit the lotto."

They all looked at him, but none were willing to speak.

"I may have! I mean we may have," said Dylan.

"We're attempting to start our own luxury drug and alcohol rehabilitation center," said Alyssa. "It's Finn's idea, but Dylan and I want in."

Trevor laughed, "You guys are crazy! You're talking about a multimillion dollar operation. Where are you going to get the funding?"

Finn explained the concept and general strategy to Trevor, but he wasn't buying into the plan.

"If you get Finn's Dad to agree, and if you get the permits and approvals from the city, and if you have enough start up cash, you're still a bunch of kids. No one will take you seriously!"

"Why not!" said Dylan. "Finn's a UCLA business school graduate."

"They'll eat you alive in the real business world along with your degrees," said Trevor chuckling.

"If we have the vision we can do it," said Alyssa looking at the other three including the skeptic. "We simply ask for it in our minds, and start acting like its happening. Eventually it will happen."

"Trevor is right!" said Finn. "It's a great point. We'll need someone older and experienced to run the operation. We'll need a CEO. None of us are ready for that, not even Trevor."

"I'm not interested," said Trevor. "Leave me out. I have other plans."

"Okay," said Finn. "Fair enough! We'll start with us three, and try to bring my Dad in as an investor with the building. If we can convince him, we'll continue from there. If not, we'll throw away the idea. I'll work a full time CEO into our costs. I'm leaving now to write it up. We'll meet at the Denny's in Santa Monica tomorrow to review it. We'll bring it to my Dad afterward. I've got to move on this thing because my Dad wants to know if I'll run that apartment building."

Finn left looking concerned and deep in thought. He didn't say goodbye to anyone.

"I'm going to head home too," said Dylan. "I have class tomorrow. Ring me up Alyssa to let me know what time we're going to meet."

Dylan said goodbye to everyone. His departure left Trevor and Alyssa on their own since they hadn't been a part of the larger conversation.

"You're not going to go through with this are you?" Trevor asked while looking at Alyssa with concern.

"Yes, I've got a strong feeling that I should pursue it. I'm very good at interpreting my instincts, and they're saying go."

"Instincts are the right word," said Trevor. "If by some miracle you get by Finn's Dad, you're going to need to grow some teeth. You'll need more of a business face and a kill or be killed attitude. Don't bring your God or Buddha mumbo-jumbo into it. If you do, you'll get crushed. It's nice to have a vision, and ask the universe nicely for what you want, but when you're done, go out and bust your butt to make it happen. Buddha won't make it happen for you. Brains, hard work, and perseverance make things happen!"

Trevor's words had a sting to them that Alyssa had never experienced before. She sensed that not only was he predicting failure, but he was making light of the belief system that was a part of her. It worked well for her, and she had grown up with it. She had come around to see his point of view, so she wondered why he couldn't see hers. He also sounded jealous in some strange way. On the other hand, she knew he was right. She would need to toughen up and save her touchy-feely side for teaching her classes. She felt pain in Trevor's words, but she was stronger for it, and she loved him. She knew she loved him. She smiled and kissed him.

"Let's go," she said. "Let's go get some dinner. This place isn't working for me tonight."

"Gladly!" said Trevor standing.

Chapter 38

"**I**'ve worked out the numbers," said Finn, "and it's not as sweet as I initially thought."

"It's never as good as your first time," Dylan jokingly replied.

"It's better than working for someone," said Alyssa. "The more I think about it, the more interested I am."

Finn passed out a two page plan across the table at the Denny's on Lincoln Boulevard in Santa Monica.

"What kills us are the salaries! They account for 78% of our monthly cost. Infrastructure costs were 14%, and operating costs 8%. I was really surprised by this. I was thinking that the limiting factor would be the building. As we discussed yesterday, we'll need a full-time CEO that I estimated at $350K per year. We also need a full-time doctor at $250K. Those two positions alone are more than a half million per year, but I think we need them, and we can't skimp on salary. We'll also need a psychologist and an accountant. That's another $120K each.

The bottom line is that our expenses will be approximately $22K per unit per month. We would need about $5K profit per unit per month to make it interesting. That brings the total we would need to charge to $27K per month. That's $13K more than I initially quoted you, but it's still $40K below what the Hillside-Zuma Recovery Center charges.

"You can go to a regular one for about $10K to $12K," said Dylan. "I'm not sure if we're priced right for a luxury experience. They might not come because we're not priced high enough. The price tag screens out what they consider to be the undesirables."

"We can let the expensive CEO set our price," said Alyssa. "That's what we'll be paying him for. I would also agree that we should go higher, but we should offer an introductory rate since we're new."

"All good points," said Finn, "and things we need to consider. There's one more thing to discuss. If we had more units, we could make more efficient use of our staff, and that would bring costs down. Obviously, there's only one building available, but I have that noted for our presentation. Look through it and make sure you agree before we go final."

Finn's Proposal to Open a Rehab Center

Executive Summary

$306.65K per month costs

$21.9K per month per unit costs

$27K per unit per month charge (23% markup)

$5.1K per unit per month profit

$71.4K per month profit

$856K per year profit

Apartment Building

$5,500K

$1,000K down

$100K closing costs (estimated)

$4,600K principal

$35K per month payment, principal and interest.

$41K per month payment principal, interest taxes and insurance

Warehouse

$280K

$ 60K improvements and equipment

$340K total

$2,4K per month principal, interest, taxes and insurance

Shuttle

$45K

$0.8K per month principal, interest, taxes and insurance

Total Infrastructure Costs

$5,985K

$44.2K/month

Labor
$350K CEO
$250K Doctor, General Practitioner
$120K Psychologist
$120K Accountant
$ 80K Administrative
$ 80K President
$ 65K Maintenance
$200K Room Cleaning (4 people)
$600K Patient Attendants/Nurses (10 people)
$1,865K Subtotal
$1,000K Costs due to employment (approx 60%)
$2,865K Total
$239K per month salary costs
Insurance
$15K Medical
$ 2K Liability
$17K Total
Operating
$2.0K Gas and Electric
$1.4K Water
$2.0K Cable
$1.0K Maintenance
$0.5K Landscaping
$6.9K Total

"I think we need a lot more detail for a business plan," said Dylan. "You've also forgotten the costs of establishing the business. There are permits and fees. You'll have attorney's fees, and incorporation costs."

"Good point, let's pencil $10K in for permits and legal fees," said Finn. "That sounds low, but it shows that we've thought of it. Do we agree?"

"Yes, for a simple proposal it looks good," Alyssa responded.

"Like I said, it lacks details, but the round numbers look reasonable," said Dylan. "I guess I agree."

"No guessing," said Finn with a serious look. "Do you agree?"

"Yes, I agree," said Dylan.

"Okay, let's go pitch it," said Finn.

"Right now?" asked Dylan.

"Yes, right now. I know I can get at my Dad right now, and he wants an answer on the property. I'm already late in responding, but I warned him that I have an unusual proposal."

"Are you sure you want us there?" Dylan asked.

"Yes, you're either in or you're not."

"Okay, let's go!" said Alyssa.

"I'll drive, and drop you back off at your cars when we're done."

There was very little discussion as they drove to Finn's Dad's house in Laurel Canyon. They pulled into a nice neighborhood of modest homes, but made another turn. Finn's Dad's house was right on Laurel Canyon Boulevard. It was an older tri-level construction built into the Hillside. Alyssa guessed that it was built during the post-war construction of the 1950s.

"Let me do all the talking at first," said Finn. "I'll introduce you guys, then I'll go through it. If he asks any questions at the end, go ahead and answer him."

"Yes Sir!" said Dylan smiling.

They all went in and prepared to present their case. Dylan's Dad entered the dining room very calmly wearing half glasses for reading. He smiled and introduced himself, and was very pleasant with a corny sense of humor and obvious laugh lines in his face. He appeared to be in his mid-fifties with a full head of hair but grey at the temples. He was good looking and friendly. Before they started he wanted to get to know both Alyssa and Dylan questioning them about their families, their backgrounds, and their hopes and dreams. He dwelled on the hopes and dreams for several minutes. Dylan's hopes and dreams seemed to be to get married, have a big family, and live on a ranch near Atascadero with horses and more than one big dog. Alyssa's dream sounded as if she wanted to run a homeless shelter, but the details were vague. She wanted a public place with a lot of beds where she could teach meditation, martial arts, and spirituality so that she could help the lost and misguided see their full potential. When asked what that was specifically, she didn't know.

"I've been doing it all my life, and I like it," she finally stated flatly after pondering the specifics of her dreams.

Alyssa wondered if this could possibly be the man that Finn complained about when they first met. She would have thought he was more of a redneck construction worker, but he turned out to be a successful business man.

"Okay John, show me what you've got!" said Finn's Dad.

Alyssa and Dylan weren't accustomed to hearing Finn called by his first name, and looked around the room for John, but Finn started speaking. He explained the whole concept and the start-up strategy. Alyssa and Dylan were very impressed with his delivery. They were seeing a side of Finn they had only recently noticed. He was very direct, articulate, and businesslike. His Dad smiled when he noticed their surprise with Finn's presentation capability and attention to detail. He didn't use notes and was speaking from memory.

"If we're smart we could work a deal with Cedar Sinai Hospital. It's very nearby to our proposed rehab center. They could transfer their detox cases over to us," said Finn.

"Another important factor to consider is the cost of labor. Labor is 78% of our expense, and with only 14 units, we're not using it efficiently. If we could expand later to a second building, we could use our staff more effectively. Our salary costs per patient would drop by about one third.

That's about it," said Finn. "I don't think it's worth buying as a luxury apartment building, but as a luxury rehab center we could make some real cake and help the community at the same time!"

303

"It's a novel idea," said Finn's Dad. "I would have never thought of it. I was interested in flipping the property after a period of one to three years. It's way undervalued as currently priced. It's a steal, and once this market recovers, it will be worth a lot. In your proposal you have it priced a little high. You must have used the listing price."

"I tried to use worst case numbers," said Finn. "I wanted to make sure I was turned off if the numbers didn't work. I don't want to be chasing a bad idea."

Mr. Finn stood, and started to speak.

"You have some big holes in your proposal," he said. "Since your team is young and learning, I won't tell you all of them. You need to figure things out on your own. You need to learn. The biggest hole is cash flow. You're quoting expenses of $300K a month. You need three to six months start-up money to make your lease and pay salaries. That equates to one or two million dollars up front."

Mr. Finn stopped smiling, and the three looked at each other as if they had forgotten the kitchen sink. Mr. Finn paused for a minute letting the revelation settle in, and then continued.

"Another big item is getting the City of Los Angeles to approve the proposal. The building is zoned commercial, but right now it's residential, and they may not want you to convert it. On the other hand, it helps the community, and shouldn't be any additional pressure on the neighborhood. If you present it right, it may get approved."

Finn started to speak, but his Dad cut him off.

"Just a few more things John, and then we'll discuss it as a group. Your liability insurance quote may be low. It may seem outrageous to you, and it is, but we need to deal with it."

The three friends looked at each other quickly when Finn's Dad said "we need to deal with it". That was the first hint that he may accept their proposal.

"The reason I didn't want to buy the warehouse is because I can't really afford it. I have too many things going on. It wasn't that I thought it was a bad deal. I think you would definitely need it for this venture."

Mr. Finn was pacing around the dining room table at this point holding his chin in his hand and removing his reading glasses.

"You'll need to find another investor for the warehouse as well as the cash required to convert it to what you need."

They all looked at each other again and started to smile because it appeared that he was going to accept their proposal.

"Lastly, I noticed you have a CEO listed here at $350K per year. The fact that a group of young adults like you recognizes the need for such a person is extraordinary! There's a very unique skill set required to operate an enterprise like the one you're proposing. As smart and ambitious as you may be, it's unlikely that you have that skill set. Furthermore, you're young and inexperienced. People in the business world may not take you seriously. Your insight into your limitations is a large factor in motivating me to accept your proposal. Beyond that, it's a good idea! If Betty Ford can do it we can do it!"

They all looked at each other again knowing that it was Trevor's idea to add the CEO. Trevor had also told them that people in the business world wouldn't take them seriously. Finn swallowed hard at the realization.

"Who's Betty Ford?" asked Dylan.

"A former U.S. President's wife," Mr. Finn replied. "She started a rehab center in Palm Springs."

"There are a few things we need to do before we know if your proposal will really work. We need to find out if we can get a two million dollar line of credit payable in salary increments. I'll work on that. John, I want you to go to City Hall and inquire about zoning and permits. I also want you to get actual quotes for both malpractice and liability insurance. Alyssa and Dylan, I want you to find an investor for the warehouse. If we can overcome these initial problems, I think we'll have a business. I'll continue my efforts to buy the building, and the new business can lease it from me at cost."

"I think I may have an investor," said Alyssa.

"That was fast!" said Mr. Finn smiling. "Who may I ask is it?"

"My Dad," Alyssa stated.

Both Finn and Dylan dropped their lower jaw at the statement and looked at Alyssa.

"Yes, I met my Dad for the first time last August," said Alyssa looking at Dylan with a glare and ignoring the Finns. "We've been getting together once or twice a month. When I first met him he said he was looking for a new investment opportunity."

"Great!" said Mr. Finn. "Feel the bumps on his head. He may like the proposal. That may be one problem solved."

"I suggest we meet back here in a week," said Finn. "We can assess progress and assign new tasks. Are you available Dad?"

"Yeah sure," said Mr. Finn. "Let's say 7 PM. Congratulations are in order for your team. You've done some nice work!"

The next evening they made the same presentation to Brad Stone. He also accepted the proposal, and was even more enthusiastic about it than Mr. Finn.

"This is a great opportunity," he said smiling at Alyssa. "It's not only a great investment, it's an opportunity to get to know my daughter a little more."

Finn had success in investigating zoning and permits with the city. They gave him a preliminary approval, but the new business was required to submit a proposal along with an environmental impact statement. His investigation of liability and malpractice insurance was disappointing. As Finn's Dad had expected, malpractice insurance was more than what Finn had first estimated, but having malpractice insurance made it easier to hire a doctor. If the doctor provided his own insurance, they would be required establish a contract with that doctor. If they had their own, they could hire the doctor as an employee. The trouble with hiring their own doctor was that very few, if any, would want to work for a start up company. The final result of his investigation was that the new business would be forced to contract for medical services until they were better established.

Mr. Finn made no progress with banks, but through his contacts with his neighbors in the film industry, he found a group of investors that were interested in providing start-up capital. Besides a high interest rate, there was another catch. They wanted a seat on the board of directors. Furthermore, they wanted their attorney to incorporate the business, and establish the management hierarchy at a cost of $50K. Mr. Finn explained to them that, although the price was high, they would have to incorporate anyway. Since that task would be done, they could hold off on actually hiring the CEO until after startup. That would save them at least $75K, as a result, they were essentially incorporating for free, and they could take more time searching for the right CEO.

After discussing their options, the team decided that giving up some control on the board was better than being completely stalled due to lack of funding. They counter offered, and asked for a buyout option. If they could pay back the entire amount plus interest within 18 months, the investment firm would relinquish any rights to the company. The counter offer was accepted.

Mr. Finn's offer for the luxury apartment building was also accepted, and since he was pre-qualified for the loan, the sale went straight into escrow. The building would be his in 90 days. The change of ownership required him to alert the current tenants of his intent. After considerable discussion, they selected a start-up date of autumn equinox on September 21st, 2007. They gave notice to the current tenants of their intent, and although the eviction date was months away, some moved out at their first opportunity in accordance with their lease. Loss of rent was an unexpected expense, but it gave them the opportunity to set up their first apartment for rehabilitation, and they could use this apartment as a model. The activity revealed another item that the team had overlooked. They needed luxury furniture, and that wasn't in their budget. Mr. Finn's many business connections proved to be invaluable. He and Finn worked a deal with a furniture company to equip the rooms as they were vacated and prepare for patients. A lump sum payment amount was negotiated at a discount, and they began to make interest-free payments for 24 months.

Brad Stone's efforts to acquire the warehouse proceeded much faster than the apartment building. The building was already vacant, and Brad was paying cash, so the escrow period was 30 days or less depending on how fast the paperwork could be processed. Alyssa and Dylan were set to work with him on a design for the building; and to their surprise, Brad hired a professional architect once they had their ideas on paper. Plans for renovating the building were completed by the end of March, and construction started shortly thereafter. The apartment building was on Burton Way in Los Angeles, but the Gym was next to the Beverly Center Shopping Mall on West 3rd Street. They needed a shuttle to move patients back and forth. Without Alyssa's knowledge, Brad purchased a used shuttle van in like new condition. He had it renovated to match the style and design of both the apartment interiors and the gymnasium color scheme. His efforts were very well thought out, and much appreciated when in April, on Alyssa's 19th Birthday, he handed her the deed to the Gym. It was in her name. The keys to the shuttle van were wrapped up in a little gift box, and the title was in the name of the business.

"I can never make up for what I lost with you," said Brad. "Missing your childhood as a result of my own selfish ways is beyond stupidity on my part. This is by no means an attempt to buy your love. You're too important to me to try something so foolish. This is a demonstration of intent on my part. I would like to be a part of your life and a part of your business venture. Giving you the building helps make up for the monetary support that I never provided. It's very good timing for a big gift. You're taking a risk, and you need the help right now. The shuttle van is my contribution. When you incorporate and create privately owned shares of the business, you can compensate me by throwing a few shares my way. I can help with maintenance and building renovations."

Daisy, Grandpa Jack, and Trevor were stunned by the gesture. Alyssa didn't know what to think. She looked at her Dad and said thank you. She became uncharacteristically emotional and gave him a hug. Franken and Dylan both smiled.

"I would really like to meet my sister one day," she said whisking away the tears with her finger tips. "We need to take care of her too."

"If she's living in Cupertino, she's probably well taken care of," said Dylan with bold sarcasm.

Everyone looked at Dylan, and then looked at each other. They all started to laugh. Grandma Lin set up the cake to blow out candles. Alyssa missed several in her attempt to extinguish the flames. She looked up.

"There's nothing left to wish for," she said to everyone with tears in her eyes. "I already have everything!"

The next day Alyssa drove down to Venice and spent the day at Muscle Beach trying to find Frenchy. He never showed, but there was another Vietnamese man there who knew him, and gave her a tip. He was working in a Mexican restaurant in Santa Monica. Alyssa had cut classes that morning anyway, so she waited for him to finish work.

"Why are you working in a Mexican restaurant?" asked Alyssa.

"Because they were hiring," said Frenchy smiling. "I'm learning a little Spanish too. Did you expect me to work in a Panda Express?"

They both started laughing.

"I'm starting a business with some friends. I wasn't motivated by money to start with, but now I'm not so sure. I was confident in myself until last night. My Dad handed me the deed to a new gymnasium free and clear. All of a sudden I doubt myself and I don't know why."

"You need to treat it," Frenchy replied. "Meditate, calm your mind, and ask the universe for the answer. The path forward will become clear for you. I would guess that the path is already clear. You see mountains of work in the future, and the thought is very daunting. This is where your spiritual training comes in. You go forward fearlessly, and work at a healthy pace each day. Little by little, you chip away at the mountain of work. You remain happy, healthy, and balanced, but yet, you stay focused on the task of the mountain. Before you know it, the mountain has been conquered."

"Yes! That's it!" Alyssa said. "I was forgetting my training. One day of work at a time, and eventually, I will complete the task!"

"You already had the answer!" said Frenchy, "Why did you find me?"

"Because you were one of my great mentors, and I love you," Alyssa said.

Frenchy smiled, and it looked like a tear came to his eye.

"You were one of my finest students, and I love you too," he said. "What else were you going to ask me?"

"How did you know I was going to ask something?"

"You're sending me that type of energy."

"I was going to ask you to help me teach. I can't do it alone."

"I will help you, and that completes the circle," said Frenchy.

"Yes, I was thinking that too. You handed off to me, and now I've handed back off to you. It has both a Yin and Yang quality."

"When do I start?"

"You start in September, but I want you to take my weekend classes until school lets out. The class is just North of Malibu near Zuma Beach."

"You know that I don't drive."

"You can take the train. The Metrolink Express will pick you up in the morning and bring you back at night. I'll pay your entire day both Saturday and Sunday including train fare."

"Okay, then I can keep my job here for a few more months. That will be good!" said Frenchy.

"I also want you to call me if you need anything," said Alyssa. "You'll be working for the business starting September 21st. You're family now."

"Yes! Agreed," said Frenchy. "I'll need to be able to spend the night. I don't need much."

"You'll have an office, but you can't officially live there. There are showers and everything you need. It's a legal problem. You can't legally live there, but I'm sure you'll keep a room in Venice like you always have. That makes it legitimate."

"Venice is home!" Frenchy said.

Alyssa hugged him, and with the hug, she secured her first employee and left her job at Hillside-Zuma Recovery Center. Frenchy would cover for her until June. Her contract would be complete, and she could resign at any time.

On her way home Alyssa realized how she had set aside years of spiritual training in favor of Trevor's philosophical point of view. She loved him so much that he had molded her to his liking without her realizing it. She had been running off instinct alone, and it had helped her immensely at first, but without that connection to her spiritual nature, she had been running herself ragged without recharge. She had recognized the animal body that she lived in, but in her discovery, she had forgotten what got her there in the first place.

"Living in a human body has a Yin and Yang aspect to it too," she thought. "As incarnate spiritual beings we must consider both sides of ourselves."

For the next ten or eleven days Trevor and Alyssa spent most of their time together. They were in-separable. They had time to be together for the first time in months, and took advantage of it. Mid-terms were over, and it wasn't time to gear up for finals yet. For Alyssa, without work on the weekend, she could easily keep up with her studies, and more than ever wanted to be with Trevor. She longed to be in his arms, and was slightly irritated whenever he wasn't around. When he was busy, she pined for him, sent him perfumed letters, and obsessed over him.

She stayed on campus only to catch up with friends. If she didn't have classes she usually showed up with Trevor. They hung out with Kaylee, or with the whole group of friends. They rode along in other people's cars, and stuck their nose in the affairs of others long enough to get invited somewhere. They became known among their friends and along the coast as "The Swizzlers" because Trevor was almost always drinking. Everyone assumed Alyssa was too, but she never drank. She had never liked drinking, but she loved him, and played along with his social games. They were an item, and were recognized anywhere they went in Santa Monica, Venice, or along the coast. They were a sight to behold.

With the regular group at Gladstones they weren't as celebrated. Their friends wondered why they dropped by since they were always in their own world ignoring everyone else. They spent their time kissing each other, teasing, and playing around until they completely annoyed those around them. "Get a room," was heard quite often when they were present, but they laughed at the remarks, and continued with their antics.

Several nights Alyssa arrived home at four in the morning. Her Grandparents let it slide the first few times, but when it became a regular thing, Grandma Lin confronted her.

"Alyssa, you're only 19, a full time student, and about to start a multi-million dollar business," are you sure you should be carrying on like this?"

"Grandma, you know I've always done the right thing. I've been on my own before." Alyssa replied.

"I know dear. I'm just starting to worry about you and Grandpa Jack is too."

"Grandma, this is my last opportunity to enjoy myself and my time with Trevor before I dive headfirst into this business. I'm fully committed to the endeavor. I'm ready to go. This is my last shot at some time off for what could be a very long time."

"Okay honey, as long as you have a handle on it, we're okay. It's just that Grandparents can sense things that young people sometimes don't. We're just trying to help."

"I know Grandma. I love you, and I appreciate it. There's just a few more days left, and my life is going to change forever."

Chapter 39

Alyssa's life did change dramatically. She made sure she spent a few hours a week with her Dad, and did her best to make him feel like he was a part of her life. She met Daisy for meals at least once a week, but sometimes more, and kept her up to date on the workings of the new business. She of course saw her Grandparents every evening while she finished up her courses and prepared for finals.

Before the end of the semester, she signed up for both summer sessions at school taking as many units as she could fit in. She knew that once September came, and the business started, she would have little time to study. At the rate she was going, she could easily finish her degree by the end of the next school year, but she scuttled those plans so that she had more time for the business. Starting in the fall she would take lighter loads planning to finish her degree in June 2009.

She began to see Finn much more than Trevor. After the semester ended they worked late into the night preparing paperwork, planning the business, and renovating the apartment building. During the day, they interviewed potential employees.

They took notes and voice recorded most interviews, but even with their diligence, their notes became confused. They lost track of who was who, and were forced to call several people back for a second interview. After their daytime sessions, they would go out together for dinner or a cold beverage, and again when they finished late they went out for a snack or a walk around the block. Their friends made note of the sudden change. Alyssa had always been seen with Trevor, but now it was always Finn. People began to talk. Finn was easygoing, mature, and most of all, a smooth operator; whereas, Trevor was always a little uptight. People assumed that she had finally made the wiser choice.

Trevor had always been in control of his relationship with Alyssa. She knew this, and let him have his way. He was such a good decision maker that she had complete trust in him. He led her around on a string. It was subtle at first, but became obvious as time passed. Besides Finn, it bothered her closest friends. They thought she was being used and treated poorly. Finn knew better. He knew that underneath obvious appearances, Alyssa was truly in control. He had full confidence in her, but for most people it was driving her friends crazy. None were more bothered by it than Dylan. Dylan finally confronted Trevor. Trevor laughed at him, and called him a buffoon. They almost came to blows, but Alyssa stepped between them. Now, however, the shoe was on the other foot. Alyssa had reigned in Trevor, and taken full control much to the applause of those that cared about her.

"Trevor, this is the hardest thing I've ever done," she started. "It truly breaks my heart to tell you this, but I need to spend some time alone for a while. I have a really strong feeling that I need to put everything I have into this business for awhile. This is my one shot. It's my moment, and I need to step up while the timing is right. It's unlikely that I'll ever have a chance like this again. I want to put our relationship on hold for a few months! I need time!"

Trevor was speechless, and didn't know what to say. He suddenly felt things he had never felt before. He felt love, he felt loss, and most of all, and he felt vulnerable. He had completely lost control, and for the first time, was at someone else's mercy."

"Are you breaking up with me?" he asked.

"No, absolutely not, I just need time for this thing! This is my time. This is me! Once it's started and functioning on its own, I'll have more time. We can be together again. You know, just like before."

"You're saying you want to be with me, but later, and you don't know how much later."

"Trevor, I'm just asking for some time. I have this thing I need to do. I feel it so strongly. I hear it loud and clear. I need to do it. I need to do it now!"

Trevor was speechless again. He furrowed his brow, squinted his eyes, focused distantly, and then returned his attention to Alyssa."

"Well okay then," he said looking at the ground and back up. "I guess we'll have some time apart. Take all the time you need!"

Alyssa could sense a change in him. She didn't want that change. She had hoped that it wouldn't come. She hoped he loved her and would understand, but instead she felt him harden. The feeling hurt her to the core. It hurt her down deep. She felt a pit in her stomach, and it was starting to grow. She almost staggered, looked for a chair to sit, but managed to stay standing. She took a chance and said something that she had wanted to say for a long time.

"Trevor I love you! I love you! I want us to be together. I want you to trust me. Give me this chance. I need it. Give me this chance!"

Alyssa became overwhelmed, tears broke out, and within seconds she was sobbing. Her tears caught Trevor off guard, the hardening stopped momentarily. He wanted to tell her he loved her too, but he couldn't formulate the words. He wanted to run to her.

315

He wanted to comfort her, but pride welled up inside him. His survival instincts flared, and his ego took over. For an instant, he had an opportunity to make it all good, to accept the inevitable, and take back control with love, but instead, he thought of himself. He maneuvered to protect himself.

"Take all the time you want," he said suddenly looking around as if to collect his things for an escape. "I have projects of my own you know. I need time too. Yes, of course, as soon as you're ready give me a call. We'll go out."

"Trevor! I don't want to break up. I just need some time. Please!"

"No, No, I get it. No, we're not breaking up. I'm telling you! Take all the time you need. When you're ready, I'll be there."

There was no sincerity in Trevor's voice.

"Trevor!" Alyssa called.

"I've gotta go. I'll call you tomorrow."

With those words he was out the door, and Alyssa broke down sobbing.

For the next few days the pit in Alyssa's stomach stayed with her. She returned to the constant low-level unsettled feeling she had when they first met. She randomly broke down into tears and found it hard to concentrate. She caught herself staring at the walls. For moments at a time she could focus on what she was doing, but her thoughts would inevitably drift back to Trevor.

Days passed with no word from Trevor. She started to improve, and began to function again. Everyone around her was understanding and supportive. Of all the people in her world, the most overworked was Finn. While she was dealing with her pain, he had taken up the slack. When she started to come around he was there for her. Working turned into her best medicine, and she began to function again. The first summer session started, and the pace of the classes kept her focused on work. She and Finn began to collaborate again late into the evening. Sometimes she would do homework, while he worked the business. Sometimes they worked together. One evening they were working late together at Grandpa Jack's and Trevor showed up at the door. Finn went to the door with Alyssa, and the three of them stood on the porch together.

"You've been spending a lot of time with Alyssa Finhead!" said Trevor.

Finn hadn't heard his old nickname for a long time, and was momentarily thrown off.

"For months now we've been working hard to stay on schedule to start this business in September!" said Finn with a look of understanding. "There's a lot of money at stake Trevor. We have a lot of people counting on us."

"I want to know what your intentions are. I think you're trying to steal her away from me. You two are always together, and you're together late into the night," said Trevor.

Alyssa was already in tears, but remained quiet.

"Look Granderson," said Finn, "I've known Alyssa a lot longer than you! As far as I'm concerned, I've known her forever. We have a strong bond, but I assure you, we have no romantic interest in each other. We're friends and that's all. We're very close friends."

"I think you're having sex with her! Don't deny it!" said Trevor.

Finn laughed out loud.

"Trevor!" cried Alyssa. "Trevor stop. Trevor don't disrespect me!"

"Granderson you're a fool. As I've said, and as I've demonstrated over many years, I'm not interested in Alyssa in that way. You're too caught up in yourself to notice how special she is. She's a natural leader Granderson. She's gifted. She leads both spiritually and physically in this crazy world. She can make sense of it all, and inspires others to do what's right and good. I'm her follower you moron, not her lover! I'm one of her many followers! Don't you see!"

Alyssa had stopped crying and was staring at Finn. Trevor's mouth was hanging open and was staring at him too as if the prophet was speaking."

"But you're the leader on this business venture," said Trevor.

"Maybe on the business side. Maybe in appearances only, but without her, I never would have attempted this in the first place. She's the leader you fool! She's the one!"

Now both Trevor and Alyssa were staring at Finn. Grandpa Jack came to the door.

"I really don't want to interfere," said Grandpa Jack calmly opening the door. "I'm getting older, and you kids are going to inherit this world. You need to make sense of it, but Trevor, you need to get along now. Finn, you go inside and collect your things. Alyssa, you head on up to bed."

"Yes Mr. Daingerfield," said Finn going back inside.

Alyssa gave Trevor a kiss on the lips that completely took him by surprise.

"Trevor," Alyssa said firmly, "go away. Call me in a few days when you've cooled off."

She turned, went through the door, and closed it behind her.

Although it was so very uncomfortable, the confrontation helped Alyssa. Now she knew that Trevor cared, and that he loved her. She could see the love in his eyes.

"He just couldn't bring himself to say that he loved me," she thought to herself as she readied herself for bed. "He does love me, and it's only a matter of time before he comes back to me."

The comforting thoughts helped significantly as she entered the second half of the first summer track at Cal State LA. Classes were accelerated, and there were significant amounts of homework every night. Work on the new business also subsided. The extra time was welcomed, but it bothered her that Finn was working 12 hour days and getting ready for opening day. She helped Finn as often as she could. He assured her that long hours were approaching for her too, and that it was a good idea to get as many classes as she could out of the way now.

Frenchy had taken up his office in the newly completed gym. He met Brad Stone on the first day, and they hit it off well. They laughed at each others situation because Brad didn't drive and Frenchy didn't own a car, yet they both lived a considerable distance away. Between them, they knew every method of public transportation, the tricks associated, and they compared notes. Their relationship became symbiotic by helping each other get to work as well as run the enterprise. Frenchy managed the activities of the gym, and started his own evening classes. Brad managed building operations, maintenance, and security. Anything that went wrong, he was immediately ready to handle it. The operation was already successful before its parent company even opened its doors.

Since the gym operated each day of its own accord, and Frenchy's classes were already generating income, Alyssa was free to focus on school. She did well in her classes, and although she was overworked, felt good about what she was getting accomplished. She fully expected to be largely taken up by work at this point, and was relieved that she actually had some free time.

She spent what free moments she had with Trevor. He was taking summer classes at Pepperdine, and they would meet at the beach in Santa Monica when there wasn't any marine layer and their schedules coincided. The relationship improved. Alyssa loved him more than ever, enjoyed his company, and looked forward to their rendezvous. Trevor kept her going. He encouraged her to be bold and go after what she wanted aggressively.

"Take no prisoners," he said one day at the beach. "If anyone gets in your way just mow them down. It's you against the world."

"It's us against the world," she corrected him smiling.

They were getting along better than they ever had, and the change made Alyssa wonder about the cause. She was fully in control of their relationship now. He accommodated her. He met

319

her schedule, and gave her whatever she needed. Before their confrontation, he was in complete control and led her along on a string. He was mildly abusive of his advantage, and thought he'd always have her no matter what. He was completely thrown off when she prioritized her work over him, and forced him to wake up to what he had. He realized he could lose her, and that the alternatives were less than desirable. Without having waged a battle she had won, and now controlled both of their destinies. In her heart, however, she detected that he resented her being in the driver's seat. He felt that he should be dominant. He was the alpha male, and she was his female, but somehow the roles were reversed, and it bothered him.

As summer session was finishing up at Cal State LA, work demands returned to the business team larger than ever. The father and son team of Finn was finishing up, but the center was preparing to open, so they began to meet three evenings a week to coordinate their efforts. They decided to name the business Hollywood-Sunset Recovery Center continuing to work off the model that Alyssa's former employer had provided them. Several employees were hired with various start dates. Most would report Monday, September 10th. They would prepare for the Grand Opening on September 21st, the remainder of those already hired would start Monday, October 1st. The search was on for a CEO, but their efforts to date were fruitless without a single candidate to interview.

On Monday, August 20th, one month prior to opening, Mr. Finn made an announcement to the rest of the group.

"I took a risk in not telling you this earlier," he started. "It may not have been very smart on my part, but this is a learning experience for you. Sometimes learning the hard way makes the lesson stick better. This may be one of those times. We open in about a month, and we're going to need customers. As you know, we'll refer to them as patients, but our patients are also our customers. There was no allowance for advertising in your original business plan. I noticed that from the start, but thought you may have an alternate plan to bring in business. It's very obvious now that you don't. We need to start soliciting customers in some fashion because in a few days we'll be responsible for payroll, and the only income we have is from Frenchy's fledgling evening classes. Alyssa, we look to you to lead this effort because you have the connections in the industry. We may need to bite the bullet and advertise. If we do advertise the sooner the better."

While Mr. Finn was talking, the rest of the group was gasping and glancing back and forth between each other. It was an obvious hole in their plans, and a huge oversight. The reality of their situation finally set in. They were opening a multimillion dollar business in one month; they needed customers, and had to do some fast thinking.

"I can't believe we forgot that!" said Finn. "We were so thorough!"

Alyssa stood and quickly started to speak.

"We can't afford to waste any time," she said in a commanding tone. "That includes looking back. If we made a mistake, then so what! We correct it and move forward. We'll make more mistakes in the coming months and we can't dwell on them or assign blame. We can't afford any emotional damage to our team. We're in this together, and we must work together.

"I'll beat the bushes and see what I can come up with. I'll report back Friday, and we'll make a decision then. In the meantime, ask around people you may know. It's unlikely our own friends can afford this service, but they may know someone."

"Where are you going to start?" asked Finn.

"I'm going to query at Cedar Sinai first," said Alyssa. "Then I'll talk to everyone I know in the business that will see me. I'll get some leads. Don't worry. We won't fail!"

"Don't you have finals this week?" asked Dylan.

"I do, but I'll be okay. I'm doing well in school. I'll study at night."

321

As the meeting broke up for the evening, there was a somber note. Everyone but Mr. Finn looked glum. He was smiling broadly, and approached Alyssa.

"You took charge just like I thought you would," said Mr. Finn. "You're our ace in the hole Alyssa. Good luck this week."

"I don't believe in luck," Alyssa responded.

"Oh yes! Okay. I'll be sending you Chi this week!"

Cedar Sinai agreed to send business their way because they were a start-up. There was a shortage of rehab beds in Los Angeles, and they wanted to encourage them. They preferred to work with Hillside-Zuma, but were intrigued with the medium priced luxury concept, and wanted to help them get started.

Since she had a positive response, she visited the administrative departments of as many hospitals as she could find in Los Angeles. It was a daunting task, and she wouldn't finish it by that Friday, but she did what she could.

She visited her original employer in Hollywood. Their services were designed to be affordable to everyone, and their prices were less than half of what Hollywood-Sunset would charge, but they promised to give them referrals for their well-off clients if they ran out of beds. Without asking her partners, Alyssa told them they would offer a significant discount to any client they referred.

When Friday arrived the mood within the group had deteriorated further.

"I've visited eleven hospitals this week including Cedar Sinai," Alyssa informed the group. Everyone promised to give us referrals. What's more, most made suggestions for advertising and listings. I found some very low cost advertising opportunities. These are definitely needed so that people can at least find us. We also need Yellow Pages adds as outdated as they may be. Some people still use them. We'll need a web site, and I know everyone here knows how to build a web site, but we need a very professional site similar to Hillside-Zuma. It will be expensive, but

322

I suggest we pay the money. We need to make a big splash when we come out, and a professional company will know how to do that. I went to the trouble of getting three estimates. Finn can decide which to accept if we decide to go that way. There are several advertising options that target our market. I suggest we hire a company now. I've made significant progress this week, but our phone hasn't rung with a single client."

"I can't believe we forgot to build a website for the business," said Finn. "I feel like I've been asleep at the wheel."

"Let's remember our agreement," said Alyssa. "There's no use in kicking ourselves in the butt for making mistakes. We correct the mistakes and move on."

"I'll get on it right away," said Finn. "I'm sure we can have something by opening day."

"I have something too that I'd like to share with the group," said Mr. Finn. "I found a CPA that is interested in the CEO job. He's well connected in the LA area, and has experience in both advertising and marketing. He has an MBA from UCLA extension program. His name is Joel Goldstein. I suggest that we hire him, but I want you to review his credentials. He agreed to take a reduced salary to work part time until the beginning of January while he winds up what he's working on. After that we'll be paying his full salary. I know we'll be bringing him on a little early, but he has some definite ideas on how to ramp up the business almost immediately."

The group voted unanimously to accept all the presented proposals, and after a week of working out the details, Joel Goldstein was hired as a consultant until the beginning of the calendar year. After the start of the year, he would become CEO. Finn hired a firm to build a website, and they tabled decisions to procure further advertising until they consulted with their new CEO.

Joel Goldstein suggested that they buy cable TV and satellite TV advertising packages that targeted areas like Palm Springs,

Santa Barbara, and Newport Beach. The television commercials would run only on cable channels and not major stations like CBS, NBC, ABC or Fox. The cost was high, but Mr. Finn suggested that they do what their CEO says, or the money they were paying him would be a waste. They approved the purchase. The commercials were scheduled to start running October 1st.

The business opened on autumn equinox without fanfare. Thanks to Alyssa's efforts, they had five beds filled, but nine beds remained empty. October 1st passed with no immediate increase in business, but the CEO assured them that advertising took time to take effect. The month of October passed without any new patients, and paid employees stood by without enough work to do.

"I find myself rooting for people to have drug and alcohol problems," said Alyssa at Gladstone's one Friday evening. "That's exactly the opposite of what I'm trained for. I'm trained to help people, and not hope that our beds fill up."

"They'll fill," said Dylan. "Have a little faith. They will fill up in short order and we'll be fine! Don't be so hard on yourself either. We hope our beds fill up so our business succeeds. If our business succeeds we'll be helping people. We're definitely doing the right thing!"

"Agree," said Finn. "The morality of it is on our side. We'll just keep chipping away at the problem until we fill up."

"You guys need to raise your rates," said Trevor. "If your prices were higher, you would attract high-end clients. The elite don't want to mix with the common folk or the party animals. High prices will filter most of those people out. If your prices aren't high enough, they won't even consider you."

"He's got a point," said Finn. "We talked about this early on. We're too low compared to Hillside-Zuma."

"That's it!" said Alyssa. "We need the party animals! The party animals drink and use drugs! How could I have forgotten! Gotta go guys! I've got an idea!"

324

She went to the other table to say goodbye to Kaylee, and bolted off to her car.

Alyssa drove home and rummaged through her junk drawer. To her delight she produced Nikki the rock star's personal card that he had given her two years ago when she treated him on her first job. She immediately called him, and to her surprise he answered.

"It's Friday night and you're not out yet?" Alyssa started sarcastically without explaining who she was.

"Everyday is happening for me," said Nikki. "There's no specific time. Every moment is precious."

"You're still as obnoxious as ever! I love it. You haven't changed a bit," said Alyssa.

"You know, hundreds of girls would literally kill to have my personal number. I gave it to you, and you don't call for two years. Now that you want something, you finally call."

"You know who this is?" asked Alyssa. "With so many girls after you, you remember one girl from two years ago?"

"You're a hard face to forget," Nikki said sarcastically.

"Who am I?"

"You're Alyssa the Rehab girl - the sly young sage. You're the mysterious one. You're the young lady that isn't impressed by wealth or fame. You have an amusing penetrating stare. When you disapprove of something, you don't even need to speak. You're expression explains everything."

"Yes, I guess that is me!" Alyssa said sheepishly. "It sounds kind of cold when you explain it. Hey, I'd like to talk to you. Are you available tomorrow?"

"I'm busy the rest of the weekend. Why don't you drop by now? It's early. I'm just here with the kids. The wife is out. We can talk all you want."

"I'll be right up," said Alyssa.

"When you get to the house, call me on this number and I'll open the gate. Park right in front of the garage on the right. You'll be fine there."

Alyssa pulled up to a large but normal looking home in the Hollywood Hills. It was by no means a mansion. She estimated the size at a comfortable 3,500 square feet. She guessed that if her grandpa Jack's house was stacked three high and redecorated, it would be approximately the same kind of thing, but Nikki's house was in a higher end neighbor hood. When she pulled up she lingered outside the gate with her car idling and her foot on the brake. Without calling Nikki, the gate opened. She decided that they had been expecting her, someone saw her, and opened the gate. It turned out her assumption wasn't true. One of Nikki's kids opened the gate and came to the front door. He was very cute with black hair and light skin, and claimed he was eight years old."

"Why did you let me in?" Alyssa asked. "What's your name?"

"You looked safe enough," he said with indifference. "My name is Brandon!"

"What if I was one of your Dad's groupies?" she asked him.

"Then you would have been sneaky," he said. "You would have had a drink in your hand, and tried to climb the fence. That's how they are. You look too normal to be a groupie."

"I see you've met my son Brandon!" said Nikki entering the room. "Come on into the family room, I'll introduce you to the rest."

Nikki had two more girls of ages four and seven. They were both darling. They were shy about meeting Alyssa, and hung onto their father's legs. Alyssa was surprised about how normal the household was, and scanned the room looking for something extraordinary but didn't find anything.

"Are you surprised about the house?" asked Nikki.

"To be honest, yes." said Alyssa. "I'm surprised it's so normal. It's not much different than my Grandparents house. It's just a little bigger and nicer."

"Thanks! I'll take that as a compliment," said Nikki grinning.

"Please do," said Alyssa without further emotion, "You have a lovely home."

"These are my two girls Misty and Rihanna," said Nikki. "This is our Nanny Elizabeth."

He motioned to a woman sitting in the corner out of the way and looking embarrassed for interrupting one of her employer's dates. Alyssa sensed this and responded.

"I'm not Nikki's date," she said to her, "we're just friends."

Elizabeth nodded her head in agreement although her expression appeared as if she didn't believe her.

Nikki laughed out loud.

"She nods yes to everything," he said. "She doesn't speak much English. I like it that way. It keeps her out of my business."

Alyssa laughed.

"How embarrassing, I wonder if any woman could resist you?" Alyssa said sarcastically.

"So what motivated you to call me after so long!" said Nikki.

"Frankly, you're right. I want something. In my defense, however, I did plan to call you when you gave me your card. It must have been obvious that I disliked you at first, but I grew to like you, and by the time you left I liked you a lot. What you say about me is true about you too. You have an inner light! There's something special about you. You're interesting and creative, and not just a drunken rock star that got lucky in the first place with a crazy band and marginal musical abilities. I just got busy with school, and I quit that job. I needed to regroup and restart. Your card got lost in the shuffle."

Nikki laughed loudly.

"So let's get to the point. What do you want?"

"Referrals!"

"Referrals?" asked Nikki with a questioning look.

"Yes, I just opened the Hollywood-Sunset Rehabilitation Center with a few business partners and some investors. We don't have enough clients. At the rate we're going we'll be out of business within a year. It's a luxury concept for people like you who are busy and value their privacy."

"Are you still teaching martial arts, meditation, Tai Chi and that kind of thing?"

"Yes, we opened a gym near our center. I'll be teaching classes there. We also plan to add massage, manicure, pedicure, and acupuncture."

"Sounds good!" said Nikki.

"Will you help me?"

"I already have. Why should I help you again? You never call."

"What do you mean, you already have?"

"Who do you think got you the job at Hillside-Zuma?"

Alyssa was rendered speechless momentarily realizing that Nikki had been behind her last job.

"So that was you who got me in there?" she asked sheepishly.

"It wasn't much on my part. They had a lousy instructor. They wanted to fire him anyway, and I told them about you. You're the most interesting instructor I've ever had. With you, it comes straight from the soul as if you've known it for a thousand years. You give up the knowledge freely, and marvel in your students successes. I think you're remarkable."

He stood staring at her waiting for a reaction. She stood searching her mind for a witty comeback.

"You're just buttering me up so you can add another notch to your bed post," she said.

"You're not the type of woman I'd want to cross swords with," said Nikki chuckling. "There's much more to you than meets the eye. I'm just happy to be your friend. I'm glad you finally called."

"So will you help?"

"I tell you what. I think you'd be a great influence on my kids. If you teach them about meditation, Tai Chi, and Eastern cultures,

I'll give you as many referrals as I can muster. I'll also give you a list of well known managers in the industry and their personal cell phone numbers. They're the ones that put their talent in rehab. Guys like me just go reluctantly when we're told we're screwing up far too much."

"That's all I'm asking for," said Alyssa. "If you could refer anyone you know, and give me a few leads I'd be very grateful."

"Do we have a deal then?" asked Nikki. "You'll teach my kids?"

"Yes, we have a deal!" said Alyssa smiling. "How can any woman say no to you?"

Nikki laughed.

"Well you come back up here once a week. I have a different number to call to make the arrangements. Hopefully, I'll get to see you from time to time, and we can talk."

"Definitely," said Alyssa. "I'm sorry I took so long to call."

"Don't mention it," said Nikki. "Just take care of the youngsters. It's your duty to pass some of this stuff on."

Chapter 40

After the Thanksgiving holiday the Hollywood-Sunset Rehab Center filled to 50% capacity. The source of the business wasn't always apparent, but many patients requested an interview with the modern day shaman priest. No one knew who that was, but after some inquiry, they decided that they must be referring to Alyssa. She became mildly famous in the Los Angeles area.

She suspected that her minor fame was a result of calling every manager in the music business each week drumming up business. She would drop Nikki's name as well as other musicians she had met. Nikki sometimes teased her by referring to her as the

329

witch doctor or the high priestess, and he may have used these terms while pumping her up on his end.

The early results of the center spoke for itself, and accurate or not, Alyssa was given credit for the results. She was the healer, and used a spiritual approach based on Eastern religions to achieve her results. Her programs were based on healing the inner self first prior to looking outside the body, meditation, quiet reflection, and martial arts based exercises. She sent them back happy, sober, well balanced, and ready to reenter their sphere of influence. Her proven results quickly earned her a reputation.

They had a psychologist on call, and she visited the center twice a week talking to patients about their feelings and concerns, but everyone wanted to consult with Alyssa. By default she became the head psychologist, and plans to hire one full time were put on hold.

As the days went by, Alyssa became more and more embroiled in the inner workings of recovery instead of teaching. She taught classes when she could, but the transition to the focus on people seemed natural. As anticipated, she had less time for everything else in her life. She kept up with her lighter load at school, and was looking forward to the end of the semester.

She maintained her relationship with Nikki and his family through necessity at first, but after time passed, she also maintained it for the sense of belonging it provided. She had a big impact on their lives, and had become like a part of the family.

She saw her Dad at the Gym almost daily, and spent moments with him when she could. She made time to see Daisy and her Grandparents at least every other Sunday, and although she was stretched, everything seemed to be going well.

The only casualty of her new life was her relationship with Trevor. Their romance had survived the earlier test of starting the business, but now that the business was established and becoming more robust, there were added pressures. She had many duties in various aspects of the operation. She needed to be everywhere at once. When she found time for Trevor, she was often exhausted and fell asleep in his arms.

When the center finally filled up in January, it became apparent that she must do something, or else lose Trevor. She decided to attempt to bring him into the business.

She approached the board, and they agreed to bring him on in a diminished capacity at first in order to see what he had to contribute. They would give him a very basic salary with incentives. If after the first six months he had demonstrated his abilities, he'd be hired full time, receive a lump sum payment of 25% of base pay, plus a 25% increase in salary. They would evaluate again after 12 months with the same incentives. Trevor accepted the offer and laughed.

"I'm better than your CEO," he said staring down Joel at the board meeting. "I'll show you how to run an organization, plus I'll have time to finish up what I'm doing now."

Trevor's first proposal was to increase rates to at least half of what Hillside-Zuma was charging. He complained that he had suggested this for a long time, but now that he was an employee, he wanted them to take action. Everyone on the board was familiar with his claim that the luxury client they were pursuing wouldn't consider them if they weren't priced high enough. Price served as a filter to eliminate the client that was on a budget. Only people with big wallets could afford to check themselves in.

With the center operating at capacity, the CEO agreed to phase-in the proposed rates. As Trevor had claimed, demand increased, but there was no way of knowing what the root cause was. Alyssa claimed that it was due to her marketing campaigns, and that word was finally getting out to their targeted segment of the population. The business was finally blossoming, and the new rates went straight to the bottom line. Their balance sheet went from red to black. They had a healthy profit for the first time.

Trevor went on to document their business processes, and lean out the operation. He improved efficiency in several areas, and

331

planned to do more as income allowed. He contracted out maid services and their computer services. The move proved to be effective on two fronts. They no longer had to pay social security or benefits for the employees, and if they had problems, they just made some calls and they were resolved. Their bottom line increased again, and Trevor was credited with the change.

Within six months they hired him full time and gave him his first bonus. Having him at work helped Alyssa improve their relationship as she had hoped. They often shared meals, walked at lunch, and left work together. Their passion for each other returned. It felt like when they first dated, and it was a welcome feeling.

"Let's head up to Enterprise Seafood like we did on our first date," he said excitedly one Friday night. "It's our two year anniversary. We've been together since October 2007!"

"Isn't it getting late," Alyssa said in response.

"It is, but they're still open. We'll probably get a table."

"Okay, I guess so," she said. "I'm a mess from working. Are you sure you want to do this?"

"Yes, why not do something spontaneous."

Their same table was open when they arrived. They requested it, and ate silently while staring at each other over candlelight and smiling. Very few words were exchanged, but they were thoroughly enjoying themselves. When they finished they walked outside together near the car where they first kissed.

Without touching him, she tenderly moved toward him and touched lips. She leaned in careful not to touch him anywhere else, and made it a real kiss. Understanding what she was doing, he resisted the temptation of going further too. Finally, they could take it no longer and embraced each other. They became passionate. Their hands found the curves of each other's bodies. They paused after a minute, held each other tightly, and sensed each others excitement.

He opened the door of the car for her, but to her surprise, he opened the door to the backseat. He grinned as she got in, and quickly moved to the other side getting in the back seat himself. He looked at her and smiled again as he held up his keys and hit the power door locks.

They kissed again, and their tongues found each other exploring new sensations. She instinctively moved toward him as they kissed. They began to move together with their heads tilting to accommodate. Moist lips were now completely finding each other, and with the initial moments of intimacy, they transcended into a passionate embrace. Their hands joined into the exchange gingerly exploring each other's curves. The moves became heated. Their lips pushed together. They paused again, and firmly held each other feeling the mutual excitement grow, and the energy flow back and forth between them invigorating their passion. They kissed once more, but this time their tongues touched slowly to savor the moment. Quickly, they became impassioned again to penetrate the unexplored. She slid down against the bottom of the seat. Trevor used the opportunity to dominate and kiss her from above aligning his lower body with hers so she could feel his firm excitement. He raised his upper body to look at her while pressing more firmly against her below. Her lower body responded graciously, she moaned provocatively, and his lower need fell in closer to hers. She moaned again in ecstasy, and he lowered his upper body so that his lips could find hers once more. Their tongues immediately touched and danced together while they kissed. He raised his upper body again, and began to unbutton her blouse while he gently massaged her below with his erection bulging through his clothing. She gasped in anticipation, lifted, and released her bra in one swift motion. He took her bra, flung it, and gently massaged each breast being sensitive to her responses. Their clothes became a frustration. He sat up, and began to unbuckle his pants. Alyssa stopped him.

333

"Trevor! Not here in the back seat of your car. It's not right. This is a special moment for us. I don't want it to be like this!"

"It's like our first date," he said excitedly. "This is the perfect opportunity. No one will see us."

"No Trevor! No!" she said looking at him squarely in the eye.

He paused, tilted his head slightly while studying her, and smiled.

"Okay, very well, another time then," he replied.

For the next few days Trevor was distant and preoccupied around Alyssa, she feared that the control issue was bothering him again. He had become self confident, once more felt like he controlled their relationship, and thought things were back to the way they should be. They were doing so well, but Alyssa had reaffirmed herself in one fell swoop.

It wasn't quite the same as the last time they fell out. Trevor seemed jumpy, and sometimes irritable. Between the rehab center and finishing up his other job, he was working long hours. The fatigue showed in his face. He was okay with a heavy workload and strangely eager to take on more. He had the look of someone who had been working on something big in the wee hours of the night. He had been laboring on the secret task, and had the look like he was about to complete it at long last. The whole world was soon to find out what his brainchild was, and he was about to cash in.

After lunch Alyssa sometimes suspected him of drinking. He had that acrid smell of alcohol on his breath, and acted as if he had something to hide. Like a naïve housewife, she went through his desk at work looking for a bottle but there was nothing. When she had the opportunity, she looked through his car for a flask, but came up empty again. Although she knew from her work how resourceful problem drinkers could be, she decided that she was being paranoid, and let it go.

The behavior continued, and when they were together, Trevor acted as if Alyssa wasn't even there. It bothered her that they had been so close just a few weeks ago, but now, the feeling was worse than ever. It was as if he was a different person.

Despite his supercilious and detached attitude, Trevor's work at the rehab center never missed a beat. With regard to business operations, he was the one with all the ideas, had a knack for resolving conflicts among the staff, and adjusted business processes to run smoothly. He often criticized the CEO, and claimed he could be doing a much better job if given the chance.

"You have no idea what the CEO is doing," said Alyssa one night at dinner with their little group.

"Neither do you! What could he be doing?" Trevor replied. "Little to nothing and making three times what I make."

"I agree," said Finn nonchalantly. "Trevor has all the ideas, understands the customer base, and the inner workings of the operation. Our CEO just seems to suck up to our investment group and work on our quarterly report."

"Well that needs to be done too," said Alyssa. "He's about to release our report for first quarter of 2009. It will be a record profit!"

"Mostly because I finally convinced him to raise our rates!" said Trevor.

"Yeah, that was a huge boon to our bottom line," said Finn. It took a bunch of pressure off us. We have some breathing room now, and may be able to pay our investment group back to keep them from getting control of the business."

"If he was smart, he would go out and get a regular loan right now. We have steady income. It would be a piece of cake, and we could pay those thieves off!"

"If it wasn't for those thieves, we may not have a company!" said Alyssa. "Mr. Finn's connections put us in touch with them. Mr. Finn deserves far more credit than he gets for getting us to where we are."

"But it was Trevor's idea to get a CEO in the first place!" said Dylan who had been listening from the shadows. "That's what sold

Mr. Finn on the whole idea. He accepted our proposal because we were smart enough to know we needed a CEO. It was just crazy enough to work. He liked the idea and wanted to help us move forward! Remember?"

"Yes, I remember," said Finn.

"Wait a minute!" said Trevor. "You mean it was my idea that sold Mr. Finn in the first place?"

"Why yes, didn't you know that?" asked Dylan.

Everyone laughed except Trevor who had his mouth hanging open in disbelief.

"Well doesn't that just take the cake!" said Trevor. "I definitely should be running things. This is just too much. Start-up companies are my thing! That's what I do! I help them get started, and take them public."

"You haven't taken one public yet," stated Alyssa.

"Maybe not, but I'm about to," said Trevor.

Trevor was right, the next week he closed a deal taking a medium sized cleaning supply company public. The initial public offering increased in value by 70% the first week earning Trevor $380K. He was indifferent to his profit, and acted as if the sum should have been more. He shrugged it off as no big deal. In the days following, he became more arrogant then ever, and more distant than ever with Alyssa.

Alyssa had become a minor celebrity at the Hollywood-Sunset Rehab Center. She was the primary interface to the customer, and did more one-on-one consulting than their staff psychologist. She spent her days calling managers and agents of people in the entertainment industry, and made sure they understood that the Center stood ready to accept patients in an instant. They would accept them in the most confidential manner possible, and could deal with the most arrogant, egotistical patient they could deliver. She offered discounts to repeat patients. She didn't want to see them back, but was well aware of the reality of relapse, and wanted another shot to prove that the Center's methods were state of the art. She became known all over Hollywood as the Rehab Girl.

"Don't lose control, or you'll have to visit the Rehab Girl," they would state.

Some called her "The Hammer", and others had a little jingle that they would repeat in her presence.

"Not one little drinka, or you'll fall down the abyssa. You'll want to do good-a so that Alyssa will miss ya."

They would recite the phrase to her and stare with a straight face. The goal was to get her to laugh, but even a smile was considered success, and would trigger roars of laughter.

They had a novel approach to sobriety and a diverse clientele. After Trevor's insistence on raising the rates, they were charging approximately $1000 a day for a 30 day stay. Almost everything else was extra, and for those prices they continued to advertise. All rooms were full with a waiting list, but they decided they could never rest. They must always push in the competitive world they lived in. They never let up. Their approach to advertising was also unusual. They had a full-size billboard on Sunset Strip and another on Hollywood Boulevard. They no longer advertised on television, but ran full page adds in relevant entertainment magazines. The subliminal message behind their advertising campaign was that it was fashionable to go to the modern Rehab. Rehab no longer had a stigma. It was the place to clean up, dry out, and recharge your batteries while living in the lap of luxury. It was better than a cruise ship.

Alyssa didn't like the gimmicky nature of their advertising campaign. To her, it was all serious business. She wanted to help people not entice people; but since marketing wasn't her area, she voiced her dissenting opinion, and moved on with her own responsibilities. There was so much work to do that she needed to depend on others to handle some of it.

Toward the end of March 2009 they called a major meeting of board and the investment group. The first order of business was a vote to pay off the investment group in three installments. The CEO had borrowed money from the bank through the channels of a regular business loan as Trevor had informally suggested. Trevor's suggestion was an easy course of action, but their CEO's plan turned out to be better. What was different from Trevor's plan was that the business need only to borrow about one third of the amount owed to the investors. They would depend on quarterly profit to provide the rest. The CEOs plan kept their debt low while leaving their balance sheet in good shape.

"It makes our business a great opportunity for a buy out. We can increase our salaries, and remain working for the parent company that buys us," the CEO said enthusiastically.

The measure was approved unanimously, and the CEO presented the investment group their first check. They would no longer have any interest in the business.

The second order of business was to make Alyssa chairman of the board. Both Alyssa and Trevor were speechless at the suggestion. Alyssa was surprised because she didn't see herself in that role. She was a healer not a business person. Trevor was surprised because he saw himself in that role, but he was denied. They obviously didn't value his services and took him for granted.

"Alyssa is the heart and soul of our operation," the CEO stated while glancing at Alyssa and smiling. "She's our primary interface with the customer. She ensures the success of the treatment program. She's imaginative and inspiring. She has the vision of what we are and where we need to be. Whether we know it or not, we all march to her drum."

Everyone in the room applauded. Alyssa blushed.

"She may not hold the position long," the CEO continued. "We're ripe for a buyout, but she'll very likely continue in a similar capacity with the new company. We want her as the face of the company when suitors come calling."

This proposal was approved with Trevor being the only dissenting vote. Alyssa naturally assumed it was his control issue, but this time she wondered if there was more.

"Is he jealous?" she thought to herself. "If he is, I don't understand why. He wasn't even involved in the beginning of this thing. This was Finn's brainchild. Finn should be upset if anyone is!"

As the meeting broke up, Trevor avoided Alyssa. It bothered her that he was letting business come between them. She thought they were beyond that now. She caught up to him as he was getting into his car.

"Why are you ignoring me?" Alyssa asked point blank.

"I'm not ignoring you," he replied. "I'm just tired. I want to get going."

"Can I get a kiss?" she asked.

Trevor gave her a smooch on the lips, climbed in his car, but left the door open.

"Okay Trevor, I'll see you later?"

"Yes, see you."

Trevor drove off and left Alyssa standing in the street watching him drive away.

Chapter 41

Alyssa's status came with a raise in pay as well as responsibility. Before her promotion, her performance was based on a labor of love. Now she felt obligated to work long and hard hours. Friends, family, and recent hires that she barely knew were all depending on her. The pressure of meeting other people's arbitrary standards began to take the joy out of working. For the first time, she wanted to go back to what she had been doing before. She had never experienced remorse over work. It reminded her of what she was experiencing with Trevor. She was remorseful about the way their relationship was going, and now she could add her work to the list.

For the short-term, she decided to focus on herself. Her graduation was pending with a degree in Rehabilitative Therapy. She wanted to make sure she completed that, and made it her top priority. She had also just turned 21. After the encounter with Trevor in the back seat of his car, she decided she needed a place to go. She felt like it was time to move out of her Grandparents' house, and have a place of her own. She reasoned that it may also help her relationship with Trevor. They could be alone together without worry of intrusion.

After many days of careful consideration, she gathered her parents and her grandparents in Grandpa Jack's living room, and explained. They all agreed it was a good idea, and her Dad agreed to help her through the process. Daisy was concerned about her safety being so young and living all by herself in a city like Los Angeles.

"I have the same concerns Mom," she said. "I would like to keep my room here if that's possible. I could use the new house as a studio at first and a meeting place for my friends. I can move in as I feel comfortable."

"I was just going to suggest that," said Grandpa Jack. "Just leave your room here as it is. You can come and go as you please like you've always done."

"Thanks Grandpa! I appreciate that," she replied.

She had dreamed of owning a house in Hancock Park. With the collapse of the housing market, and her new corporate income, she could actually afford one. She was pre-qualified for a loan. It was hard for her to believe when the realtor began to show her around.

"I'm seriously looking at real estate that only a year ago was way out of reach," she told her agent.

"Think of it as an investment as well as a home," her agent replied. "You may want to upgrade later."

"I'd prefer to own just one house my whole life just like my Grandparents," said Alyssa. "It may be unconventional, but I want my first house to be my dream house!"

"Real estate will increasingly become more of a national market rather than regional market," her realtor said. "Real estate prices will fluctuate on a national basis rather than locally. The price of real estate will also depend on how the nation is diluting its currency. A nation will have a tendency to dilute its own currency in order to devalue its own debt obligations. This will increase the price of a house over time, but its effective value remains the same."

"You're making it sound complicated," said Alyssa. "I've always loved these houses in Hancock Park. They're cute, they're well kept, and they're convenient to everything."

"I'm just confirming your decision," she replied. "You're making an excellent choice in a historic neighborhood. It's a great investment. Since you need a place to live, buy a house. Get it paid for as soon as you can, but don't go overboard in getting it paid off. Live for today, and steadily work toward getting it paid off by age 55 to 60. As each generation approaches retirement age, the government will attempt to dilute the value of all your assets. They'll target your largest asset the most, and your largest asset is usually your house. So it doesn't pay to pay it off too soon. In fact, generally, it doesn't help much to be miserly your whole life waiting for retirement. Only save in accordance with your income."

"That sounds like good advice," said Alyssa. "I can't afford to pay it off, but if I could, it would be very tempting."

Once Alyssa selected a home on South Citrus in Hancock Park, her Dad handled the rest of the transaction.

"Everything's work," she told her Dad. "Even something as exciting as buying your first house is taxing."

341

"Nothing good comes easy," Brad replied. "You know that better than anyone! I'll handle it for you. I love real estate. You help people through rehab, and I deal in real estate. We work well together!"

Alyssa hadn't heard from Trevor for several days. It hurt her to think that she was of no consequence in his life. Power, status, success and money were more important to him than she was. When she reflected back on the time when they first met, she should have known that it may be like this. He thought of people as animals. There was no God, and spirituality was mumbo-jumbo. To Trevor, life was just a big game of survival of the fittest.

"Even then," she thought, "he should value our relationship. Even animals value their mate. As long as we're together everything should be fine."

As she contemplated what they had, she detached herself from the outcome. She had done everything she could. She alone could do no more. If they were to go on, they needed him to contribute too."

"It doesn't hurt as much this time," she thought. "I'll just focus on school and work. I won't call him, and I won't let him get to me."

A month passed. Alyssa closed escrow on her new house. She had plenty of income, but no money. She had spent all her available cash in the home purchase, and had nothing left to buy furniture.

"If you have the income," said Daisy, "you could furnish it on credit. Just pay it back when those checks come in."

"No Mom, I don't want debt. It's a nice thought, but I'll wait until I have enough money. The important thing is that I have a house and a great mortgage with a low interest rate. I feel blessed. You never know what's going to happen. I could lose this job, or the business could go bankrupt. Sure, we're doing well now, but we can't know what the future will bring."

"Okay honey, anything you say. It's an impressive home for such a young lady. You're very fortunate, but it's not just fortune. You had vision, you worked hard, and you made your vision into a reality. That's what your house is made from."

"Thanks Mom, it feels good to hear you say that. It's easy to forget how hard I worked."

The entire family donated what they could to Alyssa's new home, but the house absorbed the items without showing much visible difference. The house still looked empty. Alyssa bought a few bean bag chairs and some temporary furniture. It made her laugh to walk into this beautiful home in Hancock Park with nothing but a few bean bags in the living room. She wanted to share her new project. Finn was busy, and Dylan was working, so she broke down and called Trevor.

"What are you doing?" she asked.

"Alyssa, it's good to here from you! I was thinking of calling you!"

"I bought a house," she stated. "I was hoping you could come and see it. It's laughable."

"I'll be over tonight," he said. "Give me the address. I'll put it in my GPS."

In retrospect, Alyssa decided that her statement could have been misinterpreted. Her home furnishings and décor were laughable, but the house itself was amazing. It was one of the more ornate designs in Hancock Park. Trevor arrived with his mouth hanging open. Alyssa was excited to see him, but he walked right past her scanning the house and evaluating the cost in his head. The extravagance of it sparked feelings in him that may have lain dormant since Alyssa became chairman of the board. He arrived drunk and was slightly slurring his words. Finally, he became aware of his rudeness. He hugged Alyssa and gave her a kiss, but his mind wasn't on her as he walked through the house marveling at the hard woods and the lavish kitchen.

"How did you manage this!" he said.

"I make good money now," said Alyssa, "but all I do is work and go to school. I need to spend it on something! Since I was a little girl, I've always dreamed of owning a house in Hancock Park. Now I do!"

Since it was a special night, Alyssa wanted to try Michael's restaurant on Third Street in Santa Monica, but Trevor insisted on Gladstone's at the corner of Sunset and PCH. It was their regular hangout, and took longer to get there. Alyssa didn't want to go, and due to traffic, Trevor became slightly agitated on the way. The evening was off to a bad start. It became apparent when they arrived, that his dilemma was primarily lack of drink. Since Alyssa was 21 now, he requested to sit at the bar. Alyssa had no interest in sitting at the bar. She had envisioned a romantic evening, and insisted on a quiet table by the window. The wait was 20 minutes. This annoyed Trevor, but Alyssa gave into his desire, and conceded to wait for a table in the bar. This appeased Trevor temporarily. He slammed two drinks while waiting, and ordered a third as they sat down at the table. Alyssa had become desensitized to his drinking, but he had reached a new level, and she wondered what was bothering him. He avoided eye contact with her, and when the food arrived he picked at it instead of eating. He seemed paranoid, scanned the room frequently, and went to the bathroom an unusual amount even for someone heavily drinking.

"Congratulations on graduation at the end of the month," said Trevor finally looking at Alyssa directly.

"Thank you! I'm impressed that you remembered!" she replied trying to lighten the mood. "It's kind of anti-climactic now that I've been working in the field for so long, and am already making good money! It may be a fledgling company, but I'm doing well."

"I still can't believe they made you chairman of the board! They chose someone with no business experience at all, and no experience running a corporation," said Trevor.

"I think that they chose me because I'm a physical representation of what they want to portray. I am rehab! I know the people, and I have the contacts. I've been in the business for four years. In my dreams, I've been a healer for lifetimes. I'm a spiritual healer as well as a rehabilitation counselor. I heal the soul as well as the body. That's why they wanted me! As you told me once about my course of study, I could say the same about yours. Business majors are a dime a dozen. I can buy and sell those like commodities. Anyone can count the beans, but to find someone who sees a great need and fills that need with a quality service is truly rare. People will pay for that."

Trevor laughed out loud.

"The great shaman is going to run a modern business! That's a good one!" he chuckled. "A female no less. They should have given me that job! I'm perfectly trained to handle it."

"We hired Joel Goldstein as CEO to handle exactly what you're talking about. Chairman of the Board is more of an oversight position. You should know that. Besides, I work my regular job there. I still teach meditation and Tai Chi classes. Most of the time, I'm on the phone cultivating new business. Everyone's heard of the Betty Ford Center, but few have heard of Hollywood-Sunset. I want to make our center a household name at least in the LA basin."

"Joel is a loser. He moves too slowly, and doesn't take enough risk. You should fire him and put me in there," said Trevor.

"I'm only one vote on the board. I think Joel's done well. He's set us up for a takeover. We'll all profit, and retain our jobs. He claims a bigger parent company can run us more efficiently.

"You know if anyone should be rewarded with a great position, it's Finn! He's worked his butt off for this company. He deserves a reward."

"Finn's one of your cronies. No, better yet, one of your apostles! He's a whipping boy. He does what he's told. He can't think for himself. He can't manage risk."

"He's smart, and he's hard working!" Alyssa replied.

"You've got a thing for him don't you?" Trevor asked.

"Oh brother, not this again!" said Alyssa. "We're friends Trevor! That's it!"

"What about Dylan?"

Alyssa laughed and smiled and looked at the ceiling.

"Oh Dylan, he's so sweat, and so dreamy. We've been friends since I was six. He's taken on new life. He has a new dry sense of humor, and he's woken up to the need to work. He wants to do something worthwhile that he loves. I think he's finding that in the new business."

Trevor looked perplexed over her response, and ordered another drink. He expected the response on Finn, but with Dylan, she didn't deny anything, and he found it curious.

"Perhaps she does like Dylan in that way," he thought to himself while studying her expressions. "On the other hand, they're probably just close childhood friends. She's too powerful to be with anyone that weak."

"So do you like my new house!" Alyssa asked trying to change the subject.

"Yes, I do, very much so. I must admit I'm jealous. You made a great choice," Trevor replied.

Alyssa couldn't believe the words he was saying.

"He actually admitted to being jealous!" she thought to herself. "There may be hope!"

"It's been neglected," said Alyssa. "It needs a lot of maintenance. It was a foreclosure property, and the previous owners didn't do much to it. I plan to fix it up! I want this to be my only house. I want to live here my whole life just like Grandpa Jack and Grandma Lin."

"Your house is a lot nicer than theirs," said Trevor.

"It's funny that I still live there! I own a house, but still live with my Grandparents!"

They both laughed out loud. It was the first time they laughed together all night. For a moment the old Trevor shined through.

"How is it that everything works out for you?" asked Trevor. "No matter what you're up against, it all seems to fall into place. For me, it's almost the opposite. No matter how hard I try it all seems to go to hell. How do you do it?"

"I think it's mostly an attitude for me. I work for the love of working doing what I believe is right. I'm serving God, so to speak, in the best way I know how, and I'm not attached to the outcome. What ever happens is just what happens, and whatever comes my way just comes my way for good or bad. Of course I try to mold things. I need to take care of myself, but for the most part, I leave my ego out of it, and work for the common good."

"That sounds high and mighty," said Trevor. "It doesn't sound humble."

"It may sound that way, but I'm as humble as I can be. You know, I think you've done quite well for yourself. You were working two jobs without a problem. You closed that big deal taking that company public and made a bunch of money. You're in great shape. Just be patient. Good things will happen for you."

"I just thought I'd be a lot farther along by now," said Trevor. "Look at you."

"You are far along now!" said Alyssa. "You can be no other way! You're everything right now."

"You're not going to get into that touchy feely spiritual stuff are you? You know I'm not into that. I'm a survival of the fittest type of guy."

"You can call it what you want," said Alyssa. "Work because you want to, and not because you get paid. Do things out of love. Money will come along on its own. Detach yourself from the outcome. Detach yourself from the desire for material things."

Trevor paused before he spoke. Moments passed with the two of them glancing at each other. He thought about the spiritual outlook she had on life, and how the most important thing was

347

serving. He thought about his own philosophy of competition and survival of the fittest, and how it wasn't working for him. For the first time in his life, he realized he could be wrong. It humbled him. He felt true humility for the first time in years. Alyssa seemed to read his thoughts and looked down at her finished dinner. The realization shook him, and took the color from his skin. He knew now he had been wrong. He knew now he had to change.

"You may have something. What you're saying could be thought of as just a strategy. It doesn't need any spiritual or religious connection. It just works," said Trevor as if he was thinking out loud.

"That's what I've been trying to tell you," Alyssa responded with wide eyes. "You can make it religious if you want to, but it's more of a philosophy. Basically, you can have anything you want. You just have to ask for it, and then start acting like you have it. You start playing the part. It seems to help if you ask for something that's not strictly for personal gain. In other words, don't be selfish about it. The more it serves the greater good, the easier it seems to come. That's just my observation. It may not be true."

She paused, looked away and looked back again.

"Yes, that's all there is. If you want something, just ask for it, and then start moving your conscious mind in that direction. Eventually it will come."

"Interesting! It's sort of a self psyche! Let's get out of here. You ready?" asked Trevor.

"I'm ready," said Alyssa.

As they left Gladstone's, Alyssa took note of what a difference there was between the start of the evening and the conclusion. The Trevor she knew and loved was back, and he seemed more accepting of her. The valet pulled Trevor's car up.

"Maybe I should drive," said Alyssa. "You've been drinking all night."

"I'm alright," Trevor replied.

348

The valet was holding out the keys listening to the conversation. Alyssa took the keys quickly, and spoke forcefully. Trevor was taken by surprise, and the mood of only seconds earlier suddenly changed.

"You may be alright," stated Alyssa, "but you're definitely illegal to drive. If we get pulled over, you're going to jail. This has been a great evening and I don't want to ruin it. You relax, and I'll get us as far as my house."

Trevor's nose was furrowed. He looked angry, but a thought crossed his mind, and he suddenly lightened up.

"Since you're driving, stop at a liquor store. I want to grab a nightcap."

Alyssa used all her concentration not to show emotion or comment. She knew he'd had enough to drink, but if she commented, the situation could quickly deteriorate further.

"If we stop, you better buy ice because I don't have any," Alyssa said gritting her teeth.

Trevor bought a whole bottle of hard liquor. It looked like some sort of whisky, but she couldn't see it in the bag. Trevor opened the bottle, and took a drink on the way home.

"Please don't do that Trevor," said Alyssa. "A ticket for an open container is mine as well as yours."

"Don't worry about it," Trevor snarled. "We won't get pulled over!"

When they arrived, Trevor filled a large drinking water glass half with ice, and the rest with straight liquor. He settled into one of the bean bag chairs. Alyssa put on some music, and sat in the other bean bag.

"You don't have TV?" he asked.

"No, I don't own a TV," Alyssa answered. "I don't have time for TV anyway."

"Well if you don't have a TV, there's only one thing left to do!" he said.

Trevor set his drink down, rolled off the bean bag, and on to the floor. He started kissing Alyssa starting with the ankle, then gently moving up to the calf, and then more frequently along the thigh. Alyssa liked it at first. She smiled at him and giggled, but when he got to her waist, he rose and lay down on top of her aggressively kissing her lips. She immediately felt uncomfortable, and was unresponsive. He started moving one hand up her skirt between her thighs while the other worked to remove her top almost tearing it. Alyssa started to squirm. She got frustrated, and with one big thrust of both arms, she pushed him off her and back on the floor. Trevor laughed.

"Trevor, this doesn't feel right," she said to him in a cross tone.

"Come on now," he replied moving into a kneeling position. "Isn't it time?"

"No Trevor, you're drunk, and your breath reeks. Let's listen to some music and get some sleep."

While she spoke, the look in Trevor's eyes had changed. He had switched from playful and aggressive to lusting animal within seconds. He was stalking her, and was ready to pounce like a cat. He stared at her from under his brow. She had never seen him like this before, and it frightened her. Instinctively, she prepared herself. He lunged at her, kissed her aggressively again, but this time ripping at her shirt with torn buttons sailing.

"Trevor stop!" she said when she could get breath. "Stop now!"

Her body had gone into emergency defense mode. Suddenly she had amazing strength. She pushed him off once more, but this time he went flying. His ass and his elbow hit the floor hard. Pain shot up his arm. He became angry and his face reddened. Alyssa stood and readied herself. Years of martial arts training put her into defense posture without any thought. Trevor crouched in a squatting position.

350

"Come on Rehab Girl!" he said glaring at her. "Come on Chairman of the Board! Don't you want a piece of this?"

He waited a brief moment for the words to sink in, and lunged at her again. With only one move and one quick hand, Alyssa used Trevor's attacking energy to her advantage. She caught him just below his center of gravity and flipped him as she stepped aside out of his way and stood ready like a matador for the second attack. Trevor landed on his back, and hit his head against the floor. The pain strengthened him, but the humiliation enraged him.

"Trevor you can sleep in the guest room or leave, it's your choice." She stated firmly standing ready.

"You're a weak little female. You think defense moves are so slick. After all we've been through you should be laying down for me passively. Men are the dominant sex of the species," he sneered. "You should be wanting me, wanting my baby, and making my home."

He charged at her, but she readied to use his energy against him a second time. He stopped himself just in time. She was left vulnerable through surprise. He hooked her ankle with one foot and knocked her down. He laughed, and jumped on her back, and began to aggressively mount her. She reached up grabbing both of his shoulders, and in one swift move flipped him over her and onto the floor once more. Before he could gather his wits, she had one arm twisted behind his back pushing the forearm up toward his neck. She rolled him, thrust his face against the floor, and put one knee into his back.

"I guess you like it rough," she stated aggressively. "Is this rough enough for you?"

He struggled briefly to get free, and she pushed his fore arm up toward his neck again. He winced in pain.

"If you move again I'll break your arm. I have no problem at all breaking your arm if that's what you want," she said holding him firmly.

351

Moments passed, and he didn't struggle. He didn't try to speak.

"I'm going to let you go. She finally said. Your only option now is to leave. Leave this house right now! If you try anything else I will hurt you, and I don't want to drive anyone to the hospital tonight. Keep in mind that you're drunk and I'm stone cold sober. I have all my wits about me. I'm ready for you."

She released him, quickly stood, and readied herself.

He stood slowly and without speaking. Blood trickled from his lip, and he wiped it with the back of his hand. He stared at her briefly. He turned, picked up his drink glass that was still standing through the commotion, and stumbled out the door with it. When she was sure he was gone, Alyssa broke down in tears.

The next day Trevor submitted his resignation to the Hollywood-Sunset Rehab Center.

Chapter 42

Alyssa grieved the loss of her relationship with Trevor. Instead of heartbreak, however, she felt numb. She had no feelings at all toward anything. She felt like an abused work horse that had become accustomed to the floggings. Her days passed on autopilot with occasional breakdowns over the sense of loss, but she didn't miss him, she missed what they once had together before her business started.

"What good is a job and money if it ruins your life?" she thought to herself. "If you're so driven that you lose everything that's important to you, then what's the use. It's as if we're desensitized to the important things in life by being drawn into the delusional society we live in. We think that money and things will make us happy, but it's our relationships with people, God, and nature that truly matter. We're very impressed when someone is promoted to a high level so that they can work so hard that they push out everything that matters in their life. We ascend to these high levels and consider ourselves pillars of the community, but all we really are when we arrive is hardened, bitter and old. There's no harmony. We can't hear the music around us. We're out of tune."

She remembered something that Youki had once told her.

"Once, long before I was born," said Youki, "there was a monk that achieved enlightenment at a very young age. When news of this broke, it rang around the town for several days. Some town's people approached the young monk when he came in for supplies. 'How does it feel to be enlightened?' they asked the monk. He looked at them without expression. "Just as miserable as ever," he replied."

She didn't think much about the story when he first told it to her, but she could relate to it in several ways now. Many things that Youki had told her were like that.

"I have much," she thought to herself, "but for some reason I don't feel whole. I wonder if I'm just being selfish, or am I just testing myself. I must let time pass without acting until the answer comes."

She had no time to feel glum or to reflect on what had transpired. She had to move on quickly. Her new position was demanding, yet she continued to perform her old duties. Staying on top of both jobs required long hours. There was constant pressure to perform, and to add to the madness, she was about to graduate from college. Finals week was fast approaching, and she still needed to study.

She retreated to the comfortable familiarity of her Grandparents' house, and left her new home in Hancock Park to sit idle until she was ready.

Her Dad came to her rescue once more and managed the property while she was busy. He started to catch up on the maintenance, and put a plan together to phase in the required renovations. He looked for any opportunity to help her, and seemed obsessed about trying to make up for lost time.

Finals week passed and graduation arrived quickly. Kaylee was graduating too, and both families joined forces to have one graduation party. Instead of having it at Grandpa Jack and Grandma Lin's house like usual, they had the party at Alyssa's Hancock Park home. All the guests were asked to bring a chair because Alyssa refused to buy furniture until she could pay cash. People were sitting in outdoor folding chairs on beautifully finished hardwood floors. Grandma Lin was worried that floors would get scratched, but Alyssa didn't care.

"The house is here to serve people Grandma," she said. "The people aren't here to serve the house."

"That's what you think," said Alyssa's Dad smiling.

The party was a great success with all Kaylee and Alyssa's friends attending accept Trevor. Mr. Finn, Finn, Dylan, and Joel Goldstein the CEO all dropped by to congratulate the graduates. Daisy's Mom spoke to her Dad for about 30 minutes. That was the longest they had spoken since Brad was invited into Alyssa's life.

When the heightened spirits of graduation returned to the steady state of everyday living, time passed by quickly. With school over, the pace was easier for Alyssa to manage. When she could, she worked on her home, and when she had time to go out, she explored Kaylee's advanced social world. They avoided Gladstone's for fear of seeing Trevor, and found new places to investigate in Belmont Shores.

"Do you find it interesting that you were already employed full time, working in your field, and well paid long before you finished your degree?" Kaylee asked Alyssa.

"No, I never thought much about the degree. I just knew what I wanted to do and thought it would be worth my while studying the subject. The degree also provides some credibility for people who don't know me. Besides, you meet a lot of great people in college. I liked college. What I didn't expect, was to be working so much so soon, but I'm finally okay with it."

"You already have a really nice house!" said Kaylee. "Most people don't get a house until much later, and your house is fine!"

"It comes with a nice loan payment every month," Alyssa said laughing. "It may be extravagant for someone my age, but I only wanted one purchase. I needed a place to live, and that place came to me. I plan to live there my whole life. Later on, if I want a place to get away to, I wouldn't mind a cottage in Big Sur."

"That's funny," said Kaylee. "I can see you going back there too. You love it there!"

"Yes, I love it there," Alyssa said staring into space.

Alyssa spent her Fourth of July with Dylan and her Dad at the Hancock Park house. They barbequed and tried various recipes. Finn stopped by for a few minutes, and her Grandparents dropped by for about an hour with Daisy and Franken. Kaylee had another new boyfriend, and failed to show. When it finally started to get dark, Dylan tagged along with Alyssa and her Dad to watch the annual fireworks display at Marina Del Rey.

After the Fourth, life became routine again for Alyssa. Days were long and repetitive, and the weather became unusually warm for Los Angeles. Alyssa wished she had air conditioning in the new house because her room in the attic at her Grandparent's was hot even with the window unit on full blast. She spent the summer nights on the floor of her new home with just an air mattress and a sheet.

Toward the end of July, the CEO of Hollywood-Sunset Rehab Center requested a meeting of the board of directors. Alyssa was surprised because the meeting for the quarter ending June 30th was already over. This was a special meeting, and he also requested to arrange a meeting for all employees in the days following. It was the only excitement in what had become the doldrums of summer.

"We've been offered a buyout from the Bowerman Investment Group," the CEO stated as he began to speak. "They're offering

$26.8 million dollars for rights to the entire enterprise. They want to purchase both real estate holdings at 15% above cost plus improvements. The 15% would be computed first. In other words, we wouldn't be making money on the improvements to the facilities. Finally, they're offering everyone in the room today with the opportunity for a position with the new company. A few of us would be required to stay on. They want continuity, and view us as essential to the operation. They'll negotiate our salaries individually, but they agree that pay should be equivalent to what you're making now.

Months ago, we discussed setting the company up for a buyout, and that's exactly what we've done. We all stand to profit substantially, but we need a two thirds vote of approval from the board. I must also warn you that this is our first offer. We could get better offers, but we may not get any additional offers. We're a new company in a niche business. There aren't a lot of investors out there looking for a company like ours. They're attracted to our profit, low debt load, and dedicated and competent workforce. They see potential. I suggest we accept their offer."

For Alyssa there wasn't much of a decision. She was already disillusioned with the greedy competitive society she lived in, and longed for simpler days and simpler times. She worked too hard, and for the first time in her life, she wanted a break. She was voting yes.

The measure was passed unanimously by the board. The business was sold for $26.8 million plus the cost of the real estate. Mr. Finn was very happy. With his place on the board, and the profit from his real estate investment, he did very well.

Finn and Alyssa were the major share holders owning 80% of the privately held shares. Dylan and the CEO owned most of the remainder. Last was Trevor who bought a few shares when he joined the company, and let it ride when he quit.

After expenses were paid, Alyssa would receive $7.4 million with the requirement that she continues in her current capacity.

Staying on with the new company would pay her an extra bonus of $500 thousand payable up front. If she quits before two years is up, she's required to pay back the entire $500K. She had additional profit from the gym. She paid her Dad back for the original investment, and kept the profit for herself. Her Dad didn't really want the money, and set up a trust in her name.

There was also a profit sharing bonus for all employees. The average payout was $50K. Alyssa benefited from that too. All told she would gross $8.1 million dollars. She paid $3.2 million in state and federal taxes, and pocketed $4.9 million.

"That's pretty good for just finishing your degree a few months ago," said Kaylee while sipping an ice tea in Belmont Shores. "Now you have money to buy some furniture."

Alyssa laughed.

"Yes, it's so weird. I can't actually say I'm retired. By contract, I have to work for two more years. If I don't it'll cost me $500K, but I could hang it all up right now. For all practical purposes, I received my degree and retired at the same time!"

They paused for a minute looking at each other, and then broke out laughing again.

"The last thing I'm thinking about is furniture," Alyssa continued. "I don't know what I'm going to do with the money yet. I want to think about it for a while. I want to do something smart."

"Your car is getting old," said Kaylee, "You should at least replace that."

"You're right," Alyssa acknowledged. "I do need a car, but I don't know what I want. I'm just going to chill for a while until the path forward becomes clear."

It didn't take long until the path became clear. Alyssa had been working for the new company for about three weeks when she was called into the board room. Seated at the table were the new board members. The environment seemed very normal for a large firm, but there was one major exception. Trevor was there. Alyssa tried to ignore him until she couldn't avoid it any longer.

Their eyes locked. She felt hatred from Trevor. It was glaring hatred and jealousy. She had no feelings at all besides being uncomfortable. She was confident she wasn't sending any energy or message whatsoever. She focused on keeping her energy tight.

"We're under contract with you," the new CEO stated after Alyssa was seated. "We have no intention of breaking that contract; however, we've hired Trevor Granderson to manage the local marketing efforts. We no longer require that service of you, and want to turn over all of that work to Trevor."

The new CEO's voice seemed very familiar. His eyes seemed familiar too, but Alyssa couldn't place him. The new CEO stood, paused, and began to pace around the room.

"We want you to work with him until he's managing that effort efficiently," the CEO continued. "We understand that you know each other, and that your relationship may be strained. We trust that you can keep your relationship professional and at the business level. There's no need to delve into personal experiences of the past. In the event you can't keep it professional, and you breach contract, Trevor will retain the $500K that you'll owe the company. Beyond that, you can continue teaching your classes and consulting patients as you see fit."

He looked her dead in the eyes as he completed his words, and with his penetrating gaze, Alyssa was absolutely sure that she had met him before. As the gravity of his words settled, she was stunned. She looked away and sat in disbelief with a deer in the headlights expression.

"Is that it?" she asked. "Are we done here?"

He rose without speaking and left the room. His assistant answered for him.

"Yes Ms. Daingerfield, we're finished. Thank you for your time."

"I'm being set up for failure," she thought as she walked out. "They want me to quit and forfeit the money. Trevor's a part of the plot. He wants me to fail too, but he wants to humiliate me first."

Alyssa knew immediately deep down inside that she should quit and give back the money. She was thrust into a no-win situation, and would be wasting her time even trying to continue. She had always trusted her inner voice, and it was speaking to her now, but her heart hardened. She wasn't about to let them take advantage of her, and she wasn't going to let Trevor have his revenge. She would fight the fight, and she would either win, or go down fighting. She felt that she was a force to be reckoned with. She would fight until there was no fight left in her.

Working with Trevor proved to be more difficult than anticipated. She provided him with the business contacts he needed, and coached him on who to call and when. She offered her philosophy on how to cultivate clients, and explained often how being in touch with the agents and managers of successful people can fill rehab beds.

In response he was cold, indifferent, and treated her like his employee. He occasionally put her down. She ignored the comments, and for the most part, avoided him, but there had to be some interface. She began to dislike going to work, and remembered vowing not to be this way when she was younger.

Several of her clients called her and complained about Trevor or his assistants. They wanted to deal with her as they had always done. They claimed that she understood the real task at hand, and that Trevor or his assistant had no clue how to get someone cleaned up.

Trevor often reeked of alcohol himself, and when she was forced to deal with him in the morning, he was obviously hung over and irritable. It took until the lunch hour until he perked up. Alyssa suspected that the improvement in attitude was due to the anticipation of his next drink.

As the weeks passed, she felt like she could go on, she had transferred most of her knowledge and techniques to Trevor as directed. She was done. For her, it came down to a race against the clock. It turned out to be a race she was about to lose.

She was called back once more to the board room.

"We had to let go of Wang Diang," the CEO stated. "You know, the one you call Frenchy. We want you to move into his office and stay out of the center. We'll handle things from here with rehabilitation."

"He only worked here as a favor to me you fools!" said Alyssa as her anger grew. "He's a veteran martial arts instructor. There are few better than Frenchy."

"Just the same," said the CEO, "he's gone. We want you to manage that building and make sure the bathrooms are kept clean."

Alyssa stared at him in disbelief. Trevor was smiling as he watched her reaction. It was clear that they were attempting to force her to quit, but it wasn't their game that had Alyssa captivated. She knew those eyes, and she knew that voice.

"Up until now I've played your little game of trying to discredit me and ruin my reputation while luring me with a half million dollars. You think that everyone is driven by money, and you think this business is based on money. Let me explain something, this business was started with love. We loved each other, we loved what we were doing, and we loved seeing people walk away clean and sober with a new lease on life. This place is all about reflection, adjustment, and rebirth. It's not about money. You can't prostitute this place. It will never work, and these high profile clients will see right through you. You'll go down in flames. I'm good at what I do because I'm not a fraud. I'm humble and I take what I do seriously. That's why I'm successful. You're nothing but hired guns in pursuit of meaningless paper that society calls money. If you stay on this path, you will fail, and your life will be miserable."

Alyssa was surprised about the words that poured from her mouth. It was as if something within her took control of her speech. Even the tone of her voice changed. Her words were hypnotic, and stung as they reached their intended recipients. She spoke to the CEO, and ignored Trevor. She had waged war against him. It was an ancient battle between the spiritual world of thought and feeling, and the material world of solid objects, survival of the fittest, power, and greed.

Trevor was shocked by Alyssa's words. The CEO was angered. He knew what he was dealing with. He had been in similar battles before, and was defeated. He needed to win.

"I'd like to be alone in the room with Ms. Daingerfield," the CEO stated as if he had the authority of the entire country behind him.

When everyone left the room he stood, and walked over to Alyssa. He was angry, but held his anger in abeyance. He rubbed his chin with his left hand as he paced back and forth in front of her without speaking. Alyssa was calm, and was careful not to anticipate his next move so that her judgment was not clouded. She cocked her head slightly without realizing it as a result of years of martial arts training. It was second nature to use her more reactive peripheral vision to monitor her opponent.

"You'll do what you're told Ms. Daingerfield, or not only will you lose your money, but you'll lose your reputation as well. You'll lose everything! I'll personally see to it. You're a part of this company now, and as an employee, you'll do what you're told like everyone else. You think you're something, but you're nothing. You're nothing without me, and you'll do what you're told or suffer the consequences."

"You're threatening me," Alyssa stated calmly.

"Yes."

When he said the word yes, he made a hissing sound at the end of the word. Alyssa finally placed the eyes and the voice. She narrowed her eyes, and looked at him anew. He was the man that attempted to rape her when she was 13 at Corey's apartment near Sunset Strip. She knew him now. He was older, bald, and had many worry lines, but it was him. It was the same man. She stood so that she could react if necessary.

"You're a coward and a rapist" Alyssa said without any emotion. "You prey on defenseless children. Why don't you go back to the streets where you belong?"

Her remarks took him by surprise. He was enraged at the statement, and the anger began to show. He managed to remain calm but his eyes were aflame. He had been sure that she hadn't recognized him.

"I should have raped you when I had the chance," he replied. "That's all you're good for. Do you think your little witch voice is going to save you now? Why don't you conjure up one of the demons within you and save yourself once more?"

Alyssa was already reacting from within. What he was suggesting she was already doing. Whether it was a demon or a saint, the process was already in motion.

"I called you a coward," she repeated. "What do your own kind call you on the street? A pussy? A wimp? You prey on children!"

He could contain his anger no longer. He stepped in toward her, and swung his fist at her face. She barely moved so that the swing went wide. She kept her balance and her concentration. She caught his wrist in one hand and elbow in the other and twisted with the force of her entire body. There was a crackling sound, but not the sound of breaking bones. As he went down, her knee caught him in the groin crushing both testicles. She looked at him lying on the floor, took out a five dollar bill, flicked the bill so that it landed on his face, and left the room. Trevor remained waiting outside.

"What happened?" he asked as she walked by.

"I bought him for five bucks," she said passing him by and striding down the hall.

Chapter 43

Alyssa felt foolish for being sucked into the exact situation that she spent her whole life trying to avoid. She had been taken in by money, power, and the games associated with them. The confrontation had been a wake-up call. It made her realize that she must stay true to herself and her belief system no matter what happened. She would work to get back on track, and devote herself to spiritual service.

She dropped everything, and spent two days reflecting and meditating.

"There's no use in charging ahead in the wrong direction," she reasoned with herself. "I must wait until the path is clear, and the decision is easy based on that inner feeling that's never let me down!"

She decided that she was unemployed, and began looking for a small office to rent in Santa Monica. She wanted a place to go that was away from home and strictly associated with work. She spent her days in Hancock Park, and her nights at her Grandparents. She had no place to be during the day, and it felt odd. On the fifth day she was served when answering the door at her Hancock Park home. She was being charged with assault and sued for breech of contract. They wanted $1 million. She expected as much, and spent the next week talking to the LAPD and consulting attorneys. She claimed he had attacked her first, and that she was acting in self-defense. Since there was no one in the room, it was her word against his, and her attorney claimed that it would never go to court.

"No jury will believe that a professional woman would physically attack a man first," her attorney stated in a matter of fact manner. "They would believe, however, that he attacked you first not knowing your skill set. That's a very plausible scenario. They know that. What they want is their money. We can drag this thing out, but eventually, you'll end up paying the $500K. I suggest we offer that now on the condition they drop all charges, and can never bring up another action. Once this is settled, it's settled for good."

"Let me think about it for a day or two," Alyssa replied.

"Don't think too long," her lawyer warned. "If we're going to take that approach, we need to do it quickly and be done with it."

Alyssa spent two more days meditating, reflecting, and remaining quiet at her Grandparent's house. She knew that what her attorney proposed was the right answer, but it bothered her. She felt like she was being taken advantage of. She felt like she should keep the money. She wanted the money. She started to think about money and remembered Youki's $5 gold piece. She pulled it out, examined it, and laid it on the table in front of her.

"What would Youki do?" she asked herself while staring at the coin.

Suddenly, the answer came to her. She slammed her hand down on the coin.

"The answer has been staring me in the face all along," she thought to herself. "I had a conflict, and this is the first temptation after the conflict. I remain hung up on the money. I'm as corrupt as they are. I have to let the money go freely. The money is meaningless."

She thought of her last meeting with Youki, and what he had said to her. He said it on two different occasions, and it had only served to annoy her. She hadn't understood. She remembered now the important difference.

"If you love something, give it up, if it comes back, it was always yours, if it doesn't, it was never yours to begin with," Youki had stated.

"He wasn't talking about people like the traditional version," she thought. "He was talking about things and people, or money

364

and people. He was making a broad statement, and it applies now! It applies perfectly!"

Alyssa called her attorney.

"I want to make the offer that you proposed," she directed him, "but I want to give it to the CEO in person with you present as a witness and their attorney present as well. I want to give it to them in cash. That's my condition. If I can't give them the money in cash and in person, we don't have a deal."

"Okay, I'll write it up and phone you when I hear back."

Three days passed with no word. Alyssa felt like they were stalling to make her sweat. On the morning of the forth day, her lawyer called.

"They've accepted your offer. All charges will be dropped on both sides, and you'll pay back the $500K originally agreed within two weeks. You can pay in cash and in person."

"Make an appointment for Friday morning," Alyssa responded.

Alyssa showed up that Friday morning with two young men. One was pushing a hand truck with two boxes.

"Are you planning to pay them in quarters?" her attorney asked when he saw them.

"Close but not quite," said Alyssa. "Watch and learn."

They were greeted in the CEOs office by two attorneys and a security officer who looked overweight. The CEO was sitting at his desk.

Before any words were spoken the young men grabbed the boxes and dumped the contents onto the CEO's desk. Gold coins came spilling out all over the desk. A good portion of the coins landed in the CEOs lap. Everyone was shocked, and stared in disbelief at hundreds of gold coins. The security guard started to speak, but Alyssa beat him to it.

"On your desk are 510 gold Krugerrands minted in South Africa. It's the international currency of the underworld that you belong to. It amounts to more than $500K at today's bullion rates. I wanted to pay you with the tokens that you worship. My attorney will stay here while you count them."

"Certainly Miss Daingerfield," her attorney replied smiling. "Anything you say. We'll make it all legal like before I leave!"

Alyssa tilted her head up, turned, and walked out.

Alyssa wasn't finished. While she waited word from her attorney that the transaction was complete and the case closed, she stood in front of the office building of the new owners and thought about the expressions on their faces when she dropped 510 one ounce gold coins on the desk. She was ready for the next portion of her plan.

She walked to the sidewalk in front of their office building, from her bag she produced a stack of paper money, and started handing out dollar bills to any passerby that would accept one. Recipients were startled at first, but news of free money traveled fast, and that outflow progressed handsomely. The first day she handed out $180. The next day she returned to the same spot with a stack of five dollar bills, and handed out over 300 within four hours. The third day she moved up to ten dollar bills, and the fourth day twenties.

She began to know all the locals that worked in the area, and delighted in handing out bills to employees of her former company. She knew that she was making a stir within their offices. It felt like their eyes were burning into her back from their second story windows. She was confident that her actions were bothering them at the root of their being.

"What is she doing?" she could imagine them saying. "Is she giving away money? Is she nuts? She's done with us now! We both got what we wanted! Why is she doing this? It was just business, and nothing personal."

She didn't know for sure, however, if they had noticed her at all.

Recipients of her generosity began to ask her about her motives. She resisted at first because it slowed her progress, but as

366

the buzz surrounding her exploits increased, she felt obligated to explain herself.

In the meantime she heard from her attorney that her case had settled, the deal was complete, and they could never again file a law suit against her.

Since the lawsuit was over, she felt free to explain her story to those that would listen. She wanted to express her need to help people, and demonstrate why she considered herself a healer. She wrote down a script that detailed her progression into rehabilitation, how she ended up starting her own center, and what triggered her unexpected departure at great personal loss when she had been working hard in good faith in accordance with her contract.

"I've been fortunate. I started with nothing but a passion and an idea, and became part of a very successful start-up business," she repeated dozens of times. "The business helped the community and made a small profit. It served a useful purpose, and we were all pleased with the results. When the company was purchased, however, a lot of the magic faded as the new management took over and made changes."

"Why are you giving away money?" several people asked her.

"My biggest point is that money wasn't the point! I just wanted to help people, and huge personal gain resulted from years of focused attention to my cause. Helping people was my point, not money. Money only has value because people believe it has value, but what's needed is to believe in each other rather than money. I'm demonstrating that by giving it away freely without expectation. In doing that, I'm returning something to the community that made me what I am, and at the same time, I expose the greed and political maneuvering of my former employer."

It was a simple explanation, and helped her come to terms with what had transpired; but Alyssa grew tired of repeating her story. She took a few days off for reflection and meditation, and at the end of it, decided to have a pamphlet made up that explained her situation. She moved up to handing out fifty dollar bills, and spent five more days giving away money and pamphlets in front of her former employer's offices.

Word spread quickly of her reinvigorated exploits and larger denomination currency, and people learned where and when to look for her.

She moved up to one hundred dollar bills, and when she did, she was very pleased.

"I've reached the denomination of the underworld!" she thought to herself, "this is the type of bill that those greed obsessed men understand. It will drive them to madness when they see me giving away hundreds on the street!"

She was giving away over $3000 a day, and began to attract crowds. People worshiped her for her ideals.

"Excessive money is evil," some chanted repeatedly.

It bothered her that they said this, and it bothered her that they exalted her for simply pointing out what should be obvious to all.

To prevent attracting too much attention too quickly, she varied her patterns, arrived at different times of day, and didn't linger more than thirty minutes.

Finally she reached her goal and moved up to one ounce gold bullion coins. She wanted to give away Krugerrands, but had difficulty obtaining large numbers of them all at once. She was forced to work in one ounce gold American Eagles and Canadian Maple Leafs. She understood that the underworld loved the Krugerrand, but she was forced to work with what was available.

Large crowds began to form and wait for her all day. They occasionally blocked traffic, and interrupted the daily business routine. They played hooky from school and work. One coin made it worth their while. People from all walks of life mixed together. Rich, poor, middle class, successful businessmen, and starving artists all had their hands out and were interested in the gimmicky nature of the new anti-establishment sentiment. Alyssa had become a spectacle and a fad. What was more, it paid to see her.

They called her the "Golden Girl", and when she arrived the crowd went into a frenzy calling her name and asking for a bullion shower.

She had no idea what was happening inside, but she knew that she was really bothering them. She was no longer a joke, she was a nuisance.

"They want me to go away," she thought smiling, "and are devising a method to get rid of me."

Only hours later, Trevor came down to the street to reason with Alyssa. He had to work his way through the crowd in order to confront her. When he finally made it to where she stood, her back was turned, but somehow he knew that she felt his presence. She continued with what she was doing. As if for show, she handed out several gold coins while her back was turned to him. He paused for a moment wondering if she really did sense him. He laughed out loud quietly to himself for such a thought. Knowing better than to underestimate her, he tapped her on the shoulder. The answer was clear from the moment their eyes locked. She knew exactly what she was doing. After a pause she smiled, and offered him a gold coin. He refused it.

"Are you crazy!?" he started with his face flushing. "You're giving away a fortune! Each one of those coins is worth a thousand dollars!"

"Crazy is a relative thing," she responded calmly and quietly. "I may be crazy by your standards, but by my standards you're crazy. Some people obsess over obtaining and holding onto money to the exclusion of everything else. They ignore the people and things they love for the lure of money. It's a strange addiction, and it's as bad as drugs or alcohol."

"You've worked hard your whole life," Trevor stated. "You sacrificed considerable childhood comforts and many nights out

369

working toward your vision. This is your big payoff! Why squander it?"

"Our time together must have meant something," Alyssa said while handing out another gold coin. "You've got it partially right. I've worked my whole life toward my vision and will continue to do so. My needs have always been met. I've been fortunate in this world, but money had very little to do with it. Giving this little bit away is like throwing handfuls of salt in the ocean. Money is like dust blowing around the earth. It makes a difference sometimes, but for the most part, it makes no difference."

Trevor smiled and chuckled, "How naïve. You've had a good life because you've always been supported by someone. Don't kid yourself. It's all about money!"

"Well here then!" she replied offering him another coin.

"Please stop this insanity!" he pleaded. "You're clear of us now! Why don't you go to your beautiful home in Hancock Park and forget about this!"

"I will," Alyssa calmly shot back. "I'll do just that, but I feel the need to give back right now. I'm not quite finished yet."

"If you're not finished yet give me a coin!" a woman yelled from the crowd and while thrusting out her hand.

"They're going to call the police on you!" said Trevor. "Please leave before they do!"

"What are they going to do?" Alyssa asked. "Arrest me for giving away money? It bothers you and the dogs upstairs doesn't it? That's why you're calling the police. You can't stand it that someone is just giving away what you so strongly desire!"

"They're accusing you of obstructing traffic and becoming a public nuisance."

Alyssa laughed out loud, "Let them arrest me then!"

"You can't say I didn't warn you," said Trevor.

"Of course," said Alyssa, "wash your hands of it. It's so easy to do and walk away from. You're doing the right thing aren't

370

you? Just working for the money. That's the right thing isn't it? Your conscience is now clear!"

Trevor's eye's bore down on Alyssa, but she didn't flinch.

"Oh what's the use!" cried Trevor.

He turned and walked away.

Within minutes the police arrived. They moved through the crowd with experienced efficiency advising people to disperse. When they made it to Alyssa she immediately offered them both a gold coin. The policemen looked at each other with incredulous expressions.

"I would love to accept your offer, but we're on official business, and your gesture could be considered a bribe."

"I'm giving the coins away to everyone!" Alyssa responded. "I'm not singling you out! Besides, policemen are very deserving. You keep us safe for not much money. No one can deny that you have a tough job. You're serving the public in the strictest sense."

"Thank you very much Miss," the policeman replied. "You sound very sincere, and I'm not one to judge the actions of others. You must have your reasons for doing what you're doing. I see a lot of unusual things out here in the streets, but I'm forced to ask you to stop. We've received a complaint, and if you continue we'll be forced to arrest you."

Alyssa laughed, "Arrest me! You're going to arrest me in front of all these people for giving away gold? You may not get the reaction you're looking for."

"Don't arrest her until she's done!" someone yelled.

"You can't just give away coins worth $1000 in the street and not expect to cause a disturbance," the officer stated bluntly. "If you want to give away your money, that's your business, but don't do it here or I'll be forced to arrest you. Start a website or something."

"I grew up on the street," Alyssa responded. "This is where I feel at home, and these are the people I want to help. I don't see how I'm doing anything wrong."

371

"You're causing a disturbance Ma'am. That's all as far as I'm concerned."

"Well arrest me then," said Alyssa holding out her wrists to the officer in anticipation of handcuffs.

A hush fell over the small crowd as word spread that they were arresting the golden girl. Murmuring rippled back and forth through the people in a wavelike motion. The intensity of the moment made the police officers take pause. They each seemed to appraise the situation in their heads.

"Out of respect Ma'am," the policeman started, "I understand your point, and I can tell that you're a good person. I can't stand here and debate the merits of our monetary, social or legal systems. I have a job to do, and all I can do in your case is enforce the law."

"Well enforce the law then!" Alyssa defiantly stated holding her wrists out a second time.

The policeman smiled and scanned the crowd with a smirk, "Let me make myself perfectly clear. I'm giving you the option to walk away and save everyone a lot of trouble. I'm not telling you that you can't do what you're doing. I'm telling you that you can't do it anymore today at this location. Do you understand? After today you can do anything you want."

Alyssa paused to think, "Yes, I understand."

By now the crowd had grown even larger with the spectacle of the golden girl's tentative arrest. Hardly anyone was speaking in anticipation of what would happen next. Those who were speaking were whispering to each other. The police officer sensed the tension in the air, and deliberately delayed speaking or moving. He was smiling, and definitely didn't want to arrest Alyssa. He wanted to help her. Alyssa sensed this, and stalled momentarily. She scanned the crowd, the police, and back to the crowd. Her expression changed. She shot a wry glance at the police officer, and then focused with intent on the crowd.

"I'll be back to give another day!" she said loudly to the crowd so that everyone could hear.

"She'll be back another day!" someone nearby yelled louder with glee.

The crowd cheered and applauded in agreement. The officers both smiled broadly.

"Could you escort me to my car?" Alyssa asked. "I have about 30 coins left, and wouldn't want to tempt anyone. Safety first!"

"Certainly Ma'am! Let us carry your bag, and we'll walk you to your car."

Alyssa suddenly felt unsafe even with a police escort. What had once been the overwhelming desire to give all her money away quickly turned to a desire to avoid the fickle crowd. She envisioned things turning riotous with the slightest emotional shift. With the amount of money she was carrying, she realized she was vulnerable.

She wanted to make a point, and had succeeded, but now that she had everyone's attention, she knew there would be those that would take advantage.

She decided she should stay at her Grandparents' house. Her intuition turned out to be accurate. There was a short clip of her confronting the police officer, and the paparazzi had found out where she lived and had staked out her house in hopes of an interview.

The news had spliced several two or three second outtakes into a 15 second clip. It depicted a mentally unstable young millionaire who wanted to give all her money away. They focused on her intense look. She could usually control it, but that day it had gotten away from her. She appeared completely crazy, and the police officer appeared callous and insensitive. The opposite was true. They had used her to create entertaining news, and the point of her actions had been lost.

Alyssa watched the clip in disbelief with her Grandparents. Grandpa Jack recognized her, but couldn't believe what she was saying.

"Those words would never come out of your mouth in that order!" he protested.

They recorded the clip on their DVR, and played it back several times. They found it very unsettling how the news managed to twist every word. They all sat in a hypnotic state without commenting, and glanced at each other in disbelief. Finally Grandpa Jack spoke again.

"They failed!" Grandpa stated firmly. "They wanted to make you appear crazy, but your inner peace came shinning through. You had peaceful determination in your actions. You knew what you were doing. People will sense that. We know that things are not always what they seem."

"Grandpa's right honey," said Grandma Lin. "Their attempts to frustrate you and make you look foolish failed. You're obviously a person of substance, and the reporters were obviously not. They were interested in creating a story, filling air, and selling commercials. You, on the other hand, were just trying to remind us of what the truth is. I think you succeeded."

Alyssa's initial reaction was one of disappointment. She knew that she had made her point within the walls of her former business, but she hadn't driven the message home with the public as she had desired. She remembered her own $5 gold coin that Youki had given her, and how it had become inspirational.

"It's not about money!" she thought to herself, "and that was my point! The money is obviously nice, but it comes and goes, and it mostly goes! What it's really about is knowing yourself, being engaged in what you're good at, persevering, and working effectively at the tasks you've selected with balance and peaceful resolve. Money will eventually come."

She sat quietly for a minute.

"If you can get beyond the dread of losing it all" she suddenly exclaimed out loud to her Grandparents, "you've developed enough spiritually to will it all back!"

With that thought she decided that the show wasn't over, and that the reporters outside her home in Hancock Park were an advantage to her. She could manipulate too.

"Tonight I'll become an actress," she said out loud while standing up. "I have an idea! I'm headed home!"

"Why go home at this hour?" asked Grandma Lin.

"I have an idea Grandma!" she said running up the stairs to her room.

She returned in 15 minutes wearing a white summer dress her Mom had given her. It was so pretty that she hadn't found the occasion to wear it yet. In that short amount of time she had also put on makeup and let her hair out. Both her Grandparents were startled by the sudden change in appearance. She was breathtakingly beautiful, sexy, and at that particular moment, she had a wild mischievous look about her.

"My word!" said Grandma Lin, you look radiant! You'll get arrested going out alone looking like that."

"That's the point Grandma," Alyssa replied while still brushing her hair.

"Would you like me to go with you?" asked Grandpa Jack. "I can keep the wolves at bay!"

"Thanks Grandpa, but you've helped me enough already. I want to attract as many werewolves as I can get! In fact, I want to attract every animal in the forest. Tonight I'm going to have a young man to protect me, and he's a young man that I've been ignoring too long. I'm bringing Dylan, but I'll be operating like Kaylee. Dylan's already on his way. I'm meeting him there."

"Sounds like a recipe for trouble if you ask me. Do you have the pepper spray I bought you?"

"Yes Grandpa."

"Well you be careful!" said Grandma Lin.

When Alyssa arrived, Dylan was already waiting in his car a few doors down from her house. She parked behind him. He spotted her, and hastily got out of the car as if trying to go unnoticed. His attempt at stealth was clumsily executed causing more noise than normal, but no one noticed. He was wearing a black suit and carrying a bouquet of flowers. She smiled at him as she got out of the car, and they hugged as close friends would hug. She kissed him on the cheek.

"Thanks for coming!" she said.

"This better be good," he stated formally. "Here are the flowers you requested."

Before she responded she arranged him adjusting his jacket and straightening his tie. She hadn't seen him for a while, and standing in his suit he looked striking. He had an air of confidence that she had never noticed before. He was smiling, calm, and ready to play her game. His look and his attitude stirred something inside her. She realized it was her old friend grown up and handsome.

She studied him for a moment without speaking.

"Thank you for the flowers," she stated slowly keeping her eyes on him.

She suddenly broke her gaze and got on task.

"All I want you to do is escort me to the door, and come inside on my cue. I'll do the rest," she said without looking at him.

"You've got it!" Dylan replied offering her his arm. "It's all yours from here."

By now the paparazzi that had been nearly asleep on her doorstep had noticed her, and in a bumbling manner, they were tripping over each other to activate their equipment and move her way.

Alyssa tilted her head back, raised her nose in the air, and proceeded forward.

"Walk as slowly as you can manage toward the front door," she whispered, "pause when I do to talk to the reporters."

Dylan smiled and proceeded without reply.

Video camera lights where immediately upon them, and the flashes from still cameras peppered the evening with a stroboscopic effect. Alyssa walked provocatively as if she had run

376

this gauntlet a thousand times. She paused occasionally to pose for pictures. Dylan's smile was barely noticeable. He remained steadfast with his eyes focused in the distance. He was the backdrop, the straight man, and the arm candy.

"Miss Daingerfield," someone called, "why do you want to give away your fortune?"

Several microphones were immediately thrust toward her.

"You always need to give a portion back," she stated to no one in particular. "You know, tithe as they say. It also takes money to make money, and I intend on making more, much more."

She flipped her hair back out of her eyes to face them, and continued their walk.

"Isn't that crazy?" the same voice asked.

She paused again to face them.

"At this moment in time," she said with an endearing look, "I can afford to be crazy."

"Why now?" someone else asked.

"It's just my time to give back," she said calmly releasing Dylan's arm and turning to face him.

She looked into his eyes.

"I'm almost done giving, but for now, it's my time."

She put both arms around Dylan's neck, and to his surprise, kissed him in a glorious public display of affection. It started as part of an act, but Dylan took it a step further by taking her in his arms and leaning into the kiss. She understood the demonstration, leaned back in his arms, and raised one foot.

It was authentic, and the people present understood. The event triggered a barrage of photographs.

His kiss was warm and inviting, and his arms felt good around her. She felt the comfort of security even with so many strangers' eyes upon them.

They paused, looked into each others eyes, and kissed again more passionately than before.

The audience broke into applause. They finished their kiss as if no one was watching, and scampered hand in hand the rest of the way to the front porch. The crowd moved in around them as if they had climbed onto a stage, and Alyssa purposely fumbled with her key.

Once the door was open, Alyssa turned and threw her bouquet of flowers into the crowd. Everyone cheered.

"Miss Daingerfield," someone called, "what about your former business? Will they be pressing charges?"

"Please call me Alyssa," she said smiling warmly. "We have a legal agreement, but they'll do what they must. It may sound like a judgmental thing to say, but I've exposed them for the manipulative greedy people that they are. They think they can use people, but they're wrong. They can't use me! If they want to save their business, they'd better think about helping people rather than harassing them."

"What will you do now?" someone asked from the back.

"After a few months off, I'll be back doing what I'm good at: spiritual counseling, Tai Chi, and drug and alcohol rehabilitation."

Everyone paused to take notes.

"As a teacher and not a patient," she added.

Everyone laughed, and Alyssa kissed Dylan again, but this time the kiss was both real and theatrical.

"Do you have any gold left?" a man asked in front.

"Of course!" Alyssa replied digging into her purse.

She produced a handful of one ounce gold coins, gently rolled them out at their feet, and returned to Dylan's arms on the porch.

Her gift caused some anxiety within the crowd. They didn't know whether to continue the story or dive for the coins.

Sensing the subtle change in mood with the appearance of the gold, Alyssa and Dylan waved goodbye and disappeared into the house.

Without knowing it consciously, Alyssa had achieved the exact effect she had wanted. The fickle crowd loved her. They had wanted a show, and she had provided them one. The person that they had originally made out to be crazy was now celebrated. The story was one of dislike to like, and those were the strongest sellers. Alyssa had succeeded in turning the tide, and the show came off without a hitch, but there were two lessons she learned.

The first lesson was more subtle: as soon as she had mentioned her former employer in a negative sense the mood of the crowd had changed; and then when the money came out it changed even more. That was her cue to get off the stage and she would be more careful in the future.

The more important lesson was that she realized that she loved Dylan, and possibly had loved him all along. She had substituted Trevor for Dylan when he didn't fit into her concept of how things should be. She was sidetracked because when they were younger Dylan couldn't keep up with her. It was a painful lesson. They had lost precious time together, but there was an upside. She had reinforced an idea that Youki had given her.

"Stop trying to make sense of the world," Youki had said casually. "Nothing makes sense, and everything makes sense. Surrender yourself to the world. Just let go."

The story of the golden girl played out in the news exactly as she had desired, and within a few days she had faded back into the obscurity that she had so suddenly risen from. Her task was complete, and her path forward clear. She would return to the profession that called her. She was a teacher, a counselor, and a healer. As she observed in her dreams, she would be changing sheets and helping people as long as she could, but for the next few months, as she had told the reporters, she would take time off.

Chapter 44

It was hot in Los Angeles in the summer of 2009. In the wake of the recession and the housing crisis, people's activities were subdued. Most families remained home on "staycations", but for Alyssa, the state of the economy didn't apply. Nothing applied. She was alone with nothing to do for the first time in her life. She didn't answer to anyone, and didn't need anyone. She was self-sufficient. She enjoyed being autonomous, but in another way she felt alone and isolated. She wanted people back in her life, and wanted to feel like she had a purpose.

Although she wanted to get back out into the world, she had an equally strong desire to take time for herself, reflect and be peaceful. She wanted to nest and work on her house. She wanted to go the library and read books, watch movies, and lounge on the beach, but it wasn't the right time. She had to get out, and forcing herself back into the world seemed to be a logical approach to rebuilding.

She decided that she would be as social as possible for one month, but when that month was over she would take time for herself, meditate, and reflect. She was long overdue to visit Big Sur, and made reservations for the end of the month. She would stay at the very same cabins that she cleaned as a summer student hire at Phiffer-Burns State Park. She loved Big Sur, and wanted to investigate more why she was so drawn to the area. She wanted to review everything Youki had taught her.

For the next week she got reacquainted with old friends, spent her time with Kaylee, and texted people from college. Most were starting careers after graduation, and didn't have time to party, but Kaylee's status hadn't faded much from her leadership role in their old social circles, and they managed to find someone willing to venture out almost any night of the week.

At first they revisited their old hangouts along Pacific Coast Highway. It made them feel good to reacquaint themselves with old familiar places, but after a week they grew bored.

"We've already done all this!" they said to each other in Malibu one afternoon, and laughed because they said it at the same time.

They formulated a plan to expand their horizons, and relocated their turf to Sunset Strip in the Hollywood area despite the bad experiences Alyssa had there as a young teenager. Now that they were older and wiser, they knew how to stay safe, and enjoyed the extreme music scene on the strip. They were legal now, could go anywhere they wanted, and were attracted to the struggling musicians trying to make it in an overcrowded market. They bounced between The Whiskey, The Roxy, Pandora's Box, The House of Blues and London Fog. To Kaylee, it was business as usual, but to Alyssa, it was all brand new. It was chaos, but it was a compelling chaos. It was raw unbridled energy, and it was uplifting to be a part of it. To Alyssa, these young musicians were entrepreneurs, and cut from the same cloth she was. They were intent on doing what they loved, and what they were good at. They were following their inner voice no matter where it took them. So was she; and even with her recent monetary fortune, she was still knocked down in the struggle to make a difference in the world. She flirted with them, and at first, they thought she was just another groupie, but after they got to know her, they realized that she was one of them. She was from another business, but she was raw unbridled energy too. She was wild. Alyssa loved it at first, but quickly the emptiness of that scene, like all scenes, began to show through, and when they got too close, she thought about Dylan and backed off.

"They're cute, wild, and out of control," said Kaylee. "I like the raw energy that seems to light up everything around them."

"Yet in another way," said Alyssa, "they're very sincere. They're focused on making music. It can be no other way for them. They'll starve first!"

Both Alyssa and Kaylee laughed.

"Some of them do look malnourished," said Kaylee, "although they could be on something. Crack, meth, ecstasy, who knows?"

"It's so loud in here," said Alyssa, "I can hardly hear you. I'm forced to yell in your ear. People might think we're bi."

"Relax, you're in Hollywood! Anything goes here. It's okay to be bi, and it's supposed to be loud!" said Kaylee. "I'll kiss you on the lips and everything will be cool!"

"I love you too but no thanks! I'd rather kiss one of these crazy guys. We don't have to marry them," said Alyssa. "We can just have fun getting to know them."

"You tease!" Kaylee responded. "We're just having fun here. Who said anything about marriage anyway? Marriage is old-fashioned and out dated. All that guys our age want is sex, a mother, and a maid. I'm not really interested in cleaning up or nagging after anyone!"

They both laughed.

"So when are you going to go back to work?" asked Kaylee changing the subject.

"I don't know," Alyssa replied, "I don't really need the money anymore. I'm not done taking a break."

"What do you mean that you don't need the money?" Kaylee asked. "I thought you gave all your money away!"

Alyssa laughed, "What do you think I'm crazy? No, you must think I'm stupid and all wrapped up in my spiritual nonsense!"

"I didn't know what to think," Kaylee responded defensively. "What would you think if I started giving away thousands a day on the street?"

"You have a point, but you must have had some idea of what I was doing!"

"Yes, but I thought you went too far. You have to take care of yourself and your family."

"I did!" replied Alyssa. "I set up a trust for my Dad and Mom. That was a million. I paid off my house in Hancock Park and set up another fund that generates enough interest to pay property taxes and food for the rest of my life. I have a healthy bank account. I lost $500K for quitting the company before my contract expired, and I gave away a little over $800K in the street. That's all of it. The rest was paid to state and federal government in taxes."

"Wow, that's a relief," said Kaylee. "I was worried. I have my Dad. I can always count on him, but who do you have with money?"

"I have my Dad now too, but I'd rather take care of myself," Alyssa stated looking away.

"That's crazy," said Kaylee. "You set yourself up before you gave the money away!"

"Of course I did! Spiritual doesn't mean stupid, but it could mean enlightened and enlightened people don't do stupid things. I'm not saying I'm enlightened. I have no idea whether I am or not, and who cares really, but I do know that I need a place to live and food to eat. If I have all my basic needs met, then I can move on to bigger and better things. Beyond that, who needs the money? The excess is really just a lot of work to take care of. I gave it away systematically and symbolically. People are so hung up on money they forget why they're alive in the first place. Of course I'm not ruling out making more money. In fact, I plan on making a lot more, but I don't think I'll ever worry about money again, and I say that in a humblest of ways "knocking on wood" as they say. I would love to be able to give more away."

"You've always had a special way about you," Kaylee said studying Alyssa with fresh eyes. "It's as if you shine a bright light on everything. I may be the social queen, but when it comes to the essence of things, you're the one. The rest of us pale in comparison. There's a lot going on behind those beautiful brown eyes of yours. You have it all, beauty, brains, political savvy, a strong sense of purpose, and spiritual insight. When people do a double take on you, they do it because there's something intriguing going on inside. You're not just another pretty girl."

"Thanks Kaylee, but it's not always fun either. It's a lot of work to control and nurture what's going on inside me. When I was younger, I thought I was a freak. I didn't fit in, I thought about things that no one else seemed to think about, and I had strange dreams. It was painful. When I learned to understand it and control it is when I blossomed. You can do it too. The potential is present in all of us."

"Yes I know!" said Kaylee. "We've known each other a long time now. You're good! I'm doing what I can. I'm good at social networking, and I'll work up from there."

"There's something else I've been meaning to tell you," Alyssa stated.

"Uh-oh, what now?" Kaylee replied.

"I'm going to start dating Dylan," said Alyssa. "I've wanted to since my performance for the press at my front door in Hancock Park. I've purposely let my feelings cool to see if it was for real, but I'm ready now."

"Dylan! Are you crazy! He's your whipping boy and a nerd. Oh my God, geek fest! Why Dylan? Guys go crazy over you! You're going to waste your time on Dylan!"

"Well, yes." Alyssa said timidly looking down at her drink. "I think I love him, and have been overlooking him for a long time for all the reasons you just stated."

"I just can't believe it!" Kaylee said. "Alyssa you're beautiful! You can have any guy you want! You need to get out more, and play the field. There are plenty of fish in the barrel!"

"I've been swimming in the barrel with them my whole life. I'm almost 22 and I haven't found anyone close. I went through high school and college. The only guy I found was Trevor, and for all the wrong reasons."

"Trevor at least had style, and he's good looking. Dylan's just a nerd."

"He's matured a lot through the last year. He's graduating soon from Cal State Northridge, and he performed very well in our business. He's smart and witty in a subtle way that I hadn't noticed until recently. He pays attention from the sidelines. Those aren't bad characteristics. He's actually attractive. Sometimes you don't see what's going on right under your nose."

"Promise me that you'll keep an open mind," Kaylee lectured. "I can't stop you from dating your childhood buddy, but keep both eyes open. The right guy for you is still out there. You don't want him to slip by when you're attention is elsewhere. You have to be accepting when he comes along."

"I can't believe you're telling me to be open-minded!" Alyssa countered. "I'm usually telling everyone else to be open-minded. Something inside me wants to investigate what we have between us on that level. It's a strong feeling. I've always felt like we were just friends until that night in front of my house with all the news watching. My whole attitude changed about Dylan. It was as if he transformed into a man right in front of my eyes. He took me, protected me, and best of all, kissed me. It was glorious, and all the energy around us shifted positive in that moment. The whole world was watching."

"Hardly, but I know what you mean," Kaylee replied. "I've felt that way about guys before, but it turned out to be infatuation. You, however, can read yourself way better than I can. You're the master. Who am I to tell you how to do it anyway? Do what you must, and I'll be here if you need me."

Kaylee's advice seemed to be taken more seriously than she expected. That night, Alyssa met a drummer from the band playing at the Roxy. They went out together the next evening. She never had a chance to call Dylan.

His name was Rodney Allen, but everyone called him Rodney Ranger or just Ranger for short. After only seeing each other a few times, it was already apparent that the only person Rodney Ranger cared about was himself, and everyone else in the world revolved around him. He never seemed serious about Alyssa unless he was sober, and he was only sober for the first few hours of the day when he got up. He never got up before noon.

"Yes I know he has an ego, but he's cute, he's wild, and he's daring," said Alyssa. "It's vain, but on the other hand, it's a refreshing attitude compared to most people who just do what they're told and walk through life without thinking or feeling."

Alyssa was more interested in exploring LA's music culture than she was in Rodney. She was intrigued with people that had no concept of a normal life, and living in squalor in hopes of making it big. They spent most of their waking hours after 9PM and before 5 AM together. She was using Rodney Ranger without realizing it.

The next few weeks were like a whirlwind of nightclubs, rental cars, dressing rooms and hotel lobbies. Kaylee and Alyssa where like groupies sowing their wild oats with the boys in the band. They were inseparable unless Ranger was present, in which case Kaylee would team up with Roadie Dave, and the four of them would terrorize Sunset Strip. If Rodney's band was playing, they would sit at a table in the front wearing ear plugs, looking smug and turning guys down to dance. If they wanted to dance they would dance with each other.

Weeks passed. Alyssa was excited to meet people from all walks of life. Everyone seemed to pass through the establishments of Sunset Strip. There were managers, agents, producers, marketers, lawyers, sound engineers, stage hands, bouncers, bartenders, and groupies. All of them had interesting stories, and all were potential rehab clients. It was a crash course for Alyssa in the charms and protocols of the entertainment industry, and the emptiness and despair of late night alcohol and drug induced socializing. Memories of reading the philosophy of Friedrich Nietzsche and Carl Marx came flooding back to her.

"The concept of "opiate of the masses" was alive and well in substance abuse rather than religion," she thought to herself, "and the concept of "beyond good and evil" is alive in the form of money worship and celebrity idols.

Although the excitement of meeting interesting successful people kept her attention through the long nights, Alyssa grew tired of the pettiness and debauchery of an alcohol soaked lifestyle. Alcohol didn't enter the mix for either she or Kaylee. Kaylee drank a little, but Alyssa didn't drink at all; and not just because alcohol tasted terrible and burned her mouth, but because of the damage she had seen it cause while working in rehab. Being sober suited her, but it had its drawbacks. Once everyone else became intoxicated, it bothered her how people behaved. She couldn't seem to communicate, and didn't relate to the conversation. It was as if one minute they were present and the next minute they were gone – checked out to another planet. They were loud, brash, and silly, and the more they drank, the more annoying they became. When the alcohol tipping point arrived, Alyssa was ready to bolt, but Rodney was just getting started, and that's where the conflict finally began.

Rodney Ranger was the life of the party, the rowdiest in the band, and the biggest drinker. He always reeked of alcohol, and sometimes seemed to act intoxicated even when Alyssa was sure he was sober. When he first started drinking he was charming, fun, and confident. He was fine-featured and handsome with dark hair and green eyes. Girls fought over him. The drinking made him even more attractive at first. It loosened him up, and he became witty, but it soon faded. He became sloppy, annoying, and finally obnoxious and mean. When he hit the obnoxious stage, he always wanted to get close to Alyssa reeking, slurring his speech in her ear, and drooling when coming in for a kiss. She liked him, but with time she could only tolerate him. He used the same lines, told

387

the same jokes, and clung to the same see-saw patterns night after spinning night. He usually passed out face up on the sofa with one leg touching the floor. She worried that he would asphyxiate, and with much effort, rolled him over. Eventually, he repulsed her, and she could no longer tolerate the smell or the mood swings. She left him passed out in his North Hollywood apartment with a note tucked in his designer shirt pocket.

"Don't call me!" signed Alyssa.

The next day she departed for Big Sur, and left the madness of Sunset Strip behind her. Kaylee went back to her boyfriend who was only the latest in a long line of boyfriends that were never good enough.

Alyssa asked her Dad, Brad Stone, to watch the house while she was gone, and alerted her Grandparents that she would be out of touch for about a month.

"You can leave a message at Phiffer-Burns State Park if you want," Alyssa told them. "That's where I'm staying, and I'll check my cell phone on Sundays, but I'm going up there to be peaceful and meditate, so I won't be trying to socialize very much."

Her statement wasn't entirely true. She had asked Dylan to go with her, and he had accepted. He was done with summer track at Cal State Northridge, and would be taking his last class in the fall prior to mid-year commencement in December.

"Things don't come as easy for me as they did for you," he told her defending his late graduation. "I have to work hard to get good grades, and I'm not good at loading up on classes. If I do that, I just screw them all up. I move slowly, but slow and steady will win the race."

Dylan had money from being bought out of the rehab business too. Unlike Alyssa, when they paid him, his employment was immediately terminated. He walked away with almost $400,000, and he hoped that after taxes he would have enough to buy a small condo in Venice where he could walk to the beach and live a simple life.

Alyssa was driving, and she took the Madonna Inn exit off the 101 in San Luis Obispo to get some food.

"Did I say anything about your graduation date?" Alyssa asked. "That was one of Frenchy's first lessons if you remember. "Set your goals but don't be in a hurry. If you're true to your goal you'll eventually get there prepared in the best of ways. You become your goal. Do you remember that?"

"Of course I remember! Frenchy was big on knowing what's in your heart and acting on it, and what's in your heart is what you should be doing."

"So what are you going to do now that you're graduating?" Alyssa asked.

"I have no idea!" Dylan responded.

They both laughed.

"Hopefully during this trip you can figure it out," Alyssa commented.

"Remember, I don't have the full 30 days," Dylan said. "I'm supposed to catch Amtrak from Salinas to get back home. School starts again soon."

"Of course!" Alyssa said. "But after two weeks you won't want to go back."

Chapter 45

Coastal marine layer covered mystical Big Sur, but the brightness of the overcast signaled the coming burn-off that would allow the sun to finally warm the rocky blue shoreline. The first beams of sunlight broke through the ancient redwood groves unleashing the full beauty of the forest and revealing the birds and wildlife that seemed dormant only moments ago.

Late summer brought more tourists to Phiffer-Burns and Fernwood in anticipation of warmer weather, and both locations were busy when Alyssa and Dylan arrived to check into peaceful

389

contemplation. Alyssa had to stop by Fernwood first just to walk around, reminisce, and imagine Youki dozing in the comfy chair near the big fireplace. She could hardly contain herself when they arrived at the cabins at Phiffer-Burns, and she saw summer hires still cleaning and changing sheets.

"That was me only a few years back," she motioned to Dylan.

"I bet you were the best ever," Dylan replied.

Alyssa looked straight up to the sky with her arms out, and began to twirl while giggling out loud.

"I'm so happy and at home here!" she cried out while twirling.

"Be careful or you'll get dizzy and fall," Dylan scolded.

Alyssa twirled closer until she purposely bumped into Dylan knocking him to the ground and landing on top of him laughing.

"You see, you see, I told you that you'd fall!"

Alyssa continued laughing with her head in his lap and watched his anger fade and turn into a smile. Then she leaned up and kissed him. Taken by surprise, he awkwardly gave in and accepted what he'd been dreaming about for a month. They were both momentarily consumed savoring the sensuality and feeling the energy flow between them. They stopped and paused to look into each others eyes.

"Let's unpack the car silly," Alyssa said jumping up, giggling, and ignoring him on the pavement.

After they unpacked, their decompression started with a hike in the trails of Phiffer-Burns under the canopy of the giant redwoods and the muffled sounds of the ancient forest. They paused several times along the path to drink from their pack bottles and scan the area for visual treasures.

"We didn't bring a camera," Dylan stated.

"You can't capture the essence of the forest in a picture anyway," said Alyssa with a slight giggle at the end. "These moments are for us, and the memories will be pictured only in our thoughts!"

Dylan smiled.

"You always have a great feel for what's happening in the moment. It's uncanny. It's as if you know before it happens."

"Even the great sages project a little Dylan," said Alyssa. "No one can stay in the moment completely."

"Maybe not," he replied.

The trail summited looking out over the valley and the coast highway many feet below. Alyssa stood gazing outward with wonder at all the beauty. Dylan walked up behind her and slipped his arms around her waste joining in her gaze.

"Dylan," she started, "I want to take this moment to tell you that I love you, and I think I'm falling in love with you all new."

Dylan was speechless.

"I know we've always been just friends, but I want to try being more than friends," she continued. "Let's just see if it will work for us."

She turned to face him.

His response took a moment to arrive.

"You know very well that I've always loved you," he said stammering. "Always, from the day we first met as little kids. You've been the leader, and it hasn't been easy standing in the background letting you lead, but I learned to accept it. We've always made a great team. I've made my feelings known before more than once. I've been waiting for you to accept me."

Instead of speaking, she kissed him. Their kiss became more passionate. Then they slowed and paused.

"I'm accepting you now. I want to see where this takes us!"

Dylan let go of her and thrust both fists in the air.

"Woohoo," he yelled looking skyward. "I get a shot after all!"

He smooched her, picked her up by the waist, and twirled her around.

"We're going to fall. We're going to fall," she said sarcastically.

She laughed and flung her hair enjoying the ride.

"Let's go back!" she whispered. "No need for words. Let's walk."

They walked back to their cabin hand in hand occasionally looking at the other and smiling. The forest seemed to glow around them, and birds lighted on neighboring branches singing songs, and chipmunks hustled up, winked, and scampered away. For the twenty minute walk they were at the center of the universe. They marveled at all the coincidental events with the plants and wildlife along their path.

They took to their cabin for just a short rest, and as soon as the sun set they were off to Fernwood to sit by the fire and eat ice cream as Alyssa had done with Youki.

They innocently slept together that night holding each other with clothing on feeling each other's excitement, but waiting. As always, Alyssa was the leader, and the timing wasn't quite right.

When events occur, no matter how insignificant or private they may be, the shift in energy may cause a chain of events to occur; and if connected correctly, these smaller events can trigger larger and larger events until large shifts in the unseen energy grid occur. Fishermen call it the perfect storm. Scientists call it the butterfly effect. Traders call it the ripple effect. In the world that's seemingly chaotic, it doesn't matter what you call it, the result is large and seemingly out of the blue coincidental.

The next day dawned clear with a breeze off the ocean rustling the leaves of the cottonwoods. There was a feeling of change in the air, and both Alyssa and Dylan felt anticipation as they started their day. They made a light breakfast, read, meditated, hiked the footpaths, and drove down to the Big Sur River, but the feeling never left them.

As evening arrived, they both had learned to ignore the feeling, and after they finished their supper, they walked down to the group campfire to hear the Park Ranger lecture as Alyssa had done so many times before. When they returned to the cabin, there was quite a surprise.

A red Porsche Turbo Carrera was parked blocking their car, and Trevor Granderson stood at their front door.

"Trevor!" Alyssa exclaimed without saying more.

"Alyssa!" said Trevor. "I've made a big mistake. I love you and I want you to take me back."

He moved toward Alyssa quickly, and Dylan instinctively moved to subdue him so that Trevor was standing between him and Alyssa, but for some reason, they both stopped short. Alyssa took two steps backward.

"Have you lost your mind?" she asked with a look of concern. "What are you doing here?"

"I've been driving most of the day from Los Angeles at speeds in excess of 100 MPH!" Trevor said excitedly. "I'm lucky I'm not in jail."

He paused but no one spoke.

"I couldn't get a hold of you!" Trevor continued as if out of breath. "I wanted to talk to you. Jack and Linda told me you were here! I couldn't wait! I had to race up as fast as I could! Alyssa I love you!"

"I should have told my Grandpa not to share my whereabouts," Alyssa responded looking to the ground.

Trevor took a step forward, and Alyssa took two more steps back. Dylan remained fixed. No one spoke for a moment.

"Why the sudden change of heart?" Alyssa finally inquired.

"You were right!" Trevor pleaded. "You were right all along. I was too hung up on money. I got caught up in the business when it was first taken over. I was wrong! I was so wrong! I wanted to be better than you, but I couldn't. For some reason I had to. I needed to be better! I was frustrated. My stupid ego got in the way. I never realized what I had with you. We're perfect for each other. We were a great couple!"

Trevor was sweating from the excitement. His sweat glistened in the light from the night sky. He was in a pitiful state groveling for the love he once had so completely locked up but was now

393

slightly beyond his reach. He was dashingly good looking, well dressed, and powerful. Alyssa stared at him without speaking for a few seconds recalling many of their special moments together. She still loved him, and she wanted to comfort him. She felt herself going down the path she had gone down before.

"What exactly made you change your mind Trevor?" Alyssa asked. "Was it really me that you wanted, or was it your hyped up idea of me? I'm the same person I've always been. You've let go of me before!"

"Actually, the moment it hit me was when I came out of the building to ask you to stop giving away gold in the street," Trevor replied.

"Did you understand that pursuing money can make you lose sensitivity to what's really important in life?"

"No, not exactly," Trevor said gently lowering his gaze momentarily. "It was the look you had in your eyes. It was a look of fire, determination, and intensity. It's difficult to describe. It's as if, for just one minute, you were someone else. It was the look of a warrior. You were fearless and all knowing. It startled me. At first I was taken aback, but then it was an attractive force. Later on, however, I did think about the money. I wondered why an all knowing person would give away money. But it was the look in your eye that made it clear. It made me change."

There was stillness in the air as he finished speaking. It seemed as if the crickets stopped chirping. No one moved.

Alyssa was overtaken with emotion. Tears emerged, and began to flow. She felt an overwhelming desire to run to him, take him in her arms, and comfort him. She thought again about all the good times, and the intimate times. She wanted to run, run into his arms. Wiping away the tears, she took a step.

The butterfly effect came into play once more. The one step triggered a series of seemingly insignificant events, but they weren't insignificant. Dylan instinctively took a step. He took one large step to the side. He came into full view of Alyssa, and what little light there was illuminated his face. He stood without emotion offset from Trevor and about three feet behind him. He stood without speaking peering past Alyssa.

It was as if that small movement hit Alyssa like a tempest wind. She stepped wide herself, steadied her legs, stood firm, and looked at Dylan. Full realization of the situation overtook her, tears welled up once more, and she could no longer look at Trevor.

"No Trevor!" Alyssa stated firmly. "We've had our chance. It didn't work out for us. I can't be with you like that anymore."

She looked to the ground.

"Perhaps with time we can be friends again. Come on Dylan lets go in! We're done here."

"No Alyssa," Trevor replied, "I love you! I'm begging you to take me back."

"No Trevor."

She stepped forward a few paces, and as she did Trevor moved in front of her as if to block her path. Dylan took one step forward toward Trevor.

"Stop," she said loudly holding up her hands with her eyes fixed to the ground. "Trevor, if you have any feelings left for me you'll stand aside and let me pass. I'm going to sleep now. I suggest you find a place to sleep yourself. There's a motel across from Fernwood."

The stillness prevailed, and for a moment, no one moved. Alyssa gently took a small step forward, and then another, and quickly stepped around Trevor heading for the door. Trevor turned to face them while they opened the door to the cabin.

"You're going to regret this!" he cried out. "You're going to regret losing me. You'll never find another man like me!"

Once inside Alyssa fell into Dylan's arms and breathed a sigh of relief.

"I've got you," Dylan said holding her. "Everything will be alright now."

She didn't speak. After waiting what seemed to be a long time, but was probably only minutes, they could hear the car door slam, and Trevor squealed away.

Chapter 46

Alyssa spent most of the next day meditating while Dylan headed to the store for some supplies. In the late afternoon, Alyssa emerged from her contemplation and they hiked together through the forest trails they both loved. Instead of spending their evening at Fernwood, they drove down to the Point Sur Lighthouse area, and watched the sunset from the car. Alyssa thought of Youki and how he seemed to suddenly appear or disappear depending on what was convenient for his lesson. She smiled when she thought of it, and looked at Dylan.

"That's the first time I've seen you smile today," said Dylan.

She didn't reply immediately.

"I remember the first time I met Youki right here at the lighthouse," she said. "He asked me if I had found what I was looking for. I told him that I had seen some really interesting things, but not what I was looking for."

"He said, "That may have been because you were looking for it. Let go of the desire, and you may find it. It could be waiting for you."

"I asked him why it would wait for me. He said, "Because you want to see it, you're being held from seeing it. You're on a mission with a preconceived notion of success. Your mind is closed to a new experience. He was right. I took the walk again, and I did find it."

"Is the confrontation with Trevor still bothering you?" asked Dylan.

"Only from a learning perspective," Alyssa responded. "I want to make sure I've learned what I can before I move on, but I don't hold anything against Trevor."

"What have you learned?" asked Dylan.

"I learned that my relationship with Trevor wasn't finished in more than one sense. Yesterday, we put the final closure on our past relation. I think that's clear now. I chose you, and that should be obvious."

Dylan's face flushed but he remained silent.

"I think that we'll have a professional relationship in the near future," she continued. "Something inside me is hinting that he has a further part to play in my life. I'll admit to you that I was momentarily tempted to go to him last night based on the good times we shared together. He's also a hotty, and he has good energy, but I was never able to bring that out in him. I'm not right for him, but perhaps he'll find the right person some day."

"So it's over then?"

"Yes."

"Are you sure?"

"Absolutely, I was tempted last night, but I made the right decision. What really happened is that I came to my senses when you stepped from behind him. It was a distinct moment in time, but I already knew it in my heart. If I had decided otherwise, it wouldn't have worked, and I'd have arrived at this same point weeks, months or even years down the road."

"I'm pleased you found closure," said Dylan. "It will only help us."

"Yes it will!" Alyssa said brightening.

Dylan and Alyssa spent the next few days meditating, hiking, and watching sunsets along the rugged coastline of Big Sur. Every other day they went into town to walk around Fisherman's Wharf in Monterey, down through Cannery Row, and all the way to Lover's Point in Pacific Grove. At Lover's Point they would sit on the rocks before they turned to walk back, and watched the sea

397

lions and otters. Sometimes they held each other, but seldom spoke. They stared off to the horizon occasionally glancing in the other's direction and smiling.

Toward the end of Dylan's stay, a heat wave hit the central coast. They had begun to take for granted the lush beauty of the ancient forests, hiking and exploring became sweaty and fatiguing, and their trips into town routine. Excitedly, Alyssa rose to her feet.

"Let's go tubing in the Big Sur River," she said to Dylan with large twinkling eyes. The river's super cold, but you get used to it. It's refreshingly cold!"

"Okay let's go!" Dylan replied.

On the way to the river Alyssa thought about tubing with Jim Nachman all those years ago when she first went to Big Sur, how the tubing experience was lustful and titillating, but how she was turned off when they first kissed. Her current thoughts were to make sure she had an even greater experience with Dylan, but then she thought of Youki and decided to let events happen naturally. What she really wanted was a whole new experience with Dylan.

When they entered the water they were both shy and afraid to look at each other, but during their first run down the river, playfulness overcame their self conscious behavior, and laughter temporarily masked their sexual awareness. They frolicked together as they had done as children, but when the laughter subsided, Alyssa became aware of herself. She had no makeup on and her hair was wet a stringy. She was a mess, but she was a provocative mess, and in the untamed setting, her savage beauty added to her appeal. He wanted her. In her bikini she was tantalizing, but he could sense her domination, and remained in check waiting for her cue. Her mischievous eyes twinkled playfully while she stared him down and gracefully appraised him as she stepped around him gingerly like a lynx.

The cold water had given her goose bumps and firm breasts. When she looked at Dylan, she could tell he was already aware of her condition and her thoughts. He was nervous to the point of being frightened, but unabashed in his staring. He appeared as though he wanted to grin, but held his expression down to a slight smile. She wanted to laugh, but instead returned his stares with increased intensity.

Even in the cold water, his arousal showed through his swim trunks. They stopped for a moment, turned to face each other, and giggled as if seeing each other naked for the first time. At the end of their amusement, Alyssa became overwhelmed with desire. She suddenly wanted him, and he wanted her. Realizing how lean and shapely his body was she took hold of him, and dropped her inner tube on the bank. The warmth took away her goose bumps. They fully embraced, and she could feel him erect against her. She wanted to take him right away, but others were in the vicinity, and she tried to calm herself. They kissed and she was comforted by tenderness of the moment. She finally controlled herself, and knew that everything would be alright. The moments passed as they embraced, and the sound of the rushing water behind them became a backdrop to their calming excitement. Every emotion climaxed within her, and she was sure she was in love.

"Come on!" she said suddenly tugging on his arm. "Let's make another run!"

They rode the river several more times making a spectacle of themselves. Every other person on the river knew instinctively what was happening to the new couple.

When they finally arrived back at the cabin, tension and awkwardness returned. Their actions were restrained at first. They showered separately giving each other plenty of room to do their own thing. When Dylan finished cleaning up, he laid on the bed in his shorts reading a magazine. A few minutes later she joined him pretending to read a paperback she had brought along. The tension thickened, and Alyssa could tell he was pretending to read too. She waited a minute, and then drawing some courage she threw her book on the floor and yanked the magazine out of Dylan's hands. He looked at her wondering what would come next. She climbed on top of him, and sat up while leaning over to turn off the light next to the bed.

The stillness of late evening was in the air, and the crickets chirping rhythmically outside set the night's peaceful tempo. It was past sunset, but the warm red glow of fading daylight gently entered their space. There was just enough light for a young couple to find each other, and there in the preternatural confines of Big Sur, Dylan and Alyssa made love for the first time.

The following days passed quickly while Alyssa and Dylan cemented their relationship in the hillsides of Big Sur and in the restaurants and Cafes of Monterey, Carmel and Pacific Grove. People stared at them and made comments wherever they went. They had the glow of a couple in love, and not only was it noticeable, but they ignited a wide range of emotions in people that saw them. Most people were happy for them, waved, said hello, or honked their car horns; others were jealous and sneered, and a few were nauseated and repulsed. Alyssa and Dylan barely noticed any of the reactions, and blissfully went through their days smiling, laughing, and teasing each other.

Alyssa turned out to be correct; when Dylan's two weeks were up he didn't want to return to Northridge. He could have given it all up right then, everything, to stay with Alyssa forever in Big Sur. With only one class to finish, however, he knew that it would be completely feeble to stay, and that if they were to be together, he needed to be strong, and find something to do with his life. With reluctance he agreed to take Amtrak from Salinas. When she dropped him off, they embraced, and he didn't want to let go of her. It made him sick to his stomach to leave her. She was all he could think about for the entire trip.

For Alyssa it was very different story. She was definitely in love, and was already feeling the pain of separation, but she was practiced at controlling her emotions, and she was ready to move on with her career. She telephoned the Hillside-Zuma Recovery Center to inquire about work, and although they had had

400

management turnover twice since she left, they were interested in bringing her in, and promised to call her back for an interview.

For the remainder of the trip she meditated, practiced Tai Chi, and reviewed lessons from both Frenchy and Youki. Most of her efforts proved to be fruitless because her mind kept drifting back to Dylan, and the only thing that seemed to help keep her mind off him was exercise intensive outings. If she was sweating, then her head was clear.

Ironically, on her second last day in Big Sur, Hillside-Zuma Recovery Center called and interviewed her over the phone. They offered a package that was equivalent to where she left off, but she would work full-time and would have full benefits. Not needing to work, she thought about it overnight, and accepted the offer the next day. The summary of her trip ended up very similar to experience she had as a college student working the summer in Big Sur. It included a lot of nature, hiking, and romance, and concluded with a job. The only element missing was Youki, but she knew in her heart that he had been there all along.

"If you love something, give it up," she remembered him saying, "if it comes back, it was always yours, if it doesn't, it was never yours to begin with."

She recalled how she may have misinterpreted what he meant relating it to people rather than things, and she wondered now if he intended multiple meanings.

"It seems like I came all the way here just to review what I already know," she thought to herself. "I wonder why it is that we need to break out of our regular environments just to rediscover what we truly are."

Chapter 47

Working at Hillside-Zuma was a welcome addition to her life upon her return to Los Angeles. It provided her with purpose, and it gave her the stability she needed to move on. She was now fully engaged in what she was trained for, and she was doing what she loved. School was over, and her essential needs were already covered, so life became comfortable for the first time in her memory. Within a month, her day became somewhat routine. Dylan was busy finishing his degree, and stayed in Northridge three nights a week to go to class and study. Most other nights they spent together at Alyssa's Hancock Park home. They cooked for each other, and set up a small table every night with elegant trimmings and dined by candlelight. They read philosophy and exchanged ideas, and occasionally, they practiced Tai Chi. It was a very simplistic existence, and they liked it that way. They wanted to be by themselves - just the two of them. It was their way of romance away from the prying eyes of the outside world, and all they needed was their little space inside her home and each other.

Alyssa's job required that she work afternoon shifts a few nights a week. It worked out for them because most of those nights fell on Dylan's school nights. In that case they were both out, but their schedules didn't always synch up perfectly, and on those nights, Dylan stayed at Alyssa's house anyway reading, watching television, and walking the neighborhood. On one such night Dylan heard the doorbell ring. Thinking it would be a solicitor, he let it go, but the caller was persistent and rang again. After a pause the bell rang a third time, and Dylan decided that he should answer it. The caller was Trevor, and he appeared drunk.

"Dylan! What are you doing here?" Trevor began. "I need to talk to Alyssa! Where is she? Can I speak to her?"

"Alyssa and I are together now Granderson. We've been together over three months. You have no business here!"

"She may want you as a boyfriend, but you're a lousy bodyguard Dylan! All I want to do is talk to her. I don't want to move in on you. I'm not after your woman. Lighten up!"

Trevor was slurring his speech worse than usual, and he finished his phrases with a light sneer.

"I'm not sure if I believe you! You have a bad habit of showing up uninvited on her doorstep," Dylan replied. "You must want something. You still want her! I know you do, and you're going to try and weasel your way in between us."

"I need her help actually, and she doesn't pick up my calls. I've tried *67, and she still doesn't pick up."

"She obviously doesn't want to talk to you Granderson!" Dylan stated flatly starting to shut the door.

"Can I talk to her? Is she here?"

"She's not here, she's working," Dylan replied.

"Can you please ask her to call me? I need her help! I'll leave you two alone I promise."

Dylan paused before he responded because there was something in Trevor's voice that he had never heard before. It was the sound of desperation. It was obvious he was in some kind of trouble, and he was sincerely pleading for help. Dylan was thrown off by his seemingly vulnerable state. He wondered if it was a well rehearsed act.

"Okay Trevor," he responded, "you sound sincere. I'll have her call you."

Trevor looked down at his feet, and then back at Dylan.

"Here's my number," he said handing Dylan a piece of paper. "Have her call me as soon as possible!"

"I'll do that. Goodnight."

"Good Night."

Dylan shut the front door with curiosity gnawing at him from inside. He found it difficult to focus on anything. He watched

403

"Wipeout" on channel 7 because it was so ridiculous it kept his mind off Trevor. Later, he couldn't sleep, so he worked on his laptop until Alyssa arrived home.

"I wonder what he wants now?" she asked Dylan while setting down her purse and twisting her face. "We've already said all there is to say!"

"Why don't you call him?" Dylan suggested.

"It's almost midnight."

"He may be up. He looked desperate."

Alyssa picked up her cell phone and dialed the number. Trevor picked up on the first ring.

"Yell-Oh."

"Hi Trevor, this is Alyssa. What's up?"

"I'm not doing so well and I could use your help."

"I'm just a spiritual healer. Why would you need me?"

Dylan was bothered by the start of the conversation and left the room.

"I'm having trouble with alcohol and cocaine. I've lost my job. I can't sleep, and I'm always paranoid. I hallucinate sometimes even during the day. I'm scared. I'm afraid of death. I'm afraid I'm going to die. I'm not ready to die, and I'm tired of hurting people. I need to learn kindness. I need to get over myself!"

Alyssa paused not knowing how to respond.

"Alyssa, are you there?" Trevor asked.

"Yes, Yes, I'm here. Sorry. I don't quite know how to react. Why me Trevor? Why not just check into rehab. You don't need me. You've made fun of my abilities in the past. You've made fun of my spiritual beliefs."

"You're right," Trevor responded, "I could just check into rehab, but I'm in bad shape. I know you're good at what you're doing. You go beyond normal science. You can get to the root of it, and help me to change!"

"I don't know Trevor. We have a history, and I'm not sure I'm ready to work with you on that level. I'm very happy with Dylan. We have something special, and I don't want to jeopardize that."

Alyssa heard something fall crashing to the floor in the kitchen, and wondered if Dylan was listening.

"I know that we're over. I feel it," Trevor replied. "I can accept that. Not only do I accept that, I accept Dylan too. I understood that night at Big Sur. That was my last shot at getting you back. Little did I know I had already lost you. I may have been in denial all along. I may have felt your loss long before that. I'm happy you're with Dylan, and that you've found love."

"Thank you, but you're asking a lot. I've helped with hundreds of rehab cases, and one of the rules is not to get too personally involved with your patients. Not only that, but most of the hard work is up to you. You need to get clean and sober. Rehab only provides the environment, teaches you how to cope, and coaches you along. Anyone can do that for you. It's really up to you. You've got to really want it!"

"I know all that, and I want you to help me. Like I said, you go beyond the medicine. You get into peoples' heads to see how they tick, and help them correct some deep rooted issues."

"Do you know that I'm back at Hillside-Zuma?" Alyssa asked. "They're your competition."

"Not any more," replied Trevor. "Remember, I was fired."

"Oh that's right. So was I."

"No you weren't! You were forced out because you cared. They wanted profit not understanding."

"Hillside-Zuma is super expensive. It's for the rich. Celebrities go there. Can you afford it?"

"I'll have to afford it! Yes, I can afford it."

"Okay, give me a day to grease the skids, and come in for an entrance interview at 10 AM." I'll call you back if there are any problems. If you don't hear from me, just show up."

"Thank you Alyssa!"

Alyssa cut him off.

"I've gotta go," she said. "Don't thank me. Just be there day after tomorrow. Goodbye."

She hung up on him.

During check in, Trevor was in much worse shape than he described. He hadn't showered in days, and smelled like a mixture of urine and body odor. There were several healing abrasions on his face as if he'd been beaten or had fallen several times. There were bruises on his body. His eyes were pink red from chronic dehydration, there were dark circles around his eyes, and he had broken blood vessels in his cheeks and nose. He must have been drinking for days on end. His resting heart rate was well over 100 beats per minute. He was near death from heart attack if nothing else.

He was admitted to detox, given intravenous fluids, and drugged to help with the withdrawal symptoms. The first day he slept, and his heart rate stabilized at about 85 beats per minute. They strapped him to the table, and slowly reduced the withdrawal drugs. He became conscious, but the hallucinations became worse. He constantly shook, and had sweats. He looked like a madman squirming in his constraints, and crying out in pain. After two days the sweating stopped. Shortly thereafter the shaking subsided. It looked like there was hope.

They held him in detox for three more days, and discharged him to a regular room without fanfare. His room had a view, but between the view and Trevor's bed was a teenage patient. The young patient was from a wealthy family that largely ignored him. When they did pay attention to him, they pointed out his inadequacies, and were constantly disappointed. He started drinking to relieve the loneliness and blot out his ineptness. His story was so similar to Trevor's that it pained him to look his way, all he could see was himself years earlier.

Alyssa visited him on the days she worked. They didn't speak much, but her presence brightened his spirits considerably. If he

406

wasn't in a talking mood, she just read magazines and sat by him for about an hour. When they did converse they talked about everything, and she found out things she never knew when they were dating. Trevor was a lonely man within his own skin.

For all practical purposes, Trevor was an alcoholic from his first drink. He started at age fourteen by stealing beer from his Dad's refrigerator in the garage, and quickly advanced to the liquor cabinet. He learned to refill the bottles with water so that his parents didn't notice. His regular drink became vodka because it was clear, and he could pass it off as water in various containers. He brought vodka to school in a water bottle so that it was ready and waiting when the school day was over, but before long, he was taking a drink at lunch. Soon after, he discovered that taking a nip in the morning would ease the pain of the previous day's drinking. He was well on his way to full fledged alcoholism before graduating from high school.

He was a brilliant student, but because of his brilliance, he never fit in anywhere, and used alcohol to dull the pain of living in a world where everyone seemed dull-witted and slow. He felt that all institutions were created to keep the masses in line. He understood the human condition at a young age, and it depressed him; but instead of finding God, he found the bottle. In high school he hung out with the chronic pot smokers who snuck out of class whenever they could to take a puff. He didn't partake in the smoke, but had his trusty water bottle filled with vodka whenever he needed it.

In college his drinking subsided temporarily because the challenge of his course work captured his interest, and the academic environment was intriguing to him. He pulled out of the habit for almost three years, but when he graduated, the pressures of being an investment executive got to him early. The social circles of investment banking revolved around drinking, and it didn't take long before he was back where he was in high school but with a flask in his business suit rather than a water bottle in his backpack.

Meeting Alyssa slowed him down again. He loved her and he wanted her. He curbed his drinking once more, but he also loved the game. He was good at the game, smarter than most and more savvy than nearly all. Success came quickly with boatloads of money and a never ending cocktail party. He forgot what money was for, and the pursuit of it became the only satisfying venture.

After closing his first few big deals, he discovered cocaine. He could work more than ever, party more than ever, and have time for Alyssa too. He found out too late that the benefits of cocaine came at a price too. Eventually, his body could take it no longer.

The first thing he lost was his charm, then his first job, then Alyssa, then his second job, and he was about to lose his life.

He pulled out of it once more; and after two weeks of rehab, he began to look normal again. The transformation was astounding. He smiled, his sense of humor returned, and he became interested in food. He flirted with the female staff.

He spent another month in rehab for a total of eight weeks before he was discharged back to his home. He paid his $120,000 in cash when he checked out.

Although Alyssa wasn't interested in him, she was attracted to him in some strange way. He was exceptionally good looking, and with his health back he was as charming and witty as ever. Alyssa decided that it was his success as her patient that she was so proud of, and left it at that.

Dylan wasn't as trusting of Trevor, and felt that deep in his heart he was playing another game. He speculated that his ultimate plan was to win her back. He was confident that it was only a matter of time before he made his move to regain the woman that he had so foolishly lost.

After Trevor was discharged, no one heard from him for at least two weeks. Thanksgiving at Grandpa Jack's came and went without word, and everyone agreed that Trevor had finally seen the light, and would now leave Alyssa alone. Even Dylan admitted that he may have been overly skeptical.

For Alyssa it was a relief that she could finally close that chapter of her life, and focus on her life with Dylan.

Chapter 48

Alyssa enjoyed her new routine. She went to work day after day, dealt with traffic, paid bills, cooked, cleaned and washed dishes. Like everyone else, she did her larger chores on the weekends, caught up with friends, and prepared for the next week. She had become bourgeois. Her life was predictable, but she enjoyed the comfort and stability of the middle class rigor, and wondered how long it would take before she yearned to break out again.

Working full time didn't leave her with much energy, and keeping up with friends and important social events lost its appeal. Instead she stayed home, or went shopping with her Mom. On weekends, like millions of other Americans, she worked on her house. Her Dad helped her with her with renovations. It gave them an opportunity to spend time together.

In the evenings, she spent time with Dylan. They traded off cooking dinner, and occasionally watched television when they were too tired to do anything else. Television was new to Alyssa, and she was taken aback by how relaxing it was.

"All you have to do is stare!" she said to Dylan. "You don't even need to think. They think for you."

She was completely surprised by how much she liked it. She quickly learned to use the DVR so that she could record shows and skip through the commercials when she had time to watch.

Dylan graduated from Cal State Northridge, but instead of buying a condominium as he had planned, he bought a small storefront on Lincoln Boulevard, and started a shoe store. The shop was tiny, but since he paid cash for the building, he significantly reduced the risk of failure. He leased the store to his business so that he essentially paid rent to himself. That helped him at tax time. He incorporated the business to protect his personal assets, and his parents and Alyssa loaned him enough money to stock the shelves. He specialized in high-end shoes, but what was unique was his purse rack. He made it possible for people of medium income to afford high-end purses. He purchased purses from wholesale companies or at outlet malls, and resold them with only a small markup to bring people into the store. He viewed his operation as a dream fulfilling service.

"Women love their purses," he told Alyssa. "Word will travel about my store if they can buy their purse at bargain rates."

Alyssa didn't think the idea would go, but she was proven wrong. It turned out that purses exceeded shoe sales, and Dylan was forced to mark them up a little more to ensure his store's survival.

With Alyssa frequently busy at work, and Dylan taken up by the store, they spent more time apart, but the space seemed to strengthen their relationship. They both looked forward to seeing each other, and when they were together, they made the most of it. When they had free time apart, they could pursue their personal interests, and it gave them a chance to express themselves as individuals.

One afternoon Alyssa was in good spirits as she prepared to leave work at Hillside-Zuma and was anticipating what she would do on her day off alone. While she walked down the hall toward the door, she saw him, but it was at a distance, and she couldn't be sure. As she approached she assured herself it was indeed Trevor Granderson, and her heart sank. She didn't really want to talk to him, but it was too late. He had already noticed her and immediately looked down at what he was doing when she spotted him. There was no escape, and her movements continued fluidly

410

without a flinch. She approached him in a matter of fact style with the deliberate gait of a busy professional woman with things on her mind. He pretended that he hadn't noticed her as she approached, and looked completely surprised when she spoke.

"Hello Trevor," what are you doing here?" Alyssa asked candidly.

"Alyssa! Yes, hello!" he replied without smiling. "I'm here for some follow up. I haven't relapsed if that's what you're wondering."

"Are you working?" she asked.

"Yes, I'm working for E-trade as a customer consultant," he replied. "It's temporary."

"That's good!" Alyssa stated with awkward enthusiasm. "I'm glad you found something."

"Look Alyssa," he stated, "I'm late checking in, and I need to get going. If you'd like to catch up. I could meet you for lunch tomorrow."

He looked at her blankly as if to say take it or leave it.

Alyssa was taken aback by the invitation. She didn't want to, but a strong feeling welled up inside her that protested. She paused looking at expressionless Trevor while she decided whether her inner voice was real, or if she just triggering off past emotions.

"There's something bigger going on here," she thought to herself. "It won't hurt to investigate."

"Yes, I'd like that!" she said looking down. "I'd like to hear about your progress."

"Okay, we'll meet at Whittier Golf Course at noon," he said distractedly. "You know which one?"

"Yes."

She always had enjoyed his take charge attitude. It gave her a break from decision making. It was a comforting feeling being taken care of.

"Okay sure, see you at noon."

"Surprisingly, she had made a date for lunch with a man she hoped she would never see again. What's more, she actually looked

411

forward to it. They had a mother-son relationship now, and she liked it. She had brought him back from the brink of complete disaster and possible death. She had accepted the role of guardian angel, and was curious about what he had been doing to rebuild his life.

They ate lunch at the snack bar where Alyssa had first worked. So many important things in her life had started there, and she couldn't help but wonder why he chose to meet in that particular location. They spoke of the weather, how good the other looked, and made remarks about other people in the room.

He tried to switch the conversation over to her, arouse her enthusiasm, and get her to spill her guts about what she had been doing. It worked. She fell prey to his born-again charm, and gushed while sipping her drink. He smiled suspiciously while she spoke, but he avoided meeting her eyes.

Although Alyssa did most of the talking, she did find out that he was living alone at the same house, he wasn't dating anyone, he hadn't spoken to family in over a year. He hated his job, and wanted to get back into the real game.

He looked lonely and forlorn without a friend in the world. He had family, but he had been cut off. They were done with his antics, and no longer willing to help him either emotionally or monetarily. He was an outcast.

Alyssa could feel his despair, the pain of his failure, and the emptiness of his soul. She really had no interest in him as a friend. They couldn't be friends with all that had transpired, but she was intrigued by the challenge of healing him. He was a test case for her skills. She wanted to bring to bear all of her training and experience through all the years of work and study. She envisioned filling him up with Chi, and wanted to see him become a functional investment banker again.

"If he's going to be a materialistic hedonist," she thought to herself, "he may as well be good at it."

412

Christmas was only a few days away, and since Trevor had no place to go, she accepted her challenge, and invited him over for Christmas dinner at her Hancock Park home.

It was her first holiday event, and she had invited most of her friends and all of her family. Grandpa Jack, Grandma Lin, Daisy, Franken, Brad Stone, and Dylan promised to be there. Finhead John and some other friends hoped to drop by later after dinner.

Since her life had stabilized, and her family and friends were supportive, she felt that she could safely bear the risk of inviting Trevor over. He had been sober for several weeks, and it was unlikely that he would spoil the event.

What she hadn't anticipated was Dylan's reaction to what she had done. His face flushed when she told him, and he immediately became angry. He was aware of his anger, and didn't want to focus his wrath on Alyssa, but with no place to go with the energy, he became frustrated and began to raise his voice. It was their first major argument as a couple.

"Why did you stop to talk to him?" Dylan repeated not really wanting an answer. "You should have walked right past him. That's what he deserves!"

"I told you I had no choice," Alyssa replied quietly. "He's my former patient, and I wasn't about to be rude. I'm a professional not a child!"

"But think of all the things he's done to you! Think of how he's treated you! He's self-centered and egotistical. He doesn't care about you. He just wants to see what else he can get from you."

At this point Dylan was yelling, and now it was directed at Alyssa.

"That may be true, but this is what I do," she replied calmly while looking past him. "I heal souls, and in this day and age that usually means dealing with a substance abuse problem first so that they can see clearly enough to heal themselves. Hillside-Zuma won't heal his soul. All they have are expensive psychologists that want to chat once or twice a week at $100 per hour. That won't heal his soul and you know it!"

"But why you, and why him?" Dylan asked while starting to calm down. "There are other people like you out there that can help him!"

"That may also be true, but who's it going to be? What will happen between now and when he finds someone else? He could relapse."

"Who cares!" Dylan stated flatly.

"I do! Alyssa replied. "This is what I do!"

"But you don't even need to work anymore," Dylan countered defensively. "You don't need to do this!"

"Rich or poor, this is what I plan to do for the rest of my life. If you're going to be with me, you need to accept it."

"I know," Dylan replied with a humble tone bowing his head. "You have a magnetism about you that attracts everyone, but especially guys! You're very special in some subtle unseen way. You're a stealth leader of sorts, or as you've dreamed, you're a priest, a shaman, or some sort of mystic. In Kaylee's words, you're a modern prophet!"

Alyssa laughed.

"Now you're taking it a too far!" Alyssa replied. "I work rehab, and that's all! I'm no prophet! I just have vivid dreams. My calling is to help people, and that's what I'm going to do. Your spiritual training should help you through periods of worry or jealousy. We need to trust each other if we're going to be together."

"I trust you," Dylan replied looking at Alyssa straight in the eye. "But I'm only human. I'll make mistakes along the way!"

Christmas Day arrived rather quickly. Alyssa's family spent Christmas Eve at Grandpa Jack and Grandma Lin's, and they broke tradition by opening gifts that night rather than in the morning. It was a pleasant evening with a simple meal; and afterwards they walked the neighborhood admiring the Christmas

414

lights. Daisy and Grandma Lin spent the night at Alyssa's, and helped her prepare food and organize the house in the morning. Seating was no longer a problem because Alyssa had decorated and furnished the house with recommendations from an interior designer Kaylee suggested. It was an odd collection of old and new classic pieces with themes that were based on Alyssa's dreams. One room was decorated like the Hawaiian island of Kauai. The living room had an Alaskan theme, and family room Romanian, but what tied everything together was the underlying thread of spiritual awareness and spiritual development. Her Grandparents loved it, but Daisy thought it was a bit odd and quirky.

"It's odd like me Mom, and its very Feng Shui!" Alyssa said smiling.

"It's fine darling!" Daisy replied. "Your uniqueness has served you well. Let it shine!"

Grandpa Jack and Franken arrived at noon with beverages, games to play, and the residual gifts. Laughter and endless conversations arrived a bit later when Kaylee dropped by with Dylan's gift before she headed over to her Dad's house.

"I'm only going to my Dad's to kiss butt, open my gifts, and make an appearance," Kaylee stated without expression. "I know this is where all the fun will be. I'll be back as soon as I can escape!"

"When Dylan arrived, they sat outside and played "Apples to Apples". Grandpa Jack recruited one at a time to play the antique lawn dart game called Jarts.

"Jarts were made illegal in fifty states," said Grandpa, "but I kept my copy."

Trevor arrived and the whole dynamic of the conversation changed. He didn't speak much as part of the group, but had discussions with people individually. There were awkward pauses, and people would speak softly to each other privately while looking his way.

He loved the fact that Grandpa's lawn dart game was illegal, and hounded everyone to play with him. He focused on Dylan, but Dylan was the most reluctant to play. Eventually, Dylan gave in but his heart wasn't in it, and Trevor beat him soundly. He then continued on to beat everyone else except Grandma Lin who had wild throws but ended up with ringers on almost every round.

"It was pure luck," said Grandma. "I'm surprised my throws didn't end up on the roof or in the neighbor's yard."

Through dinner, and for the rest of the day, Trevor seemed to focus his attention on Daisy. They would speak softly in each other's ear and occasionally break out giggling while looking at the person that was so obviously the focus of their discussion. Franken, who was accustomed to getting all of Daisy's attention, became annoyed. He complained to Grandpa Jack with his thick Eastern European accent.

"He has a thing for your daughter, yes?" asked Franken. "She is beautiful woman, if he keep with the flirt. I tell him something, No?"

"No," Grandpa Jack explained. "He's playing a game and has no interest in your wife."

"I not take it much longer, but okay," Franken replied.

As if on cue, Kaylee arrived, and Trevor immediately turned his attention to her. The energy shifted, and the source of whispering and giggling came from Kaylee and Trevor rather than Daisy. Trevor stared at Alyssa whenever he thought she wouldn't notice, and it made her uncomfortable. It was as if his eyes were burning into her. Every time she turned her back she felt it. Only in the kitchen did she feel relief from the surveillance. While she ducked into the kitchen, Daisy came in to speak to her.

"I know you think you're in love with Dylan," Daisy started, "but you shouldn't rule out Trevor. He's very good looking and so charming! He's delightful, and he has this commanding presence. He's a classy sort of macho. I wish Frank could be more like him."

"Oh Mom, you know how he is! Trevor is Trevor. He may never change, I've tried to help him, but he always seems to fall back to his old ways of competition and the need to win. He wants to be better than everyone else. I can't be with a man like that, and you're much better off with Frank who takes care of you. Frank's infatuated with your youth and beauty, but he loves you too. Love is important. A man like Trevor only loves himself."

"All I'm saying dear is not to rule him out! He may come around. He's so damned charming its frustrating!"

Brad Stone dropped by to say hello and changed the energy in the room once more. Brad was a regular house sitter for Alyssa, and loved to sit by her fireplace. The first thing he did was light the gas log, and everyone naturally gathered round. Alyssa put on some Burl Ives Christmas music that she knew that Grandpa Jack loved when he was a kid, and served the deserts. The end of Christmas took on a relaxed homey feeling with everyone comfortable with each other, and comfortable in Alyssa's peaceful home. Trevor and Kaylee had retreated to the kitchen and were nowhere in sight. Their absence added to the relaxed atmosphere in the living room, but occasional outbursts of laughter reminded everyone that they were still there.

Trevor and Kaylee decided to leave together just as Finhead John showed up.

"I didn't mean to drive you away old man," John said to Trevor as he took off his jacket.

"I'd love to stay and talk," Trevor replied, "but I need to get up early tomorrow."

"I'd like to invite everyone here over to my Dad's house for New Year's Eve," Kaylee announced. "It's an annual party, and lots of fun! There'll be well over one hundred people, so no need to feel awkward if you don't know anyone. It's formal, so the guys need a tie and the ladies need a dress. It's a diverse group of people, and always interesting, so it's worth dressing up. Besides there's great food. I hope to see you there!"

"I'll be there," said Trevor jokingly.

Everyone laughed, said their goodbyes, and left the evening to fade away as so many Christmases did.

A week later, to everyone's surprise Daisy and Franken showed up at Kaylee's Dad's New Year's Eve bash. It was a relief to see Kaylee with her buff boyfriend. Everyone had worried that she'd be with Trevor. Her boyfriend acted more like a prop than a date, and hoped to pass for younger version of Sylvester Stallone. He was interested in himself more than Kaylee, looked in the mirror every time he passed, and frequently pulled his pocket comb to touch up his hair. He continuously straightened his jacket and adjusted his tie.

Kaylee mostly ignored him and spent most of the night with Trevor. It was as if the boyfriend was an excuse to not officially be with Trevor.

Daisy and Franken left early for another party when Daisy realized that there weren't any celebrities present, and their departure seemed to cue the start of the dancing on the balcony. Kaylee finally latched on to her boyfriend for the first time that night, and he turned out to be an expert dancer.

Trevor's attention switched to Finhead John. Finhead was okay with his old nickname again because he had nothing left to prove in the business world, and had been learning his father's business. The business types liked his old nickname. He tried to shorten it to Finn, but as always, Finhead was the name that stuck.

Trevor and Finn became buddies the remainder the night laughing, joking, and drinking cranberry juice in glasses that gave the appearance of regular mixed drinks. It bothered Alyssa that every time she saw Trevor he seemed to be staring at her again. He quickly turned away every time she caught him. She knew that she had made a mistake inviting him back into her life.

Precisely when she doubted Trevor, Finhead approached her to say the same thing she had been hearing from everyone.

"You know now that he's cleaned up, Trevor's not such a bad guy," he told Alyssa while looking out at the people dancing. "He's got brains and he has style. I think he'd compliment you rather well. You and Dylan are so much alike. If you two stay together you may become a little too reclusive!"

Before Alyssa could respond, Finhead walked away and went back on the dance floor.

Within five minutes, Kaylee approached her and said something similar.

"If you don't want him I may just try him out! He has a way with the ladies! For that matter, he has a way with everyone!"

"Go ahead," said Alyssa, "date him! We've been over for a long time. If you want my blessing you have it."

Alyssa's statement was too late. Kaylee was already back out dancing. She hadn't heard a word.

Alyssa was bothered by the social conditions of the evening, and sought out Dylan to leave. Dylan was talking shop with another shoe store owner, and seemed annoyed by the interruption.

"Let's get going," Alyssa said to Dylan.

"But it's not even midnight yet! Why don't we dance!"

"No, I'd rather not. I think I'm done here. I get a weird vibe from Trevor. He seems to be staring at me. It's as if I'm being watched. It's creepy."

"Oh yeah," Dylan said. "That reminds me!"

He walked straight over to Trevor and grabbed him by the arm to make him look him in the eye. Trevor laughed and grinned.

"Don't think I'm so stupid that I don't know what you're doing Granderson! You're working Alyssa's friends and family one at a time to bring them over to your side. It won't be long until you start working on her. You think your plans are coming to fruition; and soon, you plan to take her back for your own. You think she'll throw me to the curb, but you may be surprised!"

"You flatter yourself Dylan!" Trevor replied calmly. "I have no such grandiose plans, and I have no quarrel with you."

"Well then stop staring at her, and keep away from us, or I'll make you wish you hadn't!"

Dylan had been speaking loudly so Trevor could hear him above the music, but after he said "stop staring at her" the music suddenly finished, and everyone could heard him yelling as he finished his statement. People quickly turned to get a glimpse of the action. Sensing all the attention, Trevor could do nothing but laugh and grin. He turned to face Alyssa and laughed again.

For an instant there was silence, and the focus of the entire room was upon them; but as suddenly as it had stopped, the music started again, and everyone went back to dancing knowing that nothing was going to happen.

"You better watch yourself Granderson!" Dylan warned. "I'm ready for you. Come on Alyssa, let's go!"

For the next few weeks Alyssa and Dylan were pleased to avoid social events, and with the passing of the Martin Luther King Jr. holiday, life returned to normal. There wasn't much happening socially regardless of how they felt about going out, and most of their friends were heading up to Mountain High, Mt Baldy, and Big Bear whenever they could to go snow boarding. It was the season for down time, and sleepy days were a welcomed change. Alyssa was happy to spend what free time she had with her Mom, and dropped by to see her Grandparents once a week. A few days a week it became routine to walk the mile up to Hollywood Boulevard with Dylan for the exercise. When they arrived, they would sit on a street bench, people watch for a few minutes, and then slowly walk back.

As with most situations, when life seems easy, and days get comfortable, there's trouble at the door.

Alyssa continued to have vivid dreams as she had throughout her life. In one of her most frequent dreams, she's in the Southeastern United States in what appears to be the Civil War. She's serving as a physician-nurse. She speculates that she's a trained doctor, but that she's discriminated against for being

420

female, and relegated to the duties of a nurse. She recalls going out to the battle field with a group of people after the fighting has ended looking for living bodies among the dead. They tag the bodies that are certainly dead, and estimate the chances for survival of those they find alive and breathing. For those that have a chance, she treats them, and her helpers load them onto wagons to be hauled back to town by horses. The others they leave behind to join the dead.

In recent weeks the dream had changed. When she's out in the battle field searching through the bodies for the living, she comes across soldier that's breathing, but his wounds are too severe to attempt to save with so many other wounded lying on the field. Many can be saved. She decides to leave this one, and tags him as dead, but when she looks at the soldier's face she sees a blank. It was as if his face was missing and replaced with white. There was no face.

The dream was unsettling, and she was traumatized by it. The recurrence increased until she was having the same dream almost every night. Days passed by, and it continued to bother her.

The dream morphed once more, and when she looked at the soldier's face she saw Trevor. It was Trevor! He was dying. In fact, he was almost dead. Nothing could be done for him. He couldn't be saved. She was horrified, but in her dreams she always operated in an automated mode. She tagged the body for dead, and moved on. Following the dream, she would wake suddenly soaked in sweat. It became exhausting, and she was afraid to sleep.

She needed to talk it out with somebody, but she didn't know who she could trust. She decided that she should call Trevor. She was torn because she didn't want to see him again, but she reasoned that whatever was happening inside her, it needed to play itself out. As uncomfortable as it may be, she had to tell him. But if she was going to talk to Trevor, there was someone else she had to talk to first. She would explain the dream to Dylan, and regardless of what Dylan thought, she would then talk to Trevor. She didn't want to go behind Dylan's back.

For the first time she explained her dreams to someone besides her Grandfather. She trusted Dylan enough to explain, and she hoped that he wouldn't judge her or label her as crazy. Dylan listened intently, and seemed very understanding at first.

"Everyone has dreams," he said, "and some more intensely than others. What you've been experiencing isn't that unusual."

When she explained the Civil War dream to him, however, and told him how she saw Trevor's face on the dying soldier, he immediately became irritated.

"It's nothing," said Dylan, "it will pass. You're upset over your recent experiences with him, and it's bubbling up from your subconscious into your dreams. That's all!"

"I think it's more than that," Alyssa countered. "I've never felt something so strong in my life. As much as I don't want to see him, I'm very compelled to tell him about it. It could make a difference!"

"I'm opposed to it," Dylan said hardening and looking past her. "He'll take advantage of you while you're vulnerable. Don't do it, don't see him. Please Alyssa! Don't see him!"

Alyssa sighed loudly.

"Okay," Alyssa said not knowing how to react. "I'll sit on it and see if it passes, but I'll tell you something Dylan, for the first time in my life I'm afraid. I'm afraid and I don't know why."

Two sleepless nights slowly drifted by for Alyssa and she could no longer take it. Grandpa Jack was getting older, and she didn't want to worry him with problems that he thought she had resolved long ago.

"I'm an adult now," she thought to herself, "I need to handle my own problems."

In a moment of weakness she called Kaylee.

"I'm having a weird dream about Trevor and it's keeping me up at night," she explained quickly. "I want to tell him about it."

"What are you waiting for?" Kaylee asked as if it was no big deal. "Call him."

"I want to tell him in person."

"Well then call him and meet him!"

"Well Dylan doesn't want me to."

"Dylan will get over it. Call Trevor, meet him, and get this off your chest. I know you. We've been friends for years now. I can tell it's eating you up."

"But I respect Dylan. I love him."

"Listen honey," Kaylee started. "Dylan has been in love with you since the day you met as children. He'll always be in love with you! There are probably a hundred men that have a crush on you. Look, you have great looks and a hot body, but that isn't it! There's something going on deep inside you and it drives men crazy. It's that look, and you know what I'm talking about. Now I'm telling you, Dylan will get over it. Go talk to Trevor and get free of this torment!"

"You're right. I'll go talk to him!"

Alyssa called Trevor. He wasn't the least bit surprised to hear from her, and he agreed to meet her the next day.

"Let's meet at the La Brea Tar Pits," he said.

"Why there?" she asked. "Why not just meet locally?"

"It'll be like old times," he said.

"Okay, meet me outside the museum. We can talk and walk outside. I'm worried about something, and not in the mood to look at ancient animal bones."

Alyssa arranged for an extended lunch break at work, and met Trevor at 1130 as planned outside the George C. Page Museum. Trevor hugged her upon their meeting, and she accepted the hug, but he pushed it and went to kiss her. His kiss fell flat upon her cheek.

"Now what's been bothering you?" he said with the gentle tone of someone genuinely concerned.

"You may think I'm crazy. We're very different people. I live in a world of spirits and dreams. Sometimes it seems as though the waking world is just one big dream! You live in a world of hard reality. Your world is one of solid objects, proven theories, and physical boundaries. You survive on your wits, and compete with other humans for scarce resources. On the other hand, I live on energy obtained through spiritual grace. I freely give away as much of that energy as I can to my fellow humans. That's what I thrive on. It's a different point of view, and neither is really wrong or right. It just is."

"What are you getting at?"

Alyssa explained her civil war dream, how she's had it her whole life, and how it recently evolved to include him. She explained to him about the dying soldier with his face, and how she marks him for dead and moves on.

"Is that all?" he asked. "You're worried about a dream? You're upset about a dream!!"

"It's not just a dream Trevor! That's what I'm trying to tell you. It's a recurring dream, and a feeling deep inside me. It's a dream in which you're dying, and there's nothing I can do for you!"

Trevor looked at her for a moment and paused. She looked at him intently as if about to cry and slightly bouncing on her feet as she stood hoping he would understand.

Suddenly, Trevor laughed out loud. It was a maniacal laugh, and there was pleasure in it.

Alyssa was stung, then smitten, and as the realization of his reaction sunk in, she was hurt. She was instantly deflated. She had no energy left. She had given it all away. Old memories came flooding back of how he had made fun of her abilities in the past. She felt like lying down right there on the sidewalk crushed by misunderstanding, but in that instant, enlightenment came, and she remained on her feet. She accepted what had just happened, and moved on. Suddenly strength returned, and she was relieved.

424

"Did you think that one of your dreams was important to me? Did you think it would change my behavior?" Trevor asked her still amused.

She didn't speak, and his callousness reinforced her revival. She shook her shoulders as if avoiding a chill, and unexpectedly thought of Dylan. Then she thought of her Grandpa Jack.

"I've gotta go," she finally replied.

She turned and started walking away.

"Wait," said Trevor. "I didn't mean to be cruel! Let me give you a hug and make it better!"

Alyssa never turned back. She never replied. She had said her piece and was finished. She had done everything she could. It was in his hands now.

She didn't wait in her car to compose herself. She needed to get away from him as quickly as possible. The traffic in the "Miracle Mile" area of Wilshire Boulevard actually helped her. Her mind was forced to focus on maneuvering through traffic, and it gave her relief from her pain, and brought her back to daily life. When she arrived back at work she checked her cell phone to find six missed calls, a voice mail, and a text from Dylan.

"Call me as soon as you can," Dylan said in the voice mail. "I've spoken to Kaylee and I know your going to meet Trevor. Don't do it! This has got to stop."

"Too late, it's done," she thought to herself.

"Call me urgent," Dylan said in his text.

While she was reading his text a call came in, but to her surprise it wasn't Dylan. It was Kaylee.

"I'm sorry, I'm so sorry," Kaylee said before Alyssa could speak. "He squeezed it out of me. He convinced me that you could be in danger and I sung like a spring sparrow. I couldn't live with myself if anything happened to you after the advice I gave you! I'm sorry. Will you forgive me?"

"Of course Kaylee," Alyssa replied quite calmly. "I don't blame you in this. I'm the one who went to see him."

"You went to see him? It's over then, and you're back?"

"Yes, those are appropriate words too. It's over, and I can't be around him as a friend or a counselor. He thinks I'm a quack. Dylan was right. He just wants to control me, and it bothers him that he can't."

"Thank God you're safe. I'm so relieved."

"I'm going to go Kaylee. I better call Dylan before this blows up anymore."

"Are we okay then?"

"Of course we are. We're better than ever. I'll call you later!"

Dylan was much more relaxed on the phone than she expected. She was prepared for him to be wound up as he sometimes gets in tense situations, but he was understanding and not accusatory at all.

"Are you okay?" he asked.

"Yes, he mocked me in a way. It really hurt at the time, but not so much now."

"I must apologize. I gave you bad advice," Dylan started.

"You're apologizing too!"

"Why yes. Who else is apologizing?"

"Kaylee, she was sorry for telling you about my plans."

"Oh, well she didn't stand a chance. I was very convincing. It wasn't her fault."

"I know," Alyssa finished.

"Alyssa you told me before Christmas that this is what you do, and I have to learn to accept it. I thought I had accepted it, but it turns out that I hadn't. I was so worried about losing you to him that it clouded my judgment. I gave the opposite advice that I should have, and I'm sorry. I want to be accepting of your work. I really do. I was upset when I found out, and kept ringing your cell, but since then, I've had time to calm down and consider my actions."

"In some strange way it all came out for the best. We all reacted emotionally, and as my Grandpa would say, shot from the

426

hip. The end result, however, seems to be the correct one. We all learned something. You, me and Kaylee all grew from the experience. You were right in that my ego was all wrapped up in trying to fix Trevor. I'm too close to him, and can't help him any longer. I've already hung on too long living in a fantasy of denial."

"There's no need to beat yourself up. As you're always telling others, learn from it and move on."

"He laughed at me, and it was a strange laugh as if he took extreme pleasure in humiliating me. He's always had contempt for my spiritual beliefs. His reaction to my warning just made me appreciate you more. I realized what I have with you. It confirmed that what we have is at a whole different level. I hope I never have to see him again."

"No, one more time," Dylan replied.

"What! What are you talking about?"

"I have an idea, and I want you to see him one more time. I can kill two birds with one stone. Well actually, I don't want to kill any birds, but I want to get two things done at the same time."

"I know what the statement means Dylan!" said Alyssa laughing.

"See, I got you laughing. We're making progress."

"What are you scheming," Alyssa asked.

"I can't tell you," Dylan replied. "You're going to have to trust me on this one."

"Okay, I guess I will!"

"Let's see if we can get all our friends together at Gladstone's the Thursday before President's Day as a reunion of sorts. We haven't seen some of our college friends in a long time. We'll invite Trevor. In fact, it's important that he's there. Hopefully it'll be good weather so we can be out in the porch area."

"Okay, I hope you know what your doing!"

"I'll also need your Dad's phone number. I want to invite a few relatives."

"Grandpa Jack or Brad," she asked.

427

"Brad. I know Grandpa Jack is like your Dad, but I want to speak to Brad."

Dylan was scarce for several days as the event approached. Managing his store was a twelve hour day in itself, but he seemed to want to get all their old friends in one spot for a reunion. He typed up a sheet with everyone's current address and phone number, and mailed it out with a flyer. Trevor enthusiastically agreed to attend, and asked about both Alyssa and Kaylee. Daisy and Franken were leaving town for the weekend, and wouldn't attend.

Up until the last minute Dylan couldn't contact Brad Stone, but on the day of the event he finally contacted him. Brad explained that he had returned to real estate speculation. Since the collapse of the housing bubble, there were some great opportunities in Los Angeles, and he was busy converting distressed properties into income properties. He was so busy, he couldn't stay, but he agreed to stop by for a few minutes.

Since most of Dylan's and Alyssa's friends had Friday off to take advantage of the long weekend, the party started early, and when Dylan arrived at 4 PM, most everyone was already there. The porch area of Gladstone's was already full. Most of the people were Cal State alumni from both the Northridge and Los Angeles campuses.

Trevor was there, and to Dylan's surprise he had brought a girlfriend with him. Her name was Diana Cafas, and the group had already given her the nickname DC. Diana thought that the only significance was her initials, but Dylan found out quickly that it had a double meaning. To the group it meant Dingy and Clingy to describe the way she behaved with Trevor.

Kaylee and Alyssa were actually sitting near Trevor, but Kaylee's beefcake boyfriend sat between Trevor and the girls separating conversations going on simultaneously. He wasn't interested in either conversation and appeared seriously bored.

428

Finhead John was conspicuously missing, but he had told Dylan that he might be working late that afternoon.

Dylan quickly became bored after joining the group. He had things on his mind, and was excited about what he had left to do. He was waiting for the arrival of Brad Stone, and was worried that he wouldn't show before the sun dropped too low, and people got cold and left. A yellow cab rolled up, and Brad emerged. Dylan had forgotten that Brad didn't drive, and getting a cab had delayed him.

Dylan shot up and hustled off to meet him outside. He talked to Brad for ten to fifteen minutes. The cab waited. The girls and several others shot off glances wondering what was going on, but finally, they both walked over together.

"Okay people listen up," Dylan spoke loudly to the group.

People continued their conversations at first, but a few started to chime silverware to glass to bring people's attention to order.

"If I could just have a moment," Dylan said loudly, "I have something to say that is very important."

Everyone focused on Dylan, and quiet engulfed the group. The only noise was from the restaurant and the cars whizzing by on the coast highway.

Dylan pulled out of his pocket a small statue of a Hawaiian hula dancer with a grass skirt suitable to attach to the dashboard of a car. It was a bit large for that purpose, but it could have been done. Out of his shirt pocket, he pulled out a ring, and put it on the hula statue's head.

"Okay here we go!" he said holding the hula dancer out at arms length in front of him.

He walked over to Alyssa, and slowly lowered himself down on one knee before her while holding out the hula dancer.

"Alyssa," he said loudly and emphatically so that all could hear. "Would you take the ring off the head of this hula dancer and marry me?"

Everyone was speechless. Brad Stone was the only one who expected it and was smiling slightly. A deafening silence gripped the crowd as they turned their attention to Alyssa. Alyssa was shocked surprised, and once she gathered her wits she stared at Dylan momentarily. A range of emotions showed on both of their faces, but the love was obvious.

"Yes Dylan," Alyssa replied rather calmly while looking into his eyes. "I'd be happy to marry you!"

There was a momentary silence following her acceptance followed by applause. Alyssa took the ring off the hula dancer, handed it back to Dylan, and then held out her left hand. He slipped the ring onto her finger triggering more applause.

Dylan stood.

"With that," he said to all, "we'll be off up the coast. I've set up a romantic weekend in Santa Barbara."

This time everyone laughed, and Alyssa had the look of surprise.

"I'll need to go home and pack a bag," she said.

People started approaching them individually and congratulating them and interrupting their conversation.

"Daisy already packed you one if you're ready. It's in the car. She knew in advance, and so did your Grandparents. I know that Kaylee brought you here, and that you have the weekend off. We can leave right now!"

"Before you go," said Trevor out of the blue, "I'd like to congratulate you both."

Trevor lightly hugged Alyssa, and turned to Dylan.

"There was never a problem between you and me," he said to Dylan while shaking his hand and looking at Alyssa from the corner of his eye. "I lost her long ago. I never understood what I had. She's a wonderful person, and you'll make a great couple. I wish you many years of happiness together."

Trevor was shaking Dylan's hand the entire time he spoke, and only let go after he finished speaking. Dylan was processing

430

what just transpired, but managed to glance at both Alyssa and Kaylee while Trevor's words sunk in. Kaylee shrugged her shoulders, and Alyssa silently mouthed the words "let's go", and pointed north up the Coast Highway.

"Thanks Trevor," said Dylan, "I should know better than to ever underestimate you. I confess that I didn't think you would take this well. You're a classy guy, and a gentleman. Thanks for being so gracious."

"Have fun in Santa Barbara," Trevor said.

Alyssa tugged Dylan away by the hand. Brad Stone had Dylan's car pulled up by the valet when he left in his taxi. Being at PCH and Sunset, they had to head south and get turned around. When they drove by Gladstone's again heading north, they beeped their horn and waved to the people that remained. Trevor was already gone.

A weekend in Santa Barbara was very relaxing for the young couple. They walked up and down State Street checking out the people and the shops. They ate seafood from a cup on Stearn's Wharf. On Saturday evening they spent time at the Paseo Nuevo Mall, had dinner outside at the Paradise Café on Anacapa Street, and watched a musical act at Soho's. They got back to the hotel room late, slept in the next day, and lingered playfully in the room until the sun was high. Without much energy left, they checked out of their hotel, and decided to browse through the Sunday Art Walk on Cabrillo Boulevard by the beach.

The onshore flow was strong keeping temperatures down and requiring a jacket, but most of the vendors set up anyway. They strolled along carefree and in love. People seemed to stare sensing the love between them and guessing they had just gotten married.

"We're only engaged," Alyssa responded to people that asked.

"We haven't set a date yet," Dylan would add.

"Are you going to wear a ring?" Alyssa asked Dylan.

"Well I don't know. I hadn't thought of it."

"What do you mean you haven't though of it? If I have to wear a ring, then you're wearing one!"

"I guess I'm wearing a ring then!" Dylan replied.

"We'll get you all ringed up in no time," Alyssa said smiling.

"I already have a ring in my nose," Dylan replied in jest.

"And don't ever forget it!" Alyssa confirmed.

They walked up to the end of the Art Walk, and had turned around to walk back to the car when Alyssa's phone rang.

"It's Kaylee, I better pick up. She's already called a few times."

"Go ahead," said Dylan.

"You guys need to come home right away!" said Kaylee without saying hello.

"Why, what is it?"

"There's been a tragedy," Kaylee said. "We need you here. A lot of people are shaken up by it."

Alyssa immediately thought of Grandpa Jack. Her heart sank. She thought the worst.

"Tell me what it is Kaylee!"

"I wish this wasn't over the phone, and I don't mean to spoil your special weekend."

"Tell me Kaylee!"

"Trevor Granderson was found dead in his car of an apparent heart attack. I'm sorry Alyssa."

Alyssa paused at the news, but for some reason she wasn't surprised.

"Trevor's dead," she repeated to Dylan. "What happened?"

"Apparently he relapsed," Kaylee said. "He was binge drinking all weekend long. A little old Filipino man found him slumped in his car parked on the street near Oxnard College. They found methamphetamine in his car too. The police said that his system probably couldn't take it, and he died."

"I warned him," said Alyssa.

"What do you mean you warned him?" Kaylee asked.

Alyssa thought it would be better not to explain her whole recent experience with Trevor. She also felt relief that it wasn't her family, but then guilt for having the thought.

"Oh nothing really," Alyssa replied. "I've been warning him since he started into recovery. I told him he can't relapse! I told him he'd already done too much damage, and that his body wouldn't be able to take it anymore.

"How did you find out?"

"The police called me. Apparently, I was the last call he placed on his cell phone, so they called me, but I had no missed calls from him. He hadn't called me in over a week! All I can figure is that he hasn't been calling anyone! He may have relapsed before he met us at Gladstone's Thursday. Who knows? This may have been going on for a while. He might have been drinking alone for weeks."

"What was he doing up in Oxnard?"

"The police think that he bought the meth in downtown Oxnard. Apparently there's a lot of tweekers in Ventura County. They think he pulled over on the way back to the coast highway to take a blast so he could get home. He may have been too drunk to drive, and he thought the crank would tweek him sober enough. It's all speculation at this point. They're going to do an autopsy and a toxicology test."

"Well we've both found peace," she thought to herself.

In her mind, Alyssa said goodbye to him, and in the acceptance of his passing the tears started to flow. She wasn't crying, but she couldn't hold back the tears. The grieving process began. She grieved for the loss of Trevor, and she grieved for her own mortality. Dylan had kept his ear close to Alyssa's cell phone, and heard the whole conversation. He was visibly upset and shaking. He forced himself to sit down.

"We're on our way Kaylee," said Alyssa. "Thanks for calling and letting me know. I'll give you a call when we get back to Hancock Park."

"Okay, be careful and drive safely! If you're too upset, wait awhile before you drive."

"Will do, okay bye."

"Bye."

The next few days were a whirlwind of activities. Kaylee ended up making nearly all of the arrangements. Trevor was an only child, and his mother had passed away years ago. He didn't have a close relationship with his Dad, and when they finally contacted him, his Dad was neither surprised nor interested. Kaylee ended up visiting him so that he could sign papers for Trevor's final arrangements.

Trevor's body was cremated and the ashes scattered at sea. Alyssa paid for everything, and she and Kaylee held a service with a small group of friends on the beach near the Santa Monica Pier on the day that Trevor's ashes were scattered. Afterwards, they had a party at Alyssa's house.

Kaylee had invited everyone she could find that knew Trevor, but very few showed. To the surprise of everyone, Trevor's father showed up late. He carried a picture of his son on a deep sea fishing trip at Cabo San Lucas. Trevor had caught a Yellow Tail, and was proudly displaying the fish while his Dad had his arm around him.

Trevor's Dad was obviously distraught, but spoke about Trevor as if he was still alive. He bragged about Trevor's Pepperdine education, his success in the business world, and his political savvy. Nothing he said was new to anyone present. His friends seemed to know more about him than his Father, but they all listened politely as he cornered them one by one to talk about his son.

After a while he lost energy, and sat in a comfortable chair and mumbled to himself for over an hour. Dylan offered to drive him home, and Alyssa followed in his car. They ended up walking him into his house, leaving his car keys, and locking the front door by turning the button on the handle and pulling the door shut. They were reluctant to leave him alone in such a state, but he assured them that he could take care of himself, and thanked them for all they had done.

Over a month passed, daylight savings time arrived, and a few weeks later the first few days of spring. A new optimism filled the air. Everyone was in good spirits both at home and at work when Alyssa received a phone call at home from an attorney.

"Miss Daingerfield," the attorney started.

"Yes, that's me!"

"I'm told that you knew Trevor Granderson, and that you were close."

"We dated at one time," Alyssa replied. "He was my first steady boyfriend. Since then, I guess you could say we were just friends."

"According to him you were very close."

"Okay, so we were! What's this about?"

"He left the majority of his estate to you. You're to inherit $1.7 million dollars in cash and investments. He considered you his common law wife. That's how he wrote up his living trust."

"I never lived with him. We were close at one time, but we broke up. I was very young and impressionable, and he was a very handsome and charming."

"Regardless, you've inherited his estate, and it's quite legal. You need to make an appointment. If you have an attorney, I would contact him before you make the appointment. If you have an accountant, you may want to contact him too."

"Okay," said Alyssa in a dazed contemplative tone. "I'll have my attorney contact you to make an appointment. What about his Dad?"

"I'm not calling with regard to his family, but I do know that they're very wealthy. This amount isn't a lot of money to them. I would suggest you take it. If you don't, it will very likely go to the State of California."

"Well thank you for the call. I'll be in touch."

As Alyssa hung up the phone, she thought of Youki and what he had said the last time he saw her.

"If you love something, give it up, if it comes back, it was always yours, if it doesn't, it was never yours to begin with."

She thought of sacrificing $500K to break a contract and leave her old company. She thought of the almost a million dollars in money and gold she had given away near the front door of her old company's headquarters.

"I parted with a million and a half," she thought to herself. "I let it go by choice, and now, out of the blue in a very strange way, almost the same amount comes back to me. It's all so strange - so surreal. How did Youki know? What was it about that hunchback little old guy that made him tick. It was as if he knew what I was going to do, and what I would go through. Maybe it was obvious to him what I needed to go through! How did he know what would transpire? It's crazy! How did he know? Why did I give the money away? What compelled me to do that? By almost anyone's standards it wasn't a smart thing to do; but I did it, and then it came back to me. Unbelievable! If God, or the universe, or whatever forces are out there wanted me to have this money, why would I have to go through that cycle of losing it and regaining it? Why did it come back? Why me to begin with, and why not somebody else? Why do these things that seem supernatural happen to me and not other people?"

As she sat questioning the nature of the significant events in her life, she noticed a hand bouquet of flowers across the room that Frenchy had given her as a child. She had dried them and saved them. The flowers made her think of the Yin and the Yang aspect of living, the circle of life, and the eternal reoccurrence. Every thought, every emotion, every feeling, seemed to have a mirror image that wasn't noticeable, but was always there. Every action had an equal and opposite reaction. Frenchy had told her so long ago that "whatever you happen to be doing at the time is the right thing to do". She found the statement absurd, but now she realized

436

it was true. The answers to her self-questioning never came to her, but she found peace in what had come to pass, peace in what material objects had come her way, and peace in her existence.

Chapter 49

As a 22nd birthday gift to herself, Alyssa made arrangements to drop down to part time status at work. To remain on the payroll, she was required to work 26 hours a week, so she accepted the new hours, and devoted the extra time to her fiancée's business.

Instead of moving to Rodeo Drive as Dylan had dreamed, they leased shelf space in two other retail clothing stores already on that strip. Dylan had developed a list of contacts and references, and consulted with store owners to match his merchandise with their seasonal offerings. He targeted clothing ensembles that store owners were already pushing, and early success garnered healthy business relationships. Owners were happy to see him. He teamed with Alyssa, and like most people, they were happy to see her too. The solution wasn't the ultimate end state that Dylan had wanted, but it was profitable, and there was no pressure to make the lease every month. Lease rates were so high in Beverly Hills that he would have had to struggle to keep his store out of the red. He was better off staying in Santa Monica and catering personally to desirable clients in the LA basin.

Alyssa's free time focused on buying a vacation home in Pacific Grove near Monterey. She wanted to visit Big Sur whenever she could, and wanted a ready place to stay when the opportunity arose.

She found a small cottage built in the 1920s with a big lot, lush landscaping and a very private backyard. The cottage was quaint with the original tile and plumbing fixtures in the single bathroom. Original ornate moldings and detailed woodwork were preserved in the remainder of the house. The kitchen was completely remodeled with modern appliances and cabinets, but the look and feel of the original design was adhered to as much as possible. Each room contributed to an overall theme of the roaring '20s, and provided a feeling of stepping back in time when entering the house.

The young couple dreamed of a simpler era when families had more time for each other, and the warm and fuzzy cottage offered them such a place as well as a refuge from the demands of their busy lives in LA.

Alyssa used her inheritance to pay for the cottage with cash, and as she had done with her Hancock Park home, she set up an account that generated enough income annually to pay her property taxes. The only bills she would be responsible for were the month to month utilities.

When escrow finally closed, they decided to use the property for their wedding reception, and picked a date of Saturday, June 26th, 2010 in hopes of avoiding traffic associated with the July 4th holiday the following weekend.

At Alyssa's request, Dylan agreed to have the wedding ceremony at the Point Sur Lighthouse, but it turned out to be too difficult. There was no way of obtaining a permit, and getting to the lighthouse required a short hike as well as negotiating stairs and foot bridges.

"Why don't we just get married at Lover's Point Park in Pacific Grove right by the cottage," Dylan suggested one morning when they had given up on Big Sur. "It's close by, and easy to get to!"

The idea turned out to be brilliant, and they both wondered why they hadn't thought of it earlier. For them, Big Sur had been more about Alyssa and Youki; whereas, Lover's Point had been a new chapter in both of their lives. It was a spot they had made their own as a couple, and was significant in their early days together.

438

They arranged for a small afternoon ceremony of 40 people, and planned it for 4PM. The late start would give the June fog a chance to burn off, and allow for a reception right across the street at Latitudes Restaurant.

"We'll leave the cooking and the dirty dishes to the restaurant," suggested Alyssa.

"Yes, and afterwards, we can retreat to the cottage for a party with all our friends," Dylan added.

With that, the plan solidified. Both families were delighted thinking that they were taking on too much with a remote ceremony at Big Sur and the stress of managing a reception at home. The only plans for the cottage were music, dancing, hors d'oeuvres wedding cake, and desserts.

The fog never completely burned off during the ceremony as they had hoped. The sun tried it's hardest to break through, but only showed itself briefly during the reception allowing for pictures. Every other part of the day proceeded flawlessly.

Grandpa Jack arrived in a tie-dye suit that was special ordered to match the tie-dye ankle length dress that Grandma Lin wore while holding up a tie-dye parasol.

"The sun may not be out," Grandma said, "but I'm using my parasol anyway. I don't get much of an opportunity to be clever."

Grandpa Jack was clearly nervous prior to the ceremony, and was unwrapping and eating Starburst Fruit Chews as fast as he could one after the other in anticipation of the event starting. Brad Stone arrived with a date that was taller than he was and quite thin. People started to whisper as soon as they walked up. Brad was in a tux, and his date in a formal gown, but they didn't match. Separately, the each looked fantastic, but standing together they contrasted.

"I wanted to get some use out of this tux," Brad stated in his defense. "I got a bargain on it in LA's garment district."

Daisy and Franken were both dressed impeccably, and looked perfect together as a couple. Daisy wore all white, looked young

439

for her age all fixed up, and could have easily been mistaken for the bride. She was accused throughout the day of being one of Alyssa's friends. Franken looked older in his suit, but not out of place. He was clearly enjoying being with one of the most beautiful women at the event, and Daisy relished in fitting in with the young people. Finhead John arrived with Kaylee. He was in sport jacket and tie, and she in a modest dress. When they walked up, the whispering started again, people wondered if they had become a couple.

Dylan's parents and family had driven down from Idaho, and had combined the wedding with a makeshift vacation. They looked sunburned and tired from spending the last three days at Lake Shasta, but still managed to be energetic and mingle with the other guests.

There was, of course, nowhere to sit at Lover's point. Guests were asked to bring folding chairs. Some did sit down, but most people stood talking about the Lakers championship run against the Celtics, and whether the Dodgers or the Giants would have a better season.

Frenchy was a licensed minister, and served as the officiant. No one had seen him since he left the business. What hair he had left had turned completely gray. The change gave him a distinguished look, and provided a commanding appearance in the role of master of ceremonies.

Frenchy had hired a guitarist for the event. The guitarist played Mason Williams' "Classical Gas" and Simon and Garfunkel's "The Boxer" over and over while people were assembling. With a cue from Frenchy, he called the event to order, and with a second cue, he began to play the "Hawaiian Wedding Song".

Alyssa wore a simple off-white dress with a small tiara and veil. Although simple, it complimented her by emphasizing her inner beauty that so many people found striking when they met her, and yet there was just enough detail in the lace to suggest an

440

intricate personality. For people who knew the family, they could tell that she worked together with Daisy to find something appropriate.

Grandpa Jack walked Alyssa halfway down the isle, and Brad Stone took over from there to deliver the bride to her new husband.

She walked very elegantly with head held high but kept her eyes focused ahead yet slightly downward affirming the presence of a higher power.

Kaylee served as maid of honor, and Finhead as best man. The wedding itself went very smoothly until the vows. Frenchy stumbled on the lines for Dylan to repeat, and Dylan said "lawfully wedded wife" instead of husband. Alyssa corrected him, and everyone laughed. The laughter helped both Daisy and Grandma Lin who were sobbing while seated and ruining their makeup. The laughter gave them a break from the tears.

After the ceremony was over, the guitarist launched into "Classical Gas" once more, and Dylan found out later that he could only remember three songs. Most people began migrating across the street to Latitudes Restaurant, some milled around talking loudly, and others participated in the picture taking, but several people skipped the dinner and headed straight over to the party.

Dinner proceeded rather quickly with people occasionally clinking their glasses in hopes of getting the couple to kiss, but as dinner proceeded, the attention seemed to shift toward the party. People wondered what they were missing, and when dinner ended, the guests wasted no time in getting to the cottage. When they arrived, celebrations were already in full swing.

Alyssa and Dylan had invited over 300 people thinking that most wouldn't make the long drive from Los Angeles. Doing the math, they thought that no more than 100 people would show up tops. Even if only 50 showed, they still worried that having only one bathroom would present a problem. They rented a portable bathroom just to make sure they were covered; and they were relieved because over 150 people signed their guest book. Even

441

with the portable, most of the ladies preferred the bathroom inside, and there was a line queued up most of the night.

Many guests were Alyssa's past students and patients, a few were Dylan's current customers, and some were strays from the neighborhood, but there were many more that no one expected. Momma Leoni showed up clean and sober with a new boyfriend in tow that was tall and gangly and looked a lot like Reech. Carol and Charlie rode up from Santa Monica on their Harley Davidsons and brought along some of their newer jewelry for show. They had intricate designs, and had crossed over into other markets beside the biker crowds. Metro Matt was there with his new wife. She was taller than he was, had shorter hair and wore loose clothing. It wasn't obvious that she was female until she spoke, and it made people uncomfortable until they could figure out which was which.

Alyssa's friend Nikki, the rock star, showed up with his family, and had made a mini vacation out of the trip. They had already been to Sequoia, Kings Canyon, Santa Cruz, and Monterey's Aquarium. The wedding was their last stop. Nikki's kids brought musical instruments, and played some sing along songs for the guests early on. They were cute, and their performance was very well received. After the impromptu show, the music started inside, but the speakers were propped up in the windows so it could be heard out back, and dancing started on the porch and the lawn and continued throughout the night.

Metro Matt had brought a bubble making machine, and fired it up in the yard to remind Alyssa of her early days in Santa Monica.

When Alyssa got ready to throw her bouquet, there were many interested single women who gathered up. Kaylee was dancing and not paying attention, and ran over at the last minute to participate. She fell down as she arrived in the nick of time. Alyssa threw the bouquet without looking. It bounced off the girls in the crowd, and hit Kaylee in the face as she was attempting to get up from the fall. She grabbed the bouquet and held it up while still on her knees, and everyone cheered.

442

Alyssa and Dylan hadn't anticipated the need to have a hotel room to escape to when the clock approached midnight, so instead, they kicked everyone out of their bedroom in the cottage, and locked the door. Brad Stone promised to keep an eye on things until the last guest drifted off, but Dylan and Alyssa could hear people in the house until past 2 AM.

When they got up the next day, several people had remained in the cottage over night. Some were awake sipping coffee, and others littered the floor asleep. Grandpa Jack had relieved Brad Stone from the watch at about 6 AM, and he and Grandma Lin sat in the kitchen reading the paper and drinking Starbucks like they belonged there.

"I had to drive into town to get a Starbucks," Grandpa said. "The one on Cannery Row. It was the only one I could find. I gotta have it! You know how I like everything that has "Star" in its name."

"Thanks for watching the house Grandpa," Alyssa replied. "We didn't think the party would be nearly that big."

"That was a great party!" said Grandpa Jack. "Everyone was having fun and there were no fights, and no one threw up."

Grandma Lin lowered her paper and stared at him momentarily, and returned to her reading.

"Considering the size of the crowd," said Dylan, "there wasn't that much drinking."

"Well it was BYO," said Grandpa Jack. "If it would have been hosted, it would have been a blow out. You have a wide range of friends. Some of them are crazy. I've been around. I grew up in the sixties. I can see it in their eyes."

"I bet you can Grandpa," said Alyssa.

"Can I call you Grandpa?" asked Dylan. "Why don't you just call me Jack," said Grandpa. "Too many people are calling me Grandpa these days. I'm starting to feel old."

"You're in your early 60s now dear," said Grandma Lin lowering the paper again.

443

"I've lost count," Grandpa replied.

"You qualify as old, but you're as young as you feel!" said Grandma turning to Dylan. "You can call me Grandma if you'd like Dylan!"

"Thanks Grandma," said Dylan smiling. "You too Jack!"

Grandpa looked at him, sipped his Starbucks and forced a fake smile without replying.

Chapter 50

It took two days for all the guests to leave town, and the little cottage became a central meeting place for all the people. As part of his wedding gift, Brad Stone kept an eye on things while people dropped by, but when Monday arrived, even Brad headed to Salinas to catch the train back to Los Angeles.

Alyssa and Dylan stayed another week. For exercise, they walked daily from their cottage, past the Monterey aquarium, up cannery row, and over to Fisherman's Wharf. It was a long walk, but the beauty of the Monterey shoreline and their love for each other kept them intoxicated with natural beauty of their situation together. They watched the otters play, the sea lions relax, and the fishing boats lumbering along to their destinations. They walked through the aquarium, and toured all the museums and tourist traps of Cannery Row.

Finally they tired of the city, and retreated to Big Sur hiking the hillsides and finding vista points while driving the rugged shoreline. They were prepared for anything with their daypacks, and whenever the spirit moved them, they made love. They preferred the canopy of the ancient redwood forests, but also found several niches along the coastline where they could slip off their clothes in the morning fog, frolic naked on the beach, and collapse

444

on their beach blanket exhausted. In minutes they were ready for more, and moved on to their next destination.

The week passed all too quickly, and Alyssa knew it was time to go home when Dylan began to worry about his store in Santa Monica, and they were spending more and more time just lounging about the cottage.

Like most owners of vacation homes, they spent their last day cleaning and securing the cottage. Before they knew it, evening arrived, and it was too late to start the long drive home.

Since they woke early the next day, they decided to take the twisted coast highway toward home so that they could see Big Sur one last time. When they arrived, they stopped at Fernwood to stock up on ice and snacks before driving. There was thick marine layer. Big Sur was shrouded in fog, and Fernwood was dark and misty. They purchased their items in the convenience store, but instead of just walking back out the door, a feeling inside moved Alyssa to walk out by the big fireplace in the next room. To her surprise there was a young Buddhist monk asleep in the chair. He was obviously Chinese, and not Japanese like Youki. He wore the traditional orange robes of a young monk, and had the shaved head of someone new to the order. Looking at him, she remembered Youki's gray robes, hunched back, and close-cropped hair. Youki was never shaved, and looked very natural in his appearance. She set down her bags for a moment, and couldn't resist waking him.

"Don't wake him!" Dylan protested. "He looks like one of their new recruits. They're probably working his rear end off! He needs the sleep! It's not your old friend. He's gone remember?"

"I know," said Alyssa, "but I just can't resist. I was an apprentice once myself."

Alyssa shook his arm.

"Youki, Youki, wake up," she said smiling knowing it wasn't him.

He opened his eyes and blinked.

"I came back for you," he said. "Did you find what you were looking for?"

"Yes," said Alyssa, "this time I really did."

"You better go back and look again," he said. "There's much work to be done!"

With that, he drifted back to sleep.

"Oh Youki," Alyssa said, "I knew you'd come back."

Dylan sighed and took Alyssa's arm as if to pull her away.

The young monk awoke again, but this time he was startled.

"Youki!" he said. "Who Youki? Who you? Leave me alone peas. Sleep much needed!"

He closed his eyes and tried to go back to sleep.

"Wait, wait just a minute," said Alyssa. "I have something for you!"

The young monk opened one eye slightly pretending to be asleep.

From her purse, Alyssa produced the $5 gold coin that Youki had left her. She held it in her fingertips and presented it to the monk.

"This is yours," Alyssa said.

The monk opened both eyes, and took the coin. He examined it.

"You crazy!" he said. "You crazy woman!"

"That's what people say," Alyssa replied.

"I have no need of such things," he said staring at her.

"I know," she said, "and that has meaning in itself. It's back where it belongs now. Keep it."

"Very well, sleep now peas. You go!"

"Yes Dylan" said Alyssa, "I'm ready to go now."

THE END

For info: http://www.pmgrates.com

446